San Diego Lightfoot Sue

San Diego Lightfoot Sue
and other stories
Tom Reamy

Introduction by
Harlan Ellison

A Reminiscence
by Howard Waldrop

Publishers
Louis Graham and Jim Loehr
Kansas City, Missouri

Acknowledgments

"Twilla" appeared in the September 1974 issue of **The Magazine of Fantasy and Science Fiction**. "Under the Hollywood Sign" appeared in **Orbit 17**, edited by Damon Knight. "Beyond the Cleft" appeared in **Nova 4**, edited by Harry Harrison. "San Diego Lightfoot Sue" appeared in the August 1975 issue of **The Magazine of Fantasy and Science Fiction**. "Dinosaurs" appeared in **New Dimensions 6**, edited by Robert Silverberg. "The Sweetwater Factor" appeared in **Lone Star Universe**, edited by George Proctor and Steve Utley. "Mistress of Windraven" appeared in **Chacal #1**, 1976. "The Detweiler Boy" appeared in the April 1977 issue of **The Magazine of Fantasy and Science Fiction**. "Insects in Amber" appeared in the January 1978 issue of **The Magazine of Fantasy and Science Fiction**. "Waiting for Billy Star" appeared in **Shayol #2**, 1978. "2076: Blue Eyes" appeared in **Shayol #3**, 1979.

SAN DIEGO LIGHTFOOT SUE and Other Stories. Copyright © 1979 by the Estate of Tom Reamy. An EarthLight Publishers book by arrangement with the author's estate. All rights reserved. Printed in the United States of America. No part of this book may be reproduced in any form or by any electronic or mechanical means including information storage and retrieval systems without the explicit permission in writing from the author's agent, except by a reviewer who may quote brief passages in a revew to be printed in a magazine or newspaper, or electronically transmitted on radio or television. For information address the author's agent: Virginia Kidd, 538 East Harford Street, Milford, Pennsylvania 18337.

"Embrace the Departing Shadow" Copyright © 1979 by Harlan Ellison.

"Tom, Tom!" Copyright © 1979 by Howard Waldrop.

Leo and Diane Dillon's artwork appears here for the first time and is Copyright © 1979 by Leo and Diane Dillon.

All characters and events portrayed in this book are fictitious.

FIRST EDITION

Library of Congress Catalog Number: 79-54396

ISBN: 0-935128-00-X (Trade Edition)
ISBN: 0-935128-01-8 (Slipcased Edition)

The following people have proven invaluable in the preparation and production of this book; the publishers wish to thank them for their assistance: Virginia Kidd, Harlan Ellison, Leo and Diane Dillon, Howard Waldrop, Pat Cadigan, Arnold Fenner, Ken Keller and Terry Matz of Nickelodeon Graphics, Jack Stone, Mary Mertens, Dave Plummer of Inter-Collegiate Press and special thanks to Richard Garrison.

EarthLight Publishers, 5539 Jackson, Kansas City, Missouri 64130

Contents

Embrace the Departing Shadow
Introduction by Harlan Ellison — ix

Twilla — 1

Under the Hollywood Sign — 30

Beyond the Cleft — 50

San Diego Lightfoot Sue — 70

Dinosaurs — 106

The Sweetwater Factor — 126

The Mistress of Windraven — 132

The Detweiler Boy — 139

Insects in Amber — 167

Waiting for Billy Star — 207

2076: Blue Eyes — 213

Tom, Tom!
A Reminiscence by Howard Waldrop — 229

For Pat Cadigan

Embrace the Departing Shadow

Introduction by Harlan Ellison

Old men sit with a chill in their bones, lamenting the struggle of the sun through the steel of the sky toward dead winter. I wake up angry every day. My friends die around me. And here I remain, a rock in the ocean; wearing away a little more each year; but here, always here; watching my friends vanish. Wait just another minute, shadows; I'm not ready to let you go yet. A minute more, for a proper goodbye; it's not that much to ask.

Oh, sorry; didn't mean to let you catch me like this. Give me a second and I'll get it together.

But if, occasionally during these words, you catch me choked up or even staring off into space murmuring softly so that you cannot tell what I'm saying, I ask your indulgence. Take no notice. Ignore it, pass by that pathetic shopping-bag lady pulling her little red wagon filled with cardboard flats, that maundering wetbrain lying with legs twisted and muscatel bottle empty in its paper sack. Go make yourself a cup of coffee and come back in a few minutes. The cleanup patrols wil have the doorways emptied and the streets free of tacky embarrassments, honest to God they will. Pretend we're all tough and cool and don't make fools of ourselves in public places. No, thanks; I have some Kleenex.

The final note, of course, whatever **else** I may say here, is that Tom is gone; and no closely-reasoned patterchat about how good or bad his stories were, or what a good guy he was, will make one twitch of difference. Don't shove no live wire up that amputated frog leg because it's cold; no galvanic twitch gonna alter the condition of gone, so leave it alone. Tom is done writing and what we're left with is his testament: two books.

One novel, BLIND VOICES; one gathering of short stories, this book.

Which will hardly serve to establish him as one of the great Lost Artists of Our Time. He was a writer getting better all the time, and there's no need to sloppify that, to moan and deify him, and try to make his passing more "significant" and thus more deserving of our sorrow. He was as good as he was when he died, and that's enough to honor. He was a teller of tales whose work had the heft and the graceful line and the vibration of creatures readying themselves to fly. He had it in him, and he set it down on paper, that quiddity that made us lift our eyes. There is a lot of sky in Tom's work. Views of the celestial regions where great songs are sung.

But he died in the middle of the work, and all we have are two books. And so I ask you, when I turn my face into the corner, that you avert your eyes. Tom would have.

"Twilla" has emerged as one of Tom's best-known stories, and it's odd that it should have captured so much attention and stayed so long in the memory of the audience. Odd, because it's such a simple story... simple in the sense of uncomplicated... but that was his way with his stories for so many years: directly to the point. (Only toward the end did Tom show signs of deepening the conceptual layers of his fables.)

It's hard to know what to say about this phylum of gently insinuative conceit. It does its job with such expertise that it has the intelligent reader by the throat before s/he knows the hex has been placed.

Goes without saying that we've had this sort of setting in contemporary fantasy many times before, most fully developed in Zenna Henderson's story-cycle of The People. But Tom brings to the familiar rural ambiance a kind of **meiosis**—a literary understatement—that ostensibly diminishes the importance of elements that are, on sum, irreducible in the plot equation. And he employs an artful psychic distance in the writing; what is referred to, in posh lit'ry circles, as the "aesthetic distance"; at some level of Tom's apprehension there was an awareness of the formal unreality of art. A distancing from the beholder, an appreciation of the aesthetic qualities that did not confuse it with reality.

For instance, he employs the Melvillean technique of "the catalogue" in the freighting of names: Gilbreath, Choate, Alice May Turner, Grace and Elizabeth Peacock, Wanda O'Dell, Carter Redwine, Ronnie Dwyer, Sammy Stocker, Raynelle Franklin, Leo Whittaker, Loretta McBride, and on and on. Three times as many names as one needs for the story, but cleverly inserted in such a way that they establish a sense of time and place and **population,** without confusing the reader by a congeries of walk-through spear-carriers without valid function in the story.

Despite its length, "Twilla" seems almost pastiche.

The plot is spare, lean, somewhat paradigmatic, the usually bolted-down overexplanations of fantastic elements nowhere in sight; the behavior of the principals is something less than rigorously logical; the prelude is rather longer than necessary to balance such an abrupt and violent ending.

And those who have read BLIND VOICES will quickly recognize the similarity of the horror visited on Yvonne Wilkins in this piece and the one that befalls Francine Latham in the longer work. This leads me to believe that "Twilla"—in ways that Tom may only dimly have realized when he wrote it—was a preliminary effort intended as a practice run for the novel, a mental note to himself. It may be that BLIND VOICES grew out of this story.

Else why such detail of Kansas, why such formidable laying-in of background for such a brief flash of plot? And like the novel, the sense and scent of the Kansas Tom remembered is here in full measure. Its length is used to

Embrace the Departing Shadow

convey a time and a place that are infinitely more important than the action.

He was a keek. Accurately and precisely, a peeping Tom; a keek. From the Scottish slang "to look."

I don't know if he was always like that, from early childhood; you might ask his mother, Gertrude Reamy. She'd probably be able to tell you if he was always like that—always seeing what others looked at but never really **saw**. But I can extrapolate from my own childhood awareness, and that of Ray Bradbury, and Frank Herbert, and other writers with whom I've discussed just that aspect of what we call "the writer's eye," and I'll be damned if I know which comes first—chicken or egg—the "eye" or the realization that the training of that eye makes one a writer. I have a hunch it's the former, that special way of seeing: living with a shard of funhouse distorting mirror wedged into the anterior chamber just behind the cornea and the Canal of Schlemm, perceiving the decades of crooked moonlit roads stretching out behind that weary-looking old woman in the supermarket check-out line, her total buy being six tins of cat food and a quart can of Hawaiian Punch. Perceiving the **story** of that old woman; how she got here; the circumstances of abandonment by those she trusted and in whom she invested love; the potentiality that she does not even live with a cat. Only the keeks of the world get all that in a flash of agonizing pain, through the "eye."

Maybe Tom **wasn't** like that all his life; but it's six, ten, and even it was **just** like that for him. Good odds only if you're one of those schmucks who thinks s/he can write . . . if only there was spare time to do it. A sucker bet, really; I **know** he was like that. He had to've been. We carnivores can spot our own kind. Keek is, as keek does.

Whatever the levels of expertise reached as a writer grows in his/her craft, there is one trained dog-&-pony act s/he can pull off in a way no other writer can. In extreme rages of dramatic or intellectual intensity, every artist, no matter how flawed or hacklike otherwise, masters one trick that often becomes the trademark so easily parodied by lesser writers who spot the pinnacle but cannot penetrate the mist and fog of the lower, equally impressive, mountain range. (Example: all the imitators of Henry James reproduce his syntactical complexities and baroque flourishes, but fail to capture the intense passion and emotionalism. Another: pipsqueak parodists of Bradbury can rattle off endless copycatisms about how the summer days were like pistachio ice cream cones melting in the mouths of our minds, but the subtle horrors of the fruit at the bottom of the bowl are beyond them. One final: brute mimics of Robert E. Howard find no difficulty in festooning their cheapjack graverobbies with bloody swords and sweaty deltoids, but the arcane mysteries of Howard's truly, individually deranged perception of reality and fantasy as merged images of the same lunatic face evade them entirely.)

"Under the Hollywood Sign," I think, is a perfect example of that one quadruple somersault from the highest bars that Tom could manage again and again, but which Reamy-clones never seem able to pull off. In this piece, as I say, we can hear the singular voice of Tom Reamy, singing a dangerous song of primal fears so deep and yet so commonplace that we automatically reject them, precisely because they may **be** universally shared. No one likes to imagine him- or herself as a potential point-beast ready to run with the slavering pack.

Clifford Simak beats everyone else at injecting the bizarre element into folksy, very placid settings. Jack Vance cannot be excelled in the creation of human-populated alien worlds that **sound** real. Kate Wilhelm does personal stress better than anyone I've read since Conrad or B. Traven. And Tom—as personified in the auctorial voice of this story—pulls off, better than anyone else in the genre I can think of, the enormously difficult trick of tapping into the deepest wells of our id, and bringing up the dippers of redolent emotional sludge we struggle to deny comes from our own commonality of desperation as flawed human beings.

This tale is, for me, one of the three best stretches of writing Tom did. Because of the fever in it, the burning, the inescapable **danger** in it . . . the horrors of the human condition we all share, with which we exist in uneasy liaison through all the moments of our lives.

How sad for you. There's the one novel, and this book of stories, and that's all of it you'll ever see. Oh, maybe there'll be another film or two after BLIND VOICES (did I mention I'm writing the screenplay even as you read this . . . perhaps it slipped my mind . . . well, it's true . . . but who knows if the film will be made . . . perhaps . . . perhaps not); there are at least thirteen Reamy scripts in various stages of completion. But from what I've seen of them—and there are a few bits and pieces herein awaiting your scrutiny and judgment—they won't add much luster to Tom's **oeuvre**. It's sad for me, too, and for all of his buddies, because he was taken away much too goddam soon. But less sad for me and for his buddies because we at least **knew** him; we got to hang out with him, sometimes.

Standard operating procedures for this kind of **hommage** include the obligatory assertion of bloodbrotherhood between the savant writing the introduction, and the subject. If, as happens here, the subject also happens to be deceased, how much easier it is to promulgate whole-cloth mythologies of the lifelong kinship of savant and subject. Well, chums and others, I ain't gonna whip that number on you. I wasn't a real close friend of Tom Reamy. We knew each other for a long time, we liked each other, we communicated often and we hung out sometimes when he was living here in Los Angeles. But if you want intimate details of Tom's personal life, or close reminiscences from the Old Boys' Network, you'd best seek out Howard Waldrop or Richard Delap or (for specific years) Al Jackson, Greg Benford, Alex Eisenstein and George Proctor (1950-1969); Bjo Trimble, George Barr or anybody who worked on the film **Flesh Gordon** (1970-1972); Ken Keller, Tim Kirk, Arnie Fenner or Pat Cadigan (1973-1977). They knew him in Kansas City and Hollywood and Dallas; and Arnie and Pat can probably furnish you with the issue of their magazine **Shayol** that contained a long interview with Tom, in which he viewed his career and his talent with very adult sensibilities.

I, on the other hand, was on the fringe of Tom's life. Mutual respect, I guess, yeah that always. I say "I guess" because I know I had respect for him and his work, but I can only assume he respected me and what I did because he asked me to write for his splendid magazine, **Trumpet;** and because we always **talked** as if we respected each other. That'll have to do.

Yet I won't entirely disappoint those of you who expect the **de rigueur** minutiae of this kind of screed. I can gift you with one of those terrific **The first time I met Tom Reamy** routines . . .

The first time I met Tom Reamy, was through the mail. It was 1954. Tom was nineteen, I was twenty. He sent me samples of his artwork, hoping I'd accept something for my fanzine, **Dimensions**. Most of you, blissfully, have forgotten that I was a science fiction fan for a few years, back in the Fifties. Even more of you may have forgotten that I published what was considered one of the half dozen or so top amateur journals in fandom.

Foreshadowing the DANGEROUS VISIONS anthologies (dedicated to the then-heretical concept that most of the science fiction being published was reactionary, semiliterate and just downright boring), I had instituted a series of stories I pompously called "taboo-breakers" in the magazine. The first one appeared in what would turn out to be my final issue of **Dimensions** (number 15, dated August-October 1954): a short story by Ray Schaffer, Jr. titled "Via Roma." God only knows whatever became of Ray Schaffer, Jr. but the full-page illustration, and a nice piece of work it was, that appeared on page 53 was rendered by someone with whom I thereafter maintained sustained, if sporadic, communication. The drawing was signed Tom Reamy.

Two years later I became a full-time professional writer. It took Tom seventeen more years to become a recognized professional writer.

If you want to talk about **jeezus what a shame**, talk about those nineteen years during which Tom did many other kinds of things, before he realized he was a storyteller; nineteen years' worth of stories that never got written. Now **that's** jeezus what a shame.

Some years ago, in the course of properly insulting some loathesome toad of my acquaintance, I said, "He's the sort of man who takes little children into the basements of churches, then rapes, murders and eats his victims . . . not necessarily in that order." Bill Rotsler has the remark in his QUOTEBOOK. Tom laughed at the remark. I don't remember if he was in Bill's and my company when I first said it but (having gotten a good laugh from my listeners the first time, and being one of the garrulous sort who never waste a livid **bon mot**) I used the line again on several occasions, making certain never to repeat it around anyone who had heard it before (thereby buttressing my reputation for always having a fresh, vicious witticism on my lips) and Tom remarked that he thought it was a sufficiently ugly concept, containing the germ of a fascinating story-idea.

I'd forgotten Tom had ever mentioned it to me, until I began reading "Beyond the Cleft"—which I'd missed when it was originally published—in order to comment on it for this introduction. It was a grisly little **bon mot**, and it's become a terrifying story. Hardly what I had in mind, and a nice example (if "nice" can be applied here in **any** way) of standing the original on its head. Herewith, Tom has the meek inheriting the strong.

Perhaps only those of us who get such ideas can read the stories of others who think similarly, without being utterly revolted. Perhaps that's why we're all part of such a tiny coterie of peculiar thinkers. Perhaps you're one, too; and perhaps you'd better watch yourself: one is known by the company kept.

"San Diego Lightfoot Sue" is a troubling story.

There is much of Tom himself in this piece. But who dares say what parts are mere fictional construct and what parts the pain known and stored for later translation?

In some ways this is a story too simplistic, too calculatedly heart-tugging to be taken seriously. Nonetheless, defying codification, in other ways, utterly contradictory ways, it is too strong and familiar a story to be ignored. Its power, I think, lies in the realization that each of us, no matter how well we think we live our lives, has somewhere along the map of the battlefield lost the innocence of childhood or nature that sustained us. We all grow older. Some of us may even grow a bit wiser, or kinder, or more courageous. Yet we all wish someone dear could have seen us at an earlier stage of our life: when we were fifteen . . . or twenty . . . or thirty.

And please notice: there is an almost total absence of evil in this story. At every juncture where we suspect John Lee will be masticated by the fangs of the corrupt, innocence wins the day. Goodness follows him. The sad and the bent and the damaged are compelled to treat him fairly, with affection, with honor. They are made better than usual by their association with him. Is this Tom, after experiences in Los Angeles that must have been alien and shattering to him, reasserting the potency of innocence? Even when an engine of destruction is turned loose on John Lee, in the form of the unrealized implement named Jocko, even then no evil can touch him.

And yet, there is foreshadowing. When Sue goes to San Diego and returns in the dead of night to sketch John Lee's portrait in black and white, it is a weary job of work. He looks older, tired . . . twenty. Why did Sue have to go to San Diego? Why did she return that night? Why did she need to sketch John Lee that night? How much urgency do we feel for her doing it? Why did she leave immediately for San Diego again? What did she know, or suspect, or have a vision of, that came through in the sketch? What was Tom trying to say about his own youth, his own discovery of the world seen (in Hemingway's words) "complete and as a whole"? And what was he saying about the coin in which we pay for love?

A troubling story.

Too simple and almost sophomorically romantic for serious consideration; too powerful and demanding to be ignored. I've always believed that much Great Art goes unheralded, simply because it is so uncomplicated that it looks easy.

Embrace the Departing Shadow xv

Oscar Wilde once said, "There are only two kinds of people who are really fascinating—people who know absolutely everything and people who know absolutely nothing." Tom was one of the former. His well of obscure information was seemingly bottomless. And his fascination with the little details of life manifested itself not only in good, long conversations late into the night, but in the stories, as well.

Much of it came from being a keek. But even more of the minutiae of history, science, various crafts and skills, people and nature came from his peregrinations. Tom was born in Woodson, Texas but because his father's work demanded frequent resiting, Tom saw a lot of the country when he was young. He lived for extended periods in Kansas, in Los Angeles, in Dallas. And he filed it all away. He read voraciously. His memory was encyclopedic. And beyond the simple mimetic skills of an intelligent human being, he was able to make intellectual linkages between obscure bits of data that brought sense out of chaos when trying to unravel a tangled plot-twist.

He was extremely good company.

And he already had the writing skills in the fifties, when his friends were reading his stories and begging him to send them off for possible acceptance by the sf magazines. But Tom never did it. God only knows why. He wasn't that shy a man, though he did tend to be laid-back in groups where the proportion of strangers was greater than that of people he knew.

One would have thought that all the years as a fan, with a high profile in publishing, would have given him the ready confidence to start sending his work out to market. In the fifties and sixties his critical writings in the fan community were professional, closely-reasoned, always gentlemanly without being asskissing; but there wasn't much fiction. Then in the early Sixties he started publishing **Trumpet**, a magazine so refined and of such a high caliber that he made the Hugo finalist ballot three or four times. And there, too, his writing shone.

But it wasn't until the Seventies that he actually began working as a professional. First in film, out here where the blue sky merchants sold him several bills of goods on the if-come, and he wrote a bunch of treatments and screenplays that kept him busy, may have made him an inadequate living, but probably won't add much to posterity's judgment of his talent.

In 1975 he moved to Kansas City and established a new magaine, **Nickelodeon**, with Ken Keller. It was a swell magazine. But that was already a five-finger exercise for Tom—though he spent more time at it than those of us who respected his serious writing might have wished. Because on the same day in 1973 he sold his first two stories, "Twilla" and "San Diego Lightfoot Sue." And there was nothing but the top of the mountain in sight. Tom was finally, at last, at long last, off and running. Everyone smiled. The dream was coming true. On November 4th, 1977 the dream ended with throat-gagging frustration for all of us who had watched and waited . . . and smiled.

On November 4th, 1977 Tom Reamy died a writer's death.

At the not-nearly-enough age of forty-two, Tom Reamy had a heart attack while sitting at his typewriter doing a story for Ed Ferman's **Magazine** of *Fantasy & Science Fiction*; a story Ed had been calling him about regularly; and he was only seven pages into it when the fist closed; and he was gone; and oh God it wasn't right! It just wasn't fair!

Keep tough. Don't get sentimental and let it dishonor all he did that was first-rank by praising that which he did to make a buck, to survive in the meanest town this side of Beirut. Deal with the lesser stuff quickly, get it said, and get back to the diamonds.

Like much of the work Tom did either in or for Hollywood, "Sting!" is a snippet of an idea both trashy and time-wasting. For reader and for Tom, who might better have been working on stories intended to be stories, not treatments for low-budget potboiler films.* It is a classic example of how destructive to the artistic intellect the lure of glamourous C*I*N*E*M*A can be.

To be precise, using the words of Saul Bellow, "Writers are not necessarily corrupted by money. They are distracted—diverted to other avenues."

Tom should have been writing novels and stories; fresh, hot, demanding stories that would have been his own, untouched by inhuman hands and by the studio mentality that obtains even with the fly-by-night independents for whom Tom worked . . . the "art by committee" philosophy that emerges from insecurity, absence of original thinking, the debased concepts attendant on **let's make a fast buck**. It was a scuzzy arena for Tom to walk into, relatively unarmed. He was too gentle, too anxious to please.

So instead of all the stories we might have had from him during that first bold flash of creative energy, 1970-1973 approximately, he wrote a plethora of film treatments, a few screenplays (a 186 page screenplay of Tom's adaptation of Sturgeons' MORE THAN HUMAN is still kicking around, and two of his five "adult" screenplays, **The Goddaughter** and **The Mislaid Genie**, were produced in 1972-1973), and he worked as prop manager on the sometimes X-rated, sometimes R-rated **Flesh Gordon**.

He loved movies, had been a movie projectionist, and the thrill of working in films took him away, diverted him, distracted him from what surely had to have been his chosen calling . . . the writing of stories. And much of what we've been left now seems so tragically time-wasting in retrospect. Items like "Sting!" which, even had it been carried to term, even had it been filmed, would have been nothing better than another dumb giant ant story. Tom had more than that to offer the world.

The same can be said about "Blue Eyes" and "Insects in Amber."

The former is another slight piece. An unfinished symphony. We cannot know how adventurous Tom would have been with this item. Again, Tom

---

* There exist two versions of "Sting": the original screenplay which appeared in 1976 in **Six Science Fiction Plays**, edited by Roger Elwood and a proposed first chapter and outline for the now defunct, Elwood-edited, Laser Books. It was decided, after the Introduction was written, not to include the original screenplay version, due to its extreme length (107 printed pages in its original paperback form) in an already large story collection, nor the inferior first chapter and outline (which Harlan is referring to) since the screenplay/novel adaptation of "2076: Blue Eyes" was already being included as an example of an uncompleted work in progress.

Embrace the Departing Shadow   xvii

was trying to break into the big time of screenwriting. This film treatment was registered with the Writers Guild in Hollywood on October 10th, 1972. For a short-line producer named Wilbur George, Mandala Productions, whose offices were in the bedroom suburb of Monrovia, a location about as relevant to Hollywood as Secaucus, New Jersey is to Broadway.

It's pretty basic after-the-bomb material; a touch of the world of "A Boy and His Dog" and a touch of AmerIndian hoopdedoo. The plot as outlined in the full treatment reads a lot like John Christopher's juvenile trilogy about the Tripods (THE WHITE MOUNTAINS, THE CITY OF GOLD AND LEAD, and THE POOL OF FIRE), a little like **Zardoz**, a little like WAR OF THE WORLDS and a lot like THE WIZARD OF OZ, the great-grandfather of all such odyssey tales, with the most distant ancestor being, of course, Homer's vast template.

Like "Sting!", there isn't much to comment on, and not much to recommend for serious readers of Reamy, save in one particular.

The scene of the birth of the mutant child, and the slaughter of the mother, carries an emotional freighting that is genuinely arresting. Even when slanting his work for that most superficial of mediums, the B flick, Tom could not help but bring to his work an operative sensibility on the highest levels of craft, and a passion that raised the construct above the usual mud of its ilk and genre.

As for the last of the three "stories" intended as narrative molds out of which films could be fashioned, "Insects in Amber," well, I'm afraid the best thing about it is the title, which I wish to God Tom had saved for a story worthy of its imagery.

It is, as presented here, clearly, obviously, painfully, selfconsciously, a narrative version of the low-budget horror film Tom originally conceived it to be.

Predictable, derivative and pretty thin stuff. Weak, watery blood; the kind of humour and vapor one gets when a bug is squashed. I don't for a moment believe Ben; I find Tannie the kind of cute li'l kid I'd like to drop-kick; Mom and Dad are tissue-paper cliches; and the stranded cadre of "insects" just one more example of rigidly structured, constricted thinking when it comes to a film intended to terrify. Your standard plot in which a disparate group of people are trapped in an enclosed space with a nameless thing that kills them off one by one a la Agatha Christie's TEN LITTLE INDIANS or, more contemporaneously, the Dan O'Bannon-Ridley Scott film **Alien**.

When the film didn't go, Tom obviously tried to salvage the work already expended by rewriting it as a short story. I cannot lie to you: unlike most of the other work in this fine collection, I find "Insects in Amber" an embarrassment.

Tom wasn't a science fiction writer, no matter how inconvenient that pragmatic reality may be for the loons and categorizers who need ready labels as a substitute for fresh thought. Even so, many of us who work in styles of our own creation have dabbled in the genre; and I think it's an unarguable truth that the work done clearly in the science fiction idiom is our least effective. For the Nivens, the Dicksons, the Heinleins and Clarkes, who feel comfortable with the rigors of pure science fiction, it is a boundaryless (and boundless) terrain on which they can run amok. But for fantasists like Tom and me, it was always a nightmare of restrictions, rules, accepted templates, fannish expectations and very much like asking us to swim the 1500 meter freestyle with anvils chained to our ankles and catchers' mitts on our paws.

It is tragically inevitable that when this book gets reviewed, it will, by all odds, wind up with the other "sci-fi" titles when, in fact, it is no more science fiction than the latest Stephen King or William Kotzwinkle novel. And even when a reviewer has the simple sense to realize it **ain't** sf, some mention of that will surface in the review: "This book should reach much farther than the usual science fiction crowd . . ." the review will say, and thereby damn it simply by the use of those words.

And that's a shame. Tom's work should be known to a much broader range of readers: those who respect writers who deal with the human condition; those who need no fasterthanlight rationales for improbable behavior; those who do not shy away from the darker side of the spirit. In short, those who respect fine writing above tinkertoy problems.

If the notes struck by the preceding little song rankle the True Believers for whom the sun rises and sets on the phrase (but not necessarily the actuality) "science fiction," well, I shrug and smile bravely. They should not be surprised; it's a song I've sung before. And that's the name of **that** tune.

I'm still here to sing the song, but Tom isn't. Though it was a refrain I've heard from him, in gentler tones, on any number of occasions. And if the True Believers find it awkward, gauche and ill-placed for such words to appear here, I offer as testament to the validity of the assertion, the story titled "Dinosaurs" in this volume.

Railing against the restrictions, Tom's natural bent when he conceived a story was not toward the accepted and acceptable science fiction ideas, but toward the dark fantasies of urban and rural life—"Under the Hollywood Sign", "Twilla", "The Detweiler Boy."

As far as I can tell, "Dinosaurs" is the only fully-formed, **actually** science fiction story Tom ever wrote. Like so many of us tarred with the wrong brush, Tom was frequently referred to as a "sci-fi guy" by the illiterati, even though he was obviously a fantasist. Just because some of his stories appeared in sf magazines. Which is like saying if you happen to rent a room in a cheap hotel that caters to pimps and whores, you must be either a pimp or a whore.

His interests and expertise never were in the areas of scientific extrapolation (though he had a wonderful grasp of the physical and biological sciences) or gadgetry. He cared about prying up the flat rocks in the human spirit and cataloguing with an unerring eye the slithery oogies that wriggled out to walk the streets. And so this story seems the assumption of an uncomfortable persona for Tom. Bluebabies and breathers and dreamers and whispering stones . . . all the la-de-dah of the prototypical sf whiplash are here, and frankly they whiz past me without getting in the wind very much.

But like all of us who were fans once, who have been gulled momentari-

Embrace the Departing Shadow

ly by the dreams we had as children, who have taken our unsuccessful flings at writing what others write better ... Tom did his and it's here for your comparison with other works that he wrote out of necessity, rather than curiosity or a misguided sense of **noblesse oblige**.

In the event my heavy hand becomes too oppressive in trying to deal with the stories in this book as attempts at **Art**—whether successful or otherwise—free of the misty-eyed, lachrymose, dishonest approbation slathered on the frequently-substandard literary legacies of writers termed "giants" by self-aggrandizing "critics" (that seem to proliferate in the world of science fiction every time a kindergarten class graduates to long pants and Norforms), know this:

Just because my friend has died, does not mean my brain or my critical faculties have turned to suet. Art is Art, and Friendship is Friendship; and respect for the latter means unswerving allegiance to the former. Even so, writing this candidly about Tom, for the eyes of strangers and friends and Tom's relatives, is a tightrope walk. He was a very private man, and he would often allude to places he'd been, experiences he'd had, things he knew first-hand ... but they were always only glancing references. He kept his own counsel and kept stages of his life separate from one another, and from the people he knew on those stages. It is not my place to talk about any of that. Tom would not approve.

But just to make certain I hadn't gone over the line in places where my own high-verbal tendencies deprived me of a sense of balance in the critical analyses, I called several of Tom's friends mentioned herein; and I read them all that has preceded this paragraph. They assured me I'd been cool. In fact, Richard Delap laughed and said Tom would have adored my comments about "Insects in Amber." Richard said, "Tom **hated** that story. He was amazed when Ed Ferman bought it ... and he could never understand what Ed saw in it. It brought in some food money and Tom was pleased Ferman had picked it up, but he despised the story."

Wheeew!

He also apprised me of an error earlier in this essay: the first two stories Tom sold, for which he received checks on the same day—from Damon Knight and Harry Harrison—were not "Twilla" and "San Diego Lightfoot Sue." They were "Beyond the Cleft" (first sale only because he opened Harrison's envelope first) and "Under the Hollywood Sign."

Sometimes, having Delap around is better than having a self-correcting typewriter.

But as a result of having been (as the est-holes put it) validated in my comments about Tom and his work, I can race toward a conclusion with comments about the four remaining stories that comprise this collection, three of which are among the best, thereby allowing me to ride out with upbeat thoughts.

"The Sweetwater Factor," I think you'll find, is a puckish, lightly intellectual variation on the O. Henry "sting in the tail" story. A one-punch entertainment, neither particularly well-developed nor particularly deep ... simply amusing. Which is no doubt just what Tom intended. He was accomplished at relaxing, and this kind of story, done by others, always amused him; I take it as a given that he should attempt to return the favor.

It reads as if Tom didn't really have any idea where the story was going when he envisioned the man sitting on the bench and the giant nose coming after him. It's a story that just grew, like Topsy. We all do it from time to time, in almost exactly the way a good jazz musician does it: just jamming. Crank it up and let it wail. It's a technique more widely used by fantasists than is generally acknowledged: free-forming it, letting the wild surmise take you where it chooses.

Bold assumptions drawn from insufficient evidence, you say? Putting yourself in Reamy's mind a bit too arrogantly, aren't you, you say? Second-guessing, Monday morning quarterbacking, you say?

As a student of fantastic literature, as a man who has worn out five separate editions of Strunk & White's ELEMENTS OF STYLE, as a serious literary critic steeped in the wisdom of two thousand years of classical literature, as a creative intellect whose credentials for worthiness include that I am looked on with disfavor by such lousy critics as Baird Searles, Paul Walker and Lester del Rey, I assure you I'm absolutely correct in this bit of auctorial detectivework, and offer as interior evidence to support my supposition Tom's introduction of the "personifications of abstractions" in the persons of History and Mother Nature in this story.

And besides, Tom **told** me that's how he wrote it.

For me, the best story in the book is one of the shortest. Don't ask me why. These things have no logic to them. "The Detweiler Boy" is probably the **strongest** story in the book; "Under the Hollywood Sign" is probably the **best written**; "San Diego Lightfoot Sue" is probably the **most emotional**; and each of them is, seriously considered, better than my favorite.

Nonetheless, I **adore** "The Mistress of Windraven." Adore, do you hear!

Sensational. Just a real, no fooling, knocks-me-out, card-carrying, righteous lollapalooza! It is a ring-tailed doozy of a variation on the old "Miniver Cheevy" kind of s/he who hates her/his life and runs off into a painting. You've read or seen it done a million times.

(Rod Serling misappropriated the idea at least twice, if I recall correctly.)

I remember a version of the idea, uh, how good's my memory, in an early issue of **Fantastic** magazine, back around 1953: "Room with a View" by Esther Carlson, if memory serves, which it probably doesn't, but I'm getting old, so be kind.

Story of a person who hates reality, paints her/himself into a wish-fulfillment picture. And wasn't there one by Clark Ashton Smith? "The Willow Landscape" it was called . . . if memory ain't failing.

Where was I?

Oh. Yeah. Right. This is Tom's entry in the I-can't-stand-it-no-more-lemme-outta-here! Sweepstakes.

And a super entry it is.

Which leaves two stories yet to comment upon. Now, if you've been

Embrace the Departing Shadow

keeping track, I've gotten around to each story in the order I'd been advised by Jim Loehr of EarthLight Publishers that they would appear in the book.* Only exception has been grouping the three intended-as-movies pieces so I could get them out of the way quickly. But now I depart from the table of contents to discuss "Waiting for Billy Star" penultimately, leaving "The Detweiler Boy" for last.

"Waiting for Billy Star" is easy to talk about. It's a poignant, unadorned version of the traditional ghost-returns-for-its-true-love story. But highly effective, of its kind, not only because it's told simply and straightforwardly, but because Tom demonstrates another of his strong points: an uncanny ability to establish locale. A feeling that you know what the landscape, the background, looks like.

Very hard to do. Even some of our most vaunted "masters" of the fantasy story fail to limn the background. Their tales take place in an echoing void, sans color, sans scent, sans all.

But even in this snippet Tom was able to create the world inside and outside that roadside truck stop in Caprock, Texas.

Another thing: because this is such a familiar trope, you know the ending before it hits. You know it when Cliff speaks to the narrator, Wade, at the cash register on his way out, when he tells Wade, "She said she'd wait for him here." Hell, you know it from the title and from the moment that Cliff tells Susanne that Billy Star is dead. You just know what's coming.

But consider Tom's skill. Unlike the long-winded Hawthorne or the wearisome Eliot (George, that is), who tip their ending ten thousand words before the conclusion and then plod along point by obvious point with dreary narrative that expends thirty-three hundred words telling you what you're going to see, thirty-three hundred words showing it to you, and thirty-three hundred words telling you what you've just been shown (one assumes because they viewed their audiences as dull-witted and slow on the uptake), Tom races to his denouement with staccato dialogue and one final paragraph of beautifully tragic imagery.

He was an instinctive storyteller; even with this most obvious and predictable form of fantasy, Tom knew how to manipulate the reader to let the reader enrich him/herself.

Like John Lee in "San Diego Lightfoot Sue," Tom had a way of allowing people to be better than they were ordinarily. Like this story, the quality that is most universally remembered about Tom by those who knew him, was that he was a **nice** man.

A nice man wrote this nice little story.

Bringing me, at last, to the last story, the one that lasts longest in the memory. "The Detweiler Boy."

Trying to talk about Tom's work, so deeply informed by his life and his

---

* It should be noted that there are two unpublished stories in the Reamy **ouevre**, not available for inclusion in this volume because they will be appearing in **The Final Dangerous Visions** ("Potiphee, Petey and Me") and in **New Voices IV** ("M is for the Million Things", which Tom wanted to re-title "They Sleep So Poorly While They Live").

nature, without (as I've said earlier) treading in territory that is clearly **terra incognita**, is difficult. I have always believed that a writer is a self-cannibalizing creature using everything s/he has ever known, learned, felt or suspected in transmogrified literary terms. Writers are keeks, taking guided tours through other people's lives, and reporting back in. But this isn't fiction, it's **hommage**, and . . .

"The Detweiler Boy" is Tom filing a report on some of the places he had been, some of the people he had known, interpreting in a singular way some of the secrets those people would rather die than have revealed. As a result, there are psychosexual aspects to this truly frightening narrative that open doors into the darkness of our souls, doors that take integrity and great courage to open. Doors that give onto a labyrinth of torments created by over five thousand seven hundred years of the Judeo-Christian Ethos.

In the creation of this extraordinary black diamond, Tom is in the loftiest tradition of the High Art dreamers—Poe, Kafka, Mary Shelly, Bierce. His descent into the maelstrom out-eldritches even the three stories by Lovecraft one might correctly call excellent.

A fable that speaks to our own hidden fears and seldom-acknowledged hungers.

The shadows that walked the streets for Tom in Hollywood were terrible creatures indeed; and in this story he manages to capture them for a burning instant in the dark glass of his artistry, in a way that I don't think anyone who reads "The Detweiler Boy" will ever be able to completely flense from memory.

It is a surprising and excellent . . . awful story.

I hope no one mistakes my use of the word **awful**.

And now the pages turn brown. And now the glue that binds the covers begins to consume the endpapers. And now the spine cracks. And now the fragile triangles of the corners fall. And now the story ends.

It is dark where I sit writing. One light above the lover with which I share my dreams, this machine like Tom's machine, intended for the spinning of webs beautiful and terrible beyond any telling. Over such a machine he spent his last moments.

And now the story ends, and now the words run out.

And now, shadows, you can go.

HARLAN ELLISON
Los Angeles
12 September 79

Twilla

Twilla Gilbreath blew into Miss Mahan's life like a pink butterfly wing that same day in early December the blue norther dropped the temperature forty degrees in two hours. Mr. Choate, the prinicpal, ushered Twilla and her parents into Miss Mahan's ninth grade home room shortly after the tardy bell rang. She had just checked the roll: all seventeen ninth graders were present except for Sammy Stocker who was in the Liberal hospital having his appendix removed. She was telling the class how nice it would be if they sent a get-well card when the door opened.

"Goooood morning, Miss Mahan," Mr. Choate smiled cheerfully. He always smiled cheerfully first thing in the morning, but soured as the day wore on. You could practically tell time by Mr. Choate's mouth. "We have a new ninth grader for you this morning, Miss Mahan. This is Mr. and Mrs. Gilbreath and their daughter, Twilla."

Several things happened at once. Miss Mahan shook hands with the parents; she threw a severe glance at the class when she heard a snigger—but it was only Alice May Turner, who would probably giggle if she were being devoured by a bear; and she had to forcibly keep her eyebrows from rising when she got a good look at Twilla. Good Lord, she thought, and felt her smile falter.

Miss Mahan had never in her life, even when it was fashionable for a child to look like that, seen anyone so perfectly . . . pink and . . . doll-like. She wasn't sure why she got such an impression of pinkness, because the child was dressed in yellow, and had golden hair (**that's** the color they mean when they say golden hair, she thought with wonder) done in, of all things, drop curls, with a big yellow bow in back. Twilla looked up at her with a sweet, radiant, sunny smile and clear periwinkle-blue eyes.

Miss Mahan detested her on sight.

She thought she saw, when Alice May giggled, the smile freeze and the lovely eyes dart toward the class, but she wasn't sure. It all happened in an instant, and then Mr. Choate continued his Cheerful Charlie routine.

"Mr. Gilbreath has bought the old Peacock place."

"Really?" she said, tearing her eyes from Twilla. "I didn't know it was for sale."

Mr. Gilbreath chuckled. "Not the entire farm, of course. I'm no farmer. Only the house and grounds. Such a charming old place. The owner lives in Wichita and had no use for them."

"I would think the house is pretty run down," Miss Mahan said, glancing at Twilla still radiating at the world. "No one's lived in it since Wash and Grace Elizabeth died ten years ago."

"It is a little," Mrs. Gilbreath said pleasantly.

"But structurally sound," interjected Mr. Gilbreath pleasantly.

"We'll enjoy fixing it up," Mrs. Gilbreath continued pleasantly.

"Mis Mahan teaches English to the four upper grades," said Mr. Choate, bringing them back to the subject, "as well as speech and drama. Miss Mahan has been with the Hawley school system for thirty-one years."

The Gilbreaths smiled pleasantly. "My . . . ah . . . Twilla seems very young to be in the ninth grade." That get-up made her look about eleven, Miss Mahan thought.

The Gilbreaths beamed at their daughter. "Twilla is only thirteen," Mrs. Gilbreath crooned, pride swelling her like yeast. "She's such an intelligent child. She was able to skip the second grade."

"I see. From where have you moved?"

"Boston," replied Mr. Gilbreath.

"Boston. I hope . . . ah . . . Twilla doesn't find it difficult to adjust to a small town school. I'm sure Hawley, Kansas, is quite unlike Boston."

Mr. Gilbreath touched Twilla lovingly on the shoulder. "I'm sure she'll have no trouble."

"Well," Mr. Choate rubbed his palms together. "Twilla is in good hands. Shall I show you around the rest of the school?"

"Of course," smiled Mrs. Gilbreath.

They departed with fond murmurings and goodbyes, leaving Twilla like a buttercup stranded in a cabbage patch. Miss Mahan mentally shook her head. She hadn't seen a family like that since Dick and Jane and Spot and Puff were sent the way of **McGuffey's Reader**. Mr. and Mrs. Gilbreath were in their middle thirties, good looking without being glamorous, their clothes nice though as oddly wrong as Twilla's. They seemed cut with some out-dated Ideal Family template. Surely, there must be an older brother, a dog, and a cat somewhere.

"Well . . . ah, Twilla," Miss Mahan said, trying to reinforce the normal

Twilla

routine, "if you will take a seat; that one there, behind Alice May Turner. Alice May, will you wave a flag or something so Twilla will know which one?" Alice May giggled. "Thank you, dear." Twilla moved gracefully toward the empty desk. Miss Mahan felt as if she should say something to the child. "I hope you will . . . ah . . . enjoy going to school in Hawley, dear."

Twilla sat primly and glowed at her. "I'm sure I shall, Miss Mahan," she said, speaking for the first time. Her voice was like the tinkle of fairy bells—just as Miss Mahan was afraid it would be.

"Good," she said and went back to the subject of a get-well card for Sammy Stocker. She had done this so often—there had been a great many sick children in thirty-one years—it had become almost a ritual needing only a small portion of her attention. The rest she devoted to the covert observation of Twilla Gilbreath.

Twilla sat at her desk, displaying excellent posture, with her hands folded neatly before her, seemingly paying attention to the Great Greeting Card Debate, but actually giving the rest of the class careful scrutiny. Miss Mahan marveled at the surreptitious calculation in the girl's face. She realizes she's something of a green monkey, Miss Mahan thought, and I'll bet my pension she doesn't let the situation stand.

And the class surveyed Twilla, in their superior position of established territorial rights, with open curiosity—and with the posture of so many sacks of corn meal. Some of them looked at her, Miss Mahan was afraid, with rude amusement—especially the girls, and especially Wanda O'Dell who had bloomed suddenly last summer like a plump rose. Oh, yes, Wanda was going to be a problem. Just like her five older sisters. Thank goodness, she sighed, Wanda was the last of them.

Children, Miss Mahan sighed again, but fondly.

Children?

They were children when she started teaching and certainly were when she was fifteen, but, now, she wasn't sure. Fifteen is such an awkward, indefinite age. Take Ronnie Dwyer: he looks like a pre-pubescent thirteen at most. And Carter Redwine, actually a couple of months younger than Ronnie, could pass for seventeen easily and was anything but pre-pubescent. Poor Carter, a child in a man's body. To make matters worse, he was the best looking boy in town; and to make matters even worse yet, he was well aware of it.

And, she noticed, so was Twilla. Forget it, Little Pink Princess. Carter already has more than he can handle, Miss Mahan chuckled to herself. Can't you see those dark circles under his eyes? They didn't get there from studying. And then she blushed inwardly.

Oh, the poor children. They think they have so many secrets. If they only knew. Between the tattle-tales and the teachers' gossip, she doubted if the whole student body had three secrets among them.

Miss Mahan admonished herself for having such untidy thoughts. She didn't use to think about things like that, but then, fifteen-year-olds didn't lead such overtly sexual lives back then. She remembered reading somewhere that only thirty-five per cent of the children in America were still virgins at fifteen. But those sounded like Big City statistics, not applicable to Hawley.

Then she sighed. It was all beyond her. The bell rang just as the get-well card situation was settled. The children rose reluctantly to go to their first class: algebra with Mr. Whittaker. She noticed that Twilla had cozied up to Alice May, though she still kept her eye on Carter Redwine. Carter was not unaware and, with deliberate, lordly indifference, sauntered from the room with his hand on Wanda O'Dell's shoulder. Miss Mahan thought the glint she observed in Twilla's eyes might lead to an interesting turn of events.

Children.

She cleared her mind of random speculation and geared it to **Macbeth** as the senior class filed in with everything on their minds but Shakespeare. Raynelle Franklin, Mr. Choate's secretary, lurked nervously among them, looking like a chicken who suddenly finds herself with a pack of coyotes. She edged her middle-aged body to Miss Mahan's desk, accepted the absentee report, and scuttled out. Miss Mahan looked forward to Raynelle's performance every morning.

During lunch period, Miss Mahan walked to the dime store for a get-well card which the ninth grade class would sign that afternoon when they returned for English. She glanced at the sky and unconsciously pulled her gray tweed coat tighter about her. The sky had turned a cobalt blue in the north. It wouldn't be long now. Though the temperature must be down to thirty-five already, it seemed colder. She guessed her blood was getting thin, she knew her flesh was. Old age, she thought, old age. Thin blood, thin flesh, and brittle bones. She sometimes felt as if she were turning into a bird.

She almost bumped into Twilla's parents emerging from the dry goods store, their arms loaded with packages. Their pleasant smiles turned on. Click, click. They chatted trivialities for a moment, adding new dimensions to Twilla's already flawless character. Miss Mahan had certainly seen her share of blindly doting parents, but this was unbelievable. She had seen the cold calculation with which Twilla had studied the class, and that was hardly the attribute of an angel. Something didn't jibe somewhere. She speculated on the contents of the packages, but thought she knew. Then she couldn't resist; she asked if Twilla were an only child. She was. Well, there went that.

She looked at the clock on the high tower of the white rococo courthouse, and, subtracting fourteen minutes, decided she'd better hurry if she wanted to eat lunch and have a rest before her one o'clock class.

The teachers' lounge was a reasonably comfortable room where students were forbidden to enter on pain of death—though it seemed to be a continuing game on their part to try. Miss Mahan hung her coat on

Twilla

a hanger and shivered. "Has anyone heard a weather forecast?" she asked the room in general.

Mrs. Latham (home economics) looked up from her needlepoint and shook her head vaguely. Poor old dear, thought Miss Mahan. Due to retire this year, I think. Seems like she's been here since Creation. She taught me when I was in school. Leo Whittaker (math) was reading a copy of **Playboy**. Probably took it from one of the children. "Supposed to be below twenty by five," he said, then grinned and held up the magazine. "Ronnie Dwyer."

Miss Mahan raised her eyebrows. Loretta McBride (history/civics) tsked, shook her head, and went back to her book. Miss Mahan retrieved her carton of orange juice from the small refrigerator and drank it with her fried egg sandwich. She put part of the sandwich back in the Baggie. She hardly had any appetite at all anymore. Guess what they say is true: the older you get . . .

She began to crochet on her interminable afghan. The little squares were swiftly becoming a pain in the neck, and she regretted ever starting it. She looked at Mrs. Latham and her needlepoint. She sighed, I guess it's expected of us old ladies. Anyway, it gave her something to hide behind when she didn't feel like joining the conversation. But today she felt like talking, though it didn't seem as if anyone else did.

She finished a square and snipped the yarn. "What do you think of the Shirley Temple doll who joined our merry group this morning?"

Mrs. Latham looked up and smiled. "Charming child."

"Yes," said Loretta, putting away the book, "absolutely charming. And smart as a whip. Really knows her Amercian History. Joined in the discussion as if she'd been in the class all semester." Miss McBride was one of the few outsiders teaching in Hawley who gave every indication of remaining. Usually they came and went as soon as greener pastures opened up. Most were like Miss Mahan, Mrs. Latham, and Leo Whittaker, living their entire lives there.

It was practically incestuous, she thought. Mrs. Latham had taught her, she had taught Leo, and he was undoubtedly teaching part of the next crop. Miss Mahan had to admit that Leo had been something of a surprise. He was only twenty-five and had given no indication in high school that he was destined for anything better than a hanging. She wondered how long it would be before Leo connected his students' inability to keep secrets from the teachers with his own disreputable youth.

Now here he was. Two years in the army, four years in college, his second year of teaching, married to Lana Redwine (Carter's cousin and one of the nicest girls in town) with a baby due in a couple of months. You never can tell. You just never can tell.

"Well, Leo," Miss Mahan asked bemused, "what did you think of Twilla Gilbreath?"

"Oh, I don't know. She seems very intelligent—at least in algebra.

Quiet and well-behaved—unlike a few others. Dresses kinda funny. Seems to have set her sights on my cousin-in-law." He grinned. "Fat chance!" Miss Mahan wouldn't say Leo was handsome—not in the way Carter Redwine was—but that grin was the reason half the girls in school had a crush on him.

"Oh? You noticed that too? I imagine she may have a few surprises up her sleeve. I don't think our Twilla is the fairy tale princess she's made out to be." She began another square.

"You must be mistaken, Miss Mahan," Loretta said wide-eyed. "The child is an absolute darling. And the very idea: a baby like that running after Carter Redwine. I never heard of such a thing!"

"Really?" Miss Mahan smiled to herself and completed a shell stitch. "We shall see what we shall see."

The norther hit during the ninth grade English class, bringing a merciful, if only temporary, halt to the sufferings of Silas Marner. The glass in the windows rattled and pinged. The wind played on the downspouts like a mad flautist. Sand ticked against the windows and the guard lights came on in the school yard. Outside had become a murky indigo, as if the world were under water. Miss Mahan switched on the lights, making the windows seem even darker. Garbage cans rolled down the street, but you could hardly hear them above the howl of the wind. And the downtown Christmas decorations were whipping loose, as they always did at least once every year.

The sand was only temporary; a cloud of it blown along before the storm, but the wind could last all night or all week. Miss Mahan remembered when she was a girl during the great drought of the thirties, when the sand wasn't temporary, when it came like a mile-high, solid tidal wave of blown away farmland, when you couldn't tell noon from midnight, when houses were half buried when the wind finally died down. She shuddered.

"All right, children. Settle down. You've all seen northers before."

Leo and Loretta were right about one thing: Twilla was intelligent. She was also perceptive, imaginative . . . and adaptable. She had already dropped the Little Mary Sunshine routine, though Miss Mahan couldn't imagine why she had used it in the first place. It must have been a pose—as if the child had somehow confused the present and 1905.

The temperature had dropped to eighteen by the time school was out. The wind hit Miss Mahan like icy needles. Her gray tweed coat did about as much good as tissue paper. She grabbed at her scarf as it threatened to leave her head and almost lost her briefcase. She walked as fast as her aging legs would go and made it to her six-year-old Plymouth. The car started like a top, billowing a cloud of steam from the exhaust pipe to be whipped away by the wind.

She sat for a moment, getting her breath back, letting the car warm up. She saw Twilla, huddled against the wind, dash to a new black

Twilla

Chrysler and get in with her parents. The car backed out and moved away. Miss Mahan wasn't the least surprised that little Miss Gilbreath wasn't riding the school bus. The old Peacock place was a mile off the highway at Miller's Corners, a once-upon-a-time town eight miles east of Hawley.

Well, I guess I'm not much better, she thought. I only live four blocks away—but I'll be darned if I'll walk it today. She always did walk except when the weather was bad, and, oddly enough, the older she got, the worse the weather seemed to get.

She pulled into the old carriage house that served equally well with automobiles, and walked hurriedly across the yard into the big, rather ancient house that had belonged to her grandfather. She knew it was silly to live all alone in such a great pile—she had shut off the upstairs and hadn't been up in months—but it was equally silly not to live there. It was paid for and her grandfather had set up a trust fund to pay the taxes. It was a very nice house, really; cool in the summer, but (she turned up the fire) a drafty old barn in the winter.

She turned on the television to see if there were any weather bulletins. While it warmed up, she closed off all the downstairs rooms except the kitchen, her bedroom, and the parlor, putting rolled up towels along the bottoms of the doors to keep the cold air out. She returned to the parlor to see the television screen covered with snow and horizontal streaks of lightning.

She knew it. The aerial had blown down again. She turned off the set and put on a kettle for tea.

The wind had laid somewhat by the time Miss Mahan reached school the next morning, but still blew in fitful gusts. The air was the color of ice and so cold she expected to hear it crackle as she moved through it. The windows in her room were steamed over and she was busily wiping them when Twilla arrived. Although Miss Mahan had expected something like this, she stared nevertheless.

Twilla's hair was still the color of spun elfin gold but the drop curls were missing. Instead it fell in soft folds to below her shoulders in a style much too adult for a thirteen-year-old. But, then, this morning Twilla looked as much like thirteen as Mrs. Latham. All the physical things were there: the hair, just the right amount of makeup, a short, stylish skirt, a pale green jersey that displayed her small but adequate breasts, a lovely antique pendant on a gold chain nestling between them.

But it wasn't only the physical things—any thirteen-year-old would have appeared more mature with a similar overhaul—it was something in the face, in her bearing: an attitude of casual sophistication, a confidence usually attainable only by those secure in their power. Twilla smiled. Shirley Temple and Mary Pickford were gone; this was the smile of a conqueror.

Miss Mahan realized her face was hanging out, but before she was forced to say anything, several students, after a prelude of clanging locker doors, barged in. Twilla turned to look at them and the moment was electric. Their inane chatter stopped as if someone had thrown a switch. They gaped. Twilla gave them time for the full effect, then strolled to them and began chatting as if nothing were new.

Miss Mahan sat at her desk feeling a little weak in the knees. She waited for Carter Redwine to arrive as, obviously, was Twilla. When he did, it was almost anticlimactic. His recently acquired worldliness and sexual sophistication melted away in one callow gawk. But he recovered quickly and his feelers popped up, testing the situation. Twilla moved to her desk, giving him a satisfied smile. Wanda O'Dell looked as if she'd eaten a bug.

Miss Mahan had to admit to the obvious. Twilla was a stunning beauty. But the whole thing was . . . curious . . . to say the least.

The conversation in the teachers' lounge was devoted almost exclusively to the transformation of Twilla Gilbreath. Mrs. Latham had noted it vaguely. Loretta McBride ceded reluctantly to Miss Mahan's observations of the previous day. Leo Whittaker expressed a masculine appreciation of the new Twilla, earning a fishy look from Loretta. "I never saw Carter act so goofy," he said grinning.

But neither they nor any of the others noted the obvious strangeness of it all. At least, Miss Mahan thought, it seems obvious to me.

That day Miss Mahan set out on a campaign of Twilla-watching. She even went upstairs to her grandfather's study and purloined one of the blank journals from the bottom drawer of his desk. She curled up in the big chair, after building a fire in the parlor fireplace—the first one this year—and opened the journal to the first page ruled with pale blue lines. She wrote **Twilla**, after rejecting **The Twilla Gilbreath Affair, The Peculiar Case of Twilla Gilbreath**, and others in a similar vein.

She felt silly and conspiratorial and almost put the journal away, but, instead, wrote further down the page: **Is my life so empty that I must fill it by spying on a student?**

She thought about what she had written and decided it was either unfair to Twilla or unfair to herself, but let it remain. She turned to the second page and wrote **Tuesday, the 5th** at the top. She filled that page and the next with her impressions of Twilla's first day. She headed the fourth page **Wednesday, the 6th** and noted the events of the day just ending.

On rereading, she thought perhaps she might have over emphasized the oddities, the incongruities, and the anachronisms, but, after all, that was what it was about, wasn't it?

It began snowing during the night. Miss Mahan drove to school through a fantasy landscape. The wind was still blowing and the steely flakes came down almost horizontally. She loved snow, always had, but she preferred the Christmas card variety when the big fluffy flakes floated down through still, crisp air like so many pillow fights.

She knew there had been developments as soon as Carter Redwine entered the room. His handsome face was glum and sullen and looked as if he hadn't slept. He sat at his desk with his head hunched between his shoulders and didn't look up until Twilla came in. Miss Mahan darted her eyes from one to the other. Carter looked away again, his neck and ears glowing red. Twilla ignored him; more than that—she consigned him to total nonexistence.

Miss Mahan was dumbfounded. What on earth . . . ? Had Carter made advances and been rebuffed? That wouldn't explain it. Surely he had been turned down before. Hadn't he? Of course, she knew he had. Leo, who viewed his cousin-in-law's adventures with bemused affection, had been laughing about it in the teachers' lounge one day. "He'll settle down," Leo had said, "he just has a new toy." Which made her blush after she'd thought about it a while.

Surely, he hadn't tried to take Twilla . . . by force? She couldn't believe that. Despite everything, Carter was a very decent boy. He had just developed too early, was too handsome, and knew too many willing girls. What then? Was it the first pangs of love? That look on his face wasn't love-sickness. It was red, roaring mortification. Then she knew what must have happened. Carter had not been rebuffed, maybe even encouraged. But, whatever she had expected, he had been inadequate.

Twilla had made another error. She had failed to realize Carter, despite the way he looked, was only fifteen. Then the ugly enormity of it struck her. My God, she thought, Twilla is only thirteen. What had she wanted from Carter that he was too inexperienced or naive to give her?

Friday, the 8th

Billy Jermyn came in this morning with a black eye. It's all over school that Carter gave it to him in Gym yesterday when Billy teased him about Twilla. What did she do to humiliate him so? I've never known Carter to fight. I guess that's one secret that'll never penetrate the teachers' lounge.

Twilla is taking over the class. I've seen it coming since Wednesday. It's subtle but pretty obvious when you know what to look for. The others defer to her in lots of little ways. Twilla is being very gracious about it. Butter wouldn't melt in her mouth. (Wonder where that little saying came from?—doesn't make much sense when you analyze it.)

I also wonder who Twilla's got her amorous sights on, now that Carter failed to make the grade. She hasn't shown an interest in anyone in particular that I've noticed. And there's been no gossip in the lounge. The flap created by Carter has probably shown her the wisdom of keeping her romances to herself. She's adaptable.

Sonny Bowen offered to put my TV aerial back up for me. I knew one of them would. Bless their conniving little hearts.

TGIF!

Miss Mahan closed the journal and sat watching a log in the fireplace that was about to fall. The whole Twilla affair was curious, but no more curious than her own attitude. She should have been scandalized (you didn't see too many thirteen-year-old combinations of Madame Bovary and the Dragon Lady—even these days), but she only felt fascination. Somehow it didn't seem quite real; more as if she were watching a movie. She smiled slightly. Wonder if it would be rated R or X, she thought. R, I guess. Haven't seen anyone with their clothes off yet.

The log fell, making her jump. She laughed in embarrassment, banked the fire, and went to bed.

The snow was still falling Monday morning, though the fierceness of the storm had passed. There was little wind and the temperature had risen somewhat. That's more like it, Miss Mahan said to herself, watching the big soft flakes float down in random zig-zags.

The bell rang and she turned away from the windows to watch the ninth grade home room clatter out. The Gilbreaths must have been out of town over the weekend, she observed. Twilla didn't get that outfit in Hawley. But she was still wearing that lovely, rather barbaric pendant around her neck. She sighed. Two days away from Twilla had made her wonder if she weren't getting senile; if she weren't making a mystery out of a molehill; if she weren't imagining the whole thing. Twilla was certainly a picture of normalcy this morning.

Raynelle Franklin came for the absentee report looking more like a frightened chicken than ever. She followed an evasive course to Miss Mahan's desk and took the report as if she were afraid of being struck. There were only two names on the report: Sammy Stocker and Yvonne Wilkins.

Raynelle glanced at the names and paled. "Haven't you **heard?**" she whispered.

"Heard what?"

Raynelle looked warily at the senior class shuffling in and backed away, motioning for Miss Mahan to follow. Miss Mahan groaned and followed her into the hall. Students were milling about everywhere, chattering and banging locker doors. Raynelle grimaced in distress.

"Raynelle, will you stand still and tell me!" Miss Mahan commanded in exasperation.

"Someone will hear," she pleaded.

"Hear **what?**"

Raynelle fluttered her hands and blew air through her teeth. She looked quickly around and then huddled against Miss Mahan. "Yvonne Wilkins," she hissed.

"Well?"

"She's . . . she's . . . **dead!**"

Miss Mahan thought Raynelle was going to faint. She grabbed her arm. "How?" she asked in her no-nonsense voice.

"I don't know," Raynelle gasped. "No one will tell me."

Miss Mahan thought for a moment. "Go on with what you were doing." She released Raynelle and marched into Mr. Choate's office.

Mr. Choate looked up with a start. He was already wearing his three

Twilla

o'clock face. "I see you've heard." He was resigned.

"Yes. What is going on? Raynelle was having a conniption fit." Miss Mahan looked at him over her glasses the same way she would a recalcitrant student.

"Miss Mahan," he sighed, "Sheriff Walker thought it best if the whole thing were kept quiet."

"Quiet? Why?"

"He didn't want a panic."

"Panic? What did she die of, bubonic plague?"

"No." He looked at her as if he wished she would vanish. "I guess I might as well tell you. It'll be all over town by ten o'clock anyway. Yvonne was murdered." He said the last word as if he'd never heard it before.

Miss Mahan felt her knees giving way and quickly sat down. "This is unbelievable," she said weakly. Mr. Choate nodded. "Why does Robin Walker want to keep it quiet? What happened?"

"Miss Mahan, I've told you all I can tell you."

"Surely Robin knows secrecy will only make it worse? Making a mystery out of it is guaranteed to create a panic."

Mr. Choate shrugged. "I have my instructions. You're late for your class."

Miss Mahan went back to her room in a daze, her imagination ringing up possibilities like a cash register. She couldn't keep her mind on **Macbeth** and the class was restless. They obviously didn't know yet, but their radar had picked up something they couldn't explain.

When the class was over she went into the hall and saw the news moving through like a shock wave. She accomplished absolutely nothing the rest of the morning. The children were fidgety and kept whispering among themselves. She was as disturbed as they and made only half-hearted attempts to restore order.

At lunch time, she bundled up and trounced through the snow to the courthouse. It was too hot inside and the heat only accentuated the courthouse smell. She didn't know what it was, but they all smelled the same. Maybe it was the state-issue disinfectant. The Hawley courthouse hadn't changed since she could remember. The same wooden benches lined the hall; the same ceiling fans encircled the round lights. No, she corrected herself, there was a change: the brass spittoons had been removed some twelve years ago. It seemed subtly wrong without the spittoons.

She was removing her coat when Rose Newcastle emerged in a huff from the sheriff's office, her heels popping on the marble floor, sending echoes ringing down the hall. Rose was the last of the three Willet girls, the daughters of old Judge Willet. People still called them the Willet girls, although Rose was considerably older than Miss Mahan. She was a widow now, her husband having finally died of insignificance.

"Hello, Rose," she said, feeling trapped. Rose puffed to a halt like a plump locomotive.

"Oh, Miss Mahan, isn't it **awful**!" she wailed. "And Robin Walker absolutely refuses to do anything! We could all be murdered in our beds!"

"I'm sure he's doing everything he can, Rose. What did he tell you?"

"**Nothing!** Absolutely nothing! If my father were still alive, I'd have that man's job. I told him he'd better watch his step come next election. I told him, as a civic leader in this town, I had a right to know what's going on. I told him I had a good mind to organize a Citizens Committee to investigate the whole affair."

"Give him a chance. Robin is a very conscientious man."

"He's a child."

"Come on, Rose. He's at least thirty. I taught him for four years and I have complete confidence in him. You'll have to excuse me. I'm here to see him myself."

"He won't tell you anything," Rose said, sounding slightly mollified.

"Perhaps," Miss Mahan said. Rose echoed off down the hall. "He might have if you haven't put his tail over the dashboard," she muttered and pushed open the door.

Loreen Whittaker, Leo's aunt by marriage, looked up and smiled. "Hello, Miss Mahan. What can I do for you?"

"Hello, Loreen. I'd like to see Robin, if I may."

Loreen chuckled. "He gave me strict orders to let no one in but the governor—right after Mrs. Newcastle left."

Miss Mahan grimaced. "I met her in the hall. Would you ask him? It's important."

Loreen arose from her desk and went into the sheriff's private office. Miss Mahan felt that she and Robin were good friends. She had not only taught him, but his sister, Mary Ellen, and his little brother, Curtis, was a senior this year. She liked all of them and thought they liked her. Robin's son was in the second grade and a little doll. She was looking forward to teaching him, too.

Loreen came out of his office, grinning. "He said you could come in but I was to frisk you first." Her smile wavered. "Try to cheer him up, Miss Mahan. It's the first . . . murder we've had since he's been in office, and it's getting to him."

Miss Mahan nodded and went in. The sheriff sat hunched over his desk. His hair was mussed where he had been running his hand through it. There was a harried look on his face but he dredged up a thin smile for her.

"You aren't gonna give me trouble, too, are you?" he asked warily.

"I ran into Rose in the hall," she smiled back at him.

He motioned her to a chair. "What's the penalty for punching a civic leader in the nose?"

"You should know that better than I."

He grunted. "Yeah." He leaned back in the chair and stretched his

Twilla

long legs. "I can't discuss Yvonne Wilkins, if that's what you're here for."

"That's why I'm here. Don't you think this secrecy is worse than the facts? People will be imagining all sorts of horrible things."

"I doubt if anything they could imagine would be worse than the actual facts, Miss Mahan. You'll have to trust me. I have to do it this way." He ran his fingers through his hair again. "I'm afraid I may be in over my head on this. There's just me and five deputies for the whole county. And we haven't anything to work on. Nothing."

"Where did they find her?"

"Okay," he sighed. "I'll tell you this much. Yvonne went out yesterday afternoon in her father's car to visit Linda Murray. When she didn't come home last night, Mr. Wilkins called the Murrays and they said Yvonne left about six-thirty. He was afraid she'd had an accident in the snow, so he called me. We found her about three this morning out on the dirt road nearly to the old Weatherly place. She was in the car . . . dead. It's been snowing for five days. There wasn't a track of any kind and no fingerprints that didn't belong. And that's all you're gonna worm out of me."

Miss Mahan had an idea. "Had she been . . . molested?"

Robin looked at her as if he'd been betrayed. "Yes," he said simply.

"But," she protested, "why the big mystery? I know it's horrible, but it's not likely to cause a . . . a panic."

He got up and paced around the office. "Miss Mahan, I can't tell you any more."

"Is there more? Is there more than rape and murder?" She felt something like panic rising in her.

Robin squatted in front of her, taking her hands in his. "If there's anyone in town I'd tell, it would be you. You know that. I've loved you ever since I was fourteen years old. If you keep after me, I'll tell you, so have a little pity on a friend and stop pushing."

She felt her eyes burning and motioned for him to get up. "Robin, you're not playing fair." She stood up and he held her coat for her. "You always were able to get around me. Okay, you win."

"Thank you, Miss Mahan," he said genuinely relieved and kissed her on the forehead. She stopped in the hall and dabbed at her eyes.

But I haven't given up yet, she thought as she huddled in her coat on the way to Paul Sullivan's office. The bell tinkled on the door and the nurse materialized from somewhere.

"Miss Mahan. What are you doing out in this weather?"

"I'd like to see the doctor, Elaine." She hung her coat on the rack.

"He's with the little Archer girl now. She slipped on the snow and twisted her ankle."

"I'll wait." She sat and picked up a magazine without looking at it. Elaine Holliday had been one of her students. Who in town hadn't, she wondered. Elaine wanted to talk about the murder as did Louise Archer when she emerged with her limping daughter, but Miss Mahan wasn't in the mood for gossip and speculation. She marched into Dr. Sullivan's sanctorium.

"Hello, Paul," she said before he could open his mouth. "I've just been to see Robin. He told me Yvonne had been raped but he wouldn't tell me what the big mystery is. I know you're what passes for the County Medical Examiner, so you know as much as he does. I've known you for fifty years and even thought at one time you might propose to me, but you didn't. So don't give me any kind of runaround. Tell me what happened to Yvonne." She plopped into a chair and glared at him.

He shook his head in dismay. "I thought I might propose to you at one time too, but right now is a good example of why I didn't. You were so independent and bull-headed, you scared me to death."

· "Don't change the subject."

"You won't like it."

"I don't expect to."

"There's no way I can 'put it delicately,' as they say."

"You don't know high school kids. I doubt if you **know** anything indelicate that I haven't heard from them."

"Even if I tell you everything I know about it, it'll still be a mystery. It is to me."

"Quit stalling."

"Okay, you asked for it. And if you repeat this to anyone, I'll wring your scrawny old neck."

"I won't."

"All right. Yvonne was . . . how can I say it? . . . she was sexually mutilated. She was split open. Not cut—torn, ripped. As if someone had forced a two by four into her—probably something larger than that."

"Had they?" Miss Mahan felt her throat beginning to burn from the bile rising in it.

"No. At least there was no evidence of it. No splinters, no soil, no foreign matter of any kind."

"My Lord," she moaned. "How she must have suffered."

"Yes," he said softly, "but only for a few seconds. She must have lost consciousness almost immediately. And she was dead long before they finished with her."

"They? What makes you think there was more than one?"

"Are you sure you want to hear the rest of it?"

"Yes," she said, but she didn't.

"I said we found no foreign matter, but we found semen."

"Wasn't that to be expected?"

"Yes, I suppose. But not in such an amount."

"What do you mean?"

"We found nearly a hundred and fifty cc's. There was probably even more. A lot of it had drained out onto the car seat." His voice was dull.

She shook her head in confusion. "A hundred and fifty cc's?"

"About a cup full."

Twilla

She felt nauseous. "How much . . . how much . . . ?"

"The average male produces about two or three cc's. Maybe four."

"Does that mean she was . . . what? . . . fifty times?"

"And fifty different men."

"That's impossible."

"Yes. I know. One of the deputies took it to Wichita to be analyzed. To see if it's human."

"Human?"

"Yes. We thought someone might . . ."

She held up her hand. "You don't need to go . . . go any further." They sat for a while, not saying anything.

After a bit he said, "You can see why Robin wanted to keep it quiet?"

"Yes." She shivered, wishing she had her coat even though the office was warm. "Is there any more?"

He shook his head and slumped morosely deep in the chair. "No. Only that Robin is pretty sure she was . . . killed somewhere else and then taken out on the old road, because there was almost no blood in or around the car. How they ever drove so far out on that road in the snow is another mystery, although a minor one. The deputy was about to give up and turn around, and he had on snow chains."

Miss Mahan was late for her one o'clock class. The children hadn't become unruly as they usually did, but were subdued and talking in hushed voices. A discussion of **Silas Marner** proved futile, so she told them to sit quietly and read. She didn't feel anymore like classwork than they did. She noticed that Twilla's eyes were bright with suppressed excitement. Well, she thought, I guess you can't expect her to react like the others. She hardly knew Yvonne.

It had stopped snowing by the time Mr. Choate circulated a memo that school would be closed Wednesday for the funeral. Apparently Robin had managed to keep a lid on knowledge of the rape. There was speculation on the subject, but she could tell it was only speculation.

When she got home, she saw the Twilla journal lying beside the big chair in front of the cold fireplace. Strange, Twilla had hardly crossed her mind all day. She guessed it only proved how silly and stupid her Twilla-watching really was. She put the journal away in the library table drawer and decided that was enough of that nonsense.

Tuesday, the 12th

This morning I saw Twilla jab Alice May Turner in the thigh with a large darning needle.

Miss Mahan stopped in the middle of a sentence and stared in disbelief. She walked slowly to Twilla's desk, feeling every eye in the class following her. "What's going on here?" she asked in a deathly quiet voice. Twilla looked up at her with such total incomprehension she wondered if she had imagined the whole thing. But she looked at Alice May and saw her mouth tight and trembling and the tears being held in her eyes only by surface tension.

"What do you mean, Miss Mahan?" Twilla asked in a bewildered voice.

"Why did you stick Alice May with a needle?"

"Miss Mahan, I didn't!"

"I saw you."

"But I didn't!" Twilla's eyes were becoming damp as if she were about to cry in injured innocence.

"Don't bother to cry," Miss Mahan said calmly. "I'm not impressed." Twilla's mouth tightened for the briefest instant. Miss Mahan turned to Alice May. "Did she jab you with a needle?"

Alice May blinked and a tear rolled down each cheek. "No, ma'am," she answered in a strained voice.

"Then why are you crying?" Miss Mahan demanded.

"I'm not crying," Alice May insisted, wiping her face.

"I think both of you had better come with me to Mr. Choate's office."

Mr. Choate wouldn't or, I guess, couldn't do anything. They both lied their heads off, insisting that nothing happened. Twilla even had the gall to accuse me of spying on her and persecuting her. I think Mr. Choate believed me. He could hardly help it when Alice May began rubbing her thigh in the midst of her denials.

Miss Mahan sent Twilla back to the room and kept Alice May in the hall. Alice May began to snuffle and wouldn't look at her. "Alice May, dear," she said patiently. "I saw what Twilla did. Why are you fibbing to me?"

"I'm not!" she wailed softly.

"Alice May, I don't want any more of this nonsense!" Why on earth did Twilla do it, she wondered. Alice May was such a silly, harmless girl. Why would anyone want to hurt her?

"Miss Mahan, I can't tell you," she sobbed.

"Here." Miss Mahan gave her a handkerchief. Alice May took it and rubbed at her red eyes. "Why can't you tell me? What's going on between you and Twilla?"

"Nothing," she sniffed.

"Alice May. I promise to drop the whole subject if you'll just tell me the truth."

Alice May finally looked at her. "Will you?"

"Yes," she groaned in exasperation.

"Well, my . . . my giggling gets on her nerves."

"What?"

"She told me if I didn't stop, I'd be sorry."

"Why didn't you pick up something and brain her with it?"

Alice May's eyes widened in disbelief. "Miss Mahan, I couldn't do that!"

"She didn't mind hurting you, did she?"

"I'm . . . I'm afraid of her. Everbody is."

"Why? What has she done?"

Twilla

"I don't know. Nothing. I'm just afraid. You promise not to let her know I told you?"

"I promise. Now, go to the restroom and wash your face."

Twilla kept watching me the rest of the period. I imagine she suspects Alice May spilled the beans. The other children were very quiet and expectant as if they thought Twilla and I would go at each other tooth and claw. I wonder who they would root for if we did.

I'll have to admit to a great deal of perverse pleasure in tarnishing Twilla's reputation in the teachers' lounge. I was a little surprised to find a few of the others had become somewhat disenchanted with her also. They didn't have such a concrete example of viciousness as I had, but she was making them uncomfortable.

I also discovered who Twilla's romantic (if you can call it that) interest is since Carter flunked out.

Leo Whittaker!

I was never so shocked and disappointed in my life. An affair between a teacher and student is bad enought but—Leo! No wonder she was being quiet about it. I thought he acted a bit peculiar when we discussed Twilla, so I said bold as brass: "I wonder who she's sleeping with?" He turned red and left the room, looking guilty as sin.

I don't know what to do about it. I've got to do something. But what? what? what? I can't do anything to hurt Leo, because it'll also hurt poor Lana.

How could Leo be so stupid?

Dark clouds hung oppressively low the morning of the funeral. They scudded across the sky so rapidly Miss Mahan got dizzy looking at them. She stood with the large group huddled against the cold outside the First Christian Church of Hawley, waiting for the formation of the procession to the County Line Cemetery. The services had drawn a capacity crowd, mostly from curiosity, she was afraid. The entire ninth grade was there, with the exception of Sammy Stocker, of course, and Twilla. Only two teachers were missing: Mrs. Bryson (first grade) who had the flu, and Leo Whittaker. Leo's absence was peculiar because Lana was there, looking pale and beautifully pregnant. She was with Carter Redwine and his parents. Carter seems to be recovering nicely from his little misadventure, she thought.

She spotted Paul Sullivan and crunched through the snow to his side. He saw her coming and frowned. "Hello, Paul. Did you get the report from Wichita?"

"Do you think this is the place to discuss it?"

"Why not? No one will overhear. Did you?"

He sighed. "Yes."

"Well?"

"It was human—although there were certain peculiarities."

"What peculiarities?"

He cocked his eyes at her. "If I told you, would it mean anything?"

She shrugged. "What else?"

"Well, it all came from the same person—as far as they could tell. At least, there was nothing to indicate that it didn't. Also all the sperm was the same age."

"What does that mean?"

"The thought occurred to us that someone might be trying to create a grisly hoax. That someone might have . . . well . . . saved it up until they had that much."

"I get the picture," she grimaced. She thought a moment. "Can't they . . . ah . . . freeze it? Haven't I read something about that?"

"You can't do it in your Frigidaire. If the person who did it had the knowledge and the laboratory equipment to do that . . . well . . . it's as improbable as the other theories."

"Robin hasn't learned anything yet?"

"I don't know. Some of us aren't as nosy as others."

She smiled at him as she spotted Lana Whittaker moving toward the Redwine car. She began edging away. "Will you keep me posted?"

"No."

"Thank you, Paul." She caught up with Lana. "Hello, dear."

Lana started and turned, then smiled thinly. "Hello, Miss Mahan."

She exchanged greetings with Mr. and Mrs. Redwine and Carter as they entered their car. "Should you be out in this weather, Lana?"

Lana shrugged. She looked a little haggard and her eyes were puffy. "I'll be all right."

Miss Mahan took her arm. "Come on. My car is right here. Get in out of the cold and talk to me. We'll have plenty of time before they get this mess untangled." Lana went unprotesting and sat in the car staring straight ahead. Miss Mahan started the car and switched on the heater although it was still fairly warm. She turned and looked at Lana.

"When you were in school," she said quietly, "you came to me with all your problems. It made me feel a little like I had a daughter of my own."

Lana turned and looked at her with love and pain in her eyes. "I'm not a little girl anymore, Miss Mahan. I'm a married lady with a baby on the way. I should be able to handle my own problems."

"Where's Leo?"

Lana leaned back against the seat and put her fingers on the sides of her nose. "I don't know," she said simply, as if her tears had been used up. "He went out last night and I haven't seen him since. I told my aunt and uncle he went to Liberal to buy some things for the baby."

"Did you call Robin? Maybe he had an accident."

"No. There was no accident. I thought so the first time."

"When was that?"

"Last Friday night. He didn't come in until after midnight. The same thing Saturday. He didn't show up until dawn Monday and Tuesday. This time he didn't come back at all."

"What did he say?"

"Nothing. He wouldn't say anything. Miss Mahan, I know he still loves me; I can tell. He seems genuinely sorry and ashamed of what he's doing, but he keeps . . . keeps doing it. I've tried to think who she might be, but I can't imagine anyone. He's so tired and worn out when he comes home, it would be funny if it . . . if it were happening to someone else."

"Do you still love him?"

Lana smiled. "Oh, yes," she said softly. "More than anything. I love him so much it . . . " she blushed, ". . . it gives me goosebumps. I was crazy about Leo even when we were in high school, but he was so wild he scared me to death. I thought . . . I thought he had changed."

"I think he has." Miss Mahan took Lana's hand as she saw Robin get in his car and pull out with the pall bearers and the hearse directly behind him. "They're starting. You'd better go back to your car. I'm glad you told me. I'll do all I can to help."

Lana opened the car door. "I appreciate it, Miss Mahan, but I really don't see what you can do."

"We shall see what we shall see."

Miss Mahan managed to hang back until she was last in the funeral procession. The highway had been cleared of snow and she hoped it wouldn't start again before they all got back to town. But she didn't know. The sky looked terrible. She turned off the highway at Miller's Corners, down the dirt road to the old Peacock place. There was nothing left of Miller's Corners now except a few scattered farm houses. The cafe had been moved into Hawley eight years ago and the Gulf station had closed when George Cuttsanger died last fall. The Gulf people had even taken down the signs.

If the Gilbreaths were fixing up the old Peacock farm, they must have started on the inside. It was still as gray and weary looking as it was ten years ago, if not more so. The black Chrysler was in the old carriage house and smoke drifted this way and that from one of the chimneys, caught by small erratic gusts of air.

She parked and sat looking at the house a moment before getting out. The snow was clean and undisturbed on the front walk. She guessed they must use the back door; it was closer to the carriage house.

No one answered her knock, but she knew they were home. She waited and knocked again. Still no response. She took a deep breath and pushed open the door. "Mrs. Gilbreath?" she called. She listened carefully but there was not a sound. She could hear the melting snow dripping from the eaves and the little ticking sounds an old house makes. She went in and closed the door behind her. "Mrs. Gilbreath?" she called again, hearing nothing but a faint echo. The house was warm but even more delapidated than the last time she was in it.

She stepped into the parlor and saw them both sitting there. "Oh!"

she gasped, startled, and then laughed in embarrassment. "I didn't mean to barge in, but no one answered my knock." Mr. and Mrs. Gilbreath sat in highback easy chairs facing away from her. She could only see the tops of their heads. They didn't move.

"Mrs. Gilbreath?" she said, beginning to feel queasy. She walked slowly around them, her eyes fixed so intently on the chairs she momentarily experienced an optical illusion that the chairs were turning slowly to face her. She blinked and took an involuntary step backward. They sat in the chairs dressed to go out, their eyes focussed on nothing. Neither of them moved, not even the slight movements of breathing, nor did their eyes blink. She stared at them in astonishment, fearing they were dead.

Miss Mahan approached them cautiously and touched Mrs. Gilbreath on the arm. The flesh was warm and soft. She quickly drew her hand back with a gasp. Then she reached again and shook the woman's shoulder. "Mrs. Gilbreath," she whispered.

"She won't answer you." Miss Mahan gave a little shriek and looked up with a jerk. Twilla was strolling down the stairs, tying the sash of a rather barbaric looking floor-length fur robe. The antique pendant she always wore was around her neck. She stopped at the foot of the stairs and leaned against the newell post. She smiled. "They're only simulacra, you know."

"What?" Miss Mahan was bewildered. She hadn't expected Twilla to be here. She thought she would be with Leo.

Twilla indicated her parents. "Watch." Miss Mahan jerked her head back toward the people in the chairs. Suddenly, their heads twisted on their necks until the blank faces looked at each other. Then they grimaced and stuck out their tongues. The faces became expressionless again, and the heads swiveled back to stare at nothing.

Twilla's laugh trilled through the house. Miss Mahan jerked her eyes back to the beautiful child, feeling like a puppet herself. "They're rather clever, don't you think?" she cooed as she walked toward Miss Mahan, the fur robe making a soft sound against the floor. "I'm glad you came, Miss Mahan. It saves me the trouble of going to you."

"What?" Miss Mahan felt out of control. Her heart was beating like a hammer and she clutched the back of Mrs. Gilbreath's chair to keep from falling.

Twilla smiled at her panic. "I haven't been unaware of your interest in me, you know. I had decided it was time to get you out of the way before you became a problem."

"Get me out of the way?"

"Of course."

"What are you?" She felt her voice rising to a screech but she couldn't stop it. "What are these things pretending to be your parents?"

Twilla laughed. "A thirteen-year-old is quite limited in this society. I had to have parents to do the things I couldn't do myself." She shrugged. "There are other ways but this is the least bothersome."

"I won't let you get me out of the way," Miss Mahan hissed, dismissing the things she didn't understand and concentrating on that single threat, trying to pull her reeling senses together.

"Don't be difficult, Miss Mahan. There's nothing you can do to stop me." Twilla's face had become petulant and then she smiled slyly. "Come with me. I want to show you something." Miss Mahan didn't budge. Twilla took a few steps and then turned back. "Come along, now. Don't you want all your questions answered?"

She started up the stairs. Miss Mahan followed her. Her legs felt mechanical. Half way up she turned and looked back at the two figures sitting in the chairs like department store dummies. Twilla called to her and she continued to the top.

A hallway ran the length of the house upstairs with bedroom doors on either side. Twilla opened one of them and motioned Miss Mahan in. The house wasn't as old as her own but it still had the fourteen foot ceilings. But the ceilings, as well as the walls, had been removed. This side of the hall was one big area, opening into the attic, the roof at least twenty feet overhead with what appeared to be some sort of trap door recently built into it. The area was empty except for a large gray mass hunched in one corner like a partially collapsed tent.

"He's asleep," Twilla said and whistled. The mass stirred. The tent unfolded slowly, rustling like canvas sliding on canvas. Bony ribs spread gracefully, stretching the canvas-like flesh into vast bat wings which lifted out and up to bump against the roof. The wings trembled slightly as they stretched lazily and then settled, folding neatly behind the thing sitting on the floor.

It was a man, or almost a man. He would have been about sixteen feet tall had he been standing. His body was massively muscled and covered with purplish gray scales that shimmered metallically even in the dim light. His chest, shoulders, and back bulged with wing-controlling muscles. He stretched his arms and yawned, then rubbed at his eyes with horny fists. His head was hairless and scaled; his ears rose to points reaching above the crown of his skull. The face was angelically beautiful but the large liquid eyes were dull and the mouth was slack like an idiot's. He scratched his hip with two-inch talons, making the sound of a rasp on metal. He was completely naked and emphatically male. His massive sex lay along his heavy thigh like a great purple-headed snake.

"This is Dazreel," Twilla said pleasantly. The creature perked up at the sound of his name and looked toward them. "He's a djinn," Twilla continued. He turned his empty gaze away and began idly fondling himself. Twilla sighed. "I'm afraid Dazreel's pleasures are rather limited."

Miss Mahan ran.

She clattered down the stairs, clutching frantically at the bannister to keep her balance. She lost her right shoe and stumbled on the bottom step, hitting her knees painfully on the floor. She reeled to her feet, unaware of her shins shining through her torn stockings. Twilla's crystal laughter peeling down the stairs hardly penetrated the shimmering white layer of panic blanketing her mind.

She bruised her hands on the front door, clawing at it, trying to open it the wrong way. She careened across the porch, into the snow, not feeling the cold on her stockinged left foot. But her lopsided gait caused her to fall, sprawling on her face, burying her arms to the elbows in the snow. She crawled a few feet before gaining enough momentum to regain her feet. Her whole front was frosted with white but she didn't notice.

She locked the car doors, praying it would start. But she released the clutch too quickly, and it bucked and stalled. She ground the starter and turned her head to see Twilla standing on the porch, her arms hugging a pillar, her cheek caressing it, her smile mocking. The motor caught. Miss Mahan turned the car in a tight circle. The rear wheels lost traction and the car fishtailed.

Take it easy, she screamed at herself. You've made it. You've gotten away. Don't end up in the far ditch.

She was halfway to Miller's Corners when the loose snow began whipping in a cloud around her. She half heard the dull boom of air being compressed by vast wings. A shadow fell over her and Dazreel landed astraddle the hood of her car. The metal collased with a hollow **whump** as the djinn leaned down to peer curiously at her through the windshield. She began screaming, tearing her throat with short, hysterical, mindless shrieks that seemed to come from a great distance.

Her screams ended suddenly with a grunt as the front wheels struck the ditch, bringing the car to an abrupt halt. Dazreel lost his balance and flopped over backwards with a glitter of purplish gray and a tangle of canvas-flesh into the snow drifts. Miss Mahan watched in paralyzed shock as he got to his feet, grinning an idiot grin, shaking the snow from his wings, and walked around the car. His wings kept opening and closing slightly to give him balance. Her head turned in quick jerks like a wooden doll, following his movements. He leaned over the car from behind and the glass of both side windows crumbled with a gravelly sound as his huge fingers poked through to grasp the tops of the doors.

The dim light became even dimmer as his wings spread in a mantle over the car. The snow swirled into the air and she could see the tips of each wing as it made a downward stroke. The car shifted and groaned and rose from the ground.

She fainted.

A smiling angel face floated out of a golden mist. Soft, pink lips moved solicitously but no sound emerged. Miss Mahan felt a glass of water at her mouth and she drank greedily, soothing her raw throat. Sound returned.

"Are you feeling better, Miss Mahan? We don't want you to have a

Twilla

heart attack just yet, do we?" Twilla's eyes glittered with excitement.

Miss Mahan sucked oxygen, fighting the fog in her brain. Then, raw, red fingers of anger tore away the silvery panic. She looked at the beautiful monstrous child kneeling before her, the extravagant robe parted enough at the top to reveal a small, perfect bare breast. The nipple looked as if it had been rouged. "I'm feeling quite myself again, thank you."

Twilla rose and moved to a facing chair. They were in the parlor. Miss Mahan looked around, but the djinn was absent. Only the parent dolls were there in the same positions.

"Dazreel is back upstairs," Twilla assured her, watching her speculatively. "You have nothing to fear." She smiled slightly. "He will have only virgins."

Miss Mahan felt the blood draining from her face and she weaved in the chair, feeling the panic creeping back. Twilla threw her head back and her crystal laugh was harsh and strident, like a chandelier tumbling down marble stairs.

"Miss Mahan, you never cease to amaze me," she gasped. "Imagine! And at your age, too."

The anger returned in full control. "It's none of your business," she stated unequivocally.

"I'm ever so glad you decided to pay me a visit, Miss Mahan. It's, what do you say? Killing two birds with one stone?"

"What do you mean?"

"Dazreel has, as I said, limited, but strong appetites. If they aren't satisfied, he becomes quite unmanageable. And don't think he will reject you because you're a scrawny old crow. He has no taste at all, and only one criterion: virginity." Twilla was almost fidgety with anticipation.

"What possible difference could it make to that monster?" I must be losing my mind, Miss Mahan thought, I'm sitting here having a calm conversation with this wretched child who is going to kill me!

Twilla was thoughtful. "I really don't know. I never thought about it. That's just the way it's always been. It could be a personal idiosyncracy, or perhaps it's religious." She shrugged. "Something like **kosher,** do you think? Anyway, you can't fool him."

"I don't understand any of this," Miss Mahan said in confusion. "Did you say he was a . . . a djinn?"

"Surely you've heard of them. King Solomon banished the entire race, if you remember." She smiled, pleased. "But I saved Dazreel."

"How old are you?" Miss Mahan breathed.

Twilla chuckled. "You wouldn't believe me if I told you. Don't let the body mislead you. It's relatively new. Dazreel has great power if you can control him. But, he's crafty and very literal. One wrong move and . . ." She ran her forefinger across her throat.

"But . . ." Miss Mahan was completely confused. "If this is all true, why are you going to school in Hawley, Kansas, for heaven's sake?"

Twilla sighed. "Boredom is the curse of the immortal, Miss Mahan. I thought it might offer some diversion."

"If you're so bored with life, why don't you die?"

"Don't be absurd!"

"How could you be so inhuman? What you did to Yvonne . . . does life mean nothing to you?"

Twilla shifted in irritation. "Don't be tiresome. How could your brief, insignificant lives concern me?"

There was a restless sound from above. Twilla glanced at the stairs. "Dazreel is becoming impatient." She turned back to Miss Mahan with a smirk. "Are you ready to meet your lover, Miss Mahan?"

Miss Mahan sat frozen, the blood roaring in her ears. "You might as well go," Twilla continued. "It's inevitable. Think of your dignity, Miss Mahan. Do you really want to go kicking and screaming? Or perhaps you'd like another run in the snow?"

Miss Mahan stood up suddenly. "I won't give you the satisfaction," she said calmly. She walked to the stairs, bobbing up and down with one shoe off. Twilla rose and ran after her, circling her in glee.

Twilla leaned against the newell post, blocking the stairs. She smiled wistfully. "I rather envy you, Miss Mahan. I've often wished . . . Dazreel knows the ancient Oriental arts, and sex **was** an art." She grimaced. "Now it's like two goats in heat!" Her smile returned. "I've often wished I had the capacity."

Miss Mahan ignored her and marched slowly up the stairs with lopsided dignity. Twilla clapped her hands and backed up ahead of her, taunting her, encouraging her, plucking at her gray tweed coat. Twilla danced around her, swirling the fur robe with graceful turns. Miss Mahan looked straight ahead, one hand on the bannister for balance.

Then, at the third step from the top, she stumbled. She fell against the railing and then to her knees. She shifted and sat on the step, rubbing her shins.

"Don't lose heart now, Miss Mahan," Twilla sang. "We're almost there." Twilla tugged at her coat sleeve. Miss Mahan clutched Twilla's wrist as if she needed help in getting up. Then she heaved with all her might. Twilla's laughter became a gasp and then a shriek as she plummeted down the stairs with a series of very satsifying thumps and crashes. Miss Mahan hurried after her but the fall had done the job.

Twilla lay on her back a few feet from the bottom step, her body twisted at the wrong angle. She was absolutely motionless except for her face. It contorted in fury and her eyes were metallic with hate. Her rose petal lips writhed and spewed the most vile obscenities Miss Mahan had ever imagined, some of them in languages she'd never heard.

"Dazreel!" Twilla keened. "Dazreel! Dazreel!" over and over. A howl reverberated through the house. It shook. Plaster crashed and wood splintered. Dazreel apeared at the top of the stairs, barely able to squeeze through the opening.

Twilla continued her call. Miss Mahan took a trembling step backward. Dazreel started down the steps. Miraculously they didn't collapse. Only the bannister splintered and swayed outward.

Miss Mahan commanded herself to think. What did she know about djinns? Very little, practically nothing. Wasn't there supposed to be a controlling device of some sort? A lamp? A bottle? A magic ring? A talisman? Something. She looked at Twilla and then at the djinn. She almost fainted. Dazreel approached the bottom of the stairs with an enormous erection.

She looked frantically at Twilla. She's not wearing rings. Then something caught her eye.

The pendant! Was it the pendant? It had slipped up and over her shoulder and beneath her neck. Miss Mahan scrambled for it. She pushed Twilla's head aside. The child screamed in horrible agony. She grasped the pendant and pulled. The chain cut into the soft flesh of Twilla's neck and then snapped, leaving a red line that oozed blood.

She looked at Dazreel. He had stopped and was looking at her tentatively. It **was** the pendant! "Give it back," Twilla groaned. "Give it back. Please. Please, give it back. It won't do you any good. You don't know how to use it." Dazreel took another step.

Miss Mahan threw the pendant at him. Twilla screamed and the hair on the back of Miss Mahan's neck bristled. It was not a scream of pain or rage, but of the damned. Dazreel's huge hand darted out and caught the pendant. He held his fist to his face and opened his fingers, gazing at what he held. He looked at Miss Mahan and smiled an angelic smile. Then he rippled, like heat waves on the desert, and . . . vanished.

Miss Mahan sat on the bottom step, weak with relief, gulping air. She looked at Twilla, as motionless as the parent dolls in the chairs. Only her face moved, twisting in sobs of self-pity. Miss Mahan almost felt sorry for her . . . but not quite.

She stood up and walked through the kitchen and out the back door. She thought she knew where it would be. Everyone kept it there. She went to the shed behind the carriage house, floundering through the snow drift. She scooped away the snow to get the door open. She stepped in and looked around. There was almost no light. The scudding clouds seemed even lower and darker and the single window in the shed was completely grimed over.

She spotted it behind some shovels, misted over with cobwebs. She pushed the shovels aside, grasped the handle and lifted the gasoline can. It was heavy. She shook it. There was a satisfying slosh. She smiled grimly and started back to the house, walking more lopsided than ever.

Then she stopped and gaped when she saw Leo Whittaker's car parked out of sight behind the house. She hurried on, letting the heavy can bounce against the ground with every other step. She opened the kitchen door and shrieked.

Mrs. Gilbreath stood in the doorway, smiling pleasantly at her, and holding a butcher knife. Without reasoning, without even thinking, Miss Mahan took the handle of the heavy gasoline can in both hands and swung it as hard as she could.

The sharp rim around the bottom caught Mrs. Gilbreath across the face, destroying one eye, shearing away her nose, and opening one cheek. Her expression didn't change. Blood flowed over her pleasant smile as she staggered drunkenly backward.

Miss Mahan lost her balance completely. The momentum of the gasoline can swung her around and she sat in the snow, flat on her skinny bottom. The can slipped from her fingers and bounced across the ground with a descending scale of clangs. She lurched to her feet and looked in the kitchen door. Mrs. Gilbreath had slammed against the wall and was sitting on the floor, still smiling her gory smile, her right arm twitching like a metronome.

Miss Mahan scrambled after the gasoline can and hid it in the pantry. She ducked up the kitchen stairs when she heard footsteps.

Mr. Gilbreath walked through the kitchen, ignoring Mrs. Gilbreath, and went out the back door. Miss Mahan hurried up the stairs. Oh Lord, she thought, I'll be so sore, I can't move for a week.

She entered the upstairs hall from the opposite end. She stepped carefully over the debris from the wall shattered by the djinn. She looked in the bedrooms on the other side. The first one was empty with a layer of dust, but the second . . . She stared. It looked like a set from a Maria Montez movie. A fire burned in the fireplace and Leo Whittaker lay stark-naked on the fur-covered bed.

"Leo Whittaker!" she bellowed. "Get up from there and put your clothes on this instant!" But he didn't move. He was alive; his chest moved gently as he breathed. She went to him, trying to keep from looking at his nakedness. Then she thought, what the dickens? There's no point in being a prude at this stage. Her eyes widened in admiration. Then she ceded him a few additional points for being able to satisfy Twilla. Why couldn't she have found a beautiful man like that when she was twenty-three, she wondered. She sighed. It wouldn't have made any difference, she guessed. It would have all turned out the same.

She put her hand on his shoulder and shook him. He moaned softly and shifted on the bed. "Leo! Wake up! What's the matter with you?" She shook him again. He acted drugged or something. She saw a long golden hair on his stomach and plucked it off, throwing it on the floor. She took a deep breath and slapped him in the face. He grunted. His head lifted slightly and then fell back. "Leo!" she shouted and slapped him again. His body jerked and his eyes clicked open but didn't focus.

"Leo!" Slap!

"Owww," he said and looked at her. "Miss Mahan?"

"Leo, are you awake?"

"Miss Mahan? What are you doing here? Is Lana all right?" He sat up in the bed and saw the room. He grunted in bewilderment.

"Leo. Get up and get dressed. Hurry!" she commanded. She heard the starter of a car grinding. Leo looked at himself, turned red, and tried to move in every direction at once. Miss Mahan grinned and went to the window. She could hear Leo thumping and bumping as he tried to put his clothes on. The car motor caught and steam billowed from the carriage house. "Hurry, Leo!" The black Chrysler began slowly backing out, Mr. Gilbreath at the wheel. Then the motor stalled and died.

He's trying to get away, she thought. No, he's only a puppet. He's planning to take Twilla away! She turned back to Leo. He was dressed, sitting on the edge of the bed, putting on his shoes. He looked at her shame-faced, like a little boy.

"Leo," she said in her sternest, most no-nonsense, unruly child voice. The car motor started again. "Don't ask any questions. Go down the kitchen stairs, and to your car. Hurry as fast as you can. Don't let Mr. Gilbreath see you. Bring your car around to the front and to the end of the lane. Block the lane so Mr. Gilbreath can't get out. Keep yourself locked in your car because he's dangerous. Do you understand?"

"No," he said, shaking his head.

"Never mind. Will you do what I said?"

He nodded.

"All right, then. Hurry!" They left the bedroom. Leo gave it one last bewildered glance. They ran down the kitchen stairs as fast as they could, Leo keeping her steady. She propelled him out the back door before he could see Mrs. Gilbreath still smiling and twitching. The black Chrysler was just pulling around to the front of the house.

She ran to the pantry, retrieved the gasoline can, and staggered into the entry hall. She could see Mr. Gilbreath getting out of the car. She locked the door and hobbled into the parlor. Twilla had been moved to the divan and covered with a quilt. He shouldn't have moved her, Miss Mahan thought, with an injury like that it could have killed her.

Twilla saw her enter and began screeching curses at her. Miss Mahan shook her head. She put the gasoline can down by the divan and tried to unscrew the cap on the spout. It wouldn't budge. It was rusted solid. Miss Mahan growled in frustration. The front door began to rattle and clatter.

Twilla's curses stopped suddenly and Miss Mahan looked at her. Twilla was staring at her in round-eyed horror. Miss Mahan went to the fireplace and got the poker. Twilla's eyes followed her. She drew the poker back and swung it as hard as she could at the gasoline can. It made a very satisfactory hole. She swung the poker several more times and tossed it away. She picked up the can as Twilla began to scream and plead. She rested it on the back of the divan and stripped away the blanket. She tipped it over and pale pink streams of gasoline fell on Twilla.

Twilla

Glass shattered in the front door. Miss Mahan left the can resting on the back of the divan, still gurgling out its contents, and went to the fireplace again. She picked up the box of matches as Mr. Gilbreath walked in. His expression didn't change as he hurried toward her. She took a handful of wooden matches. She struck them all on the side of the box and tossed them on Twilla.

Twilla's screams and the flames ballooned upward together. Mr. Gilbreath shifted directions and waded into the flames, reaching for Twilla. Miss Mahan ran out of the house as fast as she could.

She was past the black Chrysler, its motor still running, when the gasoline can exploded. Leo had parked his car where she told him. Now he jumped out and ran to her. They looked at the old Peacock house.

It was old and dry as dust. The flames engulfed it completely. The snow was melting in a widening circle around it. They had to back all the way to Leo's car because of the heat.

They heard a siren and turned to see Sheriff Walker's car hurrying down the lane, followed by some of the funeral procession on its way back to Hawley. The ones who hadn't turned down the road were stopped on the highway, looking.

"Leo, dear," she said. "Do you know what you're doing here?"

He rubbed his hand across his face, his eyes still a little bleary. "Yes, I think so. It all seems like a dream. Twilla . . . Miss Mahan," he said in pain. "I don't know why I did it."

"I do," she said soothingly and put her arm around him. "And it wasn't your fault. You have to believe that. Don't tell Lana or anyone. Forget it ever happened. Do you understand?"

He nodded as Robin Walker got out of his car and ran toward them. He looks very handsome in his uniform, she thought. My, my, I've suddenly become very conscious of good-looking men. Too bad it's thirty years too late.

"Miss Mahan? Leo? What's going on here?" Robin asked in bewilderment. "Is anyone still in there?" He looked at her feet. "Miss Mahan, why are you running around in the snow with only one shoe on?"

She followed his gaze. "I'll declare," she said in astonishment. "I didn't know I'd lost it. Leo. Robin, let's get in your car. I have a lot to tell you both."

Miss Mahan sat before the fireplace in her comfortable old house, tearing the pages from her Twilla journal and feeding them one at a time to the fire. Paul Sullivan had doctored her cuts and bruises and she felt wonderful—stiff and sore, to be sure—but wonderful. Tomorrow the news would be all over town that, with brilliant detective work, Robin Walker, aided by Leo Whittaker, had discovered that Twilla Gilbreath's father was Yvonne's killer. In an attempt to arrest him, the house had burned and all three had perished.

She had told Robin and Leo everything that happened—well,

Twilla

almost everything. She had left out her own near encounter with Dazreel and a few other related items. She had also given the impression—sort of—that the house had burned by accident. Poor, sweet, Robin hadn't believed a word of it. But, after hearing Leo's account, taking a look at her demolished car, and seeing the footprints in the snow, he finally, grudgingly, agreed to go along with it. And it did explain all the mysteries of Yvonne's death.

She knew the **public** story was full of holes and loose ends, but she also knew the people in Hawley. They wanted to hear that an outsider had done it, and they wanted to hear that he had been discovered. Their own imaginations would fill in the gaps.

Lana Whittaker didn't really believe that Leo was working with Robin all those nights he was away, but they loved each other enough. They'd be all right.

She fed the last pages to the fire and looked around her parlor. She decided to put up a tree this year. She hadn't bothered with one in years. And a party. She'd have a party. There hadn't been more than three people in the house at one time in ages.

She hobbled creakily up the stairs, humming "Deck the Halls with Boughs of Holly," considerably off key, heading for the attic to search for the box of Christmas tree ornaments.

Under the Hollywood Sign

I can't pinpoint the exact moment I noticed him. I suppose I had been subliminally aware of him for some time, though he was just standing there with the rest of the crowd. Anyway, I had other things on my mind: a Pinto and a Buick were wrapped around each other like lettuce leaves. The paramedics had two of them out, wrapped in plastic sheets waiting for the meat wagon, and were cutting out a third with a torch. He appeared to be in the Buick, but you couldn't really tell.

My partner Carnehan and I were holding back the crowd of gawkers. A couple of bike cops in their gestapo uniforms were keeping the traffic moving on Cahuenga, not letting any of them stop and get out. But there were still twenty or twenty-five of them standing there—eyes bright, noses crinkled, mouths disapproving.

All except him.

That's one of the reasons I noticed him in particular. He wasn't wearing that horrified, fascinated expression they all seem to have. He might have been watching anything—or nothing. His face was smooth and placid. I think that's the first time I ever saw a face totally without expression. It wasn't dull or blank or lifeless. No, there was vitality there. It just simply wasn't doing anything at the moment.

And he was . . . Don't get the wrong idea—my crotch doesn't get tight at the sight of an attractive young man. But there's only one word to describe him—beautiful!

I've seen my share of pretty boys—the ones that flutter and the ones that don't. It seems the prettier they are, the more trouble they get into. But he wasn't that **kind** of beautiful.

Even though the word is used these days to describe practically everything, it was the only one that fitted. I thought at first he was very young: nineteen, twenty, not more than twenty-one. But then I got the impression he was much older, though I don't know why, because he still looked twenty. He was about five-ten, a hundred and sixty-seventy pounds—one of those bodies the hero of the book always has but that you never see in real life.

His hair was red, or it might have just been the light from the flashers. There were no peculiarities of feature; just a neutral perfection. I've heard it said that perfect beauty is dull, that it takes an imperfection to make a face interesting. Whoever said it had never seen this kid.

He was standing with his hands in his pockets, watching the guys with the torch, neither interested nor uninterested. I guess I was staring at him, because his head turned and he looked directly at me.

I could smell the rusty odor of the antifreeze dribbling from the busted radiators and the sharp ozone of the acetylene and the always remembered smell of blood. A coyote began yipping somewhere in the darkness.

Then a couple of kids got too close and I had to hustle them out of the way. When I looked back, he was no longer there.

They finally got the third one out of the Buick. When they pulled him out I could see the wet brown stain all over the seat of his pants where his bowels had relaxed in death. The ambulance picked up all three of them and the wrecker hauled off the two cars still merged as one. Part of the mess was dragging on the street and I could hear the scraping for a long time. The bike cops did a few flashy turns and roared away. The crowd started to wander off, and Carnehan and I began sweeping the broken glass from the pavement.

But there was only one thing I could think of: I couldn't remember the color of his eyes.

Nothing much happened the rest of the night. We cruised the Boulevard a few times, but there wasn't anything going on. A few hustlers still lounged around the Gold Cup and the Egyptian, never giving up hope. There was no point in hassling them—they'd just say they were waiting for a bus, and we couldn't prove they weren't. It was a pretty scruffy-looking bunch this late in the morning. The presentable ones had scored a long time ago. You could probably get most of these with an offer of breakfast.

Carnehan reached behind the seat and pulled an apple from the paper sack he always kept back there. He took a bite that sounded like a rifle shot and then offered me one. "No, thanks."

"An apple a day keeps the doctor away." He grinned and took another bite.

"You're keeping the entire AMA at bay."

He laughed; partly chewed apple dribbled down his chin. He wiped it off with the back of his hand. I kept my eyes on the street. "Why don't you eat soft apples? They're quiet."

"I like hard ones."

We stopped a car with only one taillight and gave the guy a warning ticket.

Then the sun was coming up. It was hitting the tops of the Hollywood Hills and illuminating the Hollywood sign. It looked decent from this far away. You couldn't tell it was made of rotting timbers and sagging sheet metal clanging in the wind. From here you couldn't see the obscenities scrawled on it.

We went back to the station, reported, and then into the locker room. The rest of the graveyard shift were wandering in, showering, and changing out of their uniforms. Cunningham has the locker next to mine. He had been on the Pansy Patrol and was wearing a shirt unbuttoned to the waist, no underwear, and pants so tight you could count every hair on his ass.

Wharton, one of the police psychiatrists, was leaning against the lockers talking to him. Doc was on his favorite theme again. He was telling Cunningham why he, Cunningham, was so successful on the Pansy Patrol. The fags recognized a kindred spirit; the fags always knew one of their own kind; if Cunningham would only stop fooling himself, just stop deluding himself that he was straight, just know himself, just start living a conscious life, he would be a happier, more fulfilled person.

I had been on the Pansy Patrol with Cunningham a few times and had seen him operate. I wasn't completely sure Doc was wrong. Cunningham was peeling off the tight pants and I watched in fascination, although I'd seen it before, as the sizable bulge in his crotch stayed with the pants.

Poor Cunningham.

He was standing there naked with a slight smile on his face, putting the pants neatly on a hanger, listening to Doc's clarinet voice. He looked a lot like the cop on "Adam-12," whatever his name is, the kid. The boys had even called him "Adam-12" for a while until they got tired of it. I couldn't keep from comparing him to the guy I had seen at the wreck, but Cunningham didn't compare at all. He was just a good-looking kid with a slim muscular body, and not much equipment. But it didn't seem to bother him. He always grinned and said it wasn't size that counted, it was technique.

I took off my own pants and looked at myself. I wasn't as young or as good-looking as Cunningham, but I did all right on the Pansy Patrol. I was bulkier and more heavily muscled and hairier; I guess I appealed to the rough trade crowd. I was never very comfortable without underwear, and thank God I didn't have to wear padding.

Wharton finished his catalogue of Cunningham's emotional failings. Cunningham looked at me and winked. "I don't really know anything about it, Doc, but maybe the reason I'm not interested in sex with another man is because I'm just **not interested** in sex with another man."

Doc's lips got a little tight and his face was slightly flushed. I knew

Under the Hollywood Sign

Cunningham had been reading Kingsley Amis again and had probably maneuvered Doc into the whole conversation—and Doc was eminently maneuverable. I'd heard most of it before, so I got a towel and started for the showers. Cunningham followed me and Wharton followed him.

"You're right, Cunningham, you don't know anything about it!"

I turned on the water and began soaping. Cunningham got next to me and Doc stood at the door, still talking. Cunningham looked at me and grinned and said loudly, "Sorry, Doc, I can't hear you with the water running!"

There were about ten other guys in the shower, grinning at each other. Cunningham leaned toward me. "Hey, Rankin, you notice how Doc always manages to look in the showers?"

I shrugged.

"According to him everyone is either a fag or a closet queen."

"What about himself?" I asked.

He rolled his eyes and laughed. "Getting him to talk about himself is like catching fairies in a saucepan."

Carnehan came in, pitching an apple core into the wastebasket. I could see why he had never been on the Pansy Patrol. Then . . . I don't know why I thought of it, but the thought crossed my mind. I wondered what the guy at the wreck looked like naked.

I left the station and got into my five-year-old Dart. It looked like a nice day. There was enough wind from the ocean to clear away the smog. Of course, the wind was packing it into the San Gabriel Valley, but that was their problem, not mine. I went straight home and went to bed.

I was scrambling some eggs and watching **The Price Is Right** when the phone rang. They were doing the one where the screaming dame has to zero in on the prices of two objects within thirty seconds. When she names a price, the MC says "Higher" or "Lower." This keeps up until she guesses the price. You can get it in ten guesses maximum. She started at a hundred on a color TV and worked up ten dollars at a time.

"Hundred and ten!"

"Higher!"

"Hundred and twenty!"

"Higher!"

"Hundred and thirty!"

"Higher!"

She got to three-seventy before her time ran out. Dumb dame!

It was Carnehan on the phone. "Hey, Lou, Margaret wants you to come over for dinner tonight."

"Hell, Carnehan, I wish you'd said something this morning. I've already made other plans." You stupid jerk! Don't you ever wonder why your wife is always inviting me to dinner?

"Got a heavy date, Lou?"

"Something like that. Some other time, Carnehan." No other time,

Carnehan. Margaret's a pretty good-looking dame for her age, but not good enough to take chances with. You didn't even notice how her hand stayed under the table all through dinner last time.

"Margaret says how about Wednesday?"

"I'll have to let you know later." And you never even had a suspicion about what goes on after you fall asleep in front of the TV, Carnehan. If you ever found out . . .

"Okay, Lou. I'll remind you Tuesday night."

"You do that." And I'll have a good excuse ready. Not that I give a good goddamn if you do find out, but you could make a stink in the department. I don't want to lose my job, Carnehan. I like being a cop.

" 'Bye, Lou. See you later."

" 'Bye, Carnehan." I hung up the phone in time to see a granny-lady have an orgasm over winning a dune buggy.

I usually eat dinner about eight o'clock at David's. I know it's a fag hangout but the food's good and, since I let it be known I was a cop, the service is even better. I spotted him as I was leaving about nine. He went into the gay bar next to David's. It was called Goliath's, of course. I only glimpsed him from behind but I was sure of the red hair and body. Wouldn't you know he'd be a queer!

I paid my dollar and a quarter cover charge and went through the black curtains after him. I don't know what I was planning to do, but I hadn't been able to get him out of my mind. I stood for a moment, waiting for my eyes to adjust to the gloom and my ears to the plaster-cracking music. There were three small stages with naked boys dancing on them, wiggling their little round butts for all they were worth. There were also five screens showing movies of naked boys doing everything it's physically possible for naked boys to do and a few things I would have thought impossible before I joined the force.

Then there were the customers. A few were at the bar and a few were scattered around but most of them were packed like Vienna sausages against one wall. There was plenty of room and no need for the press of bodies—no need but one, and the busy hands told what that was. A few watched the movies but mostly they watched each other. One of the dancers was waving around a hardon and was getting some attention but not much. A couple of dykes at the bar watched him. I guess this is the only chance they have to see one.

I spotted the back of the red head in the middle of the mass, so I waded in. There's no way to move through something like that. No one can move out of your way; they're just as trapped as you are. You just wait and move with the current because the pack is in constant eddy as they move from one body to the next, trying to touch everything.

It was no more than thirty seconds before I felt feather touches on my ass. I thought about my wallet, but I knew that wasn't what they were after. I pushed away the first hand that closed on my crotch and saw a pout of disappointment flicker across a face in front of mine. I put my wallet in my shirt pocket anyway.

After five minutes and fifty gropes, I finally reached the redhead but he was turned the other way. I was pressed against him and could feel his hard body. By pushing with determination, I managed to get to the side of him. He was standing face to face with another guy. Both of them had their eyes closed and their mouths slightly open, occasionally coming together in a lazy kiss. Their hands were out of sight but I could feel the movement.

It wasn't him.

This was one of the pretty ones. I might even have said beautiful if I hadn't seen the other one. But, like Cunningham, he was ordinary in comparison.

He opened his eyes and saw me watching him and he smiled dreamily. I felt a hand massaging my crotch but I couldn't tell for sure if it was him. I was so disappointed I didn't push it away. Then my zipper went down and fingers expertly scooped everything out. The press was so tight I couldn't even get my arms down, much less move away. Whoever was working on me was very good and I couldn't help getting it up.

Jesus Christ!

I had a wild urge to take out my badge and shove it in every face in sight. I enjoyed my mental image of the panic it would create. But I didn't do it. I forced my arms down, pushed the clutching hands away, closed my pants, and got the hell out of there.

When I went into the locker room about eleven thirty, Carnehan already had his uniform on, sitting there reading a copy of the **Advocate** and eating an apple. He looked up when I rattled my locker.

"Hey, Lou! You missed a great dinner."

"It couldn't be helped, Carnehan."

"Don't forget about Wednesday."

"I won't."

I took off my shirt and remembered my wallet was still in the pocket. I put it on the shelf and took off my pants. I grabbed a towel and headed for the shower. I felt clammy. I must have sweated off a pound in that damn bar. Those groping bodies can generate a lot of heat.

Carnehan laughed out loud. He came toward me waving the newspaper. "Hey, Lou! Did you see this cartoon in the **Advocate**?"

"Why in hell would I be reading the **Advocate**?"

"Look, there's these two cops standing before a judge with a handcuffed fag and a hooker. One of the cops is saying, 'But Your Honor, you can get **hurt** chasing robbers and murderers.' Isn't that a scream?"

"Ha ha," I said and went on to the showers. He started rushing around the room showing it to everyone else.

I was almost finished when Cunningham came in. He turned on the water and stood under it leaning against the wall with his eyes closed and a sappy grin on his face.

"You look like the cat that swallowed the aviary," I said.

He sighed. "I am **exhausted!**"

"Let me guess from what."

"I met the most fantastic girl! A waitress at the Hamburger Hamlet on the Strip. I'm gonna give it two weeks and, if I'm **still** alive, I'm gonna propose." He rubbed his hand between his legs. "I tell you, Rankin, I didn't know I had it in me. Boy, I'd like to see Wharton try to convince **her** I'm a repressed homosexual."

I laughed dutifully. He began soaping and glanced down at me.

"You look a little shriveled up yourself. Have a big night?" He grinned goodnaturedly, wanting to share his sexual excitement.

"Yeah. Some women are just as happy with size as they are with technique."

He looked a little wistful for a moment, then the grin returned. "Shit! If I had your size and my technique, I'd quit the force, put an ad in the **Free Press,** and open a screwing service!"

And I wondered about **him** again. With that face and that body, did he worry about size and technique? How did women react to him? Were they intimidated by his beauty? Was he as beautiful in bed?

I saw him going into the Vogue Record Shop on the Boulevard. This time there was no mistake. I told Carnehan to park the car and meet me at the entrance. When I went through the turnstiles, I saw him leaning against the end of the counter. I walked into the book department and watched him from behind a rack of paperbacks.

He had his back to me and it took me a moment to figure out what he was doing. The cashier was playing the **Symphonie Fantastique**—it was the passage where the two shepherds are calling to each other on their flutes and, at the end, one doesn't answer—and he was standing there listening to the music. Then he turned slightly and I could see his face.

I could feel the skin crawling on the back of my neck.

It wasn't the same one!

It was all there: the red hair, the magnificent body, the neutral beauty of the bland face. But the features were different. He had to be the other one's brother, they were so alike.

The lights in the store were very bright. No one else was in the place but the cashier and she had her nose in a paperback volume of Toynbee. His clothes were clean and neatly pressed but they were old and hadn't cost much when they were new. His hair was neat and not very long. His face was so smooth I doubted that he shaved. And his eyes were gray—just as beautiful and as neutral as the rest of him.

Finally the record ended and he left. I glanced at the book I had been holding. The cover was a photograph of Burt Reynolds standing with his back to the camera looking over his shoulder. He was wearing nothing but a football jersey, with his bare ass hanging out. I closed the book, put it back on the rack, and for some reason thought of Betty Grable.

The cashier never even looked up when he went out. Carnehan, standing on the sidewalk looking confused, never glanced at him as he walked by. The girl was watching me. She smiled but her eyes were guarded.

"Did you know the man who just went out?" I asked, trying to sound casual.

She glanced out the door, but he had turned left toward Las Palmas. She looked back at me. "I don't think so, officer. Did he do something?"

"No. I just thought I'd seen him before. Maybe in the movies or on television."

She shrugged. "Movie stars come in here all the time. Joanne Worley was in yesterday. Wendall Burton comes in every once in a while."

"Thanks." I left before she could give me a complete catalogue of the celebrities she'd seen. She raised her voice as I went out the door.

"Chad Everett was in a couple of weeks ago but I was off that day."

I looked down the Boulevard but didn't see him. I told Carnehan to wait for me and went after him. At Las Palmas I looked in every direction but there was no sign of him. The hustlers standing around the Gold Cup pretended to ignore me, but a couple of drag queens gave me defiant looks.

There was another bad one that night on the off-ramp at Western. Four cars were scattered half a block. There were seven dead and two others who probably wouldn't see morning. And there were two of **them** in the crowd. Two different ones.

I motioned Carnehan over.

"Yeah, Lou?"

"Carnehan. See those two guys over there, the ones with red hair?"

He looked confused. "Where?"

"You see the black dame in the yellow dress? The one with pigtails all over her head that make her look like an upside-down johnny brush?"

He snickered. "Sure."

"One of them is standing right beside her. On her left. You see him?"

Slowly: "Yeah."

"What does he look like?"

He looked up at me. "What d'ya mean?"

"No! Keep looking at him!" He looked back. "You still see him?"

"Yeah."

"Describe him to me."

He thought for a moment. "Don't forget. Tomorrow's Wednesday. Margaret's expecting you for dinner."

"**Carnehan!** Concentrate on the redheaded guy. Don't think about anything else. What does he look like?"

"I don't know. He's just a guy."

"How old is he?"
"It's hard to tell. The light's not too good."
"Is he under thirty?"
He considered. "Yeah."
"Under twenty-five?"
"Yeah. Yeah, I'd say so."
"Under twenty?"

He was silent for a moment. Good old Carnehan. His little pea brain was doing its best. "Maybe . . . but probably not."

"What about his face?"
"What about it?"
"Is it an ugly face?"
"No."
"Is it a handsome face?"
"Yeah, I guess so."
"How handsome?"
"Golly, Lou."
"Very handsome?"
"Yeah."
"Better-looking than Cunningham?"

"Yeah." His voice suddenly got excited. "Hey, Lou, is that a movie star or something?"

We went through the whole thing again with the other one. Carnehan finally saw them the same way I did, but he couldn't remember the one at the record shop. Later I asked him if he remembered the two good-looking redheaded guys.

"Sure. How could you forget somebody who looks like that? Especially when there's two of 'em. Hey, you suppose they're twins?"

"Are they still there?"

"Naw. They musta left," he said, looking right at them. "Don't forget about dinner Wednesday night."

Then they both turned and looked at me with their expressionless eyes. Or were they expressionless? I thought I saw recognition and speculation, but I wasn't sure. Carnehan was right. The light **was** bad.

They kept us hopping the rest of the night. We'd barely get through with one before we were sent to another.

An old hotel on Vermont burned to the ground. Half the department was there, keeping the curious out from underfoot, rerouting traffic. My eyes were burning and watery from the smoke, but it didn't keep me from seeing them.

I counted seven. Seven beautiful redheaded young men with perfect bodies.

I leaned against my locker in pure exhaustion, wondering if I should take a shower. I was grimy from smoke and dust but I was so tired I only wanted to go to bed. Cunningham came in, looking as beat as I felt.

He looked at me and sighed, shaking his head.

"What are you doing in uniform?" I asked, not really caring. "You off the Pansy Patrol?"

He started undressing. "Yeah. They called us in about three. What got into people last night, anyway? Seems like everybody was trying to get themselves killed."

The same thought had crossed my mind, but not seriously. I had other things to think about.

Margaret called herself the next afternoon to remind me about dinner. But I'd already laid out my plan of action.

"I'm sorry, Margaret. I was just about to call you. I'm leaving for Texas in about two hours. My father is very ill and I've taken a leave of absence from the department."

"Oh, Lou, I'm so sorry. Is there anything I can do?"

"No, thank you, Margaret. Everything's taken care of."

"At least let me drive you to the airport."

"I'm not flying. I'll need my car when I get there."

"How long will you be gone?"

"I don't know. My father isn't expected to live . . ." I let my voice break a little. "Say so long to Carnehan for me."

"Of course, Lou. You're sure there's nothing I can do?"

"No. Nothing. Good-bye, Margaret."

" 'Bye, Lou, dear."

Well, it wasn't **all** a lie. My father had taken three months to die seventeen years ago when I was in high school, but nobody out here knew that. The Lieutenant hadn't much liked the idea of giving me an indefinite leave of absence, but what could he do? I packed enough supplies in the Dart to last two people six weeks, paid my landlady two months in advance, drove up La Brea to the Boulevard, and put my car in the underground garage near Graumann's Chinese. I walked down to the Vogue and caught a double feature.

It was dark when I came out. I could hear sirens in several directions. I got in the car and drove to David's for something to eat. All I had to do was get in one place and wait, no driving around, no taking extra chances of being seen.

I had almost finished eating when I heard the sirens. I didn't pay much attention because there would be plenty of time and plenty of sirens, if tonight was anything like last night. When I came out of the restaurant there were little bunches of people standing on the corners looking south down La Brea. I walked over and saw a crowd around the Gordon, standing in that tense way they do when somebody's had it. This was going to be a lot easier than I'd thought.

I crossed over Melrose past the camera store, and eased my way through the press of bodies. The colored neon of the marquee made the blood look black. The guy was under a blanket, flat on his back on the sidewalk, one brown hand poking out from under the edge. The hand had blood on it and a spot had soaked through the blanket. More of it was smeared around on the concrete.

One of the cops talking to a couple of people was named Henderson. I only knew him vaguely, so he probably wouldn't know I was supposed to be on my way to Texas. I began sorting through a number of excuses for my delay just in case.

He saw me and waved. The patrol car was behind him at the curb, the flashers turning hypnotically, but losing out to the bright marquee. A young Chicano sat in the back seat looking dazed and surly. He wiped at his mouth with the back of his hand and I saw the glint of cuffs. A girl was hunched in the front seat weeping.

Henderson finished with his witnesses and started toward me. "Hello, Rankin. Don't you get enough of this on duty?"

"Just passing by. What happened?"

He groaned and shook his head. "Couple of kids in a knife fight over a senorita. Wonder if she was worth it."

"The way she's carrying on, the wrong one musta lost."

"Yeah." Another siren approached. "Here's the ambulance. See you around, Rankin." He walked away, being very official, moving the onlookers back another inch.

I looked over the crowd and saw him almost immediately. He was about twelve feet from me, his eyes on the blanket. As usual no one was paying him the slightest attention. I edged toward him as they put the body in the ambulance. The crowd began drifting away but I kept my eyes on that beautiful boy. I wasn't sure if I had seen him before, they all looked so much alike.

He turned and walked north on La Brea. I followed him across Melrose. A few people were still milling around the intersection, but I couldn't let him get too far away from my car.

I overtook him, touched his arm, and said, "Excuse me." I had my badge in my hand when he turned with a startled look.

My face was only a foot from his. I saw the clear, healthy skin and the bewildered gray eyes that looked at me with recognition. All the artists for the last thousand years have been trying to paint that face on angels, but their poor fumbling attempts never came close. It was only for an instant but I had to look away or be overwhelmed.

The traffic on La Brea moved by us silently, like a movie with the sound turned off. But, oddly enough, I could hear the hum and click of the traffic lights as they changed. I realized I was still stupidly holding my badge in my hand, and put it away. I forced myself to look at him again.

"Will you please come down to the station with me . . ." My voice cracked. Come on, Rankin, get hold of yourself! "It's purely a routine matter."

"What do you want?"

It was only four words, but I realized I'd never heard one of them speak. How can you describe music to a deaf person? Any actor in the world would trade his prick for that voice. My own words stopped and we looked at each other. Get your shit together! You're acting like some poor fairy who's just been propositioned by Robert Redford.

"I can make . . . make this official if you refuse to cooperate."

His shoulders sagged slightly. He nodded.

He followed me to the Dart without protest. I had been a little worried because I wasn't in uniform and wasn't in a squad car, but he didn't seem to notice. I had my revolver handy when I handcuffed him to the door handle, but he sat slumped in the seat looking at nothing.

I took the Hollywood Freeway to the Pasadena Freeway. I was going down Colorado Boulevard when he said, "Why are you doing this to me?"

I glanced at him but he was still looking at nothing. I almost turned the car around. I wish I had, but I didn't.

He didn't say anything else as I got on the Foothill Freeway and headed east through the San Gabriel Valley. It was almost dawn when I pulled off the pavement winding up Mt. Baldy. I opened the gate to the gravel road down the canyon. I drove through and put on the padlock I had brought with me. I drove up the canyon a couple of miles until the road ended at a cabin. It belonged to a director friend of mine who was on location in Jamaica and would be for several more months. He'd let me use it before. Besides, what he didn't know wouldn't hurt him.

I had to break a window to get in, but that could be fixed. I'd brought a pane of glass and cutter. I turned on the electricity at the meter box and took him in. I took the chain I had brought, handcuffed one end to his ankle and the other end around the commode. Now he could use the bathroom and the bed, but the chain wasn't long enough to reach the bedroom door or the window. He didn't complain through any of this. He acted as if he didn't even know I was there.

I unloaded the car, put on a pot of coffee, scrambled some eggs, and tried to get him to eat something but he wouldn't. I finished eating, unpacked my clothes, took a shower in the other bathroom and went to sleep in the other bedroom.

He still wouldn't eat when I woke up. I took another shower and shaved. I moved a chair just out of the limit of the chain—he hadn't given me any trouble but I wasn't taking chances—and sat down to watch him.

He was still sitting on the side of the bed, where he'd been when I put on the chain, his magnificent body relaxed and his beautiful face calm. His cheeks were as smooth as ever. I knew for sure he didn't have to shave. His hands were folded in his lap and his eyes seemed to be on them. For two hours he didn't move except for gentle breathing. I didn't realize so much time had passed until the room began to get dark.

I turned on the lights and went to him, holding out my hand. "Give me your wallet." He acted as if he hadn't heard me. "Give me your wallet," I said again, louder.

He looked up at me then, puzzlement in his eyes. "I don't have one."

"Stand up," I said. He hesitated for a moment, then stood. I went over him quickly. He was telling the truth. He had no wallet; nothing but empty pockets.

I returned to my chair and sat, watching him. He stood where I had left him, stood as calmly as he had sat. "How many of you are there?" I said. He didn't seem to hear. "Look, we might as well get a few things straight. You're gonna tell me everything I want to know. We can do it easy or we can do it hard. It's up to you."

He stood for a moment in the same position, then looked at me. "I don't know." His voice still made the hair on my arms stand up.

"You must have some idea. A hundred? A thousand? Ten thousand? A million?" He shook his head. Maybe he wasn't going to let it be easy after all. I let it go; there was plenty of time. "I can fix you something to eat if you want. I'm not trying to starve you to death. Aren't you hungry?"

He said nothing.

"Look! It won't do any good to go on a hunger strike. Not one damn bit of good!" No response. I used my buddy voice. "You can have anything you want. Just name it."

He looked at me quickly. "I want to leave."

I laughed. "Anything but that."

He looked back at his hands. "I would like to bathe."

"Sure. Go ahead."

He moved his foot; the chain rattled. I dug the key out of my pocket and pitched it to him. "Unlock the cuff and throw the key back." I picked up the revolver. He unlocked the chain and tossed me the key. He started for the bathroom.

"Wait!" My heart was beating too hard. "Undress in here and leave the clothes." My mouth was dry and I swallowed. He took off his shirt and hung it on the back of the chair. He took off the shoes and socks and the pants and jockey shorts. His back was toward me but it wasn't modesty. He just happened to be standing that way. Michelangelo, you bumbling incompetent! If you could see this, you'd take a hammer to all those misshapen pieces of rock you spent so much time on.

He took a step toward the bathroom. I made a croaking sound in my throat. I tried again.

"Stop!" He stopped. "Turn around." He turned. I felt the blood singing in my ears. I don't know how long I looked at him. He stood unselfconsciously, totally unconcerned by my staring or his own nakedness. There wasn't a blemish on him. Light reddish-gold hair was scattered on his arms, legs, and chest. You could hardly see it until it caught the light. There was a darker, thicker patch of pubic hair, and he was uncircumcised. He wasn't as large as me, or as small as Cunningham. Either way would have been wrong, out of proportion, a staggering flaw. My own that I'd always been so proud of—it seemed

Under the Hollywood Sign

now gross and mutilated. I felt the pressure of it and realized I had a hardon.

The gun was pointing at him. What would he look like with a bullet there? Nothing between those perfect thighs but blood. Would he writhe screaming? Would that inhumanly placid face show human agony? "Get out of here," I said.

While he showered, I put the clothes in a grocery sack and stuck them in the closet of my bedroom. When he came out of the bathroom, he looked at the empty chair, then at me.

"You won't need them. Put the cuff back on." He sat in the chair, snapped the cuff around his ankle. I could take it only for an hour. I got my bathrobe and tossed it to him. He put it on but only because I told him to. It didn't seem to matter to him one way or the other.

I wondered if he had ever smiled. What would those perfect lips look like with a big happy grin on them? I could feel goosebumps popping out on my arms.

For three weeks I watched him do nothing. He sat in the chair and sometimes lay on the bed, but I never saw him sleep. I watched him and asked questions, but the only things I learned for sure were: he didn't eat or use the toilet. He ignored me except when I forced him to answer a question. And the answers were usually meaningless.

Some days neither of us said a word. I would just watch his face and never tire of it, the way you never tire of looking at a perfect piece of art. Then, suddenly, it would be night again. He bathed every day, but I never let him remove the robe until he was in the bathroom. I didn't want to go through that again.

Sometimes I would force him to speak—not because I expected to learn anything, but because I wanted to hear his voice again. I was trying to find out what he did when he wasn't siren-chasing. I said something inane like: "Why aren't you in the movies? You wouldn't even need talent; with your looks you could make a fortune. The movies or television would eat you up."

He turned his head toward me. "My looks?"

"Don't you know how beautiful you are?"

"I'm ugly." His fantastic voice colored the words with subtle shades of despair. "Everything is ugly."

I studied him closely. I think he believed what he said. "Don't you want to be rich? Don't you want the luxuries of life?"

"There's no point."

"Why not?"

"We're here such a short time. There's no point in gathering possessions. There's no point in anything. And there's not enough time."

"Not enough time?"

He had drifted off in a reverie. "A very short time—but it seems like forever." Impatience, hope, futility, expectation, anticipation; the voice showed it all.

"But how do you pass the time? What do you do?"

I think he sighed. "We wait," he said. "We wait."

"What are you waiting for?" I yelled in exasperation. He didn't answer. I knew better than to continue with a frontal attack. I backed up and started in at a different angle. "You said, '**We** wait.' Are the others like you?"

"Yes."

A thought occurred to me. "Do they know you're here?"

"Yes."

"Why don't they try to rescue you?"

"They're afraid."

"Afraid? Of me?"

"Yes."

"Why?"

"You're dangerous."

"Dangerous?"

"Yes. They would do anything to prevent premature interruption of the cycle."

I started to ask what the hell he was talking about, but I knew it wouldn't do any good. "How am I dangerous?"

"You can see us."

"Do you know why I can see you?"

"No."

"Am I the only one?"

"The only one we know of now."

"Now?"

"It's happened before."

I changed directions again. "Are you afraid of me?"

"Yes."

"Why? I haven't hurt you."

"There is danger that you will interrupt the cycle."

"Why did you come with me so passively?"

"I couldn't believe you would do this to me." Again subtle shadings of accusation, hopelessness, and sadness in the beautiful voice. He turned his head to look at me. For an instant, the barest instant, I felt like a real son of a bitch. Then he looked away. He sat on the side of the bed, my bathrobe too big for him, the chain snaking into the bathroom.

Don't get the idea that he had become an unexpected chatterbox. That conversation is a distillation of three weeks' questions and silences.

About a week later, I went during the night to check on him. I hadn't been sleeping very well. My mind was full of wild, impossible speculations. I won't go into them but they consisted of men from Mars and other equally incredible flights of fancy. I started to put on my bathrobe but remembered he was wearing it. I tiptoed down the hall stark naked hoping to catch him doing something—doing **anything**.

Under the Hollywood Sign

The door to his room was always left open. I looked in cautiously. I couldn't see him anywhere. I turned on the light. He was pressed against the outside wall of the room, my bathrobe crumpled at his feet. His arms were outstretched to bring as much of him against the wall as possible. He didn't seem to notice me, but then, he never did. I went to him and saw his face, the side of it flat against the wall. It was no longer expressionless. It was filled with the most overpowering hopelessness I had ever seen. I felt my throat constrict.

"What's wrong?" I whispered.

He didn't answer for a moment—not because he was ignoring me as he usually did, but because he was preoccupied. Then he said, very softly, in a voice caressed by a cold, bleak wind: "The small creatures in the forest; their deaths are so tiny and insignificant. There's hardly any life energy at all."

Then he really was aware of me. I saw him retreat until the eyes and face were neutral. I bellowed and slapped him as hard as I could. I remembered them standing around the wrecks. He fell to his knees, the crimson print of my hand on his face. I pulled him up by his armpits and looked into his empty face.

"Stop hiding from me!" I screamed and slapped him again. He slumped against me and my arms were around him, holding him up. Our naked bodies were together, exciting me. The blood rushed to my groin and my erection was painful. He was there, in the eyes, not completely, but there. I put my mouth over his. He neither drew away nor responded but his bruised lips were sweet and I didn't want to stop.

I had been looking at his placid face for a month. I knew he was capable of emotion if he would let it show. He hadn't uttered a sound or responded in any way to physical blows. He had to have a breaking point somewhere. I pushed him onto the bed on his stomach. The chain rattled. I rammed into him, trying to hurt him. He was tight, very tight. It must have been painful, but he didn't cry out or even moan. It had been a long time since the last time—a month—too long. It only took a dozen strokes, my pelvis pounding against the flawless flesh of his buttocks, before I came. I shouldn't have waited so long. It burned.

I lay on him for a moment, then reached and pulled his face around. It was vacant. I withdrew, still hard. I pulled him into a sitting position facing me. That beautiful face. That beautiful bland, bruised face. I put my hands on either side of it.

"Don't hide from me. It doesn't do any good. I can see you. I can see you!" He swam to the surface and looked at me. "Did you enjoy it? Did you even feel it?"

"Yes."

"Did it feel good? Did it hurt?"

"Yes."

"Why didn't you groan? Why didn't you scream? Why didn't you beg me to stop? Why don't you get mad? Why don't you curse me? What's inside you?" I put my hand on his breast and felt the hard nipple against my palm. "Do you have a heart? I can feel something in there. Is it a heart? What would I find if I got a knife and slit you open? Do you have sexual feelings at all?" I grabbed his penis and squeezed. It was soft but firm. "Has it ever been hard? You don't piss with it. What do you use it for?"

I put his hand on my tingling erection. He didn't pull it away. It just lay there. "That's what it's for. That's how a human uses it!" He started going away again. I slapped him. "Stay with me. Stay with me every second." I pushed him on his back. The chain clattered on the floor. I hooked his knees over my shoulders, watching his eyes the whole time. He tried to go away a few times but I slapped him back. I took a very long, slow time and I enjoyed the hell out of it.

The next morning I drove down the mountain to the village and phoned the Department. With direct dialing you can't tell where a long-distance call is coming from. My father was worse and not expected to live much longer. Yeah, too bad. I shouldn't be away much longer. Good-bye.

I started going to him every night. I hadn't meant to but I couldn't sleep without him. He didn't go away anymore and I didn't have to slap him. The bruises on his face faded finally. He was there all right, but that was all. I never succeeded in bringing emotion to his face.

Finally I began sleeping in the same bed with him, touching him all night, feeling his hard nipples under the palms of my hands.

He woke me one morning, moaning. The window was gray with light and I could see his mouth moving. I touched his face. It was hot and dry. He spoke and the music in his voice was muted. "Why have you done this to me? I never harmed you. I've never harmed anyone. All we ever want is to survive until the birth."

"What's wrong with you?"

"It's time. The end of the cycle. The birth."

"Isn't that what you've been waiting for?"

"I'm not strong enough. I haven't collected enough life energy."

"I'll let you go. I'll take you back to L.A."

"It's too late. Too late."

He never said anything again. I watched him for three days. His fever got worse and the life went from his vibrant flesh. His skin flaked away in gray scales. He was struggling with all his might against something. I don't know what. But in the end he failed. His moans were so piteous that I had to put my hands over my ears. But I couldn't take my eyes off the disintegration of that magnificent creature.

And that's all he was, wasn't he? A creature. Something not human. It wasn't my fault that, by some fluke, I could see them. I didn't know this would happen. He never told me.

On the second day a hump began forming on his back. He was curling more and more into a fetal position as the hump forced him over.

He began bleeding at the mouth. I put the shower curtain under him. When I rolled him over, my hands got covered with something like ashes.

On the third day he began to quieten and I knew it was almost over. He hadn't moved in several hours except for ragged breathing. There was a sharp cracking sound, like Carnehan biting into a new apple, only louder. The now ugly body trembled violently for a few moments, and then nothing. He lay facing me, his eyes open, the color of clay.

The breathing stopped.

It was finished.

I got out of the chair and walked around to the other side of the bed. The hump on his back had split and something white was sticking out. I reached down and pulled on it. It was a wing, a large, white wing covered with feathers. No, not feathers. Soft, white, silky hair.

There was a second wing but it was twisted and not properly developed. I pulled away all of the body and exposed what was inside it.

I cleaned up the cabin so no one would know it had been occupied. I packed everything back in the Dart. I buried them both in the woods, the body of the dead winged thing, and the husk that had held it. I drove back to Hollywood. It seemed as if I passed a wreck every half mile. I went into my apartment without noticing the apple cores in the yard. I unlocked the door, went straight to the toilet, and vomited.

I was splashing cold water on my face when I heard her.

"Lou? Is that you?" She walked in wearing a slip, her eyes red from sleep, and her hair sticking out on one side where she'd been lying on it.

"Margaret! What the hell are you doing here?"

"Oh, Lou!" She pressed against me. "It's been **awful!** Alfred found out about us!"

My head was spinning. "Who the shit is Alfred?"

She looked puzzled. "My husband!"

Jesus Christ! I'd forgotten Carnehan's first name. She was right. It was awful. "What'd he do? Do they know at the Department?"

"He hit me!" She began to blubber on my shoulder. "I was afraid. I've been hiding here for three **days!** He keeps pounding on the door but I stay quiet. He doesn't know for sure I'm here."

"How did he find out?"

"I don't **know!** He came home from work three days ago, screaming at me and hitting me. Oh, Lou. I was so frightened." She kissed me and her breath was bad. **His** breath had had no odor at all. "Come to bed with me, Lou. It's been so long," she whined.

I felt her doughy flesh through the thin slip. But it was woman flesh and I had to forget about him. I led her to the bed and began undressing. I was sticky. I hadn't bathed or shaved since he started . . . Stop it!

She pulled the slip over her head, unhooked her bra, and peeled down her pantyhose. Her tits were beginning to sag, her thighs were puffy, and there was a small roll of fat around her waist. Her skin looked muddy, not clear like . . . Stop it!

She walked toward me, smiling coyly. I wish I had been able to see . . . Stop it!

I pushed her roughly onto the bed and she squealed. Margaret liked it rough. I was about to make her very happy. She gasped deep in her throat every time my pelvis slammed against her flabby flesh. It was good—but . . . Stop it!

I lay on my back, half asleep. Margaret lay on top of me, licking my nipples and trying to coax it back up again. It hadn't lasted long enough for her, but she was wasting her time and she was heavy. I closed my eyes, trying to stay awake. I felt her hair on my face. There was a noise and her head hit mine. Her breath rushed out in one stale puff and I felt something dripping on my cheek.

I focused my eyes. Carnehan was standing over us, his nightstick raised. I couldn't move Margaret's dead weight. "Carnehan! Don't!" I yelled. The stick came down. I remembered I hadn't locked the door.

When I came out of it, it was dark. I was in a moving car. My head hurt and the car sounded as if it were driving in the bottom of a well. I could feel dried blood in my left eye; maybe mine or maybe Margaret's. I tried to wipe it away but my hands wouldn't move. I heard the clink of handcuffs and felt the door handle. My head was leaning against the glass. It felt cool. I opened my eyes and saw brush going past and a sea of lights spread out below. I could see a dozen fires burning. We must be somewhere in the Hollywood Hills.

I turned my head and looked at Carnehan driving the car. He stared straight ahead. "Carnehan, what do you think you're doing?" The words didn't come out as forcefully as I had intended. He ignored me. "Carnehan, Margaret doesn't mean anything to me." That was the wrong thing to say. Think straight! "She's not worth it, Carnehan. I'm not worth it. Neither of us is worth destroying yourself!"

He wasn't listening. "You can't hope to get away with this." Of course he didn't. "Why don't you just write it off as a mistake?"

The car had been bouncing around for a while. We must not have been on a main road. I couldn't raise myself high enough to see ahead. After a bit Carnehan stopped the car and got out. He opened the back door on my side and began dragging out Margaret's naked body. She must have been already dead, the way she flopped around like a rubber dummy. He dragged her a few feet from the car and rolled her down a hill. I could hear her crackling the brush, then silence.

Carnehan opened my door and the handcuffs pulled me out. I felt sharp rocks digging into my butt and realized I was naked too. He pulled out his revolver.

"Carnehan! Don't be a fool!"

He shot me in the stomach. Good old Carnehan. He remembered

Under the Hollywood Sign

what we'd been taught: always aim for the gut.

He unlocked the handcuffs and pulled me to the edge. All I had to do was overpower him and get away, but I decided to wait because I was very tired. I rolled down the hill like a sack of potatoes. I didn't feel the prickly pears and sharp brush. The pain in my belly was too fierce. I hit something hard and I think my shoulder broke.

I was lying on my back, my head leaning against whatever I'd hit, looking back up the hill. The car drove away. Carnehan, you bungler! I'm not dead! You wasted it all!

The sound of the car died away. It was very quiet, just crickets and the faroff rumble of traffic. You couldn't get away from that sound anywhere in Los Angeles County. A slight wind was blowing, making some loose sheet metal creak and groan somewhere near by.

I couldn't just lie here. I was bound to die if I didn't get help. I tried to move and looked up. An immense "Y" loomed over me. I was under the Hollywood sign. I couldn't see Margaret anywhere. Let me rest a moment more and get my breath back. Damn fuckin' Carnehan. Are you gonna be surprised when they haul you in and I'm there to point the finger. I looked down at my stomach. A mistake. But it doesn't hurt so much anymore. I must be in shock. I've heard that happens.

I can see my prick. It looks wrinkled and shrunken, even smaller than Cunningham's. This is a hell of a time to be thinking about pricks! My shoulder hurts worse than my gut. I can feel blood on the ground under my back. I've rested long enough.

What's that noise? Sounded like a twig cracking somewhere in the darkness. What if it's a coyote? I wonder if it will attack me. Probably not. Do coyotes react to the smell of blood the way sharks do?

Footsteps. Not a coyote. People. More than one. I'm saved! Up yours, Carnehan!

There are four of them: four redheaded young men who don't look a day over twenty. Four perfect faces that I used to think were overwhelmingly beautiful—until I saw the face of that dead winged thing. But I did see it. And I had to cover it because the beauty was too painful to look at.

Four magnificent bodies that only a few days ago would have sent the blood rushing to my penis—if I hadn't seen the pale body of the winged creature, all the more beautiful because it was sexless. A body I knew would have gleamed had it been alive.

Now these four faces seem drab and plain and the four bodies might belong to trolls.

But the eyes! They stand around me, watching me with eyes I still think beautiful because the winged creature's eyes were closed in death.

Those four pairs of beautiful, bland eyes look at me the same way Carnehan looks at an apple he's been saving for a special occasion.

Beyond the Cleft

PROLOGUE

It was born; though "born" is perhaps not the right word.

—1—

At 2:17 P.M. on Thursday afternoon, Danny Sizemore killed and ate the Reverend Mr. Jarvis in the basement of the Church of the Nazarene in the township of Morgan's Cleft, North Carolina. Danny was fifteen years old and incapable of speech. He washed the blood from his face and hands the best he could in the rain barrel behind the parsonage. There was little he could do about the mess on his shirt and it worried him. If there was one thing the Reverend Mr. Jarvis had drilled into Danny's mist-enshrouded brain, it was cleanliness and neatness.

Still wiping at his sodden shirt, Danny started home, now and then pausing to chunk a rock in the creek. He scooted his bare feet along the road; he liked the velvety feel of the dust. He had just stopped, balancing clumsily on one leg to pluck a grassburr from his big toe, when his stomach began to churn. He leaned against the split rail fence and threw up.

He stood for a moment in confusion, pink saliva running down his chin, feeling the hollowness in him and the tingling in his puffy face.

Then he thought of the quarter and took it from his pocket to look at it. The Reverend Mr. Jarvis gave him one every week for cleaning up around the church. A quarter a week wasn't much money, even in

Beyond the Cleft 51

Morgan's Cleft, but, at that, Danny was overpaid. The Reverend Mr. Jarvis used the hypothetical job as an excuse for charity even though he was reasonably sure the boy's mother wound up with the money.

His mind blank of everything but the shiny coin, Danny continued home. When he passed the Morgan's Cleft School he ignored, or perhaps was unaware of, the screams and running children.

—2—

At 2:17 P.M. that Thursday afternoon, the entire first, second, and third grades, under the tutelage of Miss Amelia Proxmire (a dour-faced warper of young minds) arose from their desks and devoured her.

Mrs. Edith Beatty (fourth, fifth, and sixth grades) heard Miss Proxmire's gurgling screams from her adjoining classroom. She lifted her copious bulk and waddled rapidly to investigate, but her way was blocked by Mandy Pritchard, age ten. Mrs. Beatty reached out her arm to gently remove the child from her path, but Mandy grabbed the arm and bit a bleeding chunk from it.

Mrs. Beatty, momentarily immobilized by shock, was dimly aware that some of the children in her classroom were attacking the others. She watched in fascination as Mandy bared her pink teeth for another bite. But she had had enough of this nonsense. She pulled her bleeding arm away and kicked Mandy in the shin with her heavy walking oxford. Mrs. Beatty kicked her again, in the head, opening a gash in her scalp, and catapulting her underneath the front row of desks.

She waded into the mass of screaming children, pulling them apart, but she could see that little was being accomplished. As soon as she released one, the child would attack again. She calmly removed her shoe and, holding it by the toe, went to each child who seemed to be the aggressor and bashed it in the head.

There were only five of them, counting Mandy. Six of the remaining seven were hysterical and Bobby MacDonald seemed to be dead. His throat was torn open. The six still on their feet were bleeding from numerous bites and scratches. Mrs. Beatty tried to calm them but the bedlam in the hall made it impossible.

Miss Proxmire's class had erupted from her room looking for plumper prey. They found Mrs. Agnes Bledsoe (junior high) and Miss Clarissa Ogilvy (high school), accompanied by their students on their way to Miss Proxmire's room. They attacked like wolves and gained a momentary advantage because of the stunned inaction of the older children.

Their attack was tenacious but not suicidal. Some of the children fought back and some of them fled. Mrs. Beatty's class had had enough and evacuated the building quickly. The entire melee rapidly moved outside with children scattering in every direction and dozens of townspeople converging on the school. The battle was brief. The three surviving teachers and the remaining children found themselves standing in the playground, numb with shock, and no one left to fight. Miss Ogilvy leaned against the johnny-stride and then slipped slowly down the pole in a faint.

There were three casualties in the school: Miss Proxmire, Bobby MacDonald, and Eloise Harper whose ill-advised flight led her down Sandy Lane. She was overtaken by six of them.

Mrs. Beatty returned to her room to find it empty. Mandy and the four others had gone, taking Bobby MacDonald's body with them. Mrs. Beatty felt very tired and weary. Her arm hurt fiercely but she was too exhausted to do anything but clutch at it. She sat at her desk and leaned back in the chair.

—3—

At 2:17 that afternoon, Betty Whitman was nursing her thirteen-month-old son. She sat rocking gently, dreamily reading of Jean Harlow in a movie magazine. She jerked and gasped when the baby bit her. He had teethed early and it was happening too often. She promised herself this was the last breast feeding and went back to her magazine.

The second time he bit her she cried out. She pulled his mouth away and watched the blood gush down her side. She put the baby on the floor and stood up. She took three steps with her hand clutched to her breast and fainted. The baby looked at her a moment and began toddling toward her.

—4—

Mavis Sizemore was a slatternly woman of indeterminate age who managed a tenuous existence by washing and ironing for other people. Her small house, connected to the town by a narrow foot bridge across Indian Creek, was as weary and woebegone as she. The backyard contained a small vegetable garden, an outhouse, a pen of disreputable-looking chickens, two scrawny pigs, and several clotheslines partially filled with drying clothes. Two black cast-iron washpots sat on kindling fires, each nearly filled with boiling water. Into one Mavis poured a can of lye and a syrup pail of cracklings left over from lard-making. She stirred the mixture with a wooden paddle and then wiped at her pewter-colored, sparrow's nest hair with the back of her hand.

She moved wearily to a galvanized washtub and drew soapy clothes from it, scrubbed them on a rub board, and then transferred them to the other boiling pot. She punched at them with a cut-off broom handle, long ago bleached white and fuzzy, to make sure they were submerged.

Beyond the Cleft 53

She left the clothes to boil and returned to the first pot, testing the contents with a chicken feather. The feather emerged blackened and curled. She added more cracklings and again stirred the thickening mixture. Her face was red and sweaty from the heat and her hands were mottled from too much lye soap and stained with bluing.

Mavis had faulty genes and in her hazy lifetime had produced eight stillbirths and Danny. She had never been married. Danny shuffled across the footbridge and came around the side of the house still lovingly engrossed with his quarter.

Her suet-colored lips began moving, making sounds at Danny. He heard them vaguely, but they meant nothing. He had long ago stopped trying to make sense of the sounds or of the woman. This was only where he went when he was sleepy or hungry. She knocked the quarter from his hand and slapped his face.

Her flesh was like putty and tasted of soap.

FIRST INTERLUDE

Not far from Asheville, North Carolina, an unpaved road leaves the state highway and wanders upward into the Blue Ridge. The road follows the path of least resistance; around hillsides of rhododendron; over ridges of white pine, yellow pine, and spruce; through valleys of hemlock, laurel, and dogwood. For the most part it follows Indian Creek, a wild mountain stream which eventually flows into the French Broad. It crosses the stream numerous times on trestle bridges of ancient timber, and then will stray away when the path of least resistance leads elsewhere.

The road passes through a few scattered villages and skirts an occasional farm or logging camp. There is less and less traffic as it penetrates deeper into the mountains. Those who live there have little reason to enter. The road rejoins Indian Creek near the logging town of Utley and becomes even more tentative as it passes through the village.

From there it rises sharply for some twenty miles to pass, with the creek, through a gap in the mountain called Morgan's Cleft. The pass and the village beyond were named for Cleatus Morgan, leader of the original settlers in the high valley. Once through the gap, the road and the stream straighten and follow the approximate center of the wide valley to the township.

Past the Church of the Nazarene, the road dwindles to little more than a pair of wheel ruts separated by grass and wild flowers. It divides many times along the fifteen mile length of the valley; each division ending at a lonely farm.

The Colonials who settled here had intended to go on to Tennessee but found themselves at a dead end. After a brief consultation with the other families, Cleatus Morgan decided this rich and fertile valley, though practically insulated from the outside world, was a definite windfall. So they settled in and prospered by their own standards. Indian Creek, which ran pure and bright and teemed with fish, provided power for a gristmill; the valley and surrounding heights were thick with Virginia deer, wild turkeys, dove, and quail. Little was needed from the outside.

—5—

Orvie Morgan, direct descendant of Cleatus Morgan and heir to the choicest farm in the valley, drove toward town with his five-year-old son at his side. The shiny black Model A Ford, one of only five automobiles in the valley—not counting the Mercantile's Model T truck—clattered and bounced in the wheel ruts. The tufted tops of the wild grasses in the center flicked against the axles with small unheard sounds. The time was 2:17 P.M. on Thursday afternoon.

Little Cleatus Morgan, this generation's proud bearer of the ancestral name, took his father's arm in his small hands. Orvie turned his head and smiled fondly at his son. The smile became a grimace of consternation when Little Cleatus' tiny sharp teeth sank in. Orvie's arm was hard muscled but the bite still brought blood.

Orvie pushed the child away with a sharp, puzzled exclamation. Little Cleatus returned with single-minded ferocity and clamped his teeth on his father's shoulder. Orvie twisted in the seat to disengage the child. His foot pressed harder on the accelerator. The narrow tire on the front wheel struck a stone in the rut and cut sharply into the high grass. The car careened through a low growth of dogwood, flushing a flock of doves which filled the air with gray blurs and whistling wings.

Orvie pinioned his son to the seat with his bleeding arm and fought the steering wheel with one hand. But it was too late. The left front wheel spun on air. The car tipped over with maddening slowness, and slid down the embankment on its roof. The glass shattered in the windshield. The car tipped again, rolled onto its wheels, then toppled once more to land upside down in Indian Creek.

Orvie's head twisted loosely with the movement of the water, his hair flowing like dark sea grass. Red flumes stretched farther and farther, leaving his head, shoulder, and arm and exiting through the empty windshield frame.

Little Cleatus fought like a trapped rat, tearing at his father's arm, clawing with his fingernails. Bubbles oozed from his nostrils and from between his clenched teeth. But he could not break Orvie's protective grip. Orvie drowned and, with love, took his would-be murderer with him.

Beyond the Cleft

—6—

Meridee Callahan put her hands to the small of her back and stretched. The nagging ache under her fingers eased slightly but resumed when she relaxed. She sighed and looked at her swollen abdomen. Only one more month, she thought and smiled. "I can take it if you can," she said out loud and patted her stomach.

She smoothed the chenille bedspread where she had taken a nap and looked at the clock. It was almost two and she had a lot of work still undone. Robbie had wanted old Ludie Morgan to help her out now that her time was drawing close. But, as much as Meridee hated to admit it, she simply didn't get along with her Grandaunt Ludie. The old woman meant well, she supposed, but she was bossy, meddling, gossipy, righteous, and had enough superstitions to do the whole valley.

Meridee lifted the cuptowel and checked the bread she had put on the back of the Sunshine stove to rise. She nodded with satisfaction. She opened the door of the fire box and stirred the coals, added shavings and kindling, let it catch, and added wood. She moved the breadpans to the kitchen cabinet away from the heat. She took a mixing bowl and a pan of string beans she had picked that morning and went to sit in the shade on the front porch.

She was snapping beans when Danny Sizemore passed on his way to the church. She watched him idly and then went back inside. She dipped water from the stove reservoir into a stewer and added the beans. The stove was hot enough so she put the breadpans in the oven, then wiped the perspiration dewing on her upper lip with the cuptowel. She rolled up the door of the high closet and took a chicken leg to nibble while waiting on the bread.

Seeing Danny reminded her she should go to Mavis' and check on her washing and ironing. She knew it was only an excuse to take a walk and get out of the hot kitchen because Mavis would bring them around when she finished. That was one thing Robbie had insisted upon. She argued she was still capable of doing her own laundry, but rather gratefully gave in when he put his foot down.

Screams of terror drifted in the kitchen window from the direction of the school.

—7—

Robbie Callahan was the constable of Morgan's Cleft. There wasn't much for a constable to do in the valley: an occasional lost child or lost cow, a little too much corn liquor on Saturday night, an infrequent territorial dispute between farmers, a boyish prank gotten out of hand. The people were hard-working, self-reliant, and God-fearing. They didn't really need a constable. Besides, everyone knew everyone else and it was virtually impossible to get away with anything. But they needed and wanted a figure of authority: someone to organize when organization was necessary, someone to collect taxes, someone to preside at town meetings, someone to help when help was wanted.

Robbie was only twenty-six, but he had broad shoulders, long legs, sandy hair, an easy grin, and could lick practically anybody who gave him trouble. He was well-liked and trusted and had married Meridee Morgan three years earlier. His connection with the Morgans hadn't hurt him at election time.

But, as there wasn't much for a constable to do, and because the job only paid ten dollars a month, Robbie worked at Watson's Mercantile. He kept the accounts, went to Utley twice a week in the truck for the mail and ice and anything else needed from the outside. For all practical purposes, Robbie had been in charge of the store since old Calvin Watson began failing six years before.

The Mercantile smelled of coffee beans, licorice, cheese, dill, and leather—especially leather. He opened another crate of harness, entering it in his inventory as he hung it up: bridles, lines, traces, pads, back and hip straps, breeching, breast straps, martingales, hames, spread straps.

Frances Pritchard, who clerked for Robbie, was showing yard goods to her mother at the front of the store. Mrs. Pritchard always found it necessary to unroll every other bolt before she made up her mind. She fingered ivory silk crepe with one hand and mais chiffon mull with the other, but Frances knew her mother was only daydreaming.

"I can't make up my mind," Mrs. Pritchard said with a whine. "Which do you like best, Frances, dear?"

Frances smiled tolerantly. "The crepe is very nice, mother, and it's two ninety-eight a yard. The mull is fifty-five and," she pushed two other bolts forward, "the chambray is nine cents a yard and the calico is ten." She cocked an eyebrow at her mother. Mrs. Pritchard sighed in resignation.

They heard a commotion from the direction of the school.

—8—

Edith Beatty sat at her desk looking at the huge smear of blood where Bobby MacDonald's body had been. Other smears led to the window where the body had been removed. Her brain felt like cotton. She couldn't think or reason. Her arm was numb. She held it tightly to stop the bleeding. She felt light-headed and her ears rang.

Several people came into the room. She recognized Mrs. Bledsoe and Robbie Callahan but the others were back in the deep shadows. Strange there should be so many shadows in the middle of the afternoon. Robbie leaned over her, talking to her, but she couldn't understand what he was saying. The shadows had overtaken Mrs. Bledsoe, covering her like a greasy black fog. Robbie was doing something to her arm but she couldn't tell what because of the shadows.

—9—

Meridee watched Morgan's Cleft through the kitchen window as she cut away the burned crust of the bread. The inside would be fine for making bread pudding, she decided. She wrapped it in a cuptowel and put in the high closet of the stove. Not tonight; she would make pudding tomorrow. It was nearly sundown but the street was filled with milling, confused, sometimes hysterical people. Robbie would be home soon, hungry as a bear.

She made biscuits and put them in the oven and warmed up the leftover chicken. Even with the beans it didn't seem like much so she fried bacon and eggs.

She had gone to the school house with everyone else. It had all seemed unreal, like she was reading a storybook. No one could explain what had happened. Everyone stood around while the stunned children told what had taken place, trying to make sense of it all. Mrs. Beatty had passed out and was carried to Doctor Morgan's office. The bite on her arm already seemed infected. The parents of some of the missing children had gone into the woods after them; they hadn't come back yet.

A team and wagon had ripped and rattled into town. The horses had been wild with panic, rearing and screaming, their eyes round and shining, bloody froth on the bits. The wagon was empty except for sacks of oats in the bed and blood on the seat.

Robbie had sent her home when Caroline Walker ran the two miles into town carrying the body of her five-year-old Pretty. Caroline's arms were covered with bites and she screamed she had killed Pretty. They couldn't get her to say anything else. She just repeated it over and over and fought them when they tried to take Pretty from her. Then she fainted and they took her to Doc.

Meridee ate the bacon and eggs because she was so hungry and fried more for Robbie.

—10—

Pauly Williams felt sick to his stomach. He had a bite on his chest and another on his arm. Both throbbed and itched. Doc Morgan had swabbed them with something that stung and bandaged them. Pauly was embarrassed and ashamed. Delton Reeves was only ten years old and Pauly was twelve, but he hadn't been able to fend off Delton's ferocious attack, hadn't been able to keep Delton from biting him twice. He had never been so grateful for anything in his life as he had been when Mrs. Beatty clobbered Delton on the head with her shoe.

He scratched at the bandage on his chest, but his mother pulled his hand away. The skin around the bandage was red and the inflammation seemed to be spreading. She felt his forehead. It was hot. He had taken a fever. She pulled the covers around Pauly's neck and told him to go to sleep. She turned the lamp low, making sure the wick didn't smoke.

She went onto the front porch and looked through the moonlight toward the road that skirted the corn field. She wished Joe Bob would get home. The chickens hadn't been fed, the eggs hadn't been gathered, and the milk still sat in the smokehouse unseparated. She had half a mind to take the lantern and do all three, but Joe Bob had told her to stay in the house with the door locked while he and the other men looked for the children.

It was hard to believe that Wayne was out there in the dark. He was only seven and had never been very strong. Pauly was the strong one. Wayne was the smart one. Thunderheads were building on the west ridge. She hoped it wouldn't rain—Wayne was sure to catch cold if it did.

She had been watching the movements of the cornstalks for several minutes before she realized what she was seeing. The tops would sway slightly as something brushed against them lower down. It was only a small area of movement. It had started at the road and crept across the field toward the creek.

She became consciously aware of it when it shifted directions and started toward the house. If we didn't have enough problems already, she thought. Now the fence is down somewhere and the deer have gotten in. They loved the young corn and could mess up a field in nothing flat. But she didn't know what she could do about it. Joe Bob had forbidden her to leave the house.

The movement drew closer and paused as it reached the fence. She leaned against the porch railing and strained her eyes to see what was there, but it was too dark. She thought she saw something crawl through the fence but she wasn't sure. Yes, she had seen something. There was another one. It wasn't deer. Deer couldn't crawl through the fence like that. Besides, it was too small.

She could see nothing but dark shapes close to the ground. There must be a dozen of them, she thought. They could be bear cubs, but she didn't think there would be so many together.

She backed toward the door, beginning to be afraid. They moved toward her with such determination and purpose. She reached behind her, feeling for the handle of the screen door. One of the shapes grew suddenly taller and moved alone toward the porch. The others waited motionlessly. She pulled open the screen and slipped inside.

The single moving shape stepped into the rectangle of light cast

Beyond the Cleft

through the open door.

"Wayne!" she cried and ran across the porch toward him. The screen door slammed behind her like a rifle shot. She stood at the top of the porch steps. She gave a little moan. He looked up at her, his clothes torn and dirty, his hair mussed, scratches on his little face and hands. She hurried down and knelt before him, throwing her arms around him, pulling him against her breast.

She saw dried blood on his neck. She pushed him from her, and held him at arm's length. Dried blood flaked from his face and stained the front of his shirt. She became aware of the other children; that they had stood up; that they were surrounding her. She rose suddenly with a frightened whimper and backed toward the porch, pulling Wayne with her.

She knew these children. She knew all of them.

Her heel caught on the edge of the step and she fell. A fierce pain shot through her elbow, numbing her whole arm. She screamed. The silent children rushed to her, covering her.

She screamed again and again. She seemed to stand outside herself watching something she couldn't believe. There was a noise like the screen door slamming. She couldn't be sure she heard it because the screams were so loud.

Delton Reeves jerked and the side of his head flew off with a little red explosion. He fell over and twisted like a rag doll. Barbara Ann Morgan clutched her hands to the front of her bloody dress, but the blood wasn't dried. It was wet and shiny.

The children ran away, scattering through the darkness like silent phantoms. A small puff of dust erupted at Wayne's feet as he ran. She pulled herself around on the steps and looked up at the porch. Pauly stood there with Joe Bob's deer rifle.

He had a satisfied look on his face.

—11—

Danny Sizemore walked slowly across the footbridge, looking around carefully. He had stayed inside all evening crouched at the window, watching the people running around the street. He had never seen so many in town at one time and it frightened him. So many horses and wagons and automobiles, leaving and coming back and leaving again, rattling the boards on the big bridge by the mill. People crying and yelling. Dogs barking and whining because they didn't understand what the commotion was about. And that big fire they built in the school yard. But no one had crossed the footbridge. No one had come near all evening as he huddled and watched.

Now the street was empty and only a few of the houses still showed lights. And he was hungry. There had been no supper though he had sat at the table and waited. The woman had never brought it.

But another compulsion overrode the hunger, forced it deep into the mists of Danny's mind. He walked through town and down the road deeper into the valley. He didn't know where he was going but he never hesitated at a juncture of the road. When the road didn't go where he had to go, he crashed through the brush, scratching his arms on the dogwood branches, flushing startled quail, never veering from his unknown destination.

Danny's lungs burned and his puffy body trembled with fatigue. He had walked for hours but his legs kept moving. Then he was slipping and scrambling down the embankment into the creek bed. He went another hundred yards keeping his footing with difficulty on the round smooth stones.

He saw them up ahead, working silently in the moonlight. They seemed to be excavating the high creek bank. Even the smallest among them carried rocks and armloads of dirt.

Probably for the first time in his dim existence, Danny **felt**. The feeling swelled in him, choking him, stretching his doughy flesh. He began running toward them, making a happy gurgling sound deep in his throat.

The children stopped their activity and turned to watch him silently. One of them reached down and plucked a smooth river rock from the stream. He threw it at Danny. The rock rattled on other rocks at his feet but Danny didn't notice. Others began throwing stones. Danny became gradually aware of the sharp pains growing on his body and stopped in bewilderment. The stones continued to pelt him. His arms came slowly up to protect his face.

He stood for a moment watching the children, the feeling inside him changing to a hurt far worse than any made by a stone. Then he turned and walked away. The children returned to their work. Danny looked back at them once, great tears rolling down his cheeks, but the children ignored him.

He tripped while climbing the embankment and didn't bother to get up. He lay with his face buried in the grass, choking on his sobs. It was the first time he had ever cried.

—12—

Meridee Callahan lay in the darkness beside her husband, feeling the warmth of his body. She couldn't sleep and thought from the sound of Robbie's breathing he couldn't either. She put her hand lightly on his bare chest. He turned facing her and put his arms around her, pulling her to him. She snuggled against him and felt his breath in her hair.

"You all right, Hon?" he asked softly.

"Mmm-huh. I just can't go to sleep."

Beyond the Cleft 61

"Me, too." His hand slid down her arm and rested gently on her stomach. She felt his face move against hers as he smiled. "I think I felt him move."

She chuckled against his neck. "It's probably gas."

"Don't say that." Robbie sat up and put his cheek against her swollen abdomen. "Hey, you in there, my son," he whispered. "If you don't hurry up and come outa there, your old man is gonna hafta pay a visit to Mavis Sizemore."

Meridee grunted and hit him on the shoulder with her small fist. He laughed and buried his face between her breasts. Her arms went around his neck squeezing him tightly to her. They lay like that for a while, her face against his hair which smelled of pine. He slid his hand under her gown and cupped her breast, rubbing his thumb across the nipple. She ran her fingernails lightly down his spine and the muscles on his back trembled. She stopped when she felt a warm hardness against her hip.

"Robbie?"

"Mmm?"

"Do you think . . . what happened to . . . to the children . . . do you think anything happened to our baby?"

He raised himself and looked into her face. "You shouldn't upset yourself with thoughts like that, Meri. Our baby will be the finest baby in the valley."

"But, how do you know . . . "

He put his fingers on her lips. "Now stop it," he said gently. "You're gonna worry yourself into a nervous fit about nothing. You hear me?"

She nodded. He slid his fingers to her cheek and touched his lips lightly to hers. "Now, go to sleep," he said and cuddled her in his arms.

But she didn't—not for a long time.

—13—

The Church of the Nazarene was packed. The pews were full and people stood three-deep around the sides. Even then, they weren't all inside. Others stood in the churchyard by the open windows where they could hear and still keep watch with the rifles and shotguns they held.

There was none of the running and playing which usually accompanied a town meeting. No children under the age of eleven were present, and most of those who were present were in the parsonage which had been converted into a makeshift hospital. All who had been bitten were running high temperatures with frequent bouts of vomiting.

Robbie stood beside the lectern with papers in his hands. The silent, pinched faces stared back at him colored with hope, despair, fear, and confusion. Robbie shuffled the paper and cleared his throat. He looked tired and kept running his fingers through his tousled hair.

"Yesterday evening and this morning," he began slowly, "we contacted everybody in the valley, to tell them about this meeting and to get a head count so we would know how many people have . . . died and how many are missing. I have it here. Do you want me to read it or pin it on the board?"

He lifted his eyes and surveyed the people pressed into the church, but there was no response. Doc Morgan, sitting in the front pew, looked around and said quietly, "Why don't you read it, Robbie."

Robbie nodded. "Okay. These are the known dead. Orvie and Little Cleatus. They drowned when Orvie's car ran off the road into the creek." A woman began weeping softly somewhere in the rear of the room. Robbie looked up briefly and then continued. "Uh . . . Edith Beatty, Caroline Walker, and Joe Bob's wife died this morning from infected wounds. Everyone bitten is sick but only those three have died. Doc can answer your questions about that. The Reverend Jarvis, Mavis Sizemore, Miss Proxmire, Betty Whitman, Bobby MacDonald were . . . killed by the children yesterday. We found the Whitman baby in the woods this morning. He had gone nearly a mile up the valley but was dead when we found him. We also found Danny Sizemore hanging from a rafter at Mavis' place. He seems to have killed himself."

Robbie wiped the moisture from his upper lip with the side of his hand. "Pete and Prissy Morgan had been . . . were dead when we went by there this morning. They had six little kids—three of them not in school yet. Barbara Ann and Delton Reeves were killed when they attacked Joe Bob's wife last night. The bodies weren't there this morning but Pauly is sure they were dead. Pretty Walker was killed when she tried to kill Caroline. The Ellis baby died after falling from her crib. She apparently tried to climb out. That's eighteen we know for sure are dead." His voice was low and without emotion.

Robbie shuffled the papers without looking up. "As for the missing . . . the best we can figure thirty-seven children were . . . affected. Two of those are eleven and the rest are ten or younger. Except for the five known dead, they've all disappeared. Seven of them are under two years old; one even younger than the Ellis baby. We don't know how they managed.

"Agnes Bledsoe and her husband went by his brother's farm last night and didn't find anyone there. Calvin Watson was gone this morning. Somebody had broken in. There was no one at my . . . my sister's place this morning. And no one at Oss Morgan's. Oss's team came into town yesterday. There was blood on the wagon. Eloise Harper hasn't been seen since she left the school house. Able Pritchard, Will and Pansy Reeves, Gil MacDonald, Sonny Morgan, and Carroll Gilmore didn't come back last night after going to look for their kids. Counting the children, over fifty people are missing."

"What about the Sullivans?" someone asked.

Doc snorted and Robbie shook his head. "I don't know. We went up

Beyond the Cleft

to the Hollow this morning but they wouldn't let us in."

"Took a shot at us!" Doc said with indignation.

"Must be a lotta kids up there," the same man said.

"Usta be." Doc grimaced. "Them Sullivans been inbreedin' up there in the Hollow like a bunch of pigs; ever since old Hiram Sullivan had a fallin' out with Cleatus Morgan nearly two hundred years ago. I don't know how many of 'em survived the diphtheria that went through there in twenty-seven. I tried to vaccinate 'em but they took a shot at me then too."

"We can't worry about the Sullivans," Leo Whitman said bitterly. "I lost my wife and baby. Nearly everybody here lost somebody. We gotta figure out what to do about it. Robbie's been pussy-footin' around, not sayin' what needs to be said. Our kids have turned into wild animals, murderin' and eatin' human flesh. We need to go in and exterminate all of 'em. Like we would a pack of wolves!"

A murmur swelled from the crowd. "I don't believe what I'm hearing!" Mrs. Pritchard's voice carried over the other sounds. "You're talking about murdering our little children! My Mandy!"

"They killed your husband," Leo pointed out.

"We don't know that Able is dead!" she cried. Frances took her mother's arm and tried to calm her. Doc stood and held up his hands. When they quieted he said, "Maybe Leo's right and maybe not. That's why we're havin' this meetin'—to decide what to do. We need to find out what's going on. Maybe it will pass. Maybe it will pass and they'll come home."

"Could you shoot one of your grandkids, Doc?"

Doc looked at the floor for a moment and then shook his head. "I don't know. Joe Bob's wife wouldn't have been able to."

"We need to keep anything like that from happening again," Robbie said. "Some of you live pretty far out. You have to take care of your fields and your stock. They've already wiped out three families."

"I'll keep my shotgun with me."

"The ones who didn't come back last night had guns."

"What are we supposed to do? Lock ourselves in our houses?"

"I don't know." Robbie leaned against the lectern and wished he could sit down. He had been on horseback since dawn. "Everybody has to be aware of the situation so we can come up with something."

"I think the first thing we have to do," Doc said quietly, "is capture one of them. Ask them why they're doing this. Ask them what has happened to them."

"Capture?"

"You're talkin' about 'em as if they were animals!"

"No." Doc shook his head. "They're not animals. Animals don't think and plan. Animals can't open doors and windows and pretend to be your children so they can get close enough to kill you. If we can't stop thinking of them as our children, we may not have a chance."

—14—

Ludie Morgan put more wood in the stove and checked the gauge on the pressure cooker. She scalded Mason jars and sliced cucumbers to soak in lime water, humming to herself all the time.

Meridee sat at the kitchen table watching her. "You don't need to do all this, Aunt Ludie," she said with considerable awe.

"Gotta get your cannin' done. Don't want to let the garden go to waste. When those green beans and pickles are done, I'll pick a bunch of those nice green tomatoes and make chow-chow."

"I wasn't really planning to can this year. I've got enough left over from last year to feed the whole town."

"Then why plant a garden?"

"Force of habit, I guess." She looked out the window but couldn't see the church from where she sat. "How long do you think the meeting will last?"

"Lord knows. Folks get to jawin', never know when to quit. I coulda told 'em bad trouble was a comin'."

Meridee knew she shouldn't say anything, but she did. "How did you know?"

Ludie moved air across her shiny face with a paper fan. "I know the signs. I didn't just come to town on a wagonload of watermelons. Only last week I heard a goatsucker two nights runnin'. I even found a crow's feather on my front stoop. And for the last three nights the lightnin' bugs have been so thick you could sew by the light. Them two old dogs of mine been layin' in the yard pantin' like lizards and the weather barely warm."

"What do your dogs have to do with it?"

"They could feel the evil in the air pressin' in on 'em, that's what. It's the Devil's work. You notice how the Reverend Mr. Jarvis was one of the first to go. I know the signs."

Meridee sighed but didn't argue. She looked at the pot of chicken and dumplings keeping warm on the back of the stove. She was starving. Ever since yesterday afternoon she couldn't seem to get enough to eat.

—15—

Robbie sat on the davenport looking up at the quilting frame suspended just below the ceiling. Meridee started on it five months ago, but hadn't worked on it lately. "My belly gets in the way," she had said. There were about a dozen people in the parlor: a few of his relatives but mostly assorted Morgans. Some were sitting anxiously and some paced nervously while others talked quietly. He hadn't been listening until he heard his name.

"What?"

"I asked how many it is now," said his seventeen-year-old cousin Travis.

"How many what?"

"How many they've killed." It wasn't necessary to explain who "they" were.

"Oh. Uh . . . . forty-two, I think, known dead and missing."

Travis turned back to Meridee's father. "That's almost a fifth of the population."

Robbie was amazed at how calmly it was discussed now after the hysteria of those first few days. He stood up and rubbed his palms on his thighs. Doc had been in there for an hour. He went to the window, protected by bars made from wheel rims by the blacksmith, and looked out. There must be fifty people in the yard, he thought.

They had been gathering since Meridee went into labor. Her worries about the baby had spread. The entire valley wanted to know if the baby would be normal or like "them."

"Only way we could do it," Meridee's father said. "We work in groups of at least ten and half of 'em do nothin' but stand guard. It works out pretty good, but while you're helpin' someone else, your own crops ruin in the fields and they kill and eat your animals. There just aren't enough people to go around. Nearly half the farms are abandoned now, with relatives movin' in with each other for protection."

"Leo thinks the only way is to hunt 'em down and kill 'em."

"I agree, but there aren't enough men to do that and the work too. Besides, he's been out half a dozen times and hasn't seen a thing."

"They found those burrows in the creek bank."

"Yeah, but they didn't find any kids. They tried to smoke 'em out and nothin' happened. Even sent one of the dogs in but the burrow collapsed and smothered him. Doc thinks they musta moved somewhere else. What beats me is how they can eat so much."

Robbie went to the bedroom door and listened but could hear nothing. He fidgeted for a moment, then went to the kitchen for a drink of water. He had thought several times of suggesting they seek outside help, but he knew it wouldn't do any good. The people in the valley had been self-sufficient for two hundred years. It would never occur to them that they couldn't handle this alone. Also, there was a certain shame involved. How could they admit to outsiders that they were unable to handle their own little children?

Robbie stepped back into the parlor when he heard the bedroom door open. Ludie stood in the doorway, her face gray. She kept rubbing her arms and not looking at him. Everyone in the room was tensely silent.

He ran into the bedroom. Doc leaned against the bassinet. He turned to Robbie and shook his head. The sheet was pulled over Meridee's face. Robbie felt the bottom of his stomach drop away. He walked slowly to the bassinet and looked in.

His daughter looked back at him and bared her teeth.

—16—

Leo Whitman hunkered down behind the mill wheel watching the creek. He held the deer rifle lightly across his knees. He particularly watched a clump of hemlock hugging the water on the opposite side. He thought he saw a movement there a few minutes ago but he wasn't sure. His eyes burned from too many hours of trying to see in the dark. He wanted to point out the movement to the others, but he was afraid to make a sound.

He shifted his position slightly to keep his leg from going to sleep again and then had to move a stone that dug into his hip.

There it was again: a less dark flicker among the hemlock branches. Leo raised the rifle to his shoulder and sighted on the bush. After several minutes his vision began to blur. He lowered the rifle slightly and blinked his eyes.

Then one of them stepped from behind the hemlock and into the water. It was naked but he couldn't tell from this distance whether it was a boy or girl. It began wading slowly across the stream, looking around as if smelling the air. It stopped in midstream, the water up to its chest, and stood motionless. Did it suspect it was walking into a trap?

Leo sighted on the figure and hoped none of the others would go off half-cocked. Then the child moved forward again. Others slipped silently into the water. God, Leo thought, how quietly they move. He counted eight of them, all naked. Okay, everybody, he said under his breath, wait until they all reach the bank.

But someone didn't. A rifle shot rattled through the night as the first one stepped out of the water. It was a boy, he could see now. The naked child jerked and flopped in the grass. Leo sighted on another and fired. It threshed in the water then floated face down. Other shots peppered the water with little geysers, but there was nothing to shoot at. The children had vanished; submerged in the creek and invisible.

"Damn!" Leo yelled and ran toward the stream. He waded into the water and hurriedly dragged out the floating corpse. The others joined him. They carried the two dead children quickly away from the creek, looking anxiously over their shoulders. But there was nothing to see, not a vagrant ripple where the children had been.

"Hurry up," Leo growled. "I don't trust 'em."

They ran down the dark street toward Doc's office. They could see him standing in the lighted window watching for them. He had the door open when they got there. Doc slammed the door and lowered the bar across it as they crowded in.

"How many did you get?" Doc asked quickly.

"Two," Leo grimaced. "Some idiot fired too soon and the rest of them ducked under water and disappeared."

"Put 'em on the table." Doc carried the lamp and held it over the bodies. There was a stunned silence as the men got their first clear look. Water puddled on the table then dripped through the cracks to drip on the floor with soft thumps.

"My God," someone whispered.

"It's Mandy Pritchard and Wayne Williams," Leo said with dull voice. "I'm glad Joe Bob isn't here."

"Is she . . . ?"

"Yes," Doc said slowly.

Mandy's body lay loosely on its back. The bullet had destroyed one of her breasts, but the other was large and full. Her hair was matted and grimy and showed a bald spot where Mrs. Beatty had kicked her. Her skin was darkly tanned and her abdomen swelled hugely.

"But, she's only . . . What? Ten?" Leo asked.

"By our reckoning, she is," Doc answered peering close, "but I doubt if that's valid anymore. You'll notice they both have a full growth of pubic hair."

"That's not all Wayne's got a full growth of," someone sniggered. "Most full-grown men wouldn't be ashamed of a pecker like that."

Doc fingered the boy's genitals. "He's fully developed all right."

"You think he's the father?"

"I don't know. He could easily be." Doc ran his hand over Wayne's stomach, pinching the cool damp skin. Then he felt Mandy's leg. "Feel their skin. It's as tough as leather. And look at their bodies. There's been a subtle change. They aren't the bodies of children any more—and Wayne seems taller, don't you think?"

There was a murmur of assent. "Now we know why they needed so much food," Doc continued.

"Why?"

"Because their bodies have been undergoing tremendous changes. Tremendous and rapid. They needed a lot of fuel for all that cell activity." He put his hand on Mandy's stomach. "I'd say she was very close to delivery."

"That's impossible," Leo blurted. "It's only been three months."

"No more impossible than the rest of it," Doc answered calmly. "But it's logical when you consider the acceleration of everything else. I imagine the baby would have been even more developed than Meri's. Probably able to take care of itself in a few weeks—maybe less."

"Then," Leo said dazed, "there'll be hundreds of them in a couple of years. In three months we've only managed to kill four. They've killed . . . What? Fifty or sixty of us?"

"I think that number can be increased considerably," Doc said, turning away from the bodies. "A bunch of us went by the Hollow this morning. There wasn't a soul around, nor any stock. Looked as if it had been deserted over a month. And the bluffs around the Hollow were riddled with burrows. We got outta there in a hurry."

"Do you think it's hopeless, Doc?"

"I can give you a better answer in seven and a half months."

"What?"

"Frances Pritchard is pregnant. She's the first I know of to conceive after that day."

"But Frances isn't married. Who . . . ?"

"She moved in with Robbie after Meri died. There was no one to marry them and, I don't know, it didn't seem to matter."

SECOND INTERLUDE

Not far from Asheville, North Carolina, a road leaves the state highway and wanders upward into the Blue Ridge. It's paved now and has been since the middle Fifties. It still follows the path of least resistance although the square turns have been rounded off and the more treacherous twists have been straightened. The many bridges across Indian Creek are new—made of steel and concrete rather than splintering timbers.

There hasn't been much change in forty years. The logging camps are gone. Camp grounds and motels with cable television have sprung up with increasing frequency. The road enjoys a great deal of traffic because it eventually ends up in the Great Smoky Mountains National Park.

The villages along the way have revived with surprising vigor after the near death of the Depression. They were quick to discover that tourists pay much better than cows, pigs, crops, or logs. They found, rather astonishingly, the very things they were eager to cast off after the coming of electricity, television, and stereophonic sound, were just as eagerly sought by the tourists.

With dumbfounded gladness they would accept money for their old polished oak iceboxes; enough money to buy new frost-free refrigerators with automatic icemakers. Money for black cast-iron washpots bought new automatic washing machines. Homemade quilts were too valuable to put on beds. Tourists bought the quilts and the villagers happily slept under electric blankets from J. C. Penney.

The city people called it Folk Art. The villagers called it Free Enterprise.

At Utley the highway makes an unexpected turn to the southwest, going nowhere near Morgan's Cleft. The old unpaved road still goes toward the pass, following Indian Creek, to a few summer cabins and outlying farms. If you tried to follow it to Morgan's Cleft, you would find yourself in the lane to the Crenshaw farm. If you backed up and tried again, you might find it—if you looked closely. The bushes are not

Beyond the Cleft

quite as thick, the trees are shorter, the ground is more level, and an occasional grading is still visible.

Some of the older people in Utley still remember those who fled the high valley nearly forty years ago. There weren't many—only a dozen or so—coming down the mountain in wagons and some on foot, scattered over several months. Some were hurt and died quickly from infected wounds. Those who lived moved on hastily without explanation, but the folk beyond the Cleft always were a strange lot.

—17—

Hollis Middleton had been to the bank that day discussing a loan. He owned a piece of very choice property that stretched from the highway to Indian Creek just in the edge of Utley. A motel there should do very nicely. But it wouldn't be just another motel. He would build a fishing veranda over the creek; the guests could fish and the motel kitchen would do the cleaning and cooking. He smiled at the idea and turned on the television set.

He yelled up the stairs for his youngest girl to turn her stereo down so he could hear the TV. He thought he detected a barely perceptible drop in the volume. He adjusted the color so Raymond Burr wouldn't look dipped in purple dye, and sat down to relax.

He groaned when he heard the dishwasher go on in the kitchen and little silver speckles began dancing across the screen. He bore his affluence with stoicism.

He heard a scream and a clatter of pots and pans from the kitchen. He arose with a sigh and went out there without too much hurry. His wife was a great screamer. She was rolling on the floor amid several pieces of her new waterless cookware. Their four-year-old grandson was wrestling with her.

Hollis shook his head and laughed. "You two sure do play rough." His grandson looked up quickly at the sound of his voice. The boy had a mouthful of flesh. Blood dribbled off his chin.

PROLOGUE (cont'd)

It grew.

Slowly and carefully, without haste or impetuosity, it grew. It had all the time in the world.

San Diego Lightfoot Sue

This all began about ten years ago in a house at the top of a flight of rickety wooden stairs in Laurel Canyon. It might be said there were two beginnings, though the casual sorcery in Laurel Canyon may have been the cause and the other merely the effect—if you believe in that sort of thing.

The woman sat cross-legged on the floor reading the book. The windows were open to the warm California night and the only sound that came through them was the distant, muffled, eternal roar of Los Angeles traffic. The brittle pages of the book crackled as she turned them carefully. She read slowly because her Latin wasn't what it used to be. She lit a cigarette and left it to burn unnoticed in the ashtray on the floor beside her.

"Here's a good one," she said to the big orange tom curled in the chair she leaned against. "You don't know where I can find a hazelnut bush with a nest of thirteen white adders under it, do you, Punkin?" The cat didn't answer; he only opened one eye slightly and twitched the tip of his tail.

She turned a page and several two-inch rectangles of white paper fell out into her lap. She picked them up and examined them, but they were blank. She stuck them back in the book and kept reading.

She found it a while later. It was a simple spell. All she had to do was write the word-square on a piece of white parchment with black ink and then burn it while thinking of the person she wished to summon.

"I wonder if Paul Newman is doing anything tonight," she chuckled.

She stood up and went to the drafting table, opened a drawer and removed a pen and a bottle of india ink. She put a masking tape

San Diego Lightfoot Sue

dispenser on the edge of the book to hold it open and carefully lettered the word-square on one of the pieces of paper stuck between the pages. She supposed that's why her mother, or whoever, had put them there—they looked like parchment, anyway.

The word-square was eight letters wide and eight letters high; eight, eight-letter words stacked on top of one another. She imagined they were words, though they were in no language she knew. The peculiar thing about the square was that it read the same sideways or upside down—even in a mirror image, it was the same.

She put the cap back on the ink and went to the ashtray, kneeling beside it. She lay the parchment on the dead cigarette butts. "Well, here goes," she said to the cat. "I wonder if it's all right to burn it with a cigarette lighter? Maybe I need a black taper made of the wax of dead bees or something."

She composed herself, trying to take it seriously, and thought of a man, not a specific man, just **the** man. "I feel like Snow White singing 'Someday My Prince Will Come,'" she muttered. She flicked the cigarette lighter and touched the flame to the corner of the piece of paper.

It flamed up so quickly and so brightly she gasped and drew back. "God!" she grunted and hurried to a window to escape the billows of black smoke that smelled of rotten eggs. The cat was already out, sitting on the farthest point of the deck railing, looking at her with round startled eyes.

The woman glanced back at the black smoke spreading like a carpet on the ceiling and then at the wide-eyed cat. She suddenly collapsed against the window sill in a fit of uncontrollable laughter. "Come on back in, Punkin," she gasped. "It's all over." The cat gave her an incredulous look and hopped off the railing into the shrubbery.

This also began about ten years ago in Kansas, the summer he was fifteen, when the air smelled like hot metal and rang with the cries of cicadas. It ended a month later when he was still fifteen, when the house in Laurel Canyon burned with a strange green fire that made no heat.

His name was John Lee Peacock, a good, old, undistinguished name in Southern Kansas. His mother and his aunts and his aunts' husbands called him John Lee. The kids in school called him Johnny, which he preferred. His father never called him anything.

His father had been by-passed by the world, but he wouldn't have cared, even if he had been aware of it. Wash Peacock was a dirt farmer who refused to abandon the land. The land repayed his taciturn loyalty with annual betrayal. Wash had only four desires in life: to work the land, three hot meals each day, sleep, and copulation when the pressures built high enough. The children were strangers who appeared suddenly, disturbed his sleep for awhile, then faded into the gray house or the County Line Cemetery.

John Lee's mother had been a Willet. The aunts were her sisters: Rose and Lilah. Wash had a younger brother somewhere in Pennsylvania—or, had had one the last time he heard. That was in 1927, the year Wash's mother died. Grace Elizabeth Willet married Delbert Washburn Peacock in the fall of 1930. She did it because her father, old Judge Willet, thought it was a good idea. Grace Elizabeth was a plain, timid girl who, he felt, was destined to be the family's maiden aunt. He was right, but she would have been much happier if he hadn't interfered.

The Peacocks had owned the land for nearly a hundred years and were moderately prosperous. They had survived the Civil War, Reconstruction, and statehood, but wouldn't survive the Depression. Judge Willet felt that Wash was the best he could do for Grace Elizabeth. He was a nice-looking young man and what he lacked in imagination, he made up in hard work.

But the Peacocks had a thin, unfortunate blood line. Only a few of the many children lived. It was the same with Wash and Grace Elizabeth. She had given birth eight times but there were only three of them left. Wash, Jr., her first born, had married one of the trashy O'Dell girls and had gone to Oklahoma to work in the oilfields. She hadn't heard from him in thirteen years. Dwayne Edward, the third born, had stayed in Los Angeles after his separation from the army. He sent a card every Christmas and she had kept them all. She wished some of the girls had lived. She would have liked to have a girl, to make pretty things for her, to have someone to talk to. But she had lost the three girls and two of the boys. She had trouble remembering their names sometimes but it was all written in the big Bible where she could remind herself when the names began to slip away.

John Lee was the youngest. He had arrived late in her life, a comfort for her weary years. She wanted him to be different from the others. Wash, Jr. and Dwayne had both been disappointments; too much like their father: unimaginative, plodding boys who had done badly in school and got into trouble with the law. She still loved them because they were her children, but she sometimes forgot why she was supposed to. She wanted John Lee to read books (God! How long since she'd read a book, she used to read all the time when she was a girl), to know about art and far away places. She knew she hoped for too much, so was content when she got a part of it.

Wash didn't pay any more attention to John Lee than he had the others. He neither asked nor seemed to want the boy's help in the fields, so Grace Elizabeth kept him around the house, helping with her chores, talking to him, having him share with her what he had learned in school. She gave him as much as she could. There wasn't money for much but she managed to hold back a few dollars now and then.

She loved John Lee very much; he was probably the only thing she did love. So, on that shimmering summer day about ten years ago, when he was fifteen, she died for him.

She was cleaning up the kitchen after supper. Wash had gone back to the fields where he would stay until dark. John Lee was at the kitchen table, reading, passing on bits of information he knew she would like to hear. She leaned against the sink with the cuptowel clutched in her hand and felt her supper turn over in her stomach. She had known it was coming for months. Now it was here.

He's too young, she thought. If he could only have a couple more years. She watched him bent over the book, the evening sun glinting on his brown hair. He's even better looking than his father, she thought. So like his father. But only on the outside. Only on the outside.

She hung the cuptowel on the rack to dry and walked through the big old house. She hadn't really noticed the house in a long time. It had grown old and gray slowly, as she had, so that you hardly noticed it happening. Then you looked at it again and it wasn't the house you remembered moving into all those years ago. Wash's father had built it in 1913 when the old one had been unroofed by a twister. He had built it like they did in those days: big so generations could live in it. It had been freshly painted when she moved in; a big white box eight miles from Hawley, a mile from Miller's Corners.

Then the hard times began. But Wash had clung to the land during the Depression and the dust. He hadn't panicked like most of the others. He hadn't sold the land at give-away prices or lost it because he couldn't pay the taxes. Things had gotten a little better when the war began, but never as good as before the Depression. Now they were bad again. At the end of each weary year, there was only enough money to do it all over again the next weary year.

She supposed, being the oldest, Wash, Jr. would get it. She was glad John Lee wouldn't. She went upstairs to his room and packed his things in a pasteboard box. She left it where he would find it and went to her own room. She opened a drawer in the old highboy that had belonged to her grandmother and removed an envelope from beneath her cotton slips. She took it to the kitchen and handed it to John Lee.

He took it and looked at her. "What is it, Mama?"

"Open it in the morning, John Lee. You'd better go to bed now."

"But it's not even dark yet." There's something wrong, there's something wrong.

"Soon, then. I want to sit on the porch a while and rest." She kissed him and patted his shoulder and left the room. He watched the empty doorway and felt the blood singing in his ears. After a while, he got a drink of water from the cooler and went to his room. He lay on the bed, looking at the water spots on the ceiling paper, and clutched the envelope in his hands. Tears formed in his eyes and he tried to blink them away.

Grace Elizabeth sat on the porch in her rocker, moving gently, mending Wash's clothes until it got too dark to see. Then she folded them neatly in her lap, leaned back in the chair, and closed her eyes.

Wash found her the next morning only because he wondered why his breakfast wasn't waiting for him. She was buried in the County Line Cemetery with five of her children after a brief service at the First Baptist Church in Hawley. Aunt Rose and Aunt Lilah had a fine time weeping into black lace handkerchiefs and clucking over Poor John Lee.

On the way back from the funeral, John Lee rode in the front seat of the '53 Chevrolet beside his father. Neither of them spoke until they had turned off the highway at Miller's Corners.

"Write a letter to Wash, Jr. Tell him to come home." John Lee didn't answer. He could smell the dust rising up behind the car. Wash parked it in the old carriage house and hurried to change clothes, hurried to make up the half day he had lost. John Lee went to the closet in the front hall and took down a shoe box, in which his mother kept such things, and looked for an address. He found it after a bit, worked to the bottom, unused for thirteen years. He wrote the letter anyway.

He had left the envelope unopened under his pillow. Now he opened it, although he had guessed what it was. He counted the carefully hoarded bills: a hundred and twenty-seven dollars. He sat on the edge of the bed, on the crazy quilt his mother had made for him, in the quiet room, in the silent weary house. He wiped his eyes with his knuckles, picked up the pasteboard box, and walked the mile to Miller's Corners.

His Sunday suit, worn to the funeral that morning, once belonging to Dwayne, and before that, Wash, Jr., was white at the cuffs from the dusty road. His shoes, his alone, were even worse. It was a scorcher. "It's gonna be another scorcher," she always used to say, looking out the kitchen window after putting away the breakfast dishes. He sat on the bench at the Gulf station, cleaning the dust off the best he could.

The cicadas screeched from the mesquite bushes, filling the hot, still air with their insistent call for a mate. John Lee rather liked the sound, but it had bothered his mother. "Enough to drive a body ravin' mad," she used to say. She always called them locusts but he had learned in school their real name was cicada. And when they talked about a plague of locusts in the Bible, they really meant grasshoppers. "Well, I'll declare," she had said. "Always wondered why locusts would be considered a plague. Far's I know, they don't do anything but sit in the bushes and make noise. Now, grasshoppers I can understand." And she would smile at him in her pleased and proud way that caused a pleasant hurting in the back of his throat.

"Hello, John Lee."

He looked up quickly. "Hello, Mr. Cuttsanger. How are you today?" He liked Mr. Cuttsanger, a string-thin man the same age as his mother, who had seemingly permanent grease stains on his hands. He wiped at them now with a dull red rag, but it didn't help.

"I'm awfully sorry about your mother, boy. Wish I coulda gone to the funeral but I couldn't get away. We were in the same grade together all through school, you know."

"Yes, I know. She told me."

"What're you doin' here still dressed up?" he asked, sticking the rag in his hip pocket and looking at the box.

"I reckon I have to catch a bus, Mr. Cuttsanger." His heart did a little flip-flop. Not the old school bus either, but a real bus.

"Where you off to, John Lee?"

"Where do your buses go, Mr. Cuttsanger?"

Mr. Cuttsanger sat on the bench beside John Lee. "The westbound will be through here in about an hour goin' to Los Angeles. The eastbound comes through in the mornin' headed for St. Louis. You already missed it."

"Los Angeles. My brother, Dwayne, lives in California." But he didn't know where. He had seen the Christmas cards in the shoe box, but he hadn't paid any attention to the return address.

Mr. Cuttsanger nodded. "Good idea, goin' to stay with Dwayne. Nothin' for you here on this played-out old farm. Heard Grace Elizabeth say the same thing. Your father ought to sell it and go with you. But I guess I know Wash better'n that." He arose from the bench with a little sigh. He went into the station and returned with a small red flag. He stuck it in a pipe welded at an angle to the pole supporting the Gulf sign. "There. He'll stop when he sees that. You buy your ticket from the driver."

"Thank you, Mr. Cuttsanger. I need to mail a letter also." He took the letter he had carefully addressed in block printing to: Delbert Washburn Peacock, Jr., Gen. Del., Norman, Okla., from his pocket and handed it to Mr. Cuttsanger. "I don't have a stamp."

Mr. Cuttsanger looked at the letter. "Is Wash, Jr. still in Norman?" He said it as if he doubted it.

"I don't know. That's the only address I could find."

Mr. Cuttsanger tapped the letter against the knuckle of his thumb. "You leave a nickel with me and I'll get a stamp from Clayton in the mornin'. Sure was a lot simpler before they closed the post office." He sat back on the bench in the shade of the car shed. John Lee followed his eyes as he looked at Miller's Corners evaporating under the cloudless sky. An out-of-state car blasted through doing seventy. Mr. Cuttsanger sighed and accepted a nickel from John Lee. "They don't even have to slow down any more. Used to be thirty-five mile speed limit signs at each end of town. Guess they don't need 'em now. Ain't nothin' here but me and the cafe. Myrtle's been saying for nearly a year she was gonna move to Hawley or maybe even Liberal. Closed the post office in fifty-five, I think it was. That foundation across the highway is where the grocery store used to be. Don't reckon you remember the grocery store?"

"No, sir, but I remember the feed store."

"Imagine that. You musta been about four-five years old."

"I was born in forty-eight."

"Closed the feed store in fifty-two. Imagine you rememberin' that far back." He continued to ramble on in his pleasant, friendly voice. John Lee asked questions and made comments to keep him going, to make the time pass faster. A whole hour before the bus would come.

But it finally did, cutting off the highway in a cloud of dust and a dragon hiss of air brakes. John Lee looked at the magic name in the little window over the windshield: LOS ANGELES. He swallowed and solemnly shook hands with Mr. Cuttsanger.

"Goodbye, Mr. Cuttsanger."

"Goodbye, John Lee. You take care now."

John Lee nodded and picked up the box and walked to the bus, his legs trembling. The door sighed open and the driver got out. He opened a big door on the side of the bus that cut right through Continental Trailways. He took the pasteboard box.

"Where you goin'?"

"I'd like a ticket to Los Angeles, please." He couldn't keep from smiling when he said the name. The driver put a tag on the box, put it in with the suitcases, and closed the door. John Lee followed him into the bus. Inside was cool like some of the stores in Liberal.

He bought his ticket and sat down in the front seat, scooting to the window as the bus lurched back onto the highway. He looked back at Miller's Corners and waved to Mr. Cuttsanger, but he was taking down the red flag and didn't see.

John Lee leaned back in the seat and hugged himself. Once more he couldn't keep from smiling. After a bit, he looked around at the other people. There weren't many and some weren't wearing Sunday clothes; so he decided it would be all right to take off his jacket. He settled back in the seat watching the baked Kansas countryside rush past the window. Strange, he thought, it looks the same way it does from the school bus. Even though he tried to prevent it, the smile returned unbidden every once in a while.

The bus went through Hawley without stopping, past the white rococo courthouse with its high clock tower; past the school, closed for the summer; over the hump in the highway by the old depot where the railroad tracks had been taken out; across the bridge over Crooked Creek.

It stopped in Liberal and the driver called out, "Rest stop!" John Lee didn't know what a rest stop was, so he stayed on the bus. He noticed that some of the other passengers didn't get off either. He decided there was nothing to worry about.

He tried to see everything when the bus left Liberal, to look on both sides at once, because it was the farthest he had ever been. But Oklahoma looked just like Kansas, Texas looked just like Oklahoma, and New Mexico looked like Texas, only each seemed a little bleaker than the one before. The bus stopped in Tucumcari for supper. John Lee

San Diego Lightfoot Sue

had forgotten to eat dinner and his bladder felt like it would burst.

He was nervous but he managed all right. He'd eaten in a cafe before and, by watching the others, he found out where the toilet was and how to pay for his meal. It was dark when the bus left Tucumcari. He tried to go to sleep, to make the time pass faster, the way he always did when the next day was bringing wondrous things. But, as usual, the harder he tried, the wider awake he was.

He awoke when the bus stopped for breakfast and quickly put his coat over his lap, hoping no one had noticed. He waited until everyone else had gotten off, then headed for the toilet keeping his coat in front of him. He didn't know for sure where he was but all the cars had Arizona license plates.

It was after dark when the bus pulled into Los Angeles terminal, though it seemed to John Lee as if they had been driving through town for two hours. He had never dreamed it was so big. He watched the other passengers collect their luggage and got his pasteboard box.

Then he went out into: Los Angeles.

He walked around the street with the box clutched in his arms in total bedazzlement. Buildings, lights, cars, people, so many different kinds of people. It was the first time he had ever seen a Chinese, except in the movies, although he wasn't absolutely sure that it wasn't a Japanese. There were dozens of picture shows, lined up in rows. He liked movies and used to go nearly every Saturday afternoon, a long time ago before the picture show in Hawley closed.

And buses, with more magic names in the little windows: SUNSET BLVD.; HOLLYWOOD BLVD.; PASADENA; and lots of names he didn't recognize, but were no less magic, he was sure, because of that.

He was standing on the curb, just looking, when a bus with HOLLYWOOD BLVD. in the little window pulled over and opened the door right in front of him. The driver looked at him impatiently. It was amazing how the bus had stopped especially for him. He got on. There didn't seem to be anything else he could do.

"Vine!" the driver bawled sometime later. John Lee got off and stood at the corner of Hollywood and Vine grinning at the night. He walked down Hollywood Boulevard, gawking at everything, reading the names in stars on the sidewalk. He never imagined there would be so many cars or so many people at night. There were more than you would see in Liberal, even on Saturday afternoon. And the strange clothes the people wore. And men with long hair like the Beatles. Mary Ellen Walker had a colored picture of them pasted on her notebook.

He didn't know how far he had walked—the street never seemed to end—but the box was heavy. He was hungry and his Sunday shoes had rubbed a blister on his heel. He went into a cafe and sat in a booth, glad to get rid of the weight of the box. Most of the people looked at him as he came in. Several of them smiled. He smiled back. A couple of people had said hello on the street too.

Hollywood was certainly a friendly place.

He told the waitress what he wanted. He looked around the cafe and met the eyes of a man at the counter who had smiled when he came in. The man smiled again. John Lee smiled back, feeling good. The man got off the stool and came to the booth carrying a cup of coffee.

"May I join you?" He seemed a little nervous.

"Sure." The man sat down and took a quick sip of the coffee. "My name is John Lee Peacock." He held out his hand. The man looked startled, then took it, giving it a quick shake and hurriedly breaking contact. "I'd rather be called Johnny, though."

The man's skin was moist. John Lee guessed he was about forty, and a little bit fat. He nodded, quickly, like a turkey. "Warren."

"Pleased to meet you, Mr. Warren. You live in Hollywood?"

"Yes."

The waitress brought the food and put it on the table. Warren was flustered. "Oh . . . ah . . . put that on my ticket."

The waitress looked at John Lee. Her mouth turned down a little at the corners. "Sure, honey," she said to Mr. Warren.

John Lee discarded the straw from his ice tea and put sugar in it. "Aren't you eating?"

"Ah . . . no. No, I've already eaten." He took another nervous sip of the coffee and John Lee heard a smothered snicker from the booth behind him. "You didn't have to pay for my supper. I've got money."

"My pleasure."

"Thank you, Mr. Warren."

"You're welcome. Uh . . . how long you been in town?"

"Just got here a little while ago. On a Continental Trailways bus; all the way from Miller's Corners, Kansas." John Lee still couldn't believe where he was. He had to say it out loud. "I sure do like bein' in Los Angeles, Mr. Warren."

"You have a place to stay yet?"

He hadn't really thought about that. "No, sir. I guess I haven't."

Warren smiled and seemed to relax a little. It was working out okay, but the kid was putting on the hick routine a little thick. "Don't worry about it tonight. You can stay at my place and look for something tomorrow."

"Thank you, Mr. Warren. That's very nice of you."

"My pleasure. Uh . . . what made you come to Los Angeles?"

John Lee swallowed a mouth full of food. "My mamma died the other day. Before she died, she gave me the money to get away."

"I want to sit on the porch a while and rest," she had said.

"It was either Los Angeles or St. Louis and the Los Angeles bus came by first." He pushed the gray memories back out of the way. "And here I am!"

Warren looked at him, no longer smiling. "How old are you?"

"I was fifteen last January." He wondered if he was expected

San Diego Lightfoot Sue

to ask Mr. Warren's age.

"God!" Warren breathed. He slumped in the seat for a moment, then seemed to come to a decision. "Look, uh . . . Johnny. I just remembered something. I won't be able to put you up for the night after all. As a matter of fact, I have to dash. I'm sorry."

"That's all right, Mr. Warren. It was kind of you to make the offer."

"My pleasure. So long." He hurried away. John Lee watched him stop at the cash register. When he left, the cashier looked at John Lee and nodded.

"Nice goin' there, John Lee Peacock, Sugah." The voice whispered in his ear with a honied Southern accent. He turned and looked nose to nose into a grinning black face. "Got yoself a free dinnah and didn't have to put out."

"What," he said, completely befuddled.

A second face, a white one, appeared over the back of the seat. It said, "May we join you?" doing a good imitation of Mr. Warren.

"Yeah, I guess so." They came around and sat opposite him, both of them skinny as Mr. Cuttsanger. He thought they walked a little funny.

The black one said, "I'm Pearl and this is Daisy Mae."

"How ja do," Daisy Mae said, chewing imaginary gum.

"Really?" John Lee asked, grinning.

"Really, what, Sugah?" Pearl asked.

"Are those really your names?"

"Isn't he **cute**?" shrieked Daisy Mae.

Pearl patted his hand. "Just keep your eyes and ears open and your pants shut, Sugah. You'll get the hang of it." He lit a pale blue cigarette and offered one to John Lee. John Lee shook his head. Pearl saw John Lee's bemused expression and wiggled the cigarette. "Nieman-Marcus," he said matter-of-factly.

"Well, if isn't the Queen of Spades and Cotton Tail." They all three looked up at a chubby young man, standing with his hand delicately on his hip. His fleshy lips coiled into a smirk at John Lee. He wore light eye makeup with a tiny diamond in one pierced ear. He was with a muscular young man who looked at John Lee coldly. "You girls stage another commando raid on Romper Room?"

"Why, lawdy, Miss Scawlètt, how you do talk!" Pearl did his best Butterfly McQueen imitation and his hands were like escaping blackbirds.

"This a Cub Scout meeting and we're den mothers," Daisy Mae said in a flat voice. The muscular young man grabbed Miss Scawlett's arm and pulled him away.

"It's a den of something!" he shot back over his shoulder.

"Did you see how Miss Scarlett looked at our John Lee?" Daisy Mae rolled his eyes.

"The bitch is in heat."

"Who was that gorgeous butch number she was with?"

"Never laid eyes on him before."

"Your eyes aren't what you'd like to lay on him," Daisy Mae said dryly.

Pearl quickly put his hands over John Lee's ears. "Don't talk like that afore this sweet child! You **know** I don't like rough trade!"

John Lee laughed and they laughed with him. He didn't know what they were talking about most of the time but he decided he liked these two strange people. "Doesn't . . . uh . . . Miss Scarlett like you?"

"Sugah," Pearl said seriously, taking his hands away, "Miss Scarlett doesn't like anybody."

"Stay away from her, John Lee," Daisy Mae said, meaning it.

"She has a problem," Pearl pronounced.

"A **big** problem," Daisy Mae agreed.

"What?" John Lee asked, imagining all sorts of things.

"She's hung like a horse." Pearl nodded sagely.

"A **big** horse." Daisy Mae nodded also.

John Lee could feel his ears getting red. Damnation, he thought. He laughed in embarrassment. "What's wrong with that?" He remembered Leo Whittaker in his room at school who bragged that he had the biggest one in Kansas and would show it to you if you would go out under the bleachers.

"Sugah," Pearl said, patting his hand again, "Miss Scawlett is a **lady**."

"It's a wonder it doesn't turn green and fall off the way she keeps it tied down. Makes her walk bow-legged."

"Don't be catty, Daisy Mae. Just count your blessings." Daisy Mae put his chin on the heel of his hand and stared morosely at nothing, like Garbo in Anna Christie. "John Lee, Sugah," Pearl continued, "was all that malarky you gave that score the truth?"

"Huh?" John Lee asked, completely confused.

"It was," Daisy Mae said in his incredible but true voice.

"You really don't have a place to stay tonight?"

"Huh-uh." He wondered why Pearl doubted him.

"And he's also really fif-**teen**," Daisy Mae said, cocking his eyes at Pearl.

"Daisy Mae, Sugah," Pearl said with utmost patience, "I'm only bein' a Sistuh of Mercy, tryin' to put a roof ovuh this sweet child's head, tryin' to keep him from bein' picked up by the po-leece fah vay-gran-cee."

Daisy Mae shrugged fatalistically.

"Why does it matter that I'm fifteen?" John Lee really wanted to know what they were talking about.

"You **are** from the boonies," Daisy Mae said in wonder.

"Sugah, you come stay with us. There's a lot you've got to learn. If we leave you runnin' around loose, you gonna get in seer-ee-us trouble. Sugah, this town is full of tiguhs and . . . you . . . are . . . a . . . juicy . . . lamb."

San Diego Lightfoot Sue 81

"Your fangs are showing," Daisy Mae said tonelessly.

Pearl turned to him, about to cut him dead, but instead threw up his arms and did Butterfly McQueen again. "Lawzy, Miss Daisy Mae, you done got a spot on yo' pretty shirt!" He turned back to John Lee with a martyred expression. "I wash and clean and iron and scrub and work my fanguhs to the bone and this slob can get covered in spaghetti sauce eatin' **jelly beans!**"

John Lee dissolved in a fit of giggles. Pearl couldn't hold his outraged expression any longer and began to grin. Daisy Mae chuckled and said, "Don't pay any attention to her, John Lee. She's got an Aunt Jemima complex."

Pearl got up. "Let's get out of this meat market. There are too many eyes on our little rump roast."

Daisy Mae put his hand on John Lee's. "John Lee, if we run into a cop, **try** to look twenty-one."

He wiped the laugh tears from his eyes. "I'll do my best." He got the pasteboard box and followed them out of the cafe. They cut hurriedly around the corner past a large sidewalk newsstand, then jaywalked to a parking lot. Pearl and Daisy Mae acted like a couple of cat burglars and John Lee had to hurry to keep up.

They got into a '63 Corvair and drove west on Hollywood Boulevard until it became a residential street, then turned right on Laurel Canyon. They wound up into the Hollywood Hills, Pearl and Daisy Mae chattering constantly, making John Lee laugh a lot. He felt very good and very lucky.

Pearl pulled into a garage sitting on the edge of the pavement with no driveway. They went up a long flight of rickety wooden steps to a small two-bedroom house with a porch that went all the way around. Pearl flipped on the lights. "It ain't Twelve Oaks, Sugah, but we like it."

John Lee stared goggle-eyed. He'd been in Aunt Rose's and Aunt Lilah's fancy houses lots of times, but they ran to beige, desert rose, and old gold. These colors were absolutely electric. The wild patterns made him dizzy and there were pictures and statues and things hanging from the ceiling.

"Golly," he said.

"Take a load off," Daisy Mae said, pointing to a big reclining chair covered in what looked like purple fur. John Lee put the box on the floor and gingerly sat down. He leaned back and was surprised at how comfortable it was. Pearl put a record on the record player but John Lee didn't recognize the music. He yawned. Daisy Mae stood over the box. "What's in this carton you keep clutching to your bosom?"

"My things."

"Pardon my nose," Daisy Mae said and opened it. He pulled out some of John Lee's everyday clothes. "You auditioning for the sixteenth road company of Tobacco Road?"

"Don't pay any attention," Pearl said, sitting beside John Lee. "She's a costumer at Paramount. Thinks she knows **every**-thing about clothes."

"Don't knock it. I had to dress thirty bitchy starlets to buy that chair you got your black ass on. I'll hang these up for you, John Lee."

John Lee yawned again. "Thank you."

Pearl threw up his hands. "Land o' Goshen, this child is ex-**haus**-ted!"

Daisy Mae carried the box into a bedroom. "Two days on a Continental Trailways bus would give Captain Marvel the drearies."

Pearl took John Lee's arm and pulled him out of the chair. "Come on, Sugah. We gotta give you a nice bath and put you to **bed**, afore you collapse." He led him to the bathroom, showed him where everything was, and turned on the shower for him. "Give a holler if you need anything."

"Thank you." Pearl left. John Lee had never taken a shower before, although he had seen them at Aunt Rose's and Aunt Lilah's. He took off his clothes and got in.

The door opened and Pearl came in, pushing back the shower curtain. "You all right, Sugah? Oh, Sugah, you are **all right**!" He leered at John Lee, but in such a way that made him laugh. His ears turned red anyway. Pearl winked and closed the curtain. "You don't mind if I brush my teeth?"

"No. Go ahead." He could hear Pearl sloshing and brushing. After a bit there was silence. He pulled back the shower curtain a little and peeped out. Pearl was leaning against the wash basin, a toothbrush in his hand, his head down, and his eyes closed. John Lee watched him, wondering if he should say anything.

"John Lee," Pearl said without looking up, his voice serious and the accent totally absent.

"Yes, Pearl?" He spoke quietly and cautiously.

"John Lee, don't pay attention when we tease you about how cute you are, or when we ogle your body. It's just the way we are. It's just the way the lousy world is."

"I won't, Pearl." He felt the hurting in the back of his throat, but he didn't know why.

Pearl suddenly stood up, the big grin back on his face. "Well. Look at me. Poor Pitiful Pearl. Now. What do you sleep in? Underwear? Peejays? Nightshirt? Your little bare skin?"

"My pajamas are in the box, I think."

"Good enough." Pearl left the bathroom and returned when John Lee was drying on a big, plush towel printed like the American flag. Pearl reached in and hung the pajamas on the doorknob without looking in. "There you go, Sugah."

"Thank you, Pearl."

He left the bathroom in his pajamas with his Sunday suit over his arm. Daisy Mae took the suit. "I'll clean and press that for you."

"You don't have to, Daisy Mae." The names were beginning to sound normal to him.

Daisy Mae grinned. "It won't hurt me."

"Thank you."

Pearl took his arm. "Time for you to go to bed." He led John Lee into the bedroom. There was an old, polished brass bed. John Lee stared at it, then ran his hand over the turned-back sheets. Even Aunt Rose hadn't thought about red silk sheets. He never imagined such luxury.

"Golly," he said.

Pearl laughed and grabbed him in a big hug and kissed him on the forehead. "Sugah, you are just not to be be-**lieved**!" John Lee grinned uncomfortably and turned red. Pearl pulled the sheet up around his neck and patted his cheek. "Sleep tight."

"Good night, Pearl."

Daisy Mae stuck his head in to say goodnight. Pearl turned at the door and smiled fondly at him, then went out, closing it. John Lee wiggled around on the silk sheets. Golly, he thought, golly, golly, golly!

Pearl walked dreamily into the living room and collapsed becomingly onto the big purple fur chair. He sighed hugely. "Daisy Mae. Now I know what it must feel like to be a mother."

The next morning John Lee woke slowly and stretched until his muscles popped. He looked at the ceiling but there was no faded, water-stained paper, only neat, white tiles with an embossed flower in the center of each. He slid to the side of the bed and felt the silk sheets flow like water across his skin. He went to the bathroom and relieved himself, splashing cold water on his face and combing the tangles out of his hair. He sure needed a haircut. He wondered if he ought to let it grow long now that he was in Hollywood.

Hollywood.

He'd almost forgotten. He bet Miss Mahan was worried about him. He sure liked Miss Mahan and a pang of guilt struck him. He should have told her he wouldn't be back in school this fall; especially after she was nice enough to come to Mama's funeral and all. Well, there was nothing he could do now. Mr. Cuttsanger would tell her—and everybody else—where he was.

He went back to his room and put on his best pair of blue jeans, a white tee-shirt and his gray sneakers. He wondered where everyone was. The house was very quiet. He guessed they had both gone to work. He went out on the back porch, only Pearl called it a deck, and saw Daisy Mae lying there on a blanket stark naked. He started to go back in, but Daisy Mae looked up. "Good morning, slugabed, you sleep well?"

John Lee fidgeted, trying not to look at Daisy Mae. "Yeah. Real good. Where's Pearl?"

"She's at work. Does windows for May Company."

"Didn't you have to work today at Paramount?" Paramount!

"Got a few days off. Just finished something called **Wives and Lovers**. Gonna be a dog. You want some breakfast, or you wanta join me?"

"Uh . . . what're you doin'?" He sure didn't seem to care if anybody saw him naked.

"Gettin' some sun, tryin' to get rid of this fish-belly white."

"You always do it with . . . uh . . . no clothes on?" You're acting like a hick again, John Lee Peacock. Damnation, he thought.

Daisy Mae chuckled. "Sure. Otherwise I'd look like a two-tone Ford. If it embarrasses you, I'll put some clothes on."

"No," he protested quickly. "No, of course it doesn't embarrass me. I think I **will** join you."

"Okay." He pointed back over his head without looking. "There's another blanket on the chaise."

John Lee spread the blanket on the porch and pulled his tee-shirt over his head. He pulled off his shoes and socks. Daisy Mae wasn't paying any attention to him. He looked around. The next house up the hill overlooked them, but that was the only one. He didn't see anybody up there. He took a deep breath, slipped off his pants and quickly lay down on his stomach. He might as well get some sun on his back first.

Daisy Mae spoke without looking at him. "Don't stay in one position more than five minutes or you'll blister."

"Okay." He estimated five minutes had passed, swallowed, and turned over on his back. He looked straight into the eyes of a woman leaning on the railing of the next house up, watching him. He froze. The bottom dropped out of his stomach. Then he jumped up and grabbed his pants. He knew he was acting like an idiot but he couldn't stop himself. He hopped on one foot, trying to get the pants on, but his toes kept getting in the way. They caught on the crotch and he fell flat on his butt. He managed to wiggle into them sitting on the floor.

Daisy Mae looked up. "You sit on a bee or something?"

"No." He motioned with his head at the woman, afraid to look at her because he knew he was beet red all over.

Daisy Mae looked up, grinned, and waved. "Hi, Sue." He didn't do anything to cover himself, didn't seem to care that she saw him.

"Hello, Daisy Mae." Her voice was husky and amused. "Who's your bashful friend?"

"John Lee Peacock from Kansas. This is Sue. San Diego Lightfoot Sue."

Damnation, John Lee thought, I'm acting like a fool, sitting here hunkered up against this shez, as Daisy Mae calls it. Doesn't anyone in Hollywood have a normal name? He forced himself to look up. She was still leaning on the railing, looking at him. Only now she was smiling. She was wearing a paint stained sweatshirt and blue jeans. Her hair was tied up in a scarf but auburn strands dangled out. She wasn't wearing any makeup that he could see. She was kinda old he thought, but really very stunning. Her smile was nice. He felt himself smiling back.

"Nothing to be bashful about, John Lee Peacock. I've seen more male privates than you could load in a boxcar." Her voice was still amused but she wasn't putting him down.

"Maybe so," he answered, "but I haven't had any ladies see mine." His boldness made him start getting red again.

She laughed and he felt goose bumps pop out on his arms. "You could have a point there, John Lee. How would you like to make a little money?"

"Huh?"

"It's okay," Daisy Mae said, getting up and wrapping a towel around his waist. "Sue's an artist. She wants you to pose for her."

John Lee looked back up at her. "That's right," she said. "I'm as safe as mother's milk."

"Well, okay, I guess. But you don't need to pay me for something like that." He got up and kicked his underwear under the chaise.

"Of course I'll pay you. It's very hard work. Come on up."

"Uh . . . how do I get up there?"

"Go down to the street and come up my steps. Front door's open, come on in. You'll find me." She smiled again and went out of sight.

He looked at Daisy Mae. "Will it be all right with Pearl?"

"Sure. We've both posed for her. She's good. Scoot." Daisy Mae went into the house. John Lee put on his tee-shirt and shoes. He wondered if he should take off his pants and put on his underwear, but decided against it.

He opened her front door and went in as she had told him. She was right about him finding her. The whole house was one big room. A small kitchen was in one corner behind a folding screen. A day bed was against one wall between two bureaus that had been painted yellow. There was a door to a closet and another to a bathroom. There were a couple of tired but comfortable-looking easy chairs, a drafting table with a stool pushed under it, and an easel under a skylight. Pictures were everywhere; some in color, mostly black and white sketches; thumb-tacked all over the walls, leaning in stacks against the bureaus, chairs, walls. A big, orange cat lay curled in a chair. It opened one eye, gave John Lee the once over, and went back to sleep.

Sue was standing at the easel, frowning at the painting he couldn't see. She had a brush stuck behind one ear and was holding another like a club. "I'm glad you showed up, John Lee. This thing is going nowhere." She flipped a cloth over it and leaned it against the wall.

John Lee stared at the pictures. Nearly all of them were of people, most of them naked, though there were a couple of the cat. Some of the people were women but most of them seemed to be men. He spotted a sketch of Pearl and Daisy Mae, leaning against each other naked, looking like a butterfly with one black and one white wing.

She watched him look for a while. "This is just the garbage. I sell the good stuff. That one of Pearl and Daisy Mae turned out rather well. It's hanging in a gay bar in the Valley. Got eleven hundred for it."

"Golly."

"You're right. It was a swindle."

"Do you . . . ah . . . want me to . . . do you want to paint my picture with my . . . clothes off?" He waved his hand vaguely at some of the nude sketches. Damn his ears!

She didn't seem to notice. "If you don't mind. Don't worry about it. It'll be a few days yet. Give you a chance to get used to the idea. I want to make some sketches and work on your face for a while." She came to him and put her hand on his cheek. "You've got something in your face, John Lee. I don't know . . . what it is. More than simple innocence. I just hope I can capture it. Hold still, I want to feel your bones." He grinned and it made her smile. "Makes you feel like a horse up for sale, doesn't it?" She ran her cool fingers over his face and he didn't want her to ever stop. He closed his eyes.

Suddenly, she caught her fingers in his hair and shook him. She laughed and hugged him against her warm, soft breasts. His stomach did a flip-flop. She released him quickly and crossed her arms with her hands under her armpits. She laughed a little nervously. "You're just like Punkin. Scratch his ears and he'll go to sleep on you."

"Punkin?"

She pointed at the cat. "Don't you think he looks remarkably like a pumpkin when he's curled up asleep like that?"

"Yeah." He laughed.

"Do you want to start now?"

"I guess."

"Okay. Just sit in that chair and relax." She pulled the stool from beneath the drafting table and put it in front of the chair. She sat on the stool with her legs crossed, a sketch pad propped on one knee. She lit a cigarette and held it in her left hand while she worked rapidly with a stick of charcoal. "You can talk if you want to. Tell me about yourself."

So he did. He told her about Miller's Corners, Hawley, the farm, school, Miss Mahan who also painted but only flowers, Mr. Cuttsanger, his mother, a lot about his mother, not much about his father because he didn't really know very much when you got right down to it. He made her chuckle about Aunt Rose and Aunty Lilah. She kept turning the pages of the sketch pad and starting over. He wanted to see what she was drawing but he was afraid to move.

She seemed to read his mind. "You don't have to sit so still, John Lee. Move when you want to." He changed positions but he still couldn't see. Punkin suddenly leaped in his lap, making him jump. The cat walked up his chest and looked into his eyes. Then he began to purr and curled up with his head under John Lee's chin.

Sue chuckled. "You are a charmer, John Lee. He treats most people with majestic indifference." John Lee grinned and stroked the cat. Punkin squirmed in delicious ecstasy. Then John Lee's stomach rumbled.

Sue put the pad down and laughed. "You poor lamb. I'm starving

San Diego Lightfoot Sue

you to death." She looked at her watch. "Good grief, it's two-thirty. What do you want to eat?"

"Anything."

"Anything it is."

He stood with Punkin curled in his arms, watching her do wonderful things with eggs, ham, green peppers, onions, and buttered toast. He said he loved scrambled eggs and she laughed and said scrambled eggs indeed, you taste my omelettes and you'll be my slave forever. She pulled down a table that folded against the wall, set out the two steaming plates with two glasses of cold milk. He was quite willing to be her slave forever, even without the omelette.

Punkin sat on the floor with his tail curled around his feet, watching them, making short, soft clarinet sounds. She laughed. "Isn't that pitiful? The cat food's under the sink if you'd like to feed him."

"Sure." He tried to pour the cat food into the bowl, but Punkin kept grabbing the box with his claws and sticking his head in it. John Lee sat on the floor having a fit of giggles. God o' mighty, he thought, everything is so wonderfully, marvelously, absolutely perfectly good.

She continued sketching after they did the dishes. He sat in the chair feeling luxuriously content. He smiled.

"May I share it?" Sue asked, almost smiling herself.

"Huh? Oh, nothin'. I was just . . . feeling good." Then he felt embarrassed. "You . . . ah . . .been painting pictures very long?"

"Oh, I've dabbled at it quite a while, but I've only been doing it seriously for a couple of years." She smiled in a funny, wry way. "I'm just an aging roundheels who decided she'd better find another line of work while she could."

He didn't know what she was talking about. "You're not old."

"I stood on the shore and chunked rocks at the Mayflower." She sighed. "I'm forty-five."

"Golly. I thought you were about thirty."

She laughed her throaty laugh that made him tingle. "Honey, at your age everyone between twenty-five and fifty looks alike."

"I think you're beautiful," he said and wished he hadn't, but she smiled and he was glad he had.

"Thank you, little lamb. You should have seen me when I was your age." She stopped drawing and sat with her head to one side, remembering. "You should have seen me when I was fifteen." Then she shifted her position on the stool and laughed. "I was quite a dish—if I do say so myself. We were practically neighbors, you know that?" she said, changing the subject. "I'm an old Okie from way back. Still can't bear to watch the **Grapes of Wrath**. We came to California in '33 and settled in San Diego. Practically starved to death. My father died in '35 and my mother went back to telling fortunes and having seances—among other things. My father wouldn't let her do it while he was alive."

"Golly," he said bug-eyed. "A real fortune teller?"

"Well," she said wryly, "I never thought of it as being very real, but I don't know anymore." She looked at him speculatively for a moment, then shrugged. "Whether she was real or not I don't know but I guess she was pretty good, 'cause there seemed to be plenty of money after that. Then the war started. And if you're twenty-three, in San Diego, during a war, you can make lots of money if you keep your wits about you." She shifted again on the stool. "Well, we won't go into that."

"Where's your mother now?"

"Oh, she's dead . . . I imagine. It was '45 I think, yeah, right after V-J Day, I went over for a visit and she wasn't there. Never heard from her again. You know, her house is still there in San Diego. I get a tax bill every year. I don't know why I keep paying it. Guess I'd rather do that than go through all that junk she had accumulated. I was down there a few years ago and went by the place. Everything was still there just as it was; two feet deep in dust, of course. I'm surprised vandals haven't stripped the place, considering what the neighborhood's become. I took a few things as keepsakes, but I didn't hang around long. It's worse than it was when she was there."

She worked a while in silence then stopped drawing again and looked at him in a way that made his stomach feel funny. "If I were twenty and you were twenty . . . you're gonna be a ring-tailed boomer when you're twenty, John Lee." She suddenly laughed and began drawing. "If I'm gonna make people older and younger, I might as well make myself fifteen—no point in wasting five years."

He didn't know what a ring-tailed boomer was, but the way she said it made his ears turn red. Her mentioning San Diego reminded him. "Why do they call you San Diego Lightfoot Sue?"

"Daisy Mae has a big mouth," she said wryly. "I'll tell you about it someday."

"I sure like Pearl and Daisy Mae," he said and smiled.

"So do I."

"Pearl is awfully nice to me."

"Some people have a cat and some people have a dog."

He sure wished he knew what people were talking about, at least some of the time.

It seemed to him hardly any time had passed when Pearl sashayed in with a May Co. carton under his arm. "It is I, Lady Bountiful, come to free the slaves," he brayed and presented the box to John Lee with a flourish. "It's a Welcome To California present."

"Golly." He took the box gingerly.

"Well, **open** it." John Lee fumbled at the string while Pearl planted a kiss on Sue's cheek. "Sugah, you look more like Lauren Bacall every **day**!"

Sue grinned. "Hello, Pearl. How are you?"

He sighed an elaborate sigh. "I am **worn** to a frazzle. I've been slaving over a tacky May Company window all day. If they would **only** let me be **cre-a-tive**!"

"Wilshire Boulevard would never survive it."

John Lee stared at the contents of the box. "How did you know what size I wore?"

"Daisy Mae has tape measures in her eyeballs." He made fluttering motions with his hands. "Well, try them **on**."

John Lee grinned and hurried to the bathroom with the box. He put it on the side of the tub and went through it. There were pants, a shirt, socks, shoes, and, he was glad to see, underwear. But he had never seen gold underwear and they looked kinda skimpy. He quickly shucked off his clothes and slipped on the gold shorts. Golly, he thought. They fit like his hide and he kept wanting to pull them up, but that's all there was to them.

The shirt was yellow and soft. He rubbed it on his face then slipped it over his head. It fit tight around his waist and the neck was open half way to his navel. He looked for buttons but there weren't any. The sleeves were long and floppy and had little pearl snaps on the cuffs.

He slipped on the pants which had alternating dark brown and light brown vertical stripes. He was surprised to find that they didn't come any higher than the shorts. He gave them an experimental tug and decided they wouldn't fall off. They were tight almost to the knees and got loose and floppy at the bottom.

He sat on the commode to put on the shoes, but stood up again to hitch up the pants in back. He slipped on the soft, fuzzy gold socks. The shoes were brown and incredibly shiny. And they didn't even have shoestrings. He stood up, gave the pants a hitch, and looked at himself in the mirror. He couldn't make himself stop grinning.

He opened the bathroom door and walked out, still grinning. Pearl made his eyes go big and round and Sue leaned against one of the yellow bureaus with her mouth puckered up. John Lee walked nervously to them, the shoes making a thump at every step. "The pants are a little bit too tight," he said and didn't know what to do with his hands.

"Oh, Sugah, you are **wrong** about that!"

"If he had his hair slicked down with pomade, he'd look like an adagio dancer . . . or something," Sue said in a flat voice.

Pearl lowered his eyebrows at her, then twirled his finger at John Lee. "Turn around."

He turned nervously, worried because Sue didn't seem pleased.

"John Lee, Sugah," Pearl said in awe, "you have **got** the **Power**!"

"Pearl. Don't you think you went a little overboard?" Sue put her hand on the back of John Lee's neck. "If he walked down Hollywood Boulevard in that, he'd have to carry a machine gun."

"Well!" Pearl swelled up in mock outrage. "At least they're not **lavender**!"

Sue laughed. John Lee laughed too, but he wasn't exactly sure why. They were saying things he didn't understand again. But he felt an overwhelming fondness for Pearl at that moment. He reached out and shook Pearl's hand. "Thank you, Pearl. I think the clothes are beautiful." Then, because he felt Pearl would be pleased, he kissed him on the cheek.

The effect was startling. Pearl's face seemed to run to putty and went through seven distinct expression changes. His mouth worked like a goldfish and he kept blinking his eyes. Then he pulled himself together and said too loudly, "Listen, you all. Dinner will be ready in exactly seveny-two minutes. We're having my world famous sow-belly and chittlin' lasagna." He hurried out, walking too fast.

John Lee was up very early the next morning. Sue opened the door still in her bathrobe. "I didn't know what time you wanted me to come over," he said apologetically. "Did I wake you up?"

Sue smiled and motioned him in. "Ordinarily, I'm not coordinated enough to tie my shoes before noon, but I woke up about two hours ago ready to go to work. I didn't even take time to dress." She indicated one wall of the room. "Check out the gallery while I put the wreck together."

All the old sketches had been cleared away from the wall. John Lee saw himself thumbtacked in neat rows. "Golly," he said, walking slowly down the rows. The sketches were all of his face: some sheets were covered with eyes, laughing, sleepy, dreamy, contemplative; others with mouths, smiling, grinning, pouting, pensive. There were noses and ears and combinations. He recognized some of the full-face sketches: this one was when he was talking about his mother; that one when he was petting Punkin; that one when he was telling of Aunt Rose and Aunt Lilah; another when he sat in rapt attention, listening to Sue.

She emerged from the bathroom dressed much as she had been the day before except that she wore a little makeup and her hair fell through the scarf, hanging long and fluffy down her back. John Lee thought she was absolutely gorgeous. "What do you think," she asked tentatively, not quite smiling.

He couldn't think of anything to say that wasn't obvious to the eye, so he just grinned in extreme pleasure. She smiled happily. "I think I've caught you, John Lee. I really feel good about it. You're just what I've been needing."

"What're you gonna draw today?"

She indicated a large canvas in position on the easel. "I'm ready to start if you are."

Oh, Lord, he thought, just don't turn red. "Yeah. I guess so."

"You can keep your pants on for a while, if it'll make you more comfortable. I'll work on your head and torso." She was businesslike, not seeming to notice his nervousness. It made him feel a little better.

He took a deep breath. "No . . . I might as well get it over with." She nodded and began puttering around with paints and turpentine, not looking at him, without seeming to be deliberately not looking at him. He pulled the tee-shirt over his head and wondered what to do with it. Quit stalling, he admonished and slipped off his sneakers and socks. He looked at her but she was still ignoring him. He quickly pulled off his pants and shorts. He stood there feeling as if there were a cyclone in his stomach. "Well," he said, "I'm ready."

She turned and looked at him as if she had seen him naked every day of his life. "You have absolutely nothing to be embarrassed about, John Lee."

"Well," he said, "well . . ."

"What's the matter?"

"I don't know what to do with my **hands**!" Then he couldn't keep from laughing and she laughed with him. "What do you want me to do?"

"Let's see . . ." She moved one of the chairs under the light. "Lean against the chair. I want you relaxed . . ."

"I'll try," he chuckled.

She smiled. "I want you relaxed and completely innocent of your nudity. Sort of the **September Morn** effect."

"You're asking a lot." He leaned against the chair, trying to look innocent.

She gave a throaty laugh and shook her head. "You look more like a chicken thief. Don't try too hard. Just relax and be comfortable, like you were yesterday."

"I had my clothes on yesterday."

"I know. You'll do okay as soon as you get used to it."

"I still don't know what to do with my hands."

"Don't do anything with them. Just forget 'em; let them find their own position. I know it's not easy. Just forget I'm here. Pretend you're in the woods completely alone. You've just been swimming in a little lake and now you're relaxing in the sun, leaning against a warm rock. Try to picture it."

"Okay, I'll try."

"You're not thinking about anything, just resting, feeling the sun on your body." She watched him. A pucker of concentration appeared over his nose. He shifted his hips slightly to get more comfortable, and his fidgety hands finally came to rest at his sides. His diaphragm moved slowly as his breathing became softer. The frown gradually disappeared from his face, and the quality she couldn't put a name to took its place. God, she thought, it brought back memories she had thought were put away forever. She felt like a giddy young girl.

"That's it, John Lee," she said very softly, trying not to disturb him. She picked up a stick of charcoal and began to work rapidly. A pleased smile flickered across his lips and then disappeared. "Beautiful, John Lee, beautiful. Don't close your eyes; watch the sun reflecting on the water."

She got the basic form the way she wanted it in charcoal, then began squeezing paint from tubes onto a palette. She applied the base colors quickly, almost off-handedly. After about fifteen minutes she said,

"When you get tired, let me know and we'll take a break."

"No. I'm fine."

After another half hour she saw his thumb twitch. "If you're not tired," she said, putting the palette down, "I am. Would you like some coffee?"

"Yeah," he said without moving. "Are you sure I can get back in the same position again?"

"I'm sure." She tossed him her bathrobe and he put it on. "Do a few knee-bends and get the kinks out." She poured two cups of coffee from the electric percolator. "I told you it was hard work."

He grinned and stretched his arms forward, rolling the muscles in his shoulders. "I'm not tired."

She handed him a cup. "You've been warned." She opened the back door when she heard a plaintive cry from outside. Punkin strolled in and looked up at her, demanding attention. She picked him up and he started purring loudly.

John Lee found it easy to keep the same position the rest of the morning. She had made him as comfortable as she could because of his inexperience. She worked steadily with concentration. He missed the easy chatter of the day before but he didn't want to disturb her. They took periodic breaks, though she sometimes became so engrossed she forgot. Then she would admonish him gently for not reminding her. When they broke for lunch, she made him do knee-bends and push-ups and then massaged his back and shoulders with green rubbing alcohol.

Daisy Mae strolled in with a foil-covered Pyrex dish. "You didn't do that when Pearl and I posed for you," he said with feigned huffiness and slipped the dish into the oven.

"Hello, Daisy Mae." John Lee grinned, putting on the robe. "Look at the sketches."

"Hello, John Lee. I knew Sue would get so absorbed she'd forget to feed you, so I brought leftover lasagna." He looked over the sketches, critically, with his fingers theatrically stroking his chin. "I think the girl shows some promise, though I see years of study ahead."

Sue kissed him on the cheek and began setting the table for three. Daisy Mae sprawled in a chair like a wilting lily. "God!" he grunted. "I got a call from Paramount this morning. I start back to work Thursday. We're doing a **west**-ern. On lo-**ca**-tion. My **God**. In **Arizona**! Centipedes! Tarantulas! Scorpions! Rattlesnakes! Sweaty starlets! If I'm not back in five weeks, send the Ma-**rines**!"

Sue laughed. "You can console yourself with thoughts of all those butch cowboys."

"Darling," he said, arching his wrist at her, "some of those cowboys are about as butch as Pamela Tiffin. I could tell you stories . . . "

"Don't bother. I've heard most of them."

"I haven't," John Lee piped in brightly.

Sue started to say something but Daisy Mae beat her to it. "Some day, John Lee. You're much too young to lose **all** your illusions."

San Diego Lightfoot Sue

When they had eaten, Sue thanked him for bringing the lasagna and shooed him out. He started to peek under the cloth covering the painting but she slapped his hand. "You know better than that."

"Can John Lee bunk over here tomorrow night? I'm giving myself a going-away party before I'm exiled to the burning deserts, and it's liable to last all night."

She stood very still for a moment. Then she nodded with a jerk of her head. "Of course." Daisy Mae waltzed out with his Pyrex dish. Sue looked after him for a moment, then at John Lee sitting bewildered on the day bed. She gave him a quick, nervous smile. "You ready?"

He took off the bathrobe, hardly feeling embarrassed at all, and took his place, bringing back the woods, the lake, and the warm rock, but needing them only for a moment to get started.

At four-thirty she covered the painting and began washing the brushes. She had said hardly anything at all since Daisy Mae left, giving him only an occasional soft-voiced direction. He put his clothes on and went to her. "Is it turning out the way you'd hoped?"

Her eyes met his. He saw sadness in them and something that had gotten lost. "Yes," she said almost inaudibly. Then she smiled. "You're a joy to paint, John Lee. Now, run along before Pearl comes traipsing in. I'd rather not have company this evening. Be over bright and early and I think we'll finish it tomorrow."

Punkin stopped him on the steps, wanting to be petted. He picked up the cat and glanced back to see Sue watching him through the window. She turned away quickly.

The painting was completed at three p.m. the next afternoon. Sue stood back from it and looked at John Lee, smiling. He went to her hesitantly, almost fearfully, still naked, and looked at it. "Golly," he breathed. When she painted a nude, she really painted everything. He felt the heat starting at his ears and flowing downward. He was almost used to being naked in front of her, but it was an astonishing shock to **see** himself being naked.

She laughed fondly. "John Lee, you're a regular traffic light."

"No, I'm not," he muttered and got even redder.

Suddenly, her arms were around him, hugging him tightly to her. He felt electricity bouncing in the bottom of his stomach. He threw his arms around her and wanted to be enveloped by her. "John Lee, my little lamb," she whispered in his ear, bending her head because she was an inch taller, "do you like it?"

"Yes!" he breathed with that peculiar pain the back of his throat again. "Oh, yes."

He shifted his head slightly so he could see. The painting was done in pale, sun-washed colors. He leaned against a suggestion of something white which might have been a large rock. It was everything she had said she wanted, and more. He seemed totally innocent of clothing, so completely comfortable was he in his nudity. His body was relaxed but there was no lethargy in it. There was something slightly supernatural about the John Lee of the painting, as if perhaps he were a faun or a wood sprite; definitely an impression of a forest creature. The various shades of pale green in the background implied a forest, and there was a dappling of leaf-shadows on his shoulder and chest—but only a suggestion. However, these were unimportant. The figure dominated the painting, executed in fine detail, like a Raphael. The face was innocent, totally uncorrupted by worldly knowledge. But there was a quality in it even purer than simple innocence. The eyes were lost in reverie.

"Do I look like that?" he asked, slightly overwhelmed.

"Well . . ." she said with a husky chuckle, "yes, you do. Although I will have to admit I idealized you somewhat."

"Is it okay if I bring Pearl and Daisy Mae over to see it?" he asked with growing excitement. "Pearl was supposed to come home at noon today to help with the party. Only she . . . I mean he, calls it a Druid ritual."

She laughed and released him. "All right."

He raced happily to the door then skidded to a halt. He hurried back, grinning sheepishly, and picked up his pants. He put them on, hopping on one foot, then out the door, clattering down the steps. She looked at the empty doorway for a moment, then rubbed at her eyes but was unable to stop the tears.

"Hell!" she said out loud. "Oh, hell!"

John Lee came over from the party about ten o'clock dressed in his new clothes and carrying a Lufthansa flight bag Pearl had packed for him. He flopped into one of the chairs, grinning. She was in the other, reading. She looked at him speculatively. Punkin leaped lightly from her lap and stretched mightily, his rear end high in the air, his chin against the floor, and his toes splayed. Then he hopped into John Lee's lap. Stroking the cat and still grinning, he met her eyes. They both burst into a fit of giggles.

"John Lee, you have **no** staying power," she choked out between gasps of laughter.

He got himself under control, gulping air. "I'd much rather be over here with you."

"I hope Pearl gave you a whip and a chair to go with those clothes."

"No, but he warned me to stay out of corners and, above all, bedrooms."

There was a light tap on the door. "I've been expecting this," she muttered. "Come on in!"

The door opened and a pale, slim, good looking young man wafted in like the queen of Rumania inspecting the hog pens. "Hello," he sighed, not quite holding out his hand to be kissed. "Pearl was telling us about the painting you did of John Lee. May I see it?" He looked at John Lee and smiled anemically.

San Diego Lightfoot Sue

"Of course." Sue got up and turned the light on over the easel. A shriek of laughter drifted over from next door. The young man strolled to the painting and stood motionless for a full two minutes staring at it.

Then he sighed. "Pearl is so lucky. My last one ran off with my stereo, my Polaroid, and knocked out three fillings."

"That's . . . ah . . . too bad," she said, valiantly not smiling.

"Yes," he said and sighed again. "I'd like to buy it."

"It's not for sale."

"I'll give you a thousand."

She shook her head.

"Two thousand."

"Sorry."

He sighed again as if he expected nothing from life but an endless series of defeats. "Oh, well. Thank you for letting me see it."

"You're extremely welcome."

He drifted to the door like a wisp of fog, turned, gave John Lee a wan smile, and departed. They both stared at the closed door.

"I feel as if I just played the last act of **La Traviata**," Sue said in a stunned voice.

"If I remember correctly," John Lee said, "that was Cow-Cow."

She lifted the painting from the easel. "There's only one thing to do if we don't want a parade through here all night. Be back shortly." She left, taking the painting with her.

When she returned half an hour later, he was dozing. "The showing was an unqualified success. I was offered se-ven thou-sand dol-lars for it. You never saw so many erotic fantasies hanging out. It was like waving a haunch of beef at a bunch of half-starved tigers." She put the painting back on the easel and stood looking at it. "It **is** good, though, isn't it, John Lee?" She sounded only partially convinced. "It really is good." She looked at him, sprawled in the chair, half asleep, smiling happily at her. "Well," she laughed, "neither the artist nor the model are qualified judges. And that crowd at Pearl's could only see a beautiful child with his privates exposed."

She sat on the arm of the chair, putting her hand on the side of his face. He closed his eyes and moved his face against her hand the way Punkin would do. "You're such a child, John Lee," she said softly, feeling her eyes getting damp. "Your body may fool people for a while, but up here," she caught her fingers in his hair, "up here, you're an innocent, trusting, guileless child. And I think you may break my heart." She closed her eyes, trying to hold back the tears, afraid she was making a fool of herself.

He looked up at her, feeling things he had never felt before, wanting things he had never wanted before. Perhaps if he hadn't been floating in the dreamlike area between wakefulness and sleep, his natural shyness might have prevented him. He slipped his arms slowly around her neck and pulled her gently to him. He felt her tense as if about to pull away, then her lips were like butterfly wings against him. She lay across him with her face buried in his neck. He stroked her hair and brushed his lips against her cheek.

"Is this what you want, John Lee?" she asked, her voice unsteady. "Is this what you really want?"

"Yes," he answered. "You're all I want."

"You're sure you're not just feeling sorry for an old lady?" she said shakily, trying to sound as if she were making a joke, but not succeeding completely.

He held her tighter. "I love you, San Diego Lightfoot Sue."

She stood up, wiping at her eyes with trembling fingers. "Daisy Mae and his big mouth," she said, half laughing and half crying. John Lee stood up also, giving the striped pants a hitch in the back. "Oh, John Lee," she said, hugging him to her, "take off those awful clothes."

He stood on tiptoe to kiss her because his mouth came only to her chin. He removed the clothes, feeling no embarrassment at all. She turned out the light and locked the door before undressing, feeling embarrassment for herself for the first time in nearly thirty years. She turned back the cover on the day bed and they lay in the warm night, listening to the shrieks of strained laughter from Pearl's, feeling, exploring, each trying to touch every part of the other's body with every part of his own. Then, she showed him what to do and kissed him when he was clumsy.

They lay together, drowsily. Flamenco music drifted over from the party next door. Sue had her arms around John Lee, her breasts pressed against his back, her face against his neck. "John Lee?"

"Mmmm?"

"John Lee, when you're twenty . . . have you thought, I'll be fifty?"

"I love you, Sue. It doesn't matter to me."

She was silent for a moment. "Perhaps it doesn't now. You're too young to know the difference, and I still have a few vestiges of my looks left. But in a few years you'll want a girl your own age and in a few years I'll be an old woman." He started to protest but she put her fingers on his lips, brushing them with feathery touches. "Your lips are like velvet, John Lee," she whispered. He opened his mouth slightly and touched her fingers with his tongue. Then she clamped her arms around him and began weeping on his shoulder. "My God, John Lee! I don't want to be like your favorite aunt, or even your mother! I don't want to see you married to some empty-headed girl, some pretty, **young** girl, having your babies like a brood sow, living in a tract house in Orange County. I want to be the one to have your babies, but I'm too old . . ."

He twisted in her arms to face her and stopped her words with his mouth. The second time she showed him how to make it last longer, how to make it better, and he was very adept. He fell asleep in her arms where she held him like a teddy bear, but she lay awake for many hours, making a decision.

San Diego Lightfoot Sue

The next morning he moved his things from Pearl's to Sue's.

When he had gone, Pearl began to sob, large tears rolling down his face. His hands clutched at each other like graceful black spiders. Daisy Mae put down the glass of tomato juice with the raw egg and Tabasco he had made for his hangover, and took Pearl in his arms.

"Oh, Pearl, you knew it would happen. Just like it always happens," he soothed.

"But John Lee was different from the others," he forced out between heaving sobs.

"Yes, he was. But he's just next door. He's still our friend. We can see him anytime."

"But it's not the same. Sue will be taking care of him, not me! Oh, Daisy Mae," he wailed, "if this is what it's like to lose a child, I don't think I want to be a mother any more!"

Sue began a new painting that morning. "I want you like you were last night," she told John Lee, "sitting all asprawl in the chair, half asleep, with Punkin in your lap, but **not** in those same clothes." They went through his meager wardrobe. She selected a pair of khaki-colored jeans and gave him one of her shortsleeve sweatshirts. She showed him how to sit. "Leave your shoes off. I have a foot fetish." She ran her fingernails quickly across the bottom of his foot. His leg jerked and he grabbed her, giggling, and pulling her in his lap. She submitted happily to his kisses for a moment, then pulled away.

"Okay," she said, laughing, "calm yourself. We've got work to do."

"Yes, ma'am," he said primly, striking a pose and beaming at her.

Thank God, she thought, he doesn't seem to have any regrets.

"My **Gawd**!" Pearl shrieked, seeing the new painting for the first time. He bulged his eyes and hugged himself. "**Sue**! That's the most erotic thing I've ever seen in my **life**! It's practically porno-**graphic**! If I look at it any longer, I'm gonna embarrass myself." He turned away dramatically and saw John Lee grinning and blushing.

"I embarrass myself a little with that one," Sue admitted. "Talk about erotic fantasies."

The painting was in dark, brooding colors, but a light from somewhere fell across John Lee, sitting deep in the chair, one bare foot tucked under him and the other dangling. One hand lay on his thigh and the other negligently stroked the orange cat in his lap. His face was sleepy and sensual. His eyes looked directly at you. They were the eyes of an innocent fawn, but they were also the eyes of a stag in rut.

"You're not . . . ah . . . gonna show it to a bunch of people, are you?" John Lee asked tentatively.

When he woke the next morning, the bed beside him was empty. He rubbed the sleep from his eyes and unfolded the note lying on her pillow. "John Lee, my love," it read in her masculine scrawl, "I had to go to San Diego for the day and didn't want to wake you. I'll be back tonight late. Sue."

He was asleep when she came in. She sat on the edge of the bed and moved her hand lightly across his chest. "John Lee. Wake up, honey."

He squirmed on the bed. "Sue?" he mumbled without opening his eyes. He turned over on his stomach, burying his head, fighting wakefulness.

She pulled back the covers and slapped him lightly on his bare bottom. "Wake up. I want to do another painting. Get dressed."

"Now?" he complained. "I'm too sleepy. Leave your number and I'll call you."

"Okay, smarty," she said, laughing, "you've got thirty seconds before I get out the ice cubes."

"White slaver," he grinned, sitting up and kissing her.

"Where did you hear that?"

"I spent the day with Pearl and Daisy Mae."

She kissed him and stood up. "Come on, get a move on." She put a new canvas on the easel. "Why wasn't Pearl at work? And I thought Daisy Mae had left for, my God, Arizona."

"Today is Saturday," he said and went into the bathroom.

"So it is. I sorta lose track." She began squeezing black and white paint from tubes.

John Lee washed his face and ran a comb through his hair. He came out of the bathroom and put on the same clothes he had worn for the last painting. "These okay?" she nodded. "Shoes or foot fetish?" he grinned.

She wrinkled her nose at him. "Shoes."

He put on his Sunday shoes rather than the sneakers. "Daisy Mae doesn't leave for a couple of weeks yet. They're having fittings and things. Wardrobe gave her . . . him an 1865 ladies' riding skirt with a **zipper** on the side. Any **welder** in **Duluth** would know better than that. What do you want me to do?"

"Nothing in particular. Just stand there." Her voice was tense and hurried.

"Stand?" he groaned. "Don't you want to do another one of me sitting down?" He snapped his fingers. "Do one of me asleep in bed!" She didn't laugh at his joke so he stood where she indicated. She began, using only black and white. "Don't artists need the northern light, or something?" he asked hopefully, pointing to the dark skylight.

She smiled. "That's just an excuse artists have been using for the last few thousand years when they didn't feel like working. Be patient with me, John Lee. You can sleep all day tomorrow. I have to go back to San Diego."

"Can't I go with you?"

"No, John Lee." Her voice was so serious he didn't say anything else.

She finished just before dawn. He was about to fall asleep standing, so she undressed him and put him to bed. He put his arms around her and kissed her, wanting her to stay a little while. "No," she said, running her fingers through his hair, "you're too sleepy. I'll be back in a few days and we can stay in bed for a week."

He smiled and his eyelids began to droop. "That'll be nice."

"Yes, my little lamb, very nice." She kissed him gently on the mouth. He was asleep before she got out the door.

He woke up late Sunday afternoon and immediately looked at the painting. It wasn't as well done as the other two, he thought. It had a hurried look. It was also in black and white. The John Lee in the painting was just standing there, his arms hanging at his sides, looking at you from beneath lowered brows. John Lee looked at the floor where he had been standing when he posed, but nothing was there. Yet, in the painting, there were lines on the floor. He was standing within a pentagram. And he looked different, he looked older, at least five years older, at least twenty.

Tuesday night Pearl and Daisy Mae took him to Graumann's Chinese where he thought the movie was great and had a wonderful time standing in the footprints, though he had never heard of most of the people who had made them. After the movie they went to a Chinese restaurant where he ate Chinese food for the first time. He didn't really like it but he told Pearl he did because it made him happy. It was nearly midnight when he got back to Laurel Canyon. Pearl wanted him to stay in his old room, but he said he'd better not because Sue might come home during the night and he wanted to be there.

He went up the wooden steps feeling incredibly content. If Sue were only there. Punkin came down the bannister like a tightrope walker, making little soft sounds of greeting. John Lee picked him up and made crooning noises. The cat butted his head against John Lee's chin, making him chuckle. He carried Punkin into the house and turned on the light.

His head exploded. His legs wouldn't hold him up any longer and he fell to his knees, dropping the cat. There was something white beside him but he couldn't make his eyes focus. He thought he heard a voice but he wasn't sure because of the wind screaming through his head. The white thing grabbed him and pulled him to his feet. It shouted more words at him but he couldn't understand what they were. Something crashed into his face. The fog cleared a little. There was man dressed in white, holding the front of his shirt. He could smell the sour whiskey on his breath. He slapped John Lee again and shoved him against the wall, but he managed to stay on his feet.

The wind was dying in his head. He heard the man's angry words. "Jesus Christ!" he said, looking at the picture of John Lee sitting in the chair. He took a knife from his pocket and slashed through the canvas.

"Stop it!" John Lee croaked and took an unsteady step in the man's direction.

He whirled, pointing the knife at John Lee. "Jesus Christ!" he said again, in amazement. "You're just a little kid! She threw me over for a little kid!" The man's face seemed to collapse as he lunged at John Lee with the knife. John Lee grabbed his arm but the man was far too strong. Then the man stepped on Punkin's tail. The cat screeched and sank his claws in his leg. The man bawled and fell against John Lee. They both went to the floor, the man on top, his face beside John Lee's.

"Jesus God," the man whispered in bewilderment. Then his breath crept out in an adenoidal whine and didn't go back in again. John Lee squirmed from beneath him. The man rolled onto his back. The knife handle stuck straight up in his chest, blood already clinging to it. John Lee tried to get to his feet, but could only make it to his knees. He saw Pearl and Daisy Mae run in but there was something very wrong with them. They floated slowly through the air, running toward him but getting farther away. Their mouths moved but only honking sounds came out. Then the floor hit him in the face.

The first thing John Lee felt was someone clutching his hand. He opened his eyes and they felt sticky. Pearl's tense and worried face leaned over him, smiling tentatively. "Pearl?" His face hurt and his mouth wouldn't work properly. He sounded as if he were talking with a mouth full of cotton.

"Don't try to talk, John Lee, Sugah," Pearl said anxiously. "You're in the hospital. They said you had a mild concussion. I was scared to death. You've been unconscious for ages. This is **Thursday**."

John Lee put his hand to his face and felt bandages on his mouth and a compress under his lip. "What happened," he had to swallow to get the words out, "happened to my mouth?" It hurt to talk.

"You got a split lip. It's all purple and swelled up. But don't sweat it, Sugah. It makes you look ve-ry sex-y."

John Lee grinned but stopped when it hurt too much. "Is Sue back?"

"She sat with you all night. I made her go home and sleep. They put you in a tacky ward but Sue had you moved to this nice private room."

"The man . . ." He tried hard to remember what happened. "The man . . ."

"He's dead, Sugah. You never saw so many police cars and ambulances and red lights. I don't know what they're gonna do, John Lee." Pearl was distraught.

Sue came in. "Don't upset him, Pearl. Everything will be all right." She smiled brightly and John Lee felt everything would be. "How are you feeling, little lamb?"

"Awful," he groaned and tried to laugh, but it hurt too much.

Pearl gave his arm a pat and said, "I'd better get back to work before May Co. fires my little black fanny. Bye, Sugah."

"Bye, Pearl." Pearl left with a big grin. Sue sat in the chair he had vacated. She took John Lee's hand and held it to her face.

"I'm so sorry," she said as if in pain.

He wanted to bring back her bright smile. "You're looking particularly beautiful today." He had never seen her dressed up before. She wore

San Diego Lightfoot Sue

a silk suit in soft green, her auburn hair loose and long.

She did smile. "Thank you—and thank Playtex, Maidenform, and Miss Clairol. You look . . . pretty awful." But she said it as if she didn't mean it.

"Pearl said I looked ve-ry sex-y."

She grinned and then her face was serious. "John Lee, are you lucid enough to listen and understand what I have to say?" He nodded. "All right. There'll be a . . . hearing . . . or something in a few days, when you're feeling better, with the juvenile authorities. You won't be in any trouble, because they know Jocko attacked you. They know it was an accident . . ."

"Who was he?" he interrupted.

She looked at him for a moment. "Someone I used to know," she said softly.

"Did you love him? Was he your lover?" He didn't know if he was saying it right. He wanted to know but he also wanted her to know that he didn't care.

"They're not exactly the same thing, but, yes, to both." She didn't look at him.

"You gave him up for me," he said in wonder, loving her so much it hurt.

She looked at him then, and smiled, but there was a funny look in her eyes. "I'd give up most anything for you, John Lee."

The next couple weeks were a blur. A bunch of people talked to him: men in blue suits and tight-faced women in gray. He told them everything that happened and they went away to be replaced by others, but none of them would let him see Sue again. There was one lady he liked, who said she was a judge. He told her that his grandfather was a judge, but he died a long time ago. She asked him about everything and he told her. She had a kind voice and made the others behave the way Miss Mahan would.

"But, Your Honor," one of the men said, pacing the floor of her office, "this child has killed a drunken sailor in a knife fight over a prostitute."

The judge laughed pleasantly. "Really, Mr. Maley, there's no need for exaggeration. You're not addressing a jury. John was merely protecting himself when attacked. The man's death resulted when he fell on his own knife."

"You can't deny he's been living with a known prostitute. I wouldn't be surprised if she hasn't seduced him."

"Please, Mr. Maley," the judge frowned, displeased, "don't speak that way in front of the child."

"You saw those paintings! Disgusting!"

The judge stood up and began putting on her coat. "Artists have been painting nudes for several thousand years, Mr. Maley. You should see the collection in the Vatican. And these are very good paintings. I made the artist an offer for the nude myself. Come along, John. I'll take you to dinner. Good evening, gentlemen."

Dwayne came to see him one day, but John Lee would never have recognized him. He hadn't seen him since he went away to the army seven years before. Dwayne was twenty-nine, big and good looking like all the Peacock men. He shook hands with John Lee, saying little, and went away after talking to the judge.

Aunt Rose and her husband flew out from Hawley. She touched him a lot and clucked a lot. Of course, she'd **like** to take care of him, him being the youngest son of her late sister and all, but the way things were, the economy and the cost of living and all, she just didn't see how she could.

It was a terrible thing, her sister marrying into the Peacock family; such an unfortunate family. Poor Grace Elizabeth's husband had died the same day she was buried; the very day John Lee had left on the bus. He had fallen off the tractor and been run over by his own plow. He had crawled almost all the way to the house before he bled to death. Such a tragic family, the Peacocks. Her sister had lost six of her children, five of them in infancy and poor Wash, Jr.

They had tracked him down in Oklahoma because the farm was his now; or, she should say, they had tracked down his wife; or, she should say, his ex-wife. Wash, Jr. was killed six years ago when a pipe fell off a rig and crushed his skull. His wife hadn't even notified the family. Then she married a Mexican driller from Texas and was living in Tulsa, but what could you expect from one of them trashy O'Dell girls. It was a good thing she had had none of Wash, Jr.'s children, just three stillbirths, because she had no claim on the family at all now. Of course, she had two fat brown babies by her new husband, but you know how Mexicans are: like rabbits.

Dwayne hadn't wanted the farm. He just told them to sell it and send him the money. Dwayne was the logical person to take John Lee, being his closest kin. Her sister, Lilah, was in no shape to take care of him. If Dwayne couldn't, then she didn't know what would happen to the poor thing, him living with a prostitute and all.

Aunt Rose and her husband flew back to Hawley.

The judge told him how sorry she was but, if one of his relatives didn't assume custody, as a minor he would have to be declared a ward of the state. But it wouldn't be too bad. He'd have a nice place to live, could finish school, and would have the company of lots of other boys his own age. He asked her why he couldn't live with Sue, but she said it was out of the question and wouldn't discuss it further.

But Dwayne did assume custody and he moved into the small apartment on Beachwood near Melrose. "Half the money from the sale of the farm is rightfully yours," Dwayne said, dressing for work. "You'll have to go to school this fall. The judge said so. Other than that, your time is your own. But you're not supposed to see that woman again." He showed John Lee how to turn the couch into a bed, and left for work. He

San Diego Lightfoot Sue

was a bartender at a place on Highland and worked from six until it closed at two in the morning.

John Lee caught the bus at Melrose and Vine and rode to Hollywood and Highland. He took a taxi to the house on Laurel Canyon. Sue wasn't at home and he couldn't find Punkin. The three paintings had been framed and were hanging. She had repaired the damaged one. No other paintings were in sight. Everything had been pushed against the walls, leaving most of the floor bare. There were blue chalk marks on the bare boards that had been hastily and inadequately rubbed out. The room smelled odd.

He found an envelope on the kitchen table with his name on it. He removed the folded piece of notepaper. "John Lee, my little lamb," it read, "I knew you would come, although they told us we mustn't see each other again. You must stay away for a while, John Lee. Only a little while, then it won't matter what they say. There'll be nothing they can do. I love you. Sue."

Pearl wasn't at home either, so he went back to Dwayne's apartment, watched television for a while, took a bath, and went to bed on the convertible sofa. He didn't know when Dwayne came in about two-thirty.

Dwayne always slept until nearly noon. John Lee found little to talk to him about and Dwayne seemed to prefer no conversation at all. John Lee watched television a lot, went to many movies, and waited for Sue.

He fell asleep in front of the television a few days later and was awakened by Dwayne and the man who was with him. Dwayne frowned at him and the man smiled nervously. The man said something to Dwayne, but he shook his head and led the man into the bedroom, closing the door. John Lee went to bed and didn't know when the man left.

The next morning he looked into the bedroom. Dwayne was sprawled on the bed, naked, still asleep. A twenty dollar bill lay beside him, partially under his hip. John Lee closed the door and fixed breakfast.

Dwayne came in while he was washing the dishes. He didn't say anything for a while, fixing a cup of instant coffee. He sat at the table in his underwear, sipping the coffee. John Lee continued with the dishes, not looking at him. Then he felt Dwayne's eyes on him and he turned. "I don't want you to think I'm queer," Dwayne said flatly. "I don't do anything, just lay there. If those guys want to pay me good money to swing on my joint, it's no skin off my nose." He turned back to his coffee.

John Lee hung up the dishtowel to dry. "I understand," he said but he wasn't sure that he did. "It's all right with me."

Dwayne didn't answer, but went on sipping coffee as if John Lee weren't there. He made sure, from then on, he was asleep before Dwayne came home.

Sue called a few nights later. He had never heard her voice over the phone, but it sounded different: brighter, less throaty, younger. "Come over, John Lee, my little lamb," she laughed gleefully. "I'm ready. Come over for the showing."

The taxi had to stop a block away because of the police cars and fire trucks. John Lee ran terrified through the milling crowd but when he reached Sue's house there was nothing to see. The rickety wooden steps went up the hill for about twenty feet and ended in mid-air. There was nothing beyond them, only a rectangle of bare earth where the house had been. But nothing else, not even the concrete foundation.

He felt a touch on his arm. He whirled to stare wide-eyed at Pearl. He couldn't speak, his throat was frozen. His heart was pounding too hard and he couldn't breathe. Pearl took his arm and led him into the house where he had spent his first night in Hollywood.

Pearl gave him a sip of brandy which burned his throat and released the muscles. "What happened? Where's Sue?" he asked, afraid to get an answer.

"I don't know," Pearl said without any trace of corn pone accent. He seemed on the verge of hysteria himself. "There was a fire . . . "

"A fire?" he asked, uncomprehending.

"I think it was a fire . . ." Pearl nervously dropped the brandy bottle. He picked it up, ignoring the stain on the carpet.

"Where's Sue?"

"She . . . she was in the house. I heard her scream," he said rapidly, not looking at John Lee.

John Lee didn't feel anything. His body was frozen and numb. Then, he couldn't help himself. He began to bawl like a baby. It was all slipping away. He could feel the good things escaping his fingers. Pearl sat beside him on the purple fur chair and tried to comfort him. "She was over there all evening, singing to herself. I could hear her, she was very happy. I went over but she wouldn't let me in. She said I knew better than to look at an artist's work before it was finished. She said anyway it was a private showing for you. I didn't hear her singing for an hour or so and then, a little while ago, I heard a noise like thunder or an explosion. I looked over and there was a bright green light in the house, like it was burning on the inside, but not like fire either. I heard her scream. It was an awful, terrible scream. There was another voice, a horrible gloating voice, I couldn't understand. Then the whole house began to glow with that same green light. It got brighter and brighter, but there was no heat from it. Then it went away and the house wasn't there anymore."

Pearl got up and handed John Lee an envelope. "I found this on the deck. She must have tossed it down earlier." John Lee took the envelope with his name on it. He recognized her handwriting, but more hurried and scrawled than usual. He opened it and read the short note.

He went back to school that fall and lived with Dwayne. He said his name was Johnny, because John Lee was home and Sue. He met a lot of girls who wanted him, but they were pallid and dull after Sue. He went with them and slept with them but was unable to feel anything for them.

He never turned down any man who propositioned him either, and there were many. He didn't care about the money, he only needed someone to relieve the pressures that built up in his loins. It didn't make any difference, man or woman, it was all the same to him. He let lonely, middle-aged women keep him, but he never found what he was looking for.

By the time he was eighteen he had grown a couple of inches and had filled out. He moved out of the apartment on Beachwood and got a place of his own. He never saw Dwayne again.

The envelope with his name on it was soiled and frayed from much handling. He read it every night. "John Lee, my little lamb," it read. "I tried very hard, so very hard. I thought I had succeeded but something is going wrong. I can feel it. I wish you could have seen me when I was fifteen, John Lee. I wish you could have seen me when I was fifteen. I'm afraid." It was unsigned.

Dinosaurs

The bluebaby swam suddenly in a tight circle. The maneuver caught the others by surprise and their outstretched arms failed to make contact. Gleeful thoughts rippled between them.

But, even in victory, the bluebaby had tired of the game. It swam downward, shutting out the joyful thoughts of the other bluebabies as they continued to race about. It paused near a dreamer and poked among the stones until it found one to its taste. It deposited the stone in its mouth and listened idly to the dream.

It was supposed to be a very special dream, but the bluebaby found it tedious and dull. It had listened on a number of occasions since its hatching in the spring and found the dream never changing.

The dream was about the surface. In the dream the surface was green and thick, and liquid flowed in large grooves. Two-legged surface creatures moved about haphazardly and lived in odd structures. The dream made the bluebaby impatient and it couldn't understand why it kept returning to listen.

A dreamer without a dream had attempted to explain it. The dreamer, with a faint note of envy in his thought, had explained that it was a very special dream because it was about the time before the world; before there were dreamers (or bluebabies, either); when there were only surface creatures.

If it was before the world, the bluebaby questioned, how did the dreamer know anything about it?

The thought of the dreamer without a dream was amused. That's the reason it is a very special dream.

The bluebaby swam away in search of a more exciting dream

and paused suddenly.

There was something on the surface. It sensed a spot of heat where a surface creature was remaining in one place.

Curious, it swam upward.

Flan raised the edge of the breather slightly and scratched the corner of his mouth with a stubby finger. He took one sip of water from the tube snaking to the pouch under his arm and leaned back against the gravel dune with a sigh. He let his muscles relax almost completely; his rest would be a short one. A few bits of gravel dislodged and rolled down the slope of the dune with soft clicks. Flan was unconcerned. His own movement had caused it.

He dropped his hairless head back against the cold gravel and looked at the sky. The stream of debris from the fractured moon stretched from horizon to horizon like bits of broken glass. Flan tried to imagine how it had looked a million years ago, but couldn't.

He raised a pale hand and jiggled the breather, settling it more comfortably over his mouth and nose. It smelled of ancient breath; breath so ancient the exhaled molecules had become a physical part of the plastic and metal. And the pack snuggled under his chin was definitely making an audible noise. He had thought so for years, but had dismissed it as imagination and apprehension. How much longer would it last? A hundred years? Two hundred? It didn't really seem to matter. Already there were many, many spares.

The cold crept quickly through the surface suit and into his bones. He wrapped the cloak tighter about him and hunched his shoulders against his neck, shivering slightly. The odors of the cloak were as ancient as those of the breather. His effort had little effect. When he was younger, when obstacles were trivial and easily overcome, the cold had bothered him not at all. Besides, it was hardly **cold**, only early autumn. Flan sighed again, admitting his years. All fourteen of them.

But he had sired the child.

The breather moved with his smile. He had sired the only child that year. No shame on him or Triz. Seven in all; two surviving; the new one not yet old enough for naming—but in a few days. He had long ago decided on the name for the new son.

He thought of the other, his first born: Sith, the arrogant, prideful young pup. Prancing and displaying the instrument that would produce a child every year—maybe even two at a time. Poor Sith—eight years old and still childless. Naturally, he put the blame on sweet, hapless Brin. He knew he had no real reason for disliking Sith other than his own peevishness, but Sith wore his glory not well.

Flan slipped his fingers into the small pouch he wore on a cord around his neck and felt the warmth of the whispering stone. His fingertips caressed it for a moment, then slid it into his hand. It was circular and flat, thicker in the center and tapering to a rounded edge. It was half as wide as his palm, white, and faintly translucent like porcelain. It began to whisper.

Flan had seen others. There were always a few lying around. They had a simple beauty and the children liked to play with them. But this one was different. He had found it when Sith was a baby; picked it up where the child had left it lying. It had grown warm in his fingers, seemed to mold to his hand, though it had not changed its shape in any way. It had not begun to whisper until years later.

No one knew the purpose of the little discs; they were pretty stones that amused the children. Even Old Frel, an ancient of almost thirty years, who had a theory about everything, could not produce one for the stones. There had been interest and curiosity when he told of the way it warmed in his hand, but it remained cool in the hands of others and the interest waned. He had not mentioned the whispering because he knew that only he could hear it.

He huddled in his cloak, resting against the gravel dune and listened to the whisper. It was, as always, maddeningly on the edge of understanding.

Flan felt an almost imperceptible movement in the gravel. His rest had been shorter than he expected. He put the stone back in the pouch and the whisper died away. He stood quickly, with no noticeable effort, and stretched to his full four-foot height. He rolled the heavy muscles in his shoulders, working out the kinks. He checked the direction machine strapped to his forearm and walked away toward the north.

Gray-blue chitinous claws like small shovels probed tentatively at the warmer area where Flan had been sitting. Finding nothing but rapidly cooling surface gravel, the claws withdrew from sight. Then the gravel bulged and rolled away as the bluebaby poked its head up to see the source of the warmth that had attracted it.

The bluebaby's eyes were small and limited but they caught Flan's receding figure. It watched curiously, nose-deep in the gravel, until distance made detail a vague dark blur. It thought of following but knew the surface creature moved too rapidly. It had never seen one quite like it, but it did seem to be very similar to the ones in the dream.

The bluebaby poked among the surface stones with hard wide fingers and selected one with a greenish tinge. It popped the stone into its mouth. Another blue head emerged silently nearby. The thoughts of the two bluebabies compared the flavor of the surface stones to those below and agreed that, while the surface stones might be the tastier of the two, the awesome **openness** was somewhat disturbing. The other head sank from sight.

The bluebaby looked again in the direction of the surface creature, but could see only a small dark spot moving in the distance. It scratched absently at the fine wiry tendrils that had only recently begun sprouting from the joints of its horny body. The itching grew uncomfortable. It sank and swam away in the gravel sea, feeling the movement of the stones bringing delicious relief. The bluebaby's digestive system was already at work on the greenish stone, breaking it down, releasing oxygen and water and other nutrients for the healthy young body.

Flan's stride was not hurried, but it ate away at the distance, bringing him nearer to the People and the summer Home, nearer to Triz and the child. His feet crunched at each step, sinking slightly. The gravel sea stretched to the limit of his vision in every direction, undulating in low dunes like frozen ocean waves. Flan knew the word **ocean** but found difficulty in grasping its meaning. He topped a dune and saw the thin white line across the flat northern horizon. He had made good time. The sun was only at twenty degrees in the west, small and white. He had over six hours before it set, but already the night wind was stirring his cloak. He hastened his step though he knew he would be there in two hours, long before the wind grew too strong. By sundown a man would be unable to keep his feet in the gale, and a few hours later, the gravel dunes would begin to shift.

Flan passed the wreckage of the air bus. He hardly noticed. It was a familiar landmark on the southward trek in the autumn as well as the northward trek in the spring. The air bus wasn't exactly **wrecked**, not smashed, twisted, or ruptured. It was simply inoperative, lying half-submerged like an immense windowed lozenge. It had shifted almost a mile to the south since spring.

Old Frel, a spinner of tall tales, claimed to remember riding in it as a child, claimed to have been riding in it when it crashed. Flan neither believed him nor disbelieved him. Who was to know if Old Frel spoke the truth or fancy? No one else was nearly as old. But the story faintly disturbed him, nevertheless. He wished the shifting dunes would cover the air bus, as they did some years, but permanently. No one spoke but eyes looked at it, thoughts of what it would be like if the trek were made by air bus rather than afoot trickled through their minds. It was unwise to think back on better times.

The stone in the pouch around his neck began to whisper, softly, urgently, unintelligibly. It seldom whispered when he wasn't holding it in his hand, but there were times and places where it did. The air bus was one of those places. He hurried on, not wanting to hear because he couldn't understand.

The white line of the receding glacier was more pronounced. Already the gravel was growing coarser. Soon it would be smooth flat rocks, then tumbled stones as big as his head, then solid rock. The teaching machine, or memories of memories of the teaching machine, said the gravel sea was growing larger. Something about the glacier and the wind—the memory was wispy. It would reach the Home . . . when? A thousand years? Ten thousand?

The wind caught at Flan's cloak and cracked it like a whip. He reached to the breather and flipped the goggles up, covering his eyes against the dust and sand beginning to blow. He pulled the hood over his hairless head.

Less than two hours later he saw the Home. It was a low black blister set in wind-scored granite, made of a substance immune to the elements, intended to be immune even to time. It was ten feet across with a flat surface at the top; it was only the doorway to the Home.

Flan stepped onto the blister, moved to the flattened top, and clutched his cloak against the wind. The Home recognized him. The flattened section lowered. Now free of the wind, Flan released his cloak and sank through a long tube. The tube closed above him, cutting off the moan of the wind. He felt warmth. He lifted the breather from his face and filled his lungs. He smiled.

The downward movement stopped. The tube wall rotated. He stepped out to the greetings of the People. They crowded around him, anxious for news, though it never varied. Their naked hairless bodies were firm and healthy. Only Klor and Blod had noticeably swollen bellies. There would be at least two new children next spring if the sickness did not strike.

Flan removed the cloak and breather, putting them in the racks with the others. The People waited as he put the direction machine carefully in its case and emptied the water pouch, returning the water to the central store. He ran his hand from his throat to his crotch. The surface suit split open and peeled back. He stepped out of it, naked. Of all of them, only Flan wore any type of adornment: the whispering stone in its pouch around his neck.

Triz smiled at him proudly. Her breasts were back to their normal size but her belly was still flat. Flan sighed inwardly. She was too old for another child. She was sixteen, two years older than he, but still beautiful.

The child peeked impishly from behind her legs. He grinned hugely at his father. Flan's face split with pleasure. He knelt and the child ran to him. Flan grabbed him in a hug and lifted him giggling and squirming. Triz came to him and put her arm around him. The People smiled.

"How fares the gravel sea?" asked Thol, a young man in his prime and the happy cause of Blod's swollen belly.

"As always," Flan replied. "I went as far as the first way station. The bluebabies are still active. All is normal."

They nodded and drifted away. Triz said nothing but pressed her body against him. He felt her sorrow and shame with his skin. He touched his cheek to the top of her smooth head with love and understanding, and without reproach. She had mothered seven. She could feel pride, not shame. It was not her fault that she grew old. The child huddled quietly in Flan's arms, watching them with solemn eyes.

Triz slid her hand across Flan's chest and down over his hard belly. Flan felt the heat following her hand and then the pressure. Triz held the

Dinosaurs 111

swelling in her hand and was satisfied. She had to keep trying, though the conception time was past. With the child cradled in one arm and the other around Triz, Flan moved through the long gray corridor to their sleeping room.

They lay on the sleeper. Triz opened to him. The child sat beside them, watching and examining. After a bit the child laughed and said, "Look, Father!" He tugged at Flan's arm. They looked and smiled. the child pointed to his little manhood, hard and erect. "Will I have many children, Father?"

They hugged him to them. "Yes, my son," Flan murmured in contentment, "many children." The child would have all of Sith's beauty, if only he avoided Sith's arrogance.

They lay together with the child between them. He lay quietly, exploring the contours of his mother's face with his fingertips. Finished with that, he settled back and looked at the gray featureless ceiling.

"Father?"

"Yes?" Flan muttered drowsily.

"When will the trek begin?"

"Soon."

"How soon?"

"As soon as the bluebabies have gone to sleep."

"What are the bluebabies? Have I ever seen one?"

Flan smiled to himself. He remembered asking almost the same questions. "No. The bluebabies are horrible, wicked creatures who live in the gravel sea."

"Why are they horrible and wicked?"

"Because they will grab you and pull you under."

"Why?"

Did he know why? Was there a memory of a memory? "Because they are horrible and wicked. Are you hungry?"

"Yes."

"So am I. Triz?"

"Yes. I'm ready for food."

They left the sleeping room, made a short detour to walk through the cleansing machine, and entered the big room. Flan punched the delivery button of the food machine three times. Three gray cubes slid out. He gave one to Triz and one to the child and kept one. The child bit into his with tiny sharp teeth and grinned when a crumb stuck to the end of his nose. The water machine ejected three containers at Flan's touch. They sat in the exercise machines, nibbling the food and sipping the water.

The others drifted in, smiled greetings, got food and water, sat in the exercise machines. The machines purred almost inaudible purrs. Sith entered with Brin. His handsome face was clouded. He wouldn't look at her. Brin's eyes were downcast and her lips were pale. Her fingers worried each other and strayed occasionally to her childless belly.

Flan watched them, unable to understand Brin's love for his churlish elder son. But he did, deep inside. Brin was shy and gentle and lovely. She had been overwhelmed by Sith of the merry eyes and impudent grin, by his powerful young body, by the promise of his large manhood. But the promise was unfulfilled and the eyes no longer merry. Flan suspected he was cruel to her.

Food time was conversation time as well. As the end of the stay in the summer Home drew near, the conversation was almost always the same. Flan only half listened. It was for the children. This time, for the child.

"I see no reason why the trek is still necessary. Why can't we spend the entire year here, or at the winter Home?" The question had always been asked, as far back as Flan could remember.

"I like the winter Home best. Everything is nicer and it has color. It isn't all gray. It's larger and more comfortable."

"Why didn't they make two teaching machines? Why didn't they put one here?"

"The winter Home has many things not found here."

Old Frel chuckled. "The teaching machine could tell us why there is only one teaching machine."

"If we only had the knowledge to repair it."

"We do have the knowledge," Old Frel muttered. "It's in the teaching machine." The others pretended not to hear.

"We might as well wish things were back the way they used to be; when there were no bluebabies; when there was no gravel sea; when the whole world was covered with vegetation and the air was thick and rich and the People lived on the surface; covered the surface in great cities; when there were pools of water miles across. We can wish that just as easy as we can wish we knew how to fix the teaching machine."

"But that's just myth. The teaching machine is real."

"Some storyteller, like Old Frel, made it up as a fancy. That's all it is. How could there be pools of water miles wide? Where would all the water come from?"

Someone chuckled. "And how could the People have been so many? There aren't enough food machines. It's only a myth."

"The People have always been as now."

"And always will be."

"Always."

The child had heard the myth before, but the idea of not making the trek was a new one. "Why can't we stay here all the time?" he asked, putting the conversation back on the subject.

"The teaching machine said we must not." A memory of a memory.

"Why?" the child repeated.

Flan smiled. "There are things we must do without knowing why."

"I stayed here through the winter once."

Old Frel's voice silenced the others. It was a new note, an electric new note. The silence hung as heads turned and eyes narrowed. Only the faint purr of the exercise machines was heard. Was this another of Old Frel's fancies?

"Why have you not told of it before?" a voice asked, soft, but loud in the silence.

Old Frel looked not at the others, but at a memory. "There seemed no need. But now, every year the voices to abandon the trek grow louder and more insistent, and I feel this trek will be my last. Before the crash of the air bus, the trek seemed to be over in an eye-blink. The sun moved not at all between leaving and arriving. Now the trek takes many weeks of walking. Sore feet have become more important than the old ways."

"What happened?"

"The air bus crashed. It ceased to function and fell into the gravel sea. Many were killed. Many were injured. Even then, the hundreds of seats in the air bus were not filled. I was very small, but I remember. We left earlier then. There was no need to fear the bluebabies, when we flew through the air like gods.

"The crash sprang open a locker filled with breathers we knew nothing about. Had it not been for that, all would have died. We were afraid to stay in the air bus, afraid we would be covered when the winds rose in the evening. We came back here. There was nothing else to do. The bluebabies were everywhere. Many of the injured were dragged under when they paused in one place too long. We spent the winter here."

He was silent for a moment, his eyes far away. "As autumn came to an end, the wind blew all the time. It was too cold to bear. It was impossible to go outside, even in the middle of the day. When winter came the winds grew worse. The cold was unbelievable. It was difficult to keep warm even in the Home. The night winds . . ." He paused. His voice grew lower. "The wind during the day was the same as the wind, now, at night. The night winds made the Home tremble and moan. The walls, the floors, everything shook. The vibration was constant. And the noise. There was never silence.

"The next spring many more had died. Some went into the tunnels to escape the sound of the wind, and were never found. Some took their own lives. Some were found killed, we never knew by whom. Some, though living, were never . . . right again. When autumn came again, when time for the trek came again, we walked. There were those who correctly interpreted the way station chart. Now the memory of it is gone, and there are those who wish to stay."

It was several minutes before anyone spoke. "What's to prevent us staying in the winter Home? The winds don't blow there. It is far from the gravel sea. The vegetation makes it possible to stay outside for a while without breathers."

"In the summer the crawlers mate."

"Yes. We couldn't go outside while the crawlers mate. We'd have to stay inside the Home all summer, but there would be no wind, no vibrations, no sound. It was the sound and vibration, wasn't it? It was the wind?"

Old Frel nodded once. "Perhaps."

The bluebaby felt languid. It swam in the gravel sea. The mantle of steely fluff growing from the joints of its body made movement awkward, but the itching of the growth made movement necessary. The bluebaby accepted its dilemma without question.

It swam near a clutch of eggs and listened to the incoherent thoughts flowing from them. It paused. The thoughts were small and formless, soft and selfish, sweet and indulgent. The bluebaby smiled a thought at them, then moved away when the two breeders hovering over the clutch grew nervous. They knew the bluebaby was no threat to their eggs, but breeders were always nervous and fretful until the spring hatching. The bluebaby thought idly of the coming time when it would be a breeder. The thought made it uncomfortable. There would be no swimming, no frolicking with other bluebabies, no freedom. From spring to spring there would be nothing but attention to the clutch.

The bluebaby had once expressed this apprehension to a dreamer. The dreamer had told the bluebaby fondly to put such thoughts from its mind. When the time came to be a breeder, it would want nothing else. And did the bluebaby not want to be a dreamer? Everything came due in its time and its place. Now, go on with your games. I am about to begin a dream and I must decide upon one that is grand and worthwhile.

The bluebaby had left the dreamer unsatisfied. It hadn't made the thought at the time, but it wasn't too sure it liked the idea of being a dreamer any more than it did being a breeder. Now, it swam near a different dreamer encased in its impenetrable shell and listened a moment to the dream. But the bluebaby was restless and itchy and the dream seemed inconsequential.

It thought again of the peculiar surface creature and swam upward. Its head poked into the scream of the night winds. It saw nothing but the creeping dunes.

Flan lay in sleep, touching Triz, touching the child who slept between them. The sleeping room monitored them, adjusted the temperature here up a degree and there down a degree. The room's almost sentient circuits hummed in soundless contentment. It was capable of contentment in its own way—as well as regret. Regret that the cycle was ending, that its units would be out of its care until the next cycle began. A unit turned in its sleep. The room adjusted the temperatures in less than a microsecond.

The whispering stone in its pouch slipped from Flan's chest as he turned and lay loosely on the sleeper by his neck. It spoke, not to Flan,

Dinosaurs

but to another part of itself miles below the surface.

It hears but does not understand, it said.

Keep trying. The unit seems nearer understanding as time passes, it replied.

Too much time is passing. This unit grows closer to the end of its existence.

It is the only hope.

It is not my original unit. Its pattern is similar but too different. Too different. It does not understand.

It must. Time passes.

Time passes and they are so few.

So few.

Growing fewer.

The new ones increase; the new ones in the gravel sea. Their vitality increases and their number grows larger.

The gravel sea grows larger.

The units have lost their history.

They cease to function so quickly.

So do I.

Yes.

I am dying.

Yes.

My death will not matter when the units are no more.

Yes.

Without them I have no purpose.

Yes.

Without me they cannot survive. I have lost my voice in Shelter 23. I cannot communicate with them. The unit must understand. It is the only hope. They need me.

Yes.

I need them.

Yes.

The exchange ended. It was not a conversation precisely, but the continuation of an introspection that had lasted millennia. It took no more than a nanosecond.

Flan turned again and woke, disoriented. More and more the whispering stone was in his dreams. He lifted the pouch, upending it. The stone slid into his hand. He felt its urgency and strained to understand. It was no use, but . . . sometimes . . . almost . . . understanding was like a phantom seen from the corner of his eye. It was a sound just outside his range of hearing.

Triz and the child were still sleeping. Then he remembered, knew why he had awakened so early. He put the whispering stone back in the pouch. This was the child's naming day.

The People gathered in the big room. The occasion was not as festive as it might have been. There was only one child to name and the knowledge dampened their spirits. They tried not to show it. Not from their own sadness would they tarnish the shining moment for Flan and Triz and the child.

The child was led in by his parents. They were swelled with pleasurable pride and could not avoid smiling at each other and at the gathering. They were greeted by murmurs and nods of respect.

Flan lifted the child to the naming platform and stood behind him. He held the child cradled against his chest and smiled. Triz sat at the child's feet. The child was nervous and bashful, but hid it with a small arrogance. His naming day was an important time in his life, second only to the birth of his first child. He stood proudly but, nevertheless, clutched at his father's arm. The People stood quietly, all eyes on the child, waiting.

Flan slipped his arms from around his son's waist. He held his arms up and out. "There is a name for the child," he said in a sing-song voice. A faint hum issued from the throats of the People. "The name for the child has been found." The hum grew louder. "The name is . . . " The hum cut short and the People stood in silence.

"The name for the child is **Roon**."

The hum returned, louder, joyous. The People smiled and nodded and murmured the name. Flan stepped away from Roon. His son was no longer a child. Roon fidgeted nervously and cast one quick glance at his parents. Triz joined Flan. Roon stood alone.

Old Frel approached Roon and held out his hand. He touched Roon's genitals and said, "Roon."

Roon blushed.

One by one, the others did the same, walked solemnly to the boy, touched his genitals, and repeated his name. Halfway through the ceremony, Roon's excitement brought an erection. The People smiled. Flan hugged Triz to him. It was a good sign.

The childless ones returned to touch again, hoping. Even Old Frel returned.

The bluebaby swam restlessly, unable to settle into the sleep. All around others were snuggled in their balls of fluff, clustered near the dreamers, sharing the dreams through the long winter. Breeders huddled at their clutches, insulating the eggs against the iron cold that would come.

The bluebaby scratched absently at its side, although the itching was growing less as the tendrils grew longer. It caught an inquiring thought from a dreamer, the one it had expressed doubts to before, the one that had still not decided on a proper dream. The bluebaby thought a greeting but did not wish to hear of what would be, did not wish to hear its restlessness would pass, did not wish to hear wise platitudes from a dreamer.

It swam to the surface and poked its head into the bright, brittle

Dinosaurs 117

stillness of midday. It searched the gravel sea with small dim eyes, but nothing moved. It remembered the surface creature's speed, moving entirely on top of the gravel.

The bluebaby, on sudden impulse, emerged completely into the open air. It tried to imitate the creature's movements, but it was not equipped for walking. It floundered clumsily and looked up. Sheer terror overcame it. It was about to fall into that vast nothing, fall until the end of time. It was suddenly back beneath the surace and didn't remember how it got there.

Every day it came to the surface, but never saw the peculiar creature. Nor did it venture out again farther than its nose.

The naming ceremony had lasted long. Songs were sung, stories were told (Old Frel was the best), and then the People had moved to the surface with the midday warmth. They basked in the waning sunlight and gloried in open space while the children raced about in games. Roon had been self-conscious at first but soon joined in.

Triz had remained below for a while, then joined Flan and spoke to him quietly, out of hearing of the others. Now he hurried through the corridor, past the occupied sleeping rooms, past the many unoccupied ones, past the vast room where the air bus had berthed. He walked gray corridors he had not seen since he explored them as a curious boy. He passed the sighing room where the air machines made breathable atmosphere. He passed rooms with purposes he could not even imagine. The stone around his neck whispered as he passed some of the rooms, louder at some than at others, and loudest of all at one section of corridor. It whispered so loudly he paused, but then hurried on.

Flan knew his destination. Everyone had been there, but once explored, no reason existed to return.

It was a large area where the corridor terminated. Other tunnels opened at intervals on the other side, black unlighted tunnels. Flan had entered the darkness of one as a boy, but a thumping heart and clammy skin had ended his penetration after a dozen steps.

Two strips of metal on the floor ran parallel into each tunnel. Flan did not know the reason for the rails, nor did he even speculate that a reason existed. Had he been told of the time that had passed since they had been used, he couldn't have grasped it. The time was so great that even the inviolate metal of the rails had darkened.

Brin stood small and lovely in the doorway of a sleeping cubicle. No one knew why sleeping cubicles were necessary in this extreme end of the Home, but several were there, tiny and austere and functional.

She stood with her head down, looking at her feet. He walked to her, concerned and puzzled.

"Brin?" he said. She raised her eyes quickly and lowered them just as quickly. "Triz said you wanted to talk with me. Why here? Why not outside in the sun with the others?"

Brin stood for a moment without answering, then whispered something he could not hear. She repeated it more clearly at his question. "I do not want Sith to know," she said. Then she sobbed silently, her hands hanging loosely at her sides.

Flan took her in his arms and made soothing murmurs until her tears stopped. She snuffled and pushed him gently away, her eyes again shifting to the floor in embarrassment.

"Has Sith been cruel to you, Brin?" Flan asked softly.

Her eyes rose to his with pleading swiftness. "Oh, no. Not the way you mean."

He said nothing.

"Sith is not cruel. But his . . . silences and his looks are more painful than beatings." Her voice sank to a whisper he could hardly hear.

Flan released his breath in an impatient sigh.

"I know you dislike Sith," she said in a small tortured voice. "Most dislike him, but you are wrong. I love him. I love him more than my life."

"That is foolish. He does not deserve your love, Brin."

Her hands clenched into small fists. "You are wrong. Sith is beautiful. Sith is gifted. Sith is bright. Sith is golden. Sith has a right. It is only . . . he is tortured because he is childless. For three years I have been empty. Sith deserves many children."

"Others are childless. They are not lost in cruel rage."

"Sith is special."

"Perhaps Sith is at fault. Not you."

She stood as stiff as stone, her eyes closed and her lips pale. Flan knew why she had called him to this forsaken place. He knew and said nothing.

Her lips quivered before she spoke, her eyes still closed. "I do not believe my golden Sith could be with such a flaw, though Triz suggested it also. I do not believe it, but in my love and desperation I will grasp at any hope."

"There is danger. Sith has too much pride."

"I know. Sith must never discover the child is not his. The knowledge would be worse than childlessness." She looked at him quickly. "However, I do not believe there will be a child. The flaw is mine, not his."

"Why did you choose me?"

"Because Roon was the only child produced this year. Because . . . Triz suggested it."

"Is it your wish, or do you only follow Triz's suggestion?"

"I must give Sith a child."

He looked at her small pinched face, at the pain and pleading in her eyes. He did not speak. He knew from the tingling in his thighs and the pressure at the base of his belly; he knew his answer was visible.

When Brin had gone, giving him only one shyly smiling glance, Flan sat in the sleeping cubicle feeling relaxed and lethargic. The corners of his mouth curled slightly. It might be good for Sith if he did find out but, no, Brin would be the one to suffer. Perhaps Sith was tormented enough; perhaps if there was a child he would find a compromise between his arrogance and his despair.

Flan sighed and stood, stretching his arms over his head and rolling his shoulders. He clenched the muscles in his thighs and buttocks and felt suddenly restless. He took the whispering stone in his hand and heard its meaningless voice urgently commanding.

"I do not understand," he said aloud.

He passed by the dark tunnels, caressing the warm stone with his thumb, sliding his feet on the smooth coolness of the metal strips. He stopped and looked in, hesitated, took a few steps into the darkness. Childhood tensions caught at him and he turned back.

In the corridor the voice of the whispering stone grew louder, even louder than before because Flan held it in his hand. He stopped and looked at the walls. Both were featureless gray. A frown creased the skin above his nose. Behind one wall was the air machine room. He turned to the other. He had always supposed, when he thought about it at all, that it concealed nothing but solid rock. He took a step toward it. It looked the same as it had always looked. He listened to the whispering and placed the tips of his fingers against the wall. It felt no different than any other wall in the Home. He spread his fingers until his palm rested flat against it. Still there was nothing, but he knew, he thought he knew, the wall was important.

He stepped sideways and let his hand slide on the gray smoothness. Then another step. He released his breath and stepped back, letting his hand drop. It was then he felt it, as his hand slid downward on the wall, just before it broke contact. He bent over and looked closely at the spot level with his chest.

There was an indentation there, a rectangle as big as his head recessed no more than a millimeter. It seemed no different than the rest of the wall and was almost impossible to see. He touched it again, running the tip of his finger around the edge. He put his hand flat against the rectangle and felt nothing.

Then—his vision was swimming and his ears were ringing—then, he placed the tip of his finger **there**, and again **there**, and once more **there**, and back again to the first place.

He understands.

No. He only follows blindly.

He touched **there** and **there** at the same time. The rectangle sank inward another half inch.

Flan gasped and jerked his hand away. And, without knowing how he got there, was pressed flat against the opposite wall of the corridor.

The wall in front of him slid to one side with a gritty sigh.

Flan stared into a great room filled with machines. They climbed to the high-domed ceiling in stair-stepping tiers, solid to the top, quiet, sleeping, the glassy eyes dark. The room steeped in silent gloom; and in the center was a sphere, a globe, a vast round ball covered with pinpoints of light: blue, red, amber, and violet lines crisscrossing as if it were encased in a net.

Flan looked for a moment, then went to get the others.

The People stood with craned necks, the eyes of the adults only slightly less goggled than those of the children. The globe towered above them like a mountain. They milled around it, trying to see it all.

"Do you see up there?" Flan said. "That white light? It's the only white one there is."

They backed away to get a better look because it was above the curve of the sphere. Yes, they agreed, it was the only white light. Flan listened to the whispers and felt the stone warm in his hand. "Old Frel," he said softly, "you know the way station chart."

"Yes." Old Frel stepped beside him and looked at the white light.

"Look at those small lights below the white one. Are they the same as the way station chart?"

"Yes," Old Frel said doubtfully. "They look the same, but there are lines and too many lights."

"Just the small lights." The others were gathering around and nodding agreement. Roon started to his father with his mouth half open in question, but Triz stopped him and held him at her side.

Old Frel dipped his head once. "Yes."

"The white light I think is here, the summer Home. Follow the way station lights as if we were making the autumn trek. It leads to that larger light that must be the winter Home."

"But," Old Frel protested, "the light is amber. It is amber like the way stations that have something wrong with them."

A violet line from the white light to the amber light suddenly brightened. It glowed for a moment then went out completely. The People looked at each other. Then another line brightened, from the white light to a blue light farther around the globe. The line remained.

Will they understand?

Wait.

Flan moved away from the others and watched the blue light. Nothing changed on the globe. He looked back at Old Frel and saw agreement glittering in the ancient's eyes.

"No," Old Frel said, coming to him. "It's too far."

"The machine is telling us to do it."

Old Frel shook his head. "It is twice as far as the winter Home. We could not make it walking. If the air bus hadn't crashed . . . "

No. No.

Another violet line brightened. It led from the white light around the globe in the other direction.

Far below the gravel sea impulses flashed through semisentient circuits unused for millennia. In the room at the end of the corridor where Flan and Brin had met, one of the darkened tunnels was suddenly lighted. Two hundred miles away a long narrow vehicle moved into the lighted tunnel. It looked something like the air bus but had only one window at the front and rode the metal rails on magnetic skids and something that was almost antigravity. It passed the speed of sound in seconds.

"Look!" Sith pointed to the new violet line and they all followed his finger. A green dot moved on the line, moved rapidly toward the white light of the summer Home.

The whispering stone sang. "The tunnels," Flan said softly. "The dark tunnels at the end of the corridor."

He understands.
Wait.

The others looked at him. "We must travel to the new Home in the tunnels."

Cybernetic relays closed here and opened there. The impulses flew joyously, for they were capable of joy in their own way. Then, there was an unthinkable sifting of impossible dust. The impulses derailed, were shunted to the wrong circuits, relays closed at the wrong time, opened at the wrong time, microscopic memory cells went insane.

Magnetic currents in the rails fluctuated. The rocketing vehicle's skids impossibly touched. Sparks flew like a meteor storm. The vehicle yawed and struck the tunnel wall as the lights went out.

Flan ground his teeth and pressed his hands against his ears. The whispering stone screamed, once, briefly, unbearably, and then was still. The green light moving along the violet line flickered and darkened.

The People waited at the end of the corridor, watched the dark tunnels. Flan waited in the room with the great globe, but the whispering stone did not whisper again.

Triz came to him in the following days. She waited with him silently and then finally she spoke. "The trek begins, Flan."

"We must go through the tunnels," he muttered.

She was silent again for a moment. "No. We could not bear the darkness. They tried. Come, Flan. We must go."

He went with her at last and left the silent white stone lying on the floor.

The bluebaby felt torpor creeping through its body, but the sensation did not produce warm lassitude and a desire to curl up in the steely fluff. It only made the bluebaby uncomfortable. It was the only one who had not entered the sleep, the only one who swam about sluggishly and irritably. More and more it caught the inquiring thoughts of the dreamer who had not found a dream, but it refused to answer.

It kept swimming, although the completed growth of fluff made movement clumsy, because it dared not rest, dared not let the sleep creep upon it unbidden. It found an especially delectable rusty stone but did not enjoy it. The stone lay in its stomach with dead weight. The digestive process had halted for the sleep. The bluebaby regurgitated and pushed the stone away.

It swam to the surface—and saw them!

The surface creatures moved by a short distance away, many of them. The bluebaby subdued the lethargy that slowed its limbs and dived. It made a swoop and returned to the surface. Excitement flowed from it with such strength, two nearby breeders awoke and crouched with poised spurs to defend their clutches.

The bluebaby watched, wondering if the one seen earlier was among them. It couldn't tell. They all looked alike except for variations in size. All were wrapped in loose flat things that stirred with the rising night winds, and all wore things over their faces. They moved in an irregular line that clumped and thinned sporadically.

The bluebaby followed.

Flan glanced occasionally at the direction machine strapped to his forearm. The indication glow remained steady with a brightness that should mean the way station would come into view within minutes. Triz walked beside him, matching his pace without effort. Roon walked at his side. The boy was tiring but never complained. He clung to Flan's cloak as they topped a large dune.

The way station lay ahead, poking its smooth black top just above the surface of the gravel sea. The others reached the top of the dune and sighed loudly and pleasurably at the end of the first day of the trek. They scooted down the other side, moving a little faster, moving with lighter feet.

The way station was one of many scattered over the vast expanse of the creeping dunes no more than a day's walk apart, put there in the same distant past when the Homes were built. It floated on the gravel sea, anchored in place, kept level by its machines. Most had never known living things, never exercised their purpose after the day the workmen departed. The machines of the way-stations purred in solitude, keeping them afloat, keeping them anchored, keeping them level. Inside, the air machines produced breathable atmosphere, the food machine and water machine stood waiting.

Except for a few. On the large charts in the Homes, several way station lights had gone dark and others had changed from clear blue to amber and red. The second way station on the trek was an amber light—the air machine no longer functioned. The People used it anyway, sleeping in their breathers. It was uncomfortable and awkward but not worth the lengthy detour. A detour was necessary near the end, four extra days of travel to skirt a darkened light on the chart. The flotation-anchoring machines had malfunctioned. The way station was awash, lost forever in the gravel sea.

The People entered in small groups, as many as the descending tube would hold at one trip. They stripped away the uncomfortable surface suits, the irritating breathers, stretched unconfined bodies, jostled and laughed in the one cramped room. They patiently waited turns at the small toilet, ate the gray cubes from the food machine, sipped at containers of water, and wished for relaxing exercise machines.

Many returned to the surface, escaping the confinement for a while. Rested and with full bellies, they wanted the freedom of space for as long as possible. Flan sat with Triz. He though regretfully of the promise of the globe in the forgotten room and didn't understand. He put his arm around Triz and pulled her to him, putting the whispering stone from his mind.

They nestled comfortably in the loose gravel, watching Roon and the other young ones play a game of chase and touch. Roon would be ready to mate when he reached five years or, if he was lucky and developed quickly, at four. Already he was the constant companion of young Glur, the daughter of Slef and Klin. Flan hoped Roon would select a mate younger than himself—if any females were produced in the next couple of years. When the female was older, the reproducing years were shortened. If Triz were his own age or younger there would be a chance of two or three more children. Now, there would be no more. He pulled Triz closer to him. She turned her eyes from her son to Flan. Her breather moved with her smile. Flan would not interfere with Roon's decision. Never once had he regretted mating with Triz, even if there would be no more children.

The bluebaby floated nose-deep in the gravel sea, watching the antics of the surface creatures. The light wind ruffled the thick fluff around its head. Some of the creatures, the smaller ones, raced about with great activity. Others reclined on the surface. As the wind rose, some of them entered the black bubble.

The bluebaby slipped below the surface and moved closer. It swam slowly and carefully, not wanting to disturb the creatures. When it emerged again the swiftly moving small ones were quite near. Their activity was not unlike its own romps with other bluebabies, though without the grace of swimming. It marveled at the rather incredible agility and speed with which they moved despite their clumsy limitations.

Roon ran in a great circle to avoid Glur's touch. She was at present concentrating on contact with Jird who was an easier target. This time he would win the game. Roon crouched behind a dune, hoping to be forgotten until after Jird had been touched.

He huddled against the low dune, breathing rapidly from exertion. He was tired and happy and content. The excitement of his first trek was very satisfying. (Although it was actually his second; he had been too young to have more than the vaguest memories of the first in the spring.)

Unease slowly rippled through Roon's contentment. He frowned behind his breather but could find no cause for his apprehension. He craned his neck slightly to peer over the dune. All was as it should be. None of the others seemed disturbed. He felt faint prickles on the back of his neck and decided to return even if it did mean losing the game. As he rose from the ground he turned and looked behind him.

At first he thought it was a round blue stone slightly larger than his head, but then he saw the eyes. They were two black smudges in horny sockets, just barely above the level of the ground. And they watched him.

Roon gasped and took a step backward. He had never seen a bluebaby, but he was sure it was one. But the bluebabies were supposed to be asleep. The southward trek didn't begin until they were asleep, and the northward trek was completed before they awoke.

The blue head sank into the gravel without a trace.

Roon turned and ran. He had taken two slithering steps up the dune when the chitinous blue claws closed around his foot.

Roon screamed but the breather muffled the sound. It was doubtful that the others would have heard anyway above the noise of the rising wind.

But Glur saw him rise above the dune and drop down again. She smiled behind her breather. So that was where he was hiding. With exaggerated stealth she crept around the dune and pounced.

No one was there. Only the edge of Roon's breather protruded from the gravel sea.

The bluebaby pulled the surface creature down with some difficulty. It squirmed and thrashed with great determination. The bluebaby also had some difficulty moving it through the loose gravel. If the creature would swim . . . but it had stopped moving altogether.

The bluebaby stopped and examined it. Something seemed to be wrong with it. Besides its cessation of activity, its outer covering was leaking fluid. It felt the creature and was surprised at its softness. The outer covering seemed filled with pulp. The bluebaby suddenly became concerned and dragged the creature quickly to the surface. It pushed it completely out and watched it for signs of activity, but there was none. It continued to leak fluid.

The bluebaby felt a great sadness and sank slowly into the gravel. It swam downward, willing the sleep to come, but it would not. A hollowness grew in the bluebaby. It swam toward the dreamer without a dream with many confused questions.

The dreamer thought comfort at the bluebaby; comfort and regret and understanding. The surface creatures are harmless, fragile things. They should not be bothered.

I meant it no harm, the bluebaby thought with remorse.

I know. The young are curious and unwise. The surface creatures are

Dinosaurs

able to live only on the surface. To bring them under means their death. You must never do it again.

What is death?

The dreamer thought amusement at the solemnity of the young. You are not mature enough to grasp such a concept. Wait until you have become a dreamer. You will have time to think of such things. Now is the time for youth. Everything will come due in its time and its place. But the bluebaby insisted and the dreamer thought it was like being hatched, only the opposite, and would think no more.

The bluebaby swam away unsatisfied, and wrapped itself in fluff near a dreamer with other bluebabies. The sleep came quickly, but the dreamer's dream seemed to involve surface creatures with leaking fluids.

The bluebaby was the first to awaken in the spring. The others still slept in balls of fluff. It swam quickly to the surface, leaving its steely fluff scattered through the gravel sea, shortly to decompose. It poked its head into bright day and looked at the black bubble floating there. No surface creatures were in sight. It swam around the bubble, touching it, feeling its faint vibrations. Had the creatures returned already? It swam to the dreamer without a dream.

The surface creatures had not returned. It was not time, but it would be soon. Why had the young one awakened so early?

I must see them again, the bluebaby thought. My sadness is still with me.

It went to the surface many times every day, but still the creatures did not return. It watched the clutches hatch and the new bluebabies swim away. Would they too destroy surface creatures? It wanted to tell them, to warn them, but their thoughts were only for frivolity. Perhaps they would never know without doing it themselves.

It watched the breeders, free of their clutches, shed their husks and emerge as new dreamers. They quickly encased themselves for eternity. It listened to their tentative inexperienced dreams and swam away restlessly.

The time for the return of the creatures had long passed, but they had not returned. Midsummer arrived before the bluebaby abandoned its vigil. It swam to the dreamer without a dream.

It was only the second time within the dreamer's memory—the dreamer was young—that the surface creatures had failed to pass over. Before that they moved through the air. The dreamer pushed aside the bluebaby's queries about moving through the air and thought on the surface creatures' failure to return. After a few days of deliberation, it decided. Yes, it was a perfect subject for a dream. It began the dream immediately.

It was a great dream and lasted nearly a thousand years.

The Sweetwater Factor

Montgomery Sweetwater felt the cast-iron bench on which he sat tremble slightly. He sighed, lowered his magazine and, putting his arm along the back of the bench, looked over his shoulder.

The nose was about twenty feet away, poking from the dry earth, twitching slightly as it tested the air. The nose was a bit larger than Montgomery's head, nakedly pink, with nostril hairs protruding like black fence wire, though, other than that, it was quite an ordinary nose. "Good grief," Montgomery muttered and turned on the bench, resting his chin on his folded arms.

The nose snuffled a few times and raised a small cloud of dust. The nostril hairs quivered. Then it turned toward Montgomery and poised, like a well-trained pointer. Montgomery watched it, his eyes half-closed and his mouth turned downward in a resigned pout.

The nose moved toward him, turning back the surface crust of the baked earth like the prow of an ice-breaker, like a plow opening a furrow, sending cracks radiating in all directions, popping concrete-hard clods into the air like tiddlywinks.

Montgomery Sweetwater watched it a moment, until it was about ten feet away. Then he turned down the corner of the magazine page he'd been reading and left it lying on the vibrating bench. He walked a short distance away, ninety degrees from the approaching nose, and turned to watch it.

The nose stopped. It paused in motionless uncertainty for a moment and began twitching again as it cast about for the scent. "I hope you don't really think you're sneaking up on me," Montgomery said with a total lack of interest.

The Sweetwater Factor 127

The nose snuffled again, raising another dust cloud, and made a ninety degree turn. It approached Montgomery, moving a little faster, straining its fleshy tip forward, spraying dry chunks of hard-packed earth as it ripped the ground.

Montgomery waited until the nose was almost to him, then drew back his foot. "You're ridiculous!" he said tiredly and kicked the nose as hard as he could. The nose froze in startled immobility for a second, its tip reddening rapidly. Then it honked. Montgomery stepped back to escape the flying dust. The nose sank from sight, honking pathetically.

The earth rumbled and folded inward at the seam torn by the nose. Montgomery yelped and grabbed for his magazine as the cast-iron bench toppled into the crevasse. Montgomery leaned over tentatively and looked in. A smooth burrow rose almost vertically where the nose, and whatever had been attached to it, came to the surface. It leveled out for twenty feet or so, made a ninety degree turn, dropped almost vertically again where the nose, and whatever had been attached to it, had made its retreat. Montgomery could hear the pained honking fading into the depths.

The bench teetered on the lip of the descending shaft, then slipped over in a cascade of dry, crumbled earth. Montgomery smiled slightly at the metallic twangs as the bench ricocheted from one side of the abyss to the other. He waited for the sudden, shrill hoot as the bench caught up with the nose, and whatever had been attached to it. Montgomery's smile broadened as he turned back toward the house.

"Monty!"

Dorothybelle's screech came from the terrace. "What was that noise, Monty?" She joggled down the steps, clutching at the railing, heaving along like a brightly colored sack of suet. "Monty!" she screeched again, but her shortness of breath turned it into a croak. Montgomery began thumbing through his magazine looking for his place. The folded corner had unfolded.

"Oh, crap!" Dorothybelle grunted. "Look at that great hole in my garden, Monty!" She breathed heavily, grasping at her lumpy bosom. "It's so **hot** out here! I wish you'd make it rain, Monty. It hasn't rained in forty-seven years, Monty!" She lurched around and pointed down the hill. "Look down there, Monty! Down at the bottom of the hill it's practically a **swamp**! It rains down there all the time, Monty! If you really loved me, Monty, you'd make it rain in my garden!"

Montgomery didn't bother to answer. They went through this practically every day—not specifically rain in the garden, but something much like it. He started toward the house with Dorothybelle Sweetwater pitching and swaying behind him on 24 carat gold and lavender satin mules. She never stopped talking all the way, though her enunciation had pretty well degenerated into wheezes and grunts. Montgomery wasn't listening anyway.

He slid open the terrace door and almost shivered at the blast of arctic air-conditioning that hit him. Dorothybelle collapsed on a molecule for molecule reproduction of a Louis XVI chaise. Dorothybelle had never heard of Louis XVI in this year of 1242 NC (New Calendar), but her friend Eloise Baumgardner had Louis XVI reproductions so, naturally, Dorothybelle had to have them also. Montgomery thought it was ridiculous.

Dorothybelle frowned at her ruined shoes and tossed them into the disposal. The VG chimed softly. She waved Montgomery from the room and thumbed a control beside the chaise. The other half of the room flickered and was replaced by a similar room half. The only major difference was the woman who sat there, on a Louis XVI chaise, frowning at Montgomery.

"Oh, Eloise!" Dorothybelle wailed. "I'm so glad you called. You won't believe what happened! There's a great hole in my garden!"

Montgomery sighed and left the room, but not soon enough to avoid hearing Eloise say, "What's he done **this** time?"

Consider for a moment that Mother Nature and History are concrete entities, personifications if you would, rather than abstractions. History would be a grandfatherly type, no doubt, with a long beard and kind, tolerant eyes. Mother Nature would be matronly, a little plump, a little gray in the hair, and a stern set to her lips—like a third grade teacher is supposed to look. They would live on some astral plane with a lot of other personified abstractions, a plane not too unlike Mount Olympus. There History would observe the world with an occasional bemused sigh, and Mother Nature . . . well . . . let's face it. Mother Nature is something of a busybody. She leaned on a marble balustrade and grunted. Which, you see is why they must be personified. Abstractions don't grunt.

History sat beside her and looked downward. "Sweetwater?" he asked.

"Of course," she said. "The Sweetwater line has been a thorn in my side for longer than I care to remember. I've traced it all the way back to the Chaldeans. It's gone from the probable to the possible to the **im**probable to the **im**possible to the **absurd**!"

"He certainly makes it interesting for me," History said and smiled tolerantly.

"Piffle!" Mother Nature said—or words to that effect. "Interesting? It's chaos!"

"I think you sometimes get carried away with your . . . ah . . . obsession for order and balance and rhythm," he said.

"Nonsense! It's the only way. The only possible way!" She turned her head and looked up at him with a smug smile. "I have, I think, eliminated the Sweetwater fly in my ointment."

He raised his craggy eyebrows. "Oh?"

"For the last twenty generations of Sweetwaters I've been . . ."

The Sweetwater Factor

"You always did do things slowly and methodically," he interrupted.

"Of course. It's the only way. Montgomery Sweetwater is the last of his unnatural line. Montgomery Sweetwater is sterile and there will not be another."

"That seems an unnecessary maneuver," History chuckled. "Have you taken a look at Dorothybelle lately?"

"Yes," she smiled. "That was an unexpected bit of good luck. Of course, I couldn't have known about Dorothybelle twenty generations ago."

"What?" he said in mock surprise. "Do my ears hear approval for the unexpected?"

"Humph!" she said and turned her gaze downward.

Montgomery entered his private sanctorum—which was not done in Louis XVI. It was done in California ranch oak, though he had never heard of a ranch nor, for that matter, California. He had seen it on a VG tape and liked the looks of the leather couch with the embossed long-horned steer on the back and the blond oak half wagon wheels for arms. He sat on the couch and propped his feet on the blond oak coffee table and got back to his magazine which, he suddenly discovered, was filled with ninety-eight page twelves. He was not unduly concerned and page twelve was the one he had been reading.

Dorothybelle came in a bit later, though she wasn't supposed to be in his sanctorum at all. "Just for a sec, Monty," she always said or, "One quickie question, Monty," or, "It's absolutely vital, Monty!"

She looked around with her sanctorum frown. "This is such a tacky room, Monty. Why don't you let me . . . ?"

"What do you want, Dorothybelle? You're not supposed to be in here, you know."

"Just for a sec, Monty. I want to go to the mainland for a while and visit Eloise."

He shrugged. "Go ahead."

"I want to be near people, Monty! I never see anyone!"

He sighed. She went through this at least once a week. She never had gone to the mainland; she always talked herself out of it by putting the words into his mouth. "The VG is all right, Monty, but it's no substitute for really being in the same room with your friends. I'll call Transportation on the VG and have them send over a shuttle in the morning. It's too bad you have to stay on the island, Monty, but I guess they know what they're doing. Strange things do happen when you're around, Monty. Just look at that great hole in my garden."

Montgomery was spared the rest of the routine by the rain. There was no warning, no distant thunder or lightning, no darkening of the room; the rain just began falling from the ceiling. Dorothybelle shrieked and ran out. Montgomery looked up and squinted his eyes against the falling droplets. The rain was pale pink and smelled of violets. Montgomery looked back at his magazine as he felt it disintegrate in his hands. Then he slipped slowly to the floor as the couch, the coffee table, and everything else in the room dissolved into blond oak sludge.

Montgomery sat in the middle of the floor in the spreading gook holding nothing in his hands and looking martyred.

"It's not just the bizarre things that happen to Sweetwater himself," Mother Nature grumbled a decade later, "but his influence spreads over the whole world. Putting his ancestors on that island two hundred years ago didn't help—except to get the more blatant idiocies out of sight. The more civilized they get, the more impossible the Sweetwater influence becomes. I've checked the line thoroughly and, as near as I can pinpoint it, the influence changed from the possible to the improbable right about the Industrial Revolution. It became the impossible about five hundred years later, and the absurd another five hundred years after that."

History ran his fingers through his beard. "Such neat little categories: probable, possible, improbable, impossible, absurd. How do you distinguish among them?"

She ticked them off her fingers. "It was probable that Cyrus would conquer Babylon. It was possible that Rome would eclipse Greece. It was improbable that Hitler would ever amount to anything. It was impossible that a six-year-old child would assassinate the Russian Premier with a rubber band and a paper clip. And it was absurd when the capital city of Africa suddenly turned into salt water taffy!"

History chuckled. "That really kept things hopping for a while."

"Chaos! Sheer and utter chaos!" Mother Nature trembled with emotion.

"But humanity thrives on adversity," History pointed out.

"Order," she said under her breath. "It's the only way."

Montgomery Sweetwater, the last of the Sweetwater line, lay on his deathbed. He felt only a vast relief. Dorothybelle was in the VG room sitting cross-legged on a Turkish pillow weeping softly. The Louis XVI reproductions had gone decades ago. Now the room was filled with filigreed brass and swooping draperies. Dorothybelle was extremely uncomfortable, but Eloise sat on an identical pillow in the VG tsk-tsking and saying perhaps it was for the best.

Montgomery looked out the window at the bananas and smiled fondly. Dorothybelle had been a bit hysterical when the first one popped up like a mushroom two weeks ago. But, when they didn't do anything but just sit there, she accepted them much as she had the chocolate icing on the roof of the house. The bananas didn't grow on trees as bananas should, but were twenty-foot giants growing endwise from the ground. And quite delicious, too, Montgomery thought.

Montgomery Sweetwater began to laugh. He couldn't stop. "It's

The Sweetwater Factor

ridiculous," he choked out between guffaws. Then he died.

Dorothybelle ran into the room and stood there staring while the curled toes of her harem slippers vibrated. She heard a **plop** and looked out the window. The chocolate icing was dripping off the house.

Within two days the bananas had turned brown. Within four days they began to rot. Dorothybelle finally went to the mainland—mostly to get away from the stench of the bananas. She missed the first rain in eighty-three years.

"That's that!" Mother Nature said with satisfaction. "Not one single absurd thing has happened since Sweetwater kicked off. All the wars have stopped. The strawberry Kool-Aid is gradually disappearing from the Baltic Sea. The invaders from Arcturus have packed up and gone home. The Chinese have started growing hair on their heads instead of parsley. It's wonderful. Order, balance, and rhythm; it's the only way!"

A thousand years later Mother Nature said, biting her lip, "I don't understand it. Everything going so well. There was absolute order and harmony. I don't understand it at all!"

History yawned. "They're probably perishing from sheer boredom," he said. "I know the last thousand years since Montgomery Sweetwater died have been the longest thousand years I ever spent." He yawned again.

"But," she said a little uncertainly, "it was the only way. Absolutely the only way."

In another thousand years the human race was totally extinct.

The Mistress of Windraven

I dreamed again last night of Windraven Hall. It was as I had seen it last, a gaunt ruin on the edge of the sea. Gulls circled the blackened fingers of stone and blackbirds nested in the creepers relentlessly covering the ugly wounds. The great stone arches of the central hall still stood, curved against the pale sky like the bones of some huge dead beast picked clean by vultures.

Only the low west wing had escaped the fire. I knew Alex was in there, in his library, perched like a blind bird among his books, seeing nothing, hearing nothing, wanting nothing.

In my dream I again left Windraven Hall as I had done that last time with my few meager possessions in my old wicker valise. I turned once more at the edge of the meadow and looked at the blind windows of the west wing. Was there a movement at the window? Did he look out at me . . . or was it only the reflection of a gull?

Windraven Hall, where my dreams began and seemingly must forever end in a dream.

"Well, darling, at least she doesn't set the tiresome things in Cornwall. Jesus! If one more gothic set in Cornwall comes across my desk, I swear I shall go screaming through the steno pool. Most of them know as much about Cornwall as I know about the far side of the moon. Why can't one of the things be set on a wheat farm in Nebraska?

"My God, the artist doesn't have to **read** them. I just tell him the location and the period and he paints the girl and the house with the light in one window. The lucky bastards! **I'm** the one who has to **read** the damn things.

The Mistress of Windraven 133

"Her real name is Agnes Gooch, or something. **We** were the ones who changed it to Valentina Hope. That's probably why the book is doing so well. The tiny brains out there look at it with their usual perception and see 'Victoria Holt.'

"No, I haven't met the woman. The book came through the mail and now she has an agent. It's just as well. Spare me from lady novelists. **Oops!** Don't let that get over to **Cosmo**; I'll be drummed out of my own sex.

"Well, darling, I did get a **tiny** bonus from R.T. for buying the book. The agent says she's started another one.

"I have to hang up now, darling. I have a luncheon engagement with Manly Armbruster. What a Cosmic Jest! Imagine anyone naming that old fruit 'Manly.' If his readers only **knew!** Cocktails tomorrow?

"Fine. The Pied Piper at seven. See you then, darling. Bye, bye."

He leaned over her shoulder and looked at the sheet of paper in the typewriter. "I dreamed again last night of Windraven Hall," he muttered and then cocked his eyes at her. "Isn't that a bit Daphne du Maurier-ish?"

She sighed and leaned back in the chair. He knew she didn't like him reading over her shoulder—and he hadn't shaved again that morning. "Actually, I thought it was a bit Jane Eyre-ish. Don't you have something to do?"

"Don't get peevish, **Valentina**," he grunted and continued to read. "Don't you think you're a little heavy on the bird imagery?"

"No."

"What's this one called?"

"I don't know." She knew he didn't care what she called it. She knew he was looking for an argument. "It doesn't make much difference. The titles usually don't mean anything, anyway. How about **Gothic Romance #792?**" She tried to keep the sarcasm from her voice.

"There must be more of them than that," he said over his shoulder, going into the kitchen. "Don't forget to leave a light burning in the window." He guffawed and she heard him open the refrigerator and pull the tab on a beer can.

"Damn you, Howard!" she said softly. "God damn you, Howard!"

I first saw Windraven the summer of my eighteenth year.

After the deaths of my dear parents from brain fever, I posted a letter to my uncle telling him of my plight. My father, though a gentle and loving man, was not a wizard with finances. My small legacy was eaten up completely by his debts, leaving me penniless and alone. My uncle, a poor but kindly man, agreed that I might live with his family until such time as I married or found a position of my own.

It was also that same day, in the summer of my eighteenth year, that I first looked into the laughing grey eyes of Alexander Culhane.

My uncle's man met the post chaise at Weymouth. We rode along the Dorset coast in a dray pulled by a dappled mare of sweet disposition and indeterminate age. It was a sugary day, warm and still, the air thick and sweet with the scent of freshly scythed hay. Larks trilled in the meadows and hedge sparrows quarreled merrily in the low hedgerows on either side of the quiet country lane. It was such a perfect English summer day my recent tragedy was put quite out of my head.

I saw the great house across the long swell of a meadow, a dark silhouette against the sea.

"What is that?" I asked, strangely affected by the somber beauty of the scene.

My uncle's man, whose name was Jaban, halted the dray. The old mare began to nibble at the sweet grass between the ruts of the lane. Jaban turned in the seat and squinted against the bright sky. He shifted the clay pipe in his mouth and spoke with it clenched in his teeth.

"That be Windraven Hall, Mistress," he said.

"Who lives there?" I asked.

"They be the Culhanes. Most for leagues around be Culhane land, even the croft where the young mistress's uncle be a freeholder."

Jaban had turned back to flick the dapple with the reins when we heard the pounding hoofbeats on the opposite side of the lane. I looked away from Windraven Hall as the night-black stallion leaped the hedgerow. The rider reined him in, just in front of the dray, and the horse reared, his skin shimmering like midnight silk.

I gasped and lay my hand to my bosom. The powerful beauty of the horse and rider quite took my breath away. Jaban tipped his hat to the young man and the young man nodded as he walked the stallion to the side of the dray. He pushed the wind-blown hair from his face, hair as black as the stallion, and stroked the horse's neck with his bare hand. The horse stepped in place impatiently and dug at the turf with a shiny black hoof. The muscles coiled under the horse's black hide much as they did in the young man's thigh under the soft cloth of his breeches.

I looked up and into sparkling grey eyes in quite the most handsome face I had ever seen.

"Good morrow, Jaban. Who is your passenger?" he asked, never taking his eyes from mine.

"This be the niece of Edward Bronwyn, Master Alex," Jaban said, tipping his hat again.

The young man on the horse smiled. "Does the niece of Edward Bronwyn have a name?"

"India Bronwyn, your Lordship," I said boldly, then lowered my bonnet to hide my blush.

The young man laughed and I looked up again. His head was thrown back in merriment. "I be no lord, Mistress. No drop of royal blood be in these veins." His speech before had been that of an educated man, but now he spoke in the peasant dialect of the district, seemingly as a jest.

"Your pardon, sir," I said, lowering my eyes from the power of his gaze.

"Granted, Mistress India." He bowed slightly and touched the stallion easily with the heels of his boots. The magnificent animal leaped away and galloped down the lane, then over the hedgerow, speeding across the meadow.

I turned in the seat of the dray as Jaban flicked the reins. The old dappled mare moved slowly and ponderously, so greatly in contrast to the beautiful black animal and his rider. As I watched the stallion was reined in and turned. Alex Culhane looked at me again from the center of the meadow, then he wheeled the horse and continued toward Windraven Hall.

"Master Alex be the best of the Culhanes, but he be also the youngest," Jaban said. "He be never master of the land."

Agnes Grover dropped towels in the pool of water spreading rapidly across the kitchen floor from the washing machine. It was the third time that month and the repair man wanted seventy-five dollars to fix it. She was squeezing towels out in the sink when the doorbell rang. She dropped the wet towel and dried her hands, but heard Howard going to the door.

He came into the kitchen a few moments later with a special delivery letter. He dropped it on the cabinet and looked at her. She picked it up and saw the return address of her agent. She knew what was in it. She put it back on the cabinet without opening it.

Howard snorted. "Doesn't the successful lady author want to know how much it is?"

"It can wait," she said and went back to work with the towels.

"Wait for what?" he said. "Wait until I'm not around so my ego won't be bruised?"

"All right, Howard," she said softly and tore the end off the envelope. She looked at the check.

"How much?" he asked.

"Fifteen hundred."

"That should keep the wolf away from the door until the new one is finished. Adding it to the other checks you used to catch up on the bills and pay my debts makes a very tidy sum."

"Howard, please."

"Now you can get the washing machine fixed; even buy a new one if you want to." He threw the words at her like stones.

"Howard, you're being ridiculous!" She clamped her lips together. She was letting him do it again, letting him lure her into an argument.

He looked at her for a moment, victory in his eyes. "Ridiculous, am I? Ridiculous because you have to support me?"

"No, Howard."

"Ridiculous because I can't find a job and have to be supported by Valentina Hope?"

"No!" she yelled. "You're ridiculous because you make so much of it. Why shouldn't I support you when I can? I'm your wife. This marriage is a partnership. We're supposed to be helping each other. Why is it so important to you?"

"Because I don't feel like a man anymore!"

"There are more important things than money that make a man. Do you want me to stop writing like you've stopped looking for a job? Do you want us to lose the house and the car? Do you want us to starve?"

He slapped her. She leaned against the sink and forced herself not to cry.

"Why didn't you go to New York like they wanted? Why didn't you go to the cocktail parties and be interviewed by the newspapers?" he growled through his teeth.

"I didn't want to go to New York."

"Maybe when you've sold a few more books we can move to New York, get a penthouse apartment, and I can stay around to answer the phone for you."

"Howard, stop it! You didn't mind when I was writing the first book. You thought it was fun. You bragged about it."

"Because I didn't think it had a chance in hell of ever selling!" He stalked from the kitchen and a moment later she heard the front door slam.

"Don't track water through the house," she said softly and began to cry.

I was awakened in the middle of the night by screams.

I sat up in bed and listened. I could hear nothing but Hagan's snores as he lay beside me, still sleeping. I thought for a moment it had been a dream, then the screams came again. It was Emmaline. I knew. I woke Hagan.

He stirred and sat up, his face so like and yet so unlike Alex's. "Emmaline has gotten out of her room," I said and then smelled the faint odor of smoke.

Hagan sniffed and jumped out of bed. We raced down the stairs of the east wing, not even taking time to put on dressing gowns over our nightclothes. The odor of smoke grew stronger and soon I saw flickering light from the direction of Emmaline's room.

"Stay here, India," Hagan said and rushed toward the open door from which came the light of the flames. He went inside and I heard Emmaline's screams grow more frenzied in her madness. Soon Hagan emerged from the room dragging a limp form.

Even at that distance and in the smoke I could see it was Alex. I ran to them. "My God, India," Hagan groaned. "She's killed Leo. I must get him out." He ran back into the flaming room.

"No, Hagan!" I cried as he was hidden from view by the smoke. Alex

The Mistress of Windraven

moaned and I looked at him. A cut bled freely on his forehead where he had been struck. I put my hand on his chest and felt his heart beating strongly.

There was a sudden crash from the burning room as something collapsed. Emmaline's mad screams rose suddenly in pitch. I went to the door but was driven back by the heat. "Hagan!" I cried, but received no answer. As I watched, something moved in the flames. It was Emmaline. She ran from the room, herself a living flame. Even now, I sometimes wake in the night and seem to hear those screams. She ran down the hallway and smashed through the glazed doors into the garden. There she fell and her screams were stilled, her tortured mind finally at peace.

I tried to pull Alex away from the fire, but his weight was more than my small strength could manage. I was almost given in to panic when I heard someone call. It was Jaban. With him was Uncle Edward and Aunt Sophie and my cousins. They pulled Alex to safety while Jaban lent me his strong arm.

Other neighbors came and, with the servants, extinguished the fire. Only Emmaline's room and the one above were damaged greatly, but Hagan was dead. Leo was dead. Emmaline was dead. All who had inhabited the great house were dead except Alex and myself.

In the summer of my twentieth year I was a widow and no longer the mistress of Windraven Hall.

Howard Grover pulled the pages from the wastebasket and looked at them. He shuffled through them and raised his eyebrows questioningly at his wife. "I thought you'd finished this thing."

"I'm changing the ending."

"Oh?"

"I decided not to burn Windraven Hall. When the middle brother's mad wife sets fire to the place, they manage to put it out. I decided to have a happy ending."

"You always were one for a happy ending."

"Please, Howard. I want to get this finished."

"Does dear, sweet little India still marry Alex's elder brother?"

"Yes. The heroine always marries the wrong man first." She looked at him but he was still scanning the pages. "It's part of the formula. Instead of having Alex become a psychotic recluse in the ruins of Windraven Hall and India leave because she can't get through to him, I'm having him come to his senses and marry her."

"And they live happily ever after."

"Of course."

"Too bad real life isn't that way." He tossed the pages back in the wastebasket and went into the kitchen. She heard him open the refrigerator door and pull the tab on a can of beer. Then he turned on the television even though he knew it made it difficult for her to work.

I stood on the grand staircase of Windraven Hall, listening to the music swell through the great house and watching the dancers whirl on the polished floor. It was the happiest moment of my life; the ball in honor of my marriage to Alex Culhane. In the summer of my twenty-first year I was again mistress of Windraven, but it was of no importance. As the wife of Hagan Culhane it had been an empty joy. Now, it meant nothing to me. My only pleasure was the love of my husband.

Alex came up the staircase toward me, his handsome face bathed in smiles and his night-black hair for once under control. He took me in his strong arms and crushed me to his chest. He laughed and motioned upward with his head.

Laughing, I ran ahead of him. The hallway was bright with light. Candles burned everywhere. Every room in the house was filled with waxen sunshine. The candle makers of Weymouth had been kept busy for months in preparation for this night at Windraven Hall.

With Alex's aid I quickly extinguished all the candles in our bedroom, then I was in his arms where I would stay forever and ever.

"Darling, you mustn't call me at the office. I'm hanging on to my job by my fingernails.

"Well, R. T. has been the teeniest bit forgiving since the book is selling in spite of everything. I don't know what came over me. I must have been possessed. Do you know a good exorcist?

"At least I had the perspicacity to change the title from Gothic Romance #792 to The Mistress of Windraven. R.T. would never have forgiven that.

"I know it doesn't mean anything, but the titles of these things never do.

"We haven't been able to find her. Agnes Gooch, or whatever her name is, has disappeared from the face of the earth. I even went to that horrid provincial town where she lives looking for her myself. Her husband hadn't seen her since she mailed the manuscript to her agent. After seeing Harold Gooch, or whatever his name is, I can't say I blame her.

"R.T. has been frantic. The first two books are selling very well and he wants another. The Mistress of Windraven is selling even better than the first one—in spite of that wretched cover.

"You haven't seen it? My God, I thought everyone in the world had seen it. I don't know what possessed that mad artist to paint it. I don't know what possessed me to accept it.

"It's too horrible to even think about. It's just the same as all the gothic covers except there's no girl in the foreground. There's just the house. And in the house all the windows are lit. All the windows are lit except one!

"Please don't call me at the office again, darling, until R.T. gets over his little snit. Cocktails tomorrow? See you then, darling. Bye, bye."

The Detweiler Boy

The room had been cleaned with pine oil disinfectant and smelled like a public toilet. Harry Spinner was on the floor behind the bed, scrunched down between it and the wall. The almost colorless chenille bedspread had been pulled askew exposing part of the clean, but dingy, sheet. All I could see of Harry was one leg poking over the edge of the bed. He wasn't wearing a shoe, only a faded brown and tan argyle sock with a hole in it. The sock, long bereft of any elasticity, was crumpled around his thin rusty ankle.

I closed the door quietly behind me and walked around the end of the bed so I could see all of him. He was huddled on his back with his elbows propped up by the wall and the bed. His throat had been cut. The blood hadn't spread very far. Most of it had been soaked up by the threadbare carpet under the bed. I looked around the grubby little room but didn't find anything. There were no signs of a struggle, no signs of forced entry—but then, my BankAmericard hadn't left any signs either. The window was open, letting in the muffled roar of traffic on the Boulevard. I stuck my head out and looked, but it was three stories straight down to the neon-lit marquee of the movie house.

It had been nearly two hours since Harry called me. "Bertram, my boy, I've run across something very peculiar. I don't really know what to make of it."

I had put away the report I was writing on Lucas McGowan's hyperactive wife. (She had a definite predilection for gas-pump jockeys, car-wash boys, and parking-lot attendants. I guess it had something to do with the Age of the Automobile.) I propped my feet on my desk and leaned back until the old swivel chair groaned a protest.

"What did you find this time, Harry? A nest of international spies or an invasion from Mars?" I guess Harry Spinner wasn't much use to anyone, not even himself, but I liked him. He'd helped me in a couple of cases, nosing around in places only the Harry Spinners of the world can nose around in unnoticed. I was beginning to get the idea he was trying to play Doctor Watson to my Sherlock Holmes.

"Don't tease me, Bertram. There's a boy here in the hotel. I saw something I don't think he wanted me to see. It's extremely odd."

Harry was also the only person in the world, except my mother, who called me Bertram. "What did you see?"

"I'd rather not talk about it over the phone. Can you come over?"

Harry saw too many old private-eye movies on the late show. "It'll be a while. I've got a client coming in in a few minutes to pick up the poop on his wandering wife."

"Bertram, you shouldn't waste your time and talent on divorce cases."

"It pays the bills, Harry. Besides, there aren't enough Maltese falcons to go around."

By the time I filled Lucas McGowan in on all the details (I got the impression he was less concerned with his wife's infidelity than with her taste; that it wouldn't have been so bad if she'd been shacking up with movie stars or international playboys), collected my fee, and grabbed a Thursday special at Colonel Sanders, almost two hours had passed. Harry hadn't answered my knock, and so I let myself in with a credit card.

Birdie Pawlowicz was a fat, slovenly old broad somewhere between forty and two hundred. She was blind in her right eye and wore a black felt patch over it. She claimed she had lost the eye in a fight with a Creole whore over a riverboat gambler. I believed her. She ran the Brewster Hotel the way Florence Nightingale must have run that stinking army hospital in the Crimea. Her tenants were the losers habitating that rotting section of the Boulevard east of the Hollywood Freeway. She bossed them, cursed them, loved them, and took care of them. (Once, a couple of years ago, a young black buck thought an old fat lady with one eye would be easy pickings. The cops found him three days later, two blocks away, under some rubbish in an alley where he'd hidden. He had a broken arm, two cracked ribs, a busted nose, a few missing teeth, and was stone-dead from internal hemorrhaging.)

The Brewster ran heavily in the red, but Birdie didn't mind. She had quite a bit of property in Westwood which ran very, very heavily in the black. She gave me an obscene leer as I approached the desk, but her good eye twinkled.

"Hello, lover!" she brayed in a voice like a cracked boiler, "I've lowered my price to a quarter. Are you interested?" She saw my face and her expression shifted from lewd to wary. "What's wrong, Bert?"

"Harry Spinner. You'd better get the cops, Birdie. Somebody

killed him."

She looked at me, not saying anything, her face slowly collapsing into an infinitely weary resignation. Then she turned and telephoned the police.

Because it was just Harry Spinner at the Brewster Hotel on the wrong end of Hollywood Boulevard, the cops took over half an hour to get there. While we waited I told Birdie everything I knew, about the phone call and what I'd found.

"He must have been talking about the Detweiler boy," she said, frowning. "Harry's been kinda friendly with him, felt sorry for him, I guess."

"What's his room? I'd like to talk to him."

"He checked out."

"When?"

"Just before you came down."

"Damn!"

She bit her lip. "I don't think the Detweiler boy killed him."

"Why?"

"I just don't think he could. He's such a gentle boy."

"Oh, Birdie," I groaned, "you know there's no such thing as a killer type. Almost anyone will kill with a good enough reason."

"I know," she sighed, "but I still can't believe it." She tapped her scarlet fingernails on the dulled Formica desk top. "How long had Harry been dead?"

He had phoned me about ten after five. I had found the body at seven. "A while," I said. "The blood was mostly dry."

"Before six-thirty?"

"Probably."

She sighed again, but this time with relief. "The Detweiler boy was down here with me until six thirty. He'd been here since about four fifteen. We were playing gin. He was having one of his spells and wanted company."

"What kind of spell? Tell me about him, Birdie."

"But he couldn't have killed Harry," she protested.

"Okay," I said, but I wasn't entirely convinced. Why would anyone deliberately and brutally murder inoffensive, invisible Harry Spinner right after he told me he had discovered something "peculiar" about the Detweiler boy? Except the Detweiler boy?

"Tell me anyway. If he and Harry were friendly, he might know something. Why do you keep calling him a boy; how old is he?"

She nodded and leaned her bulk on the registration desk. "Early twenties, twenty-two, twenty-three, maybe. Not very tall, about five five or six. Slim, dark curly hair, a real good-looking boy. Looks like a movie star except for his back."

"His back?"

"He has a hump. He's a hunchback."

That stopped me for a minute, but I'm not sure why. I must've had a mental picture of Charles Laughton riding those bells or Igor stealing that brain from the laboratory. "He's good-looking and he's a hunchback?"

"Sure." She raised her eyebrows. The one over the patch didn't go up as high as the other. "If you see him from the front, you can't even tell."

"What's his first name?"

"Andrew."

"How long has he been living here?"

She consulted a file card. "He checked in last Friday night. The 22nd. Six days."

"What's this spell he was having?"

"I don't know for sure. It was the second one he'd had. He would get pale and nervous. I think he was in a lot of pain. It would get worse and worse all day; then he'd be fine, all rosy and healthy-looking."

"Sounds to me like he was hurtin' for a fix."

"I thought so at first, but I changed my mind. I've seen enough of that and it wasn't the same. Take my word. He was real bad this evening. He came down about four fifteen, like I said. He didn't complain, but I could tell he was wantin' company to take his mind off it. We played gin until six thirty. Then he went back upstairs. About twenty minutes later he came down with his old suitcase and checked out. He looked fine, all over his spell."

"Did he have a doctor?"

"I'm pretty sure he didn't. I asked him about it. He said there was nothing to worry about, it would pass. And it did."

"Did he say why he was leaving or where he was going?"

"No, just said he was restless and wanted to be movin' on. Sure hated to see him leave. A real nice kid."

When the cops finally got there, I told them all I knew—except I didn't mention the Detweiler boy. I hung around until I found out that Harry almost certainly wasn't killed after six thirty. They set the time somewhere between five ten, when he called me, and six. It looked like Andrew Detweiler was innocent, but what "peculiar" thing had Harry noticed about him, and why had he moved out right after Harry was killed? Birdie let me take a look at his room, but I didn't find a thing, not even an abandoned paperclip.

Friday morning I sat at my desk trying to put the pieces together. Trouble was, I only had two pieces and **they** didn't fit. The sun was coming in off the Boulevard, shining through the window, projecting the chipping letters painted on the glass against the wall in front of me. BERT MALLORY Confidential Investigations. I got up and looked out. This section of the Boulevard wasn't rotting yet, but it wouldn't be long.

There's one sure gauge for judging a part of town: the movie theaters. It never fails. For instance, a new picture hadn't opened in

The Detweiler Boy

downtown L.A. in a long, long time. The action ten years ago was on the Boulevard. Now it's in Westwood. The grand old Pantages, east of Vine and too near the freeway, used to be the site of the most glittering premieres. They even had the Oscar ceremonies there for a while. Now it shows exploitation and double-feature horror films. Only Graumann's Chinese and the once Paramount, once Loew's, now Downtown Cinema (or something) at the west end got good openings. The Nu-View, across the street and down, was showing an X-rated double feature. It was too depressing. So I closed the blind.

Miss Tremaine looked up from her typing at the rattle and frowned. Her desk was out in the small reception area, but I had arranged both desks so we could see each other and talk in normal voices when the door was open. It stayed open most of the time except when I had a client who felt secretaries shouldn't know his troubles. She had been transcribing the Lucas McGowan report for half an hour, **humphing** and **tsk-tsking** at thirty-second intervals. She was having a marvelous time. Miss Tremaine was about forty-five, looked like a constipated librarian, and was the best secretary I'd ever had. She'd been with me seven years. I'd tried a few young and sexy ones, but it hadn't worked out. Either they wouldn't play at all, or they wanted to play all the time. Both kinds were a pain in the ass to face first thing in the morning, every morning.

"Miss Tremaine, will you get Gus Verdugo on the phone, please?"

"Yes, Mr. Mallory." She dialed the phone nimbly, sitting as if she were wearing a back brace.

Gus Verdugo worked in R&I. I had done him a favor once, and he insisted on returning it tenfold. I gave him everything I had on Andrew Detweiler and asked him if he'd mind running it through the computer. He wouldn't mind. He called back in fifteen minutes. The computer had never heard of Andrew Detweiler and had only seven hunchbacks, none of them fitting Detweiler's description.

I was sitting there, wondering how in hell I would find him, when the phone rang again. Miss Tremaine stopped typing and lifted the receiver without breaking rhythm. "Mr. Mallory's office," she said crisply, really letting the caller know he'd hooked onto an efficient organization. She put her hand over the mouthpiece and looked at me. "It's for you—an obscene phone call." She didn't bat an eyelash or twitch a muscle.

"Thanks," I said and winked at her. She dropped the receiver back on the cradle from a height of three inches and went back to typing. Grinning, I picked up my phone. "Hello, Janice," I said.

"Just a minute till my ear stops ringing," the husky voice tickled my ear.

"What are you doing up this early?" I asked. Janice Fenwick was an exotic dancer at a club on the Strip nights and was working on her master's in oceanography at UCLA in the afternoons. In the year I'd known her I'd seldom seen her stick her nose into the sunlight before eleven.

"I had to catch you before you started following that tiresome woman with the car."

"I've finished that. She's picked up her last parking-lot attendant—at least with this husband." I chuckled.

"I'm glad to hear it."

"What's up?"

"I haven't had an indecent proposition from you in days. So I thought I'd make one of my own."

"I'm all ears."

"We're doing some diving off Catalina tomorrow. Want to come along?"

"Not much we can do in a wetsuit."

"The wetsuit comes off about four; then we'll have Saturday night and all of Sunday."

"Best indecent propostion I've had all week."

Miss Tremaine **humphed**. It might have been over something in the report, but I don't think it was.

I picked up Janice at her apartment in Westwood early Saturday morning. She was waiting for me and came striding out to the car all legs and healthy golden flesh. She was wearing white shorts, sneakers, and that damned Dallas Cowboys jersey. It was authentic. The name and number on it were quite well-known—even to non-football fans. She wouldn't tell me how she got it, just smirked and looked smug. She tossed her suitcase in the back seat and slid up against me. She smelled like sunshine.

We flew over and spent most of the day **glubbing** around in the Pacific with a bunch of kids fifteen years younger than I and five years younger than Janice. I'd been on these jaunts with Janice before and enjoyed them so much I'd bought my own wetsuit. But I didn't enjoy it nearly as much as I did Saturday night and all of Sunday.

I got back to my apartment on Beachwood fairly late Sunday night and barely had time to get something to eat at the Mexican restaurant around the corner on Melrose. They have marvelous carne asada. I live right across the street from Paramount, right across from the door people go in to see them tape **The Odd Couple**. Every Friday night when I see them lining up out there, I think I might go someday, but I never seem to get around to it. (You might think I'd see a few movie stars living where I do, but I haven't. I did see Seymour occasionally when he worked at Channel 9, before he went to work for Gene Autry at Channel 5.)

I was so pleasantly pooped I completely forgot about Andrew Detweiler. Until Monday morning when I was sitting at my desk reading the **Times**.

It was a small story on page three, not very exciting or newsworthy. Last night a man named Maurice Milian, age 51, had fallen through the plate-glass doors leading onto the terrace of the high rise where he lived. He had been discovered about midnight when the people living below him had noticed dried blood on **their** terrace. The only thing to connect the deaths of Harry Spinner and Maurice Milian was a lot of blood flowing around. If Milian had been murdered, there **might** be a link, however tenuous. But Milian's death was accidental—a dumb, stupid accident. It niggled around in my brain for an hour before I gave in. There was only one way to get it out of my head.

"Miss Tremaine, I'll be back in an hour or so. If any slinky blondes come in wanting me to find their kid sisters, tell 'em to wait."

She **humphed** again and ignored me.

The Almsbury was half a dozen blocks away on Yucca. So I walked. It was a rectangular monolith about eight stories tall, not real new, not too old, but expensive-looking. The small terraces protruded in neat, orderly rows. The long, narrow grounds were immaculate with a lot of succulents that looked like they might have been imported from Mars. There were also the inevitable palm trees and clumps of bird of paradise. A small, discreet, polished placard dangled in a wrought-iron frame proclaiming, ever so softly, NO VACANCY.

Two willowy young men gave me appraising glances in the carpeted lobby as they exited into the sunlight like exotic jungle birds. It's one of those, I thought. My suspicions were confirmed when I looked over the tenant directory. All the names seemed to be male, but none of them was Andrew Detweiler.

Maurice Milian was still listed as 407. I took the elevator to four and rang the bell of 409. The bell played a few notes of Bach, or maybe Vivaldi or Telemann. All those old Baroques sound alike to me. The vision of loveliness who opened the door was about forty, almost as slim as Twiggy, but as tall as I. He wore a flowered silk shirt open to the waist, exposing his bony hairless chest, and tight white pants that might as well have been made of Saran Wrap. He didn't say anything, just let his eyebrows rise inquiringly as his eyes flicked down, then up.

"Good morning," I said and showed him my ID. He blanched. His eyes became marbles brimming with terror. He was about to panic, tensing to slam the door. I smiled my friendly, disarming smile and went on as if I hadn't noticed. "I'm inquiring about a man named Andrew Detweiler." The terror trickled from his eyes, and I could see his thin chest throbbing. He gave me a blank look that meant he'd never heard the name.

"He's about twenty-two," I continued, "dark, curly hair, very good-looking."

He grinned wryly, calming down, trying to cover his panic. "Aren't they all?" he said.

"Detweiler is a hunchback."

His smile contracted suddenly. His eyebrows shot up. "Oh," he said. "Him."

Bingo!

Mallory, you've led a clean, wholesome life and it's paying off.

"Does he live in the building?" I swallowed to get my heart back in place and blinked a couple of times to clear away the skyrockets.

"No. He was . . . visiting."

"May I come in and talk to you about him?"

He was holding the door three quarters shut, and so I couldn't see anything in the room but an expensive-looking color TV. He glanced over his shoulder nervously at something behind him. The inner ends of his eyebrows drooped in a frown. He looked back at me and started to say something, then, with a small defiance, shrugged his eyebrows. "Sure, but there's not much I can tell you."

He pushed the door all the way open and stepped back. It was a good-sized living room come to life from the pages of a decorator magazine. A kitchen behind a half wall was on my right. A hallway led somewhere on my left. Directly in front of me were double sliding glass doors leading to the terrace. On the terrace was a bronzed hunk of beef stretched out nude trying to get bronzer. The hunk opened his eyes and looked at me. He apparently decided I wasn't competition and closed them again. Tall and lanky indicated one of two identical orange-and-brown-striped couches facing each other across a football-field-size marble and glass cocktail table. He sat on the other one, took a cigarette from an alabaster box and lit it with an alabaster lighter. As an afterthought, he offered me one.

"Who was Detweiler visiting?" I asked as I lit my cigarette. The lighter felt cool and expensive in my hand.

"Maurice—next door," he inclined his head slightly toward 407.

"Isn't he the one who was killed in an accident last night?"

He blew a stream of smoke from pursed lips and tapped his cigarette on an alabaster ashtray. "Yes," he said.

"How long had Maurice and Detweiler known each other?"

"Not long."

"How long?"

He snuffed his cigarette out on pure-white alabaster and sat so prim and pristine I would have bet his feces came out wrapped in cellophane. He shrugged his eyebrows again. "Maurice picked him up somewhere the other night."

"Which night?"

He thought a moment. "Thursday, I think. Yes, Thursday."

"Was Detweiler a hustler?"

He crossed his legs like a Forties pin-up and dangled his Roman sandal. His lips twitched scornfully. "If he was, he would've starved. He was de-**formed**!"

"Maurice didn't seem to mind." He sniffed and lit another cigarette. "When did Detweiler leave?"

He shrugged. "I saw him yesterday afternoon. I was out last night . . . until quite late."

The Detweiler Boy

"How did they get along? Did they quarrel or fight?"

"I have no idea. I only saw them in the hall a couple of times. Maurice and I were . . . not close." He stood, fidgety. "There's really not anything I can tell you. Why don't you ask David and Murray. They and Maurice are . . . were thick as thieves."

"David and Murray?"

"Across the hall. 408."

I stood up. "I'll do that. Thank you very much." I looked at the plate-glass doors. I guess it would be pretty easy to walk through one of them if you thought it was open. "Are all the apartments alike? Those terrace doors?"

He nodded. "Ticky-tacky."

"Thanks again."

"Don't mention it." He opened the door for me and then closed it behind me. I sighed and walked across to 408. I rang the bell. It didn't play anything, just went **bing-bong**.

David (or Murray) was about twenty-five, red-headed, and freckled. He had a slim, muscular body which was also freckled. I could tell because he was wearing only a pair of jeans, cut off very short, and split up the sides to the waistband. He was barefooted and had a smudge of green paint on his nose. He had an open, friendly face and gave me a neutral smile-for-a-stranger. "Yes?" he asked.

I showed him my ID. Instead of going pale he only looked interested. "I was told by the man in 409 you might be able to tell me something about Andrew Detweiler."

"Andy?" He frowned slightly. "Come on in. I'm David Fowler." He held out his hand.

I shook it. "Bert Mallory." The apartment couldn't have been more different from the one across the hall. It was comfortable and cluttered, and dominated by a drafting table surrounded by jars of brushes and boxes of paint tubes. Architecturally, however, it was almost identical. The terrace was covered with potted plants rather than naked muscles. David Fowler sat on the stool at the drafting table and began cleaning brushes. When he sat, the split in his shorts opened and exposed half his butt, which was also freckled. But I got the impression he wasn't exhibiting himself; he was just completely indifferent.

"What do you want to know about Andy?"

"Everything."

He laughed. "That lets me out. Sit down. Move the stuff."

I cleared a space on the couch and sat. "How did Detweiler and Maurice get along?"

He gave me a knowing look. "Fine. As far as I know. Maurice liked to pick up stray puppies. Andy was a stray puppy."

"Was Detweiler a hustler?"

He laughed again. "No. I doubt if he knew what the word means."

"Was he gay?"

"No."

"How do you know?"

He grinned. "Haven't you heard? We can spot each other a mile away. Would you like some coffee?"

"Yes, I would. Thank you."

He went to the half wall separating the kitchen and poured two cups from a pot that looked like it was kept hot and full all the time. "It's hard to describe Andy. There was something very little-boyish about him. A real innocent. Delighted with everything new. It's sad about his back. Real sad." He handed me the cup and returned to the stool. "There was something very secretive about him. Not about his feelings; he was very open about things like that."

"Did he and Maurice have sex together?"

"No. I told you it was a stray puppy relationship. I wish Murray were here. He's much better with words than I am. I'm visually oriented."

"Where is he?"

"At work. He's a lawyer."

"Do you think Detweiler could have killed Maurice?"

"No."

"Why?"

"He was here with us all evening. We had dinner and played Scrabble. I think he was real sick, but he tried to pretend he wasn't. Even if he hadn't been here I would not think so."

"When was the last time you saw him?"

"He left about half an hour before they found Maurice. I imagine he went over there, saw Maurice dead, and decided to disappear. Can't say as I blame him. The police might've gotten some funny ideas. We didn't mention him."

"Why not?"

"There was no point in getting him involved. It was just an accident."

"He couldn't have killed Maurice after he left here?"

"No. They said he'd been dead over an hour. What did Desmond tell you?"

"Desmond?"

"Across the hall. The one who looks like he smells something bad."

"How did you know I talked to him and not the side of beef?"

He laughed and almost dropped his coffee cup. "I don't think Roy **can** talk."

"He didn't know nothin' about nothin'." I found myself laughing also. I got up and walked to the glass doors. I slid them open and then shut again. "Did you ever think one of these was open when it was really shut?"

"No. But I've heard of it happening."

I sighed. "So have I." I turned and looked at what he was working on at the drafting table. It was a small painting of a boy and girl, she in a soft white dress, and he in jeans and tee shirt. They looked about fifteen.

The Detweiler Boy

They were embracing, about to kiss. It was quite obviously the first time for both of them. It was good. I told him so.

He grinned with pleasure. "Thanks. It's for a paperback cover."

"Whose idea was it that Detweiler have dinner and spend the evening with you?"

He thought for a moment. "Maurice." He looked up at me and grinned. "Do you know stamps?"

It took me a second to realize what he meant. "You mean stamp collecting? Not much."

"Maurice was a philatelist. He specialized in postwar Germany—locals and zones, things like that. He'd gotten a kilo of buildings and wanted to sort them undisturbed."

I shook my head. "You've lost me. A kilo of buildings?"

He laughed. "It's a set of twenty-eight stamps issued in the American Zone in 1948 showing famous German buildings. Conditions in Germany were still pretty chaotic at the time, and the stamps were printed under fairly makeshift circumstances. Consequently, there's an enormous variety of different perforations, watermarks, and engravings. Hundreds as a matter of fact. Maurice could spend hours and hours poring over them."

"Are they valuable?"

"No. Very common. Some of the varieties are hard to find, but they're not valuable." He gave me a knowing look. "Nothing was missing from Maurice's apartment."

I shrugged. "It had occurred to me to wonder where Detweiler got his money."

"I don't know. The subject never came up." He wasn't being defensive.

"You liked him, didn't you?"

There was a weary sadness in his eyes. "Yes," he said.

That afternoon I picked up Birdie Pawlowicz at the Brewster Hotel and took her to Harry Spinner's funeral. I told her about Maurice Milian and Andrew Detweiler. We talked it around and around. The Detweiler boy obviously couldn't have killed Harry or Milian, but it was stretching coincidence a little bit far.

After the funeral I went to the Los Angeles Public Library and started checking back issues of the **Times**. I'd only made it back three weeks when the library closed. The LA **Times** is **thick**, and unless the death is sensational or the dead prominent, the story might be tucked in anywhere except the classifieds.

Last Tuesday, the 26th, a girl had cut her wrists with a razor blade in North Hollywood.

The day before, Monday, the 25th, a girl had miscarried and hemorrhaged. She had bled to death because she and her boy friend were stoned out of their heads. They lived a block off Western—very near the Brewster—and Detweiler was at the Brewster Monday.

Sunday, the 24th, a wino had been knifed in MacArthur Park.

Saturday, the 23rd, I had three. A knifing in a bar on Pico, a shooting in a rooming house on Irolo, and a rape and knifing in an alley off LaBrea. Only the gunshot victim had bled to death, but there had been a lot of blood in all three.

Friday, the 22nd, the same day Detweiler checked in the Brewster, a two-year-old boy had fallen on an upturned rake in his backyard on Larchemont—only eight or ten blocks from where I lived on Beachwood. And a couple of Chicano kids had had a knife fight behind Hollywood High. One was dead and the other was in jail. Ah, **machismo**!

The list went on and on, all the way back to Thursday, the 7th. On that day was another slashed-wrist suicide near Western and Wilshire.

The next morning, Tuesday, the 3rd, I called Miss Tremaine and told her I'd be late getting in but would check in every couple of hours to find out if the slinky blonde looking for her kid sister had shown up. She **humphed**.

Larchemont is a middle-class neighborhood huddled in between the old wealth around the country club and the blight spreading down Melrose from Western Avenue. It tries to give the impression of suburbia—and does a pretty good job of it—rather than just another nearly downtown shopping center. The area isn't big on apartments or rooming houses, but there are a few. I found the Detweiler boy at the third one I checked. It was a block and a half from where the little kid fell on the rake.

According to the landlord, at the time of the kid's death Detweiler was playing bridge with him and couple of elderly old-maid sisters in number twelve. He hadn't been feeling well and had moved out later that evening—to catch a bus to San Diego, to visit his ailing mother. The landlord had felt sorry for him, so sorry he'd broken a steadfast rule and refunded most of the month's rent Detweiler had paid in advance. After all, he'd only been there three days. So sad about his back. Such a nice, gentle boy—a writer, you know.

No, I didn't know, but it explained how he could move around so much without seeming to work.

I called David Fowler: "Yes, Andy had a portable typewriter, but he hadn't mentioned being a writer."

And Birdie Pawlowicz: "Yeah, he typed a lot in his room."

I found the Detweiler boy again on the 16th and the 19th. He'd moved into a rooming house near Silver Lake Park on the night of the 13th and moved out again on the 19th. The landlady hadn't refunded his money, but she gave him an alibi for the knifing of an old man in the park on the 16th and the suicide of a girl in the same rooming house on the 19th. He'd been in the pink of health when he moved in, sick on the 16th, healthy the 17th, and sick again the 19th.

It was like a rerun. He lived a block away from where a man was mugged, knifed, and robbed in an alley on the 13th—though the details

The Detweiler Boy

of the murder didn't seem to fit the pattern. But he was sick, had an alibi, and moved to Silver Lake.

Rerun it on the 10th: a woman slipped in the bathtub and fell through the glass shower doors, cutting herself to ribbons. Sick, alibi, moved.

It may be because I was always rotten in math, but it wasn't until right then that I figured out Detweiler's timetable. Milian died the 1st, Harry Spinner the 28th, the miscarriage the 25th, the little kid on the 22nd, Silver Lake on the 16th and 19th, etc., etc., etc.

A bloody death occurred in Detweiler's general vicinity every third day.

But I couldn't figure out a pattern for the victims: male, female, little kids, old aunties, married, unmarried, rich, poor, young, old. No pattern of any kind, and there's **always** a pattern. I even checked to see if the names were in alphabetical order.

I got back to my office at six. Miss Tremaine sat primly at her desk, cleared of everything but her purse and a notepad. She reminded me quite a lot of Desmond. "What are you still doing here, Miss Tremaine? You should've left an hour ago." I sat at my desk, leaned back until the swivel chair groaned twice, and propped my feet up.

She picked up the pad. "I wanted to give you your calls."

"Can't they wait? I've been sleuthing all day and I'm bushed."

"No one is paying you to find this Detweiler person, are they?"

"No."

"Your bank statement came today."

"What's that supposed to mean?"

"Nothing. A good secretary keeps her employer informed. I was informing you."

"Okay. Who called?"

She consulted the pad, but I'd bet my last gumshoe she knew every word on it by heart. "A Mrs. Carmichael called. Her French poodle has been kidnapped. She wants you to find her."

"Ye Gods! Why doesn't she go to the police?"

"Because she's positive her ex-husband is the kidnapper. She doesn't want to get him in any trouble; she just wants Gwendolyn back."

"Gwendolyn?"

"Gwendolyn. A Mrs. Bushyager came by. She wants you to find her little sister."

I sat up so fast I almost fell out of the chair. I gave her a long, hard stare, but her neutral expression didn't flicker. "You're kidding." Her eyebrows rose a millimeter. "Was she a slinky blonde?"

"No. She was a dumpy brunette."

I settled back in the chair, trying not to laugh. "Why does Mrs. Bushyager want me to find her little sister?" I sputtered.

"Because Mrs. Bushyager thinks she's shacked up somewhere with **Mr.** Bushyager. She'd like you to call her tonight."

"Tomorrow. I've got a date with Janice tonight." She reached in her desk drawer and pulled out my bank statement. She dropped it on the desk with a papery plop. "Don't worry," I assured her, "I won't spend much money. Just a little spaghetti and wine tonight and ham and eggs in the morning." She **humphed**. My point. "Anything else?"

"A Mr. Bloomfeld called. He wants you to get the goods on Mrs. Bloomfeld so he can sue for divorce."

I sighed. Miss Tremaine closed the pad. "Okay. No to Mrs. Carmichael and make appointments for Bushyager and Bloomfeld." She lowered her eyelids at me. I spread my hands. "Would Sam Spade go looking for a French poodle named Gwendolyn?"

"He might if he had your bank statement. Mr. Bloomfeld will be in at two, Mrs. Bushyager at three."

"Miss Tremaine, you'd make somebody a wonderful mother." She didn't even **humph**; she just picked up her purse and stalked out. I swiveled the chair around and looked at the calendar. Tomorrow was the 4th.

Somebody would die tomorrow and Andrew Detweiler would be close by.

I scooted up in bed and leaned against the headboard. Janice snorted into the pillow and opened one eye, pinning me with it. "I didn't mean to wake you," I said.

"What's the matter," she muttered, "too much spaghetti?"

"No. Too much Andrew Detweiler."

She scooted up beside me, keeping the sheet over her breasts, and turned on the light. She rummaged around on the nightstand for a cigarette. "Who wants to divorce him?"

"That's mean, Janice," I groaned.

"You want a cigarette?"

"Yeah."

She put two cigarettes in her mouth and lit them both. She handed me one. "You don't look a bit like Paul Henreid," I said.

She grinned. "That's funny. You look like Bette Davis. Who's Andrew Detweiler?"

So I told her.

"It's elementary, my dear Sherlock," she said. "Andrew Detweiler is a vampire." I frowned at her. "Of course, he's a **clever** vampire. Vampires are usually stupid. They always give themselves away by leaving those two little teeth marks on people's jugulars."

"Darling, even vampires have to be at the scene of the crime."

"He always has an alibi, huh?"

I got out of bed and headed for the bathroom. "That's suspicious in itself."

When I came out she said, "Why?"

"Innocent people usually don't have alibis, especially not one every three days."

The Detweiler Boy

"Which is probably why innocent people get put in jail so often."
I chuckled and sat on the edge of the bed. "You may be right."
"Bert, do that again."
I looked at her over my shoulder. "Do what?"
"Go to the bathroom."
"I don't think I can. My bladder holds only so much."
"I don't mean that. Walk over to the bathroom door."

I gave her a suspicious frown, got up, and walked over to the bathroom door. I turned around, crossed my arms, and leaned against the door frame. "Well?"

She grinned. "You've got a cute rear end. Almost as cute as Burt Reynolds'. Maybe he's twins."

"What?" I practically screamed.

"Maybe Andrew Detweiler is twins. One of them commits the murders and the other establishes the alibis."

"Twin vampires?"

She frowned. "That is a bit much, isn't it? Had they discovered blood groups in Bram Stoker's day?"

I got back in bed and pulled the sheet up to my waist, leaning beside her against the headboard. "I haven't the foggiest idea."

"That's another way vampires are stupid. They never check the victim's blood group. The wrong blood group can kill you."

"Vampires don't exactly get transfusions."

"It all amounts to the same thing, doesn't it?" I shrugged. "Oh, well," she sighed, "vampires are stupid." She reached over and plucked at the hair on my chest. "I haven't had an indecent proposition in hours," she said, grinning.

So I made one.

Wednesday morning I made a dozen phone calls. Of the nine victims I knew about, I was able to find the information on six.

All six had the same blood group.

I lit a cigarette and leaned back in the swivel chair. The whole thing was spinning around in my head. I'd found a pattern for the victims, but I didn't know if it was **the** pattern. It just didn't make sense. Maybe Detweiler **was** a vampire.

"Mallory," I said out loud, "you're cracking up."

Miss Tremaine glanced up. "If I were you, I'd listen to you," she said poker-faced.

The next morning I staggered out of bed at six a.m. I took a cold shower, shaved, dressed, and put Murine in my eyes. They still felt like I'd washed them in rubber cement. Mrs. Bloomfeld had kept me up until two the night before, doing all the night spots in Santa Monica with some dude I hadn't identified yet. When they checked into a motel, I went home and went to bed.

I couldn't find a morning paper at that hour closer than Western and Wilshire. The story was on page seven. Fortunately they found the body in time for the early edition. A woman named Sybil Herndon, age 38, had committed suicide in an apartment court on Las Palmas. (Detweiler hadn't gone very far. The address was just around the corner from the Almsbury.) She had cut her wrists on a piece of broken mirror. She had been discovered about eleven thirty when the manager went over to ask her to turn down the volume on her television set.

It was too early to drop around, and so I ate breakfast, hoping this was one of the times Detweiler stuck around for more than three days. Not for a minute did I doubt he would be living at the apartment court on Las Palmas, or not far away.

The owner-manager of the court was one of those creatures peculiar to Hollywood. She must have been a starlet in the Twenties or Thirties, but success had eluded her. So she had tried to freeze herself in time. She still expected, at any moment, a call from The Studio. But her flesh hadn't cooperated. Her hair was the color of tarnished copper, and the fire-engine-red lipstick was painted far past her thin lips. Her watery eyes peered at me through a Lone Ranger mask of Maybelline on a plaster-white face. Her dress had obviously been copied from the wardrobe of Norma Shearer.

"Yes?" She had a breathy voice. Her eyes quickly traveled the length of my body. That happens often enough to keep me feeling good, but this time it gave me a queasy sensation, like I was being measured for a mummy case. I showed her my ID, and asked if I could speak to her about one of the tenants.

"Of course. Come on in. I'm Lorraine Nesbitt." Was there a flicker of disappointment that I hadn't recognized the name? She stepped back holding the door for me. I could tell that detectives, private or otherwise, asking about her tenants wasn't a new thing. I walked into the doilied room, and she looked at me from a hundred directions. The faded photographs covered every level surface and clung to the walls like leeches. She had been quite a dish—forty years ago. She saw me looking at the photos and smiled. The make-up around her mouth cracked.

"Which one do you want to ask me about?" The smile vanished and the cracks closed.

"Andrew Detweiler." She looked blank. "Young, good-looking, with a hunchback."

The cracks opened. "Oh, yes. He's only been here a few days. The name had slipped my mind."

"He's still here?"

"Oh, yes." She sighed. "It's so unfair for such a beautiful young man to have a physical impairment."

"What can you tell me about him?"

"Not much. He's only been here since Sunday night. He's very handsome, like an angel, a dark angel. But it wasn't his handsomeness that attracted me." She smiled. "I've seen many handsome men in my

The Detweiler Boy 155

day, you know. It's difficult to verbalize. He has such an incredible innocence. A lost, doomed look that Byron must have had. A vulnerability that makes you want to shield and protect him. I don't know for sure what it is, but it struck a chord in my soul. Soul," she mused. "Maybe that's it. He wears his soul on his face." She nodded, as if to herself. "A dangerous thing to do." She looked back up at me. "If that quality, whatever it is, would photograph, he would become a star overnight, whether he could act or not. Except—of course—for his infirmity."

Lorraine Nesbitt, I decided, was as nutty as a fruitcake.

Someone entered the room. He stood leaning against the door frame, looking at me with sleepy eyes. He was about twenty-five, wearing tight chinos without underwear and a tee shirt. His hair was tousled and cut unfashionably short. He had a good looking Kansas face. The haircut made me think he was new in town, but the eyes said he wasn't. I guess the old broad liked his hair that way.

She simpered. "Oh, Johnny! Come on in. This detective was asking about Andrew Detweiler in number seven." She turned back to me. "This is my protege, Johnny Peacock—a very talented young man. I'm arranging for a screen test as soon as Mr. Goldwyn returns my calls." She lowered her eyelids demurely. "I was a Goldwyn Girl, you know."

Funny, I thought Goldwyn was dead. Maybe he wasn't.

Johnny took the news of his impending stardom with total unconcern. He moved to the couch and sat down, yawning. "Detweiler? Don't think I ever laid eyes on the man. What'd he do?"

"Nothing. Just routine." Obviously he thought I was a police detective. No point in changing his mind. "Where was he last night when the Herndon woman died?"

"In his room, I think. I heard his typewriter. He wasn't feeling well," Lorraine Nesbitt said. Then she sucked air through her teeth and clamped her fingers to her scarlet lips. "Do you think he had something to do with **that**?"

Detweiler had broken his pattern. He didn't have an alibi. I couldn't believe it.

"Oh, Lorraine," Johnny grumbled.

I turned to him. "Do you know where Detweiler was?"

He shrugged. "No idea."

"Then why are you so sure he had nothing to do with it?"

"She committed suicide."

"How do you know for sure?"

"The door was bolted from the inside. They had to break it down to get in."

"What about the window? Was it locked too?"

"No. The window was open. But it has bars on it. No way anybody could get in."

"When I couldn't get her to answer my knock last night, I went around to the window and looked in. She was lying there with blood all over." She began to sniffle. Johnny got up and put his arms around her. He looked at me, grinned, and shrugged.

"Do you have a vacancy?" I asked, getting a whiz-bang idea.

"Yes," she said, the sniffles disappearing instantly. "I have two. Actually three but I can't rent Miss Herndon's room for a few days—until someone claims her things."

"I'd like to rent the one closest to number seven," I said.

I wasn't lucky enough to get number six or eight, but I did get five. Lorraine Nesbitt's nameless, dingy apartment court was a fleabag. Number five was one room with a closet, a tiny kitchen, and a tiny bath—identical with the other nine units she assured me. With a good deal of tugging and grunting the couch turned into a lumpy bed. The refrigerator looked as if someone had spilled a bottle of Br'er Rabbit back in 1938 and hadn't cleaned it up yet. The stove looked like a lube rack. Well, I sighed, it was only for three days. I had to pay a month's rent in advance anyway, but I put it down as a bribe to keep Lorraine's and Johnny's mouths shut about my being a detective.

I moved in enough clothes for three days, some sheets and pillows, took another look at the kitchen and decided to eat out. I took a jug of Lysol to the bathroom and crossed my fingers. Miss Tremaine brought up the bank statement and **humphed** a few times.

Number five had one door and four windows—identical to the other nine Lorraine assured me. The door had a heavy-duty bolt that couldn't be fastened or unfastened from the outside. The window beside the door didn't open at all and wasn't intended to. The bathroom and kitchen windows cranked out and were tall and skinny, about twenty-four by six. The other living room window, opposite the door, slid upward. The iron bars bolted to the frame were so rusted I doubted it they could be removed without ripping out the whole window. It appeared Andrew Detweiler had another perfect alibi after all—along with the rest of the world.

I stood outside number seven suddenly feeling like a teen-ager about to pick up his first date. I could hear Detweiler's typewriter **tickety-ticking** away inside. Okay, Mallory, this is what you've been breaking your neck on for a week.

I knocked on the door.

I heard the typewriter stop ticking and the scrape of a chair being scooted back. I didn't hear anything else for fifteen or twenty seconds, and I wondered what he was doing. Then the bolt was drawn and the door opened.

He was buttoning his shirt. That must have been the delay; he wouldn't want anyone to see him with his shirt off. Everything I'd been told about him was true. He wasn't very tall; the top of his head came to my nose. He was dark, though not as dark as I'd expected. I couldn't place his ancestry. It certainly wasn't Latin-American and I didn't think it was Slavic. His features were soft without the angularity usually found in

The Detweiler Boy   157

the Mediterranean races. His hair wasn't quite black. It wasn't exactly long and it wasn't exactly short. His clothes were non-descript. Everything about him was neutral—except his face. It was just about as Lorraine Nesbitt had described it. If you called central casting and asked for a male angel, you'd get Andrew Detweiler in a blond wig. His body was slim and well-formed—from where I was standing I couldn't see the hump and you'd never know there was one. I had a glimpse of his bare chest as he buttoned the shirt. It wasn't muscular but it was very well made. He was very healthy-looking—pink and flushed with health, though slightly pale as if he didn't get out in the sun much. His dark eyes were astounding. If you blocked out the rest of the face, leaving nothing but the eyes, you'd swear he was no more than four years old. You've seen little kids with those big, guileless, unguarded, inquiring eyes, haven't you?

"Yes?" he asked.

I smiled. "Hello, I'm Bert Mallory. I just moved in to number five. Miss Nesbitt tells me you like to play gin."

"Yes," he said, grinning. "Come on in."

He turned to move out of my way and I saw the hump. I don't know how to describe what I felt. I suddenly had a hurting in my gut. I felt the same unfairness and sadness the others had, the way you would feel about any beautiful thing with one overwhelming flaw.

"I'm not disturbing you, am I? I heard the typewriter." The room was indeed identical to mine, though it looked a hundred per cent more livable. I couldn't put my finger on what he had done to it to make it that way. Maybe it was just the semidarkness. He had the curtains tightly closed and one lamp lit beside the typewriter.

"Yeah, I was working on a story, but I'd rather play gin." He grinned, open and artless. "If I could make money playing gin, I wouldn't write."

"Lots of people make money playing gin."

"Oh, I couldn't. I'm too unlucky."

He certainly had a right to say that, but there was no self-pity, just an observation. Then he looked at me with slightly distressed eyes. "You . . . ah . . . didn't want to play for money, did you?"

"Not at all," I said and his eyes cleared. "What kind of stories do you write?"

"Oh, all kinds." He shrugged. "Fantasy mostly."

"Do you sell them?"

"Most of 'em."

"I don't recall seeing your name anywhere. Miss Nesbitt said it was Andrew Detweiler?"

He nodded. "I use another name. You probably wouldn't know it either. It's not exactly a household word." His eyes said he'd really rather not tell me what it was. He had a slight accent, a sort of soft slowness, not exactly a drawl and not exactly Deep South. He shoved the typewriter over and pulled out a deck of cards.

"Where're you from?" I asked. "I don't place the accent."

He grinned and shuffled the cards. "North Carolina. Back in the Blue Ridge."

We cut and I dealt. "How long have you been in Hollywood?"

"About two months."

"How do you like it?"

He grinned his beguiling grin and picked up my discard. "It's very . . . unusual. Have you lived here long, Mr. Mallory?"

"Bert. All my life. I was born in Inglewood. My mother still lives there."

"It must be . . . unusual . . . to live in the same place all your life."

"You move around a lot?"

"Yeah. Gin."

I laughed. "I thought you were unlucky."

"If we were playing for money, I wouldn't be able to do anything right."

We played gin the rest of the afternoon and talked—talked a lot. Detweiler seemed eager to talk or, at least, eager to have someone to talk with. He never told me anything that would connect him to nine deaths, mostly about where he'd been, things he'd read. He read a lot, just about anything he could get his hands on. I got the impression he hadn't really **lived** life so much as he'd **read** it, that all the things he knew about had never physically affected him. He was like an insulated island. Life flowed around him but never touched him. I wondered if the hump on his back made that much difference, if it made him such a green monkey he'd had to retreat into his insular existence. Practically everyone I had talked to liked him, mixed with varying portions of pity, to be sure, but liking nevertheless. Harry Spinner had liked him, but had discovered something "peculiar" about him. Birdie Pawlowicz, Maurice Milian, David Fowler, Lorraine Nesbitt, they all liked him.

And, God damn it, I liked him too.

At midnight I was still awake, sitting in number five in my jockey shorts with the light out and the door open. I listened to the ticking of the Detweiler boy's typewriter and the muffled roar of Los Angeles. And thought, and thought, and thought. And got nowhere.

Someone walked by the door, quietly and carefully. I leaned my head out. It was Johnny Peacock. He moved down the line of bungalows silent as a shadow. He turned south when he reached the sidewalk. Going to Selma or the Boulevard to turn a trick and make a few extra bucks. Lorraine must keep tight purse strings. Better watch it, kid. If she finds out, you'll be back on the streets again. And you haven't got too many years left where you can make good money by just gettin' it up.

I dropped in at the office for a while Friday morning and checked the first-of-the-month bills. Miss Tremaine had a list of new prospective clients. "Tell everyone I can't get to anything till Monday."

She nodded in disapproval. "Mr. Bloomfeld called."

"Did he get my report?"

"Yes. He was very pleased, but he wants the man's name."

"Tell him I'll get back on it Monday."

"Mrs. Bushyager called. Her sister and Mr. Bushyager are still missing."

"Tell her I'll get on it Monday." She opened her mouth. "If you say anything about my bank account, I'll put Spanish fly in your Ovaltine." She didn't **humph**, she giggled. I wonder how many points **that** is?

That afternoon I played gin with the Detweiler boy. He was genuinely glad to see me, like a friendly puppy. I was beginning to feel like a son of a bitch.

He hadn't mentioned North Carolina except that once the day before, and I was extremely interested in all subjects he wanted to avoid. "What's it like in the Blue Ridge? Coon huntin' and moonshine?"

He grinned and blitzed me. "Yeah, I guess. Most of the things you read about it are pretty nearly true. It's really a different world back in there, with almost no contact with the outside."

"How far in did you live?"

"About as far as you can get without comin' out the other side. Did you know most of the people never heard of television or movies and some of 'em don't even know the name of the President? Most of 'em never been more than thirty miles from the place they were born, never saw an electric light? You wouldn't believe it. But it's more than just **things** that're different. People are different, think different—like a foreign country." He shrugged. "I guess it'll all be gone before too long though. Things keep creepin' closer and closer. Did you know I never went to school?" he said, grinning. "Not a day of my life. I didn't wear shoes till I was ten. You wouldn't believe it." He shook his head, remembering. "Always kinda wished I coulda gone to school," he murmured softly.

"Why did you leave?"

"No reason to stay. When I was eight, my parents were killed in a fire. Our house burned down. I was taken in by a balmy old woman who lived not far away. I had some kin, but they didn't want me." He looked at me, trusting me. "They're pretty superstitious back in there, you know. Thought I was . . . marked. Anyway, the old woman took me in. She was a midwife, but she fancied herself a witch or something. Always making me drink some mess she'd brewed up. She fed me, clothed me, educated me, after a fashion, tried to teach me all her conjures, but I never could take 'em seriously." He grinned sheepishly. "I did chores for her and eventually became a sort of assistant, I guess. I helped her birth babies . . . I mean, deliver babies a couple of times, but that didn't last long. The parents were afraid me bein' around might mark the baby. She taught me to read and I couldn't stop. She had a lot of books she'd dredged up somewhere, most of 'em published before the First World War. I read a complete set of encyclopedias—published in 1911."

I laughed.

His eyes clouded. "Then she . . . died. I was fifteen, so I left. I did odd jobs and kept reading. Then I wrote a story and sent it to a magazine. They bought it; paid me fifty dollars. Thought I was rich, so I wrote another one. Since then I've been traveling around and writing. I've got an agent who takes care of everything, and so all I do is just write."

Detweiler's flush of health was wearing off that afternoon. He wasn't ill, just beginning to feel like the rest of us mortals. And I was feeling my resolve begin to crumble. It was hard to believe this beguiling kid could possibly be involved in a string of bloody deaths. Maybe it was just a series of unbelievable coincidences. Yeah, "unbelievable" was the key word. He **had** to be involved unless the laws of probability had broken down completely. Yet I could swear Detweiler wasn't putting on an act. His guileless innocence was real, damn it, **real**.

Saturday morning, the third day since Miss Herndon died, I had a talk with Lorraine and Johnny. If Detweiler wanted to play cards or something that night, I wanted them to agree and suggest I be a fourth. If he didn't bring it up, I would, but I had a feeling he would want his usual alibi this time.

Detweiler left his room that afternoon for the first time since I'd been there. He went north on Las Palmas, dropped a large manila envelope in the mailbox (the story he'd been working on, I guess), and bought groceries at the supermarket on Highland. Did that mean he wasn't planning to move? I had a sudden pang in my belly. What if he was staying because of his friendship with **me**? I felt more like of a son of a bitch every minute.

Johnny Peacock came by an hour later acting very conspiratorial. Detweiler had suggested a bridge game that night, but Johnny didn't play bridge, and so they settled on Scrabble.

I dropped by number seven. The typewriter had been put away, but the cards and score pad were still on the table. His suitcase was on the floor by the couch. It was riveted cowhide of a vintage I hadn't seen since I was a kid. Though it wore a mellow patina of age, it had been preserved with neat's-foot oil and loving care. I may have been mistaken about his not moving.

Detweiler wasn't feeling well at all. He was pale and drawn and fidgety. His eyelids were heavy and his speech was faintly blurred. I'm sure he was in pain, but he tried to act as if nothing were wrong.

"Are you sure you feel like playing Scrabble tonight?" I asked.

He gave me a cheerful, if slightly strained, smile. "Oh, sure. I'm all right. I'll be fine in the morning."

"Do you think you ought to play?"

"Yeah, it . . . takes my mind off my . . . ah . . . headache. Don't worry about it. I have these spells all the time. They always go away."

"How long have you had them?"

"Since . . . I was a kid." He grinned. "You think it was one of those

The Detweiler Boy

brews the old witch-woman gave me caused it? Maybe I could sue for malpractice."

"Have you seen a doctor? A real one?"

"Once."

"What did he tell you?"

He shrugged. "Oh, nothing much. Take two aspirin, drink lots of liquids, get plenty of rest, that sort of thing." He didn't want to talk about it. "It always goes away."

"What if one time it doesn't?"

He looked at me with an expression I'd never seen before and I knew why Lorraine said he had a lost, doomed look. "Well, we can't live forever, can we? Are you ready to go?"

The game started out like a Marx Brothers routine. Lorraine and Johnny acted like two canaries playing Scrabble with the cat, but Detweiler was so normal and unconcerned they soon settled down. Conversation was tense and ragged at first until Lorraine got off on her "career" and kept us entertained and laughing. She had known a lot of famous people and was a fountain of anecdotes, most of them funny and libelous. Detweiler proved quickly to be the best player, but Johnny, to my surprise, was no slouch. Lorraine played dismally but she didn't seem to mind.

I would have enjoyed the evening thoroughly if I hadn't known someone nearby was dead or dying.

After about two hours, in which Detweiler grew progressively more ill, I excused myself to go to the bathroom. While I was away from the table, I palmed Lorraine's master key.

In another half hour I said I had to call it a night. I had to get up early the next morning. I always spent Sunday with my mother in Inglewood. My mother was touring Yucatan at the time, but that was neither here nor there. I looked at Johnny. He nodded. He was to make sure Detweiler stayed at least another twenty minutes and then follow him when he did leave. If he went anywhere but his apartment, he was to come and let me know, quick.

I let myself into number seven with the master key. The drapes were closed, and so I took a chance and turned on the bathroom light. Detweiler's possessions were meager. Eight shirts, six pairs of pants, and a light jacket hung in the closet. The shirts and jacket had been altered to allow for the hump. Except for that, the closet was bare. The bathroom contained nothing out of the ordinary—just about the same as mine. The kitchen had one plastic plate, one plastic cup, one plastic glass, one plastic bowl, one small folding skillet, one small folding sauce pan, one metal spoon, one metal fork, and a medium-sized kitchen knife. All of it together would barely fill a shoebox.

The suitcase, still beside the couch, hadn't been unpacked—except for the clothes hanging in the closet and the kitchen utensils. There was underwear, socks, an extra pair of shoes, an unopened ream of paper, a bunch of other stuff necessary for writing, and a dozen or so paperbacks. The books were rubber-stamped with the name of a used-book store on Santa Monica Boulevard. They were a mixture: science fiction, mysteries, biographies, philosophy, several by Colin Wilson.

There was also a carbon copy of the story he'd just finished. The return address on the first page was a box number at the Hollywood post office. The title of the story was "Deathsong." I wish I'd had time to read it.

All in all, I didn't find anything. Except for the books and the deck of cards there was nothing of Andrew Detweiler personally in the whole apartment. I hadn't thought it possible for anyone to lead such a turnip existence.

I looked around to make sure I hadn't disturbed anything, turned off the bathroom light, and got in the closet, leaving the door open a crack. It was the only possible place to hide. I sincerely hoped Detweiler wouldn't need anything out of it before I found out what was going on. If he did, the only thing I could do was confront him with what I'd found out. And then what, Mallory, a big guilty confession? With what you've found out he could laugh in your face and have you arrested for illegal entry.

And what about this, Mallory. What if someone died nearby tonight while you were with Detweiler; what if he comes straight to his apartment and goes to bed; what if he wakes up in the morning feeling fine; what if nothing is going on, you son of a bitch?

It was so dark in there with the curtains drawn that I couldn't see a thing. I left the closet and opened them a little on the front window. It didn't let in a lot of light, but it was enough. Maybe Detweiler wouldn't notice. I went back to the closet and waited.

Half an hour later the curtains over the barred open window moved. I had squatted down in the closet and wasn't looking in that direction, but the movement caught my eye. Something hopped in the window and scooted across the floor and went behind the couch. I only got a glimpse of it, but it might have been a cat. It was probably a stray looking for food or hiding from a dog. Okay, cat, you don't bother me and I won't bother you. I kept my eye on the couch, but it didn't show itself again.

Detweiler didn't show for another hour. By that time I was sitting flat on the floor trying to keep my legs from cramping. My position wasn't too graceful if he happened to look in the closet, but it was too late to get up.

He came in quickly and bolted the door behind him. He didn't notice the open curtain. He glanced around, clicking his tongue softly. His eyes caught on something at the end of the couch. He smiled. At the **cat**? He began unfastening his shirt, fumbling at the buttons in his haste. He slipped off the shirt and tossed it on the back of a chair.

There were straps across his chest.

He turned toward the suitcase, his back to me. The hump was

The Detweiler Boy

artificial, made of something like foam rubber. He unhooked the straps, opened the suitcase, and tossed the hump in. He said something, too soft for me to catch, and lay face down on the couch with his feet toward me. The light from the opened curtain fell on him. His back was scarred, little white lines like scratches grouped around a hole.

He had a hole in his back, between his shoulder blades, an unhealed wound big enough to stick your finger in.

Something came around the end of the couch. It wasn't a cat. I thought it was a monkey, and then a frog, but it was neither. It was human. It waddled on all fours like an enormous toad.

Then it stood erect. It was about the size of a cat. It was pink and moist and hairless and naked. Its very human hands and feet and male genitals were too large for its tiny body. Its belly was swollen, turgid and distended like an obscene tick. Its head was flat. Its jaw protruded like an ape's. It too had a scar, a big, white, puckered scar between its shoulder blades, at the top of its jutting backbone.

It reached its too-large hand up and caught hold of Detweiler's belt. It pulled its bloated body up with the nimbleness of a monkey and crawled onto the boy's back. Detweiler was breathing heavily, clasping and unclasping his fingers on the arm of the couch.

The thing crouched on Detweiler's back and placed its lips against the wound.

I felt my throat burning and my stomach turning over, but I watched in petrified fascination.

Detweiler's breathing grew slower and quieter, more relaxed. He lay with his eyes closed and an expression of almost sexual pleasure on his face. The thing's body got smaller and smaller, the skin on its belly growing wrinkled and flaccid. A trickle of blood crawled from the wound, making an erratic line across the Detweiler boy's back. The thing reached out a hand and wiped the drop back with a finger.

It took ten minutes. The thing raised its mouth and crawled over beside the boy's face. It sat on the arm of the couch like a little gnome and smiled. It ran its finger down the side of Detweiler's cheek and pushed his damp hair back out of his eyes. Detweiler's expression was euphoric. He sighed softly and opened his eyes sleepily. After a while he sat up.

He was flushed with health, rosy and clear and shining.

He stood up and went in the bathroom. The light came on and I heard water running. The thing was in the same place, watching him. Detweiler came out of the bathroom and sat back on the couch. The thing climbed onto his back, huddling between his shoulder blades, its hands on his shoulder. Detweiler stood up, the thing hanging onto him, retrieved the shirt, and put it on. He wrapped the straps neatly around the artificial hump and stowed it in the suitcase. He closed the lid and locked it.

I had seen enough, more than enough. I opened the door and

stepped out of the closet.

Detweiler whirled, his eyes bulging. A groan rattled in his throat. He raised his hands as if fending me off. The groan rose in pitch, becoming an hysterical keening. The expression on his face was too horrible to watch. He stepped backward and tripped over the suitcase.

He lost his balance and toppled over. His arms flailed for equilibrium, but never found it. He struck the edge of the table. It caught him square across the hump on his back. He bounced and fell forward on his hands. He stood up agonizingly, like a slow motion movie, arching his spine backward, his face contorted in pain.

There were shrill, staccato shrieks of mindless torment, but they didn't come from Detweiler.

He fell again, forward onto the couch, blacking out from pain. The back of his shirt was churning. The scream continued, hurting my ears. Rips appeared in the shirt and a small misshapen arm poked out briefly. I could only stare, frozen. The shirt was ripped to shreds. Two arms, a head, a torso came through. The whole thing ripped its way out and fell onto the couch beside the boy. Its face was twisted, tortured, and its mouth kept opening and closing with the screams. Its eyes looked uncomprehendingly about. It pulled itself along with its arms, dragging its useless legs, its spine obviously broken. It fell off the couch and flailed about on the floor.

Detweiler moaned and came to. He rose from the couch, still groggy. He saw the thing, and a look of absolute grief appeared on his face.

The thing's eyes focused for a moment on Detweiler. It looked at him, beseeching, held out one hand, pleading. Its screams continued, that one monotonous, hopeless note repeated over and over. It lowered its arm and kept crawling about mindlessly, growing weaker.

Detweiler stepped toward it, ignoring me, tears pouring down his face. The thing's struggles grew weaker, the scream became a breathless rasping. I couldn't stand it any longer. I picked up a chair and smashed it down on the thing. I dropped the chair and leaned against the wall and heaved.

I heard the door open. I turned and saw Detweiler run out.

I charged after him. My legs felt rubbery but I caught him at the street. He didn't struggle. He just stood there, his eyes vacant, trembling. I saw people sticking their heads out of doors and Johnny Peacock coming toward me. My car was right there. I pushed Detweiler into it and drove away. He sat hunched in the seat, his hands hanging limply, staring into space. He was trembling uncontrollably and his teeth chattered.

I drove, not paying any attention to where I was going, almost as deeply in shock as he was. I finally started looking at the street signs. I was on Mulholland. I kept going west for a long time, crossed the San Diego Freeway, into the Santa Monica Mountains. The pavement ends a couple of miles past the freeway, and there's ten or fifteen miles of dirt

The Detweiler Boy

road before the pavement picks up again nearly to Topanga. The road isn't traveled much, there are no houses on it, and people don't like to get their cars dusty. I was about in the middle of the unpaved section when Detweiler seemed to calm down. I pulled over to the side of the road and cut the engine. The San Fernando Valley was spread like a carpet of lights below us. The ocean was on the other side of the mountains.

I sat and watched Detweiler. The trembling had stopped. He was asleep or unconscious. I reached over and touched his arm. He stirred and clutched at my hand. I looked at his sleeping face and didn't have the heart to pull my hand away.

The sun was poking over the mountains when he woke up. He roused and was momentarily unaware of where he was; then memory flooded back. He turned to me. The pain and hysteria were gone from his eyes. They were oddly peaceful.

"Did you hear him?" he said softly. "Did you hear him die?"

"Are you feeling better?"

"Yes. It's all over."

"Do you want to talk about it?"

His eyes dropped and he was silent for a moment. "I want to tell you. But I don't know how without you thinking I'm a monster."

I didn't say anything.

"He . . . was my brother. We were twins. Siamese twins. All those people died so I could stay alive." There was no emotion in his voice. He was detached, talking about someone else. "He kept me alive. I'll die without him." His eyes met mine again. "He was insane, I think. I thought at first I'd go mad too, but I didn't. I think I didn't. I never knew what he was going to do, who he would kill. I didn't want to know. He was very clever. He always made it look like an accident or suicide when he could. I didn't interfere. I didn't want to die. We had to have blood. He always did it so there was lots of blood, so no one would miss what he took." His eyes were going empty again.

"Why did you need the blood?"

"We were never suspected before."

"Why did you need the blood?" I repeated.

"When we were born," he said, and his eyes focused again, "we were joined at the back. But I grew and he didn't. He stayed little bitty, like a baby riding around on my back. People didn't like me . . . us, they were afraid. My father and mother too. The old witch-woman I told you about, she birthed us. She seemed always to be hanging around. When I was eight, my parents died in a fire. I think the witch-woman did it. After that I lived with her. She was demented, but she knew medicine and healing. When we were fifteen she decided to separate us. I don't know why. I think she wanted him without me. I'm sure she thought he was an imp from hell. I almost died. I'm not sure what was wrong. Apart, we weren't whole. I wasn't whole. He had something I didn't have, something we'd been sharing. She would've let me die, but he knew and got blood for me. Hers." He sat staring at me blankly, his mind living the past.

"Why didn't you go to a hospital or something?" I asked, feeling enormous pity for the wretched boy.

He smiled faintly. "I didn't know much about anything then. Too many people were already dead. If I'd gone to a hospital, they'd have wanted to know how I'd stayed alive so far. Sometimes I'm glad it's over, and, then, the next minute I'm terrified of dying."

"How long?"

"I'm not sure. I've never been more than three days. I can't stand it any longer than that. He knew. He always knew when I had to have it. And he got it for me. I never helped him."

"Can you stay alive if you get regular transfusions?"

He looked at me sharply, fear creeping back. "Please. No!"

"But you'll stay alive."

"In a cage! Like a freak! I don't want to be a freak anymore. It's over. I want it to be over. Please."

"What do you want me to do?"

"I don't know. I don't want you to get in trouble."

I looked at him, at his face, at his eyes, at his soul. "There's a gun in the glove compartment," I said.

He sat for a moment, then solemnly held out his hand. I took it. He shook my hand, then opened the glove compartment. He removed the gun and slipped out of the car. He went down the hill into the brush.

I waited and waited and never did hear a shot.

Insects in Amber

The storm built in the southwest, turning the air to underwater blue, making the flat land look like the bottom of the sea. Lightning flickered in the approaching darkness and threw fleeting shimmers on the rolling clouds. Thunder that had been distant rumbles soon crackled across the Kansas prairie unhindered.

Tannie and I watched the spectacular display through the rear window of the new Buick station wagon. The rain followed us like a vague, miles-long curtain. It caught us in minutes and turned the late afternoon to night.

My father grunted and flipped on the lights and windshield wipers. He braked the station wagon carefully and hunched over the steering wheel peering into the downpour. Thunder crashed and rattled around us. The lightning flashes were so brilliant that they left a white streak floating before your eyes. The windshield wipers snicked away merrily, but futilely.

Tannie sat beside me bright-eyed with excitement. She was seven and had the kind of inquisitive mind that drove certain adults up the wall.

We were starting out on one of those vacations the auto manufacturers, the motel owners, the resort owners, the tire companies, Howard Johnsons and the curio sellers on Route 66 like to promote. We had piled into the station wagon for three weeks of butt-numbing travel. We left Lubbock that morning (my father was an associate professor of English at Texas Tech) planning to go up through Kansas, Nebraska, South Dakota, over to Wyoming and Yellowstone, then back through Colorado and home. It wasn't the kind of vacation I would have initiated, though I didn't mind it that much.

I was fifteen, not too far from sixteen, and if given a guilt-free choice, I would have probably stayed in Lubbock to goof around with my friends. But since I had a special relationship with my family, the trip was no sacrifice.

We had planned to make it to Dodge City by nightfall, but the rain seemed to have put the kibosh on that. Dad was creeping along about twenty miles an hour, barely able to see the road. It went like that for a while until we came up behind a couple of other cars going even slower. We were behind a red Firebird with Arizona plates, and it was behind an old pickup truck. Dad didn't try to pass, and the Firebird seemed content to stay where it was too.

Mom squinted at an Exxon road map. "The next town is Hawley, but it looks pretty small," she said. "It's an open circle, which means . . ." She shuffled the map. "Ah . . . under a thousand."

"Let's hope it's not too small to have a motel," Dad said, giving up on Dodge City.

"I don't care about a motel," Tannie chirped. "I just hope there's someplace to eat." She sat with her nose pressed against the window, fogging up the glass with her breath and then drawing pictures in it.

"Eat?" I laughed. "You've eaten enough today to kill a horse." I knew she really was hungry, but she liked me to tease her.

Tannie turned from the window and surveyed me coolly, but with a twinkle in her eye. I knew she was about to devastate me. She leaned back in the seat and crossed her arms. "There's a little too much sibling rivalry in this seat," she said with an ultra-ladylike air.

I groaned. She was always saying something like that. Mom and Dad laughed. I could see Tannie's mouth beginning to twitch. She wouldn't be able to hold that lofty expression very long.

"It's your own fault, Ben," Dad chuckled. "You should never have told her she was precocious."

"Yeah," Tannie said, grinning, "I looked it up."

"Uh-oh," Dad said. He stopped laughing and slowed the station wagon. I leaned on the back of the front seat and looked over Mom's shoulder. Wooden barricades with amber flashers were in the road ahead. Two cars were already stopped: a yellow Volkswagen and a dark, sedate sedan that may have been a Chevrolet. The pickup stopped behind the sedan, the Firebird stopped behind the pickup, and we stopped behind the Firebird. Everyone sat there for a bit in a neck-craning session; then a man in a raincoat got out of the passenger side of the VW.

He hurried around to the driver's side of the sedan, apparently intending to get in without comment, but the guy in the pickup stuck his head out the window and said something. The man in the raincoat hesitated, rather reluctantly, I thought, then came back to the pickup and stood there talking.

Insects in Amber

"Guess I'd better get out and see what's going on," Dad said, with a resigned sigh.

"Charles, you're gonna get soaked."

Dad twisted around in the seat. "Ben, can you get to the umbrella back there?"

I got on my knees in the seat and dug around in the back among the suitcases, blankets, cardboard boxes full of who knows what, and all kinds of vacation gear. I finally found it and handed it to him. As Dad got out in the rain, a girl got out of the VW, also with an umbrella. They met at the pickup. Then a guy got out of the Firebird and joined them. It was turning into a convention.

They stood there in the pouring rain, all four of them, talking and waving their arms and pointing this way and that. Mostly it was the man from the sedan and the guy in the pickup. He was the smart one—he was in out of the rain. Then after a while, they dispersed.

"We gotta take a detour," Dad said when he got back in.

"What's wrong?" Mom asked.

"Highway's under water up ahead."

"Could you see it?" Tannie perked up at the first sign of disaster.

"No. The girl in the VW said a highway patrolman in a yellow slicker told her the road was flooded. He stopped her, and then the old gentleman in the sedan came along. Seems they know each other."

"Did he say the detour was safe?" Mom asked, looking at the rain with a little frown.

"I don't know. The patrolman seems to have disappeared. The guy in the pickup lives around here. He said it was okay."

Tannie bounced in the seat. "Isn't this exciting?" she squeaked.

"You won't think so if we have to spend the night in the car stuck in the mud somewhere," I said.

Dad grimaced. "Hold that thought, Cheerful Charlie," he said and started the motor.

The sedan pulled around the VW and turned left onto a gravel road that cut away from the highway at the barricades. The VW followed him, then the pickup, then the Firebird, and then us. Just like a camel caravan. The road wasn't bad, a little rough with lots of standing puddles.

I turned around in the seat and looked back at the highway, but I couldn't see the flashers anymore. We must have gone over a rise, although I hadn't noticed doing so. I also thought I saw the headlights of a car go by on the highway, but with the rain I wasn't sure. It must have been lightning.

Mom and Dad didn't talk. The farther we traveled from the highway, the darker it seemed to get. Mom watched the road nervously, and Dad kept his attention on his driving. Even Tannie was quiet for a change. She had her nose against the window again, trying to see by the frequent flashes of lightning. I don't know how far we had gone. It probably seemed farther than it was because we were moving so slowly.

Then I pressed my nose against the window and looked out. I don't know if it was coincidence or not, but it couldn't have been better if it had been staged by Alfred Hitchcock. There was a tremendous rattle of thunder and a flash of lightning that lingered for an unaccountably long time. I saw a house some fifty yards from the road on top of a low hill. It looked quite old, a big boxy shape with lots of tall chimneys and gables and a tower on one corner. The lightning faded slowly, and I turned my head to follow it, but the lightning wasn't repeated.

I turned as Dad braked the station wagon to a stop. The other cars in the caravan were stopped also, their brake lights flicking on and off.

"You think somebody got stuck in the mud?" Tannie asked with a faint current of desire under the question. I think she would gladly be attacked by tigers just to find out what it was like.

"Let's hope not," Dad grunted.

Somebody up the row honked his horn. "Looks like they're calling another conference," I said.

"Looks like you're right." Dad pulled out the umbrella.

I leaned my arms on the back of the seat and watched them gather around the pickup truck again. Then the rain slacked, or something, and I could see by the headlights of the sedan a sheet of muddy water flowing across the road. Trash and debris swirled around on it; weeds and tree limbs.

After a bit they disbanded and Dad got back in, wrestling with the umbrella. "This road is flooded, too," he said in a discouraged voice. "We'll have to turn around and go back."

"Doesn't look like there's room to turn around. You might get stuck in the ditch," Mom said matter-of-factly. She was worried but wouldn't show it; she didn't want to frighten Tannie and me.

"According to the guy in the pickup, we just passed, quote, the old Weatherly place, unquote. We're supposed to back up and turn around in the drive."

"Yeah," I said, "I saw it. Looked like something out of a horror movie."

"Terrific," Dad groaned.

"I want to see!" Tannie squealed and scrambled on top of me, pasting her face against the damply cool window.

"Watch it!" I grunted. "You've got bony knees."

"Okay. Hold it down back there," Dad said, but he was smiling. He backed the car slowly, looking over his shoulder.

"Can you see where you're going?" Mom asked.

"Actually, no." He grimaced.

Dad had it the worst. The others could see by the headlights of the car behind them. Tannie and I had our noses against the window again, watching for the house. A flash of lightning came right on cue. Tannie let out a little sigh of appreciation.

Dad stopped the station wagon with a lurch. Brake lights flashed on

Insects in Amber 171

sequentially down the row. Dad raised up in the seat and examined the drive critically with a little frown on his face. A culvert crossed the ditch of rushing water, though more water seemed to be going over the drive than under it. He looked at Mom. She looked at the water. Dad shrugged, rippled a tattoo on the steering wheel with his fingernails, and pulled slowly in.

The front end had nosed in about three feet when it lurched suddenly sideways and slipped into the ditch.

"Are we stuck in the mud?" Tannie asked with cloying innocence.

"I wouldn't be at all surprised." Dad put the station wagon in reverse and tried to back out. The tires whined and the rear end slithered farther into the road. Dad cut the engine and settled back in the seat with a snort.

"Looks like it's time for another conference," I said when I saw the others converging on us.

"Don't be a wiseacre," he groaned. He grabbed the umbrella and got out. I scooted over to the other side and rolled down the window so I could hear.

"Sorry, folks," Dad said.

"Tough luck, Mr. Henderson." That was the guy from the Firebird. They had apparently introduced themselves at a previous conference.

The girl in the yellow Volkswagen was Ann Callahan. She was twenty and absolutely lovely. That was the first time I had had a good look at her. When I did I couldn't keep my eyes off her.

The old guy in the sedan was Professor Philip Weatherly. That's right: Weatherly, as in "the old Weatherly place." He was sixty, with a kindly but slightly befuddled expression. I also caught, inadvertently, a certain amount of nervous strain, but I didn't think much about it under the circumstances.

Carl Willingham was the driver of the pickup. He was about fifty, with a slightly protuberant beer belly and a cigar that he worried about in his mouth. He was wearing boots and a sweat-darkened Stetson. I think he had been sent over by central casting.

The guy from the Firebird was Poe McNeal. He was about twenty-five, with a cheerful face and a quick smile. He had a stocky muscular build and a pleasant, rather then handsome, face. I liked him immediately.

Ann Callahan and Carl Willingham went to the front of the car, as close as they could get without wading, and examined the mired wheels.

"It wasn't your fault, Mr. Henderson," she said with a voice that did funny things to me. "The pipe is clogged and the drive is badly undercut."

The others moved up to check on it. "Maybe we could put something under the wheels to give it some traction," Poe McNeal suggested.

"Won't do no good," Carl Willingham grunted. "Car's too heavy and in too deep. Have to get a tow truck." The brown water swirled around the bumper.

"Great," Dad said. "How do we do that?"

"I guess we could wait till another car comes along and send them," Poe said without much conviction.

"How will they turn around?" Trust Dad to put his finger on it. "We may have three hundred cars piled up before the night's over."

Poe grinned. "The tow truck drivers will love it."

"What about that house there?" Dad asked, squinting through the rain. A flash of lightning and a roll of thunder punctuated his question. Much too convenient; more like William Castle than Alfred Hitchcock.

"I noticed some chimneys. Maybe there's a fireplace where we can dry out and get warm." That was Ann.

Carl looked up the hill with displeasure. "Nobody lived in that house for fifty years. Like as not, it's about to fall down."

"Guess we could check it out," Poe said doubtfully. "Do you think the owner would mind a band of pilgrims taking refuge?"

Professor Weatherly spoke for the first time. "I suppose I'm the owner. You have my permission." His voice had a tenseness in it, like somebody with a pat hand.

Carl's frown grew deeper. "Don't know that I'd fancy spending the night in that house."

"Don't tell me it's haunted!" Poe cried with suppressed excitement.

"Don't rightly know," Carl answered with no trace of humor, "though I've heard folks talk."

The professor looked at Carl with a little frown, as if he'd misread one of his cards.

"I'll get a flashlight," Dad said and opened the door of the station wagon. He leaned in, trying to keep himself covered with the umbrella. "Ben, hand me the flashlight." He looked at Mom. "We're gonna check out that house to see if it's fit to spend the night in." Mom nodded and looked through the darkness, trying to see it.

I dug the flashlight out from behind the seat. "May I go with you?"

"No, you can't. If it's not fit, there's no point in your getting wet."

"Heck!" I said.

"Heck, yourself." Then he grinned. "Come on."

I got another umbrella from the back seat cornucopia and scrambled out. Poe was leaning in the window of the Firebird telling the other people what was happening. Then we all traipsed up the hill to the house.

With the darkness and the rain and trying to see where we were putting our feet, none of us really paid much attention to the house until we made it to the old-fashioned porch around three sides. Once out of the rain, we looked about without saying anything. The house was a little weather-beaten and badly needed paint, but it wasn't what one would call dilapidated. A few pieces of gingerbread were missing from

Insects in Amber

around the top of the porch, and a few boards squeaked when stepped on, but I've seen people living in a lot worse.

Dad looked at the others and opened the wide front door with a fanlight over it. He shone the flashlight around, and the rest of us crowded in behind him. My arm bumped Ann's. She smiled at me. It was just one of those friendly but noncommittal smiles you give to strangers, but I felt my face getting warm.

We were in a large entry hall—I finally noticed. A wide stairway ascended to a second floor landing at the rear. We looked at each other with no small amount of bewilderment. Everything was clean and free of dust. The carpet running down the middle of the hall and up the stairs was faded but in good condition. The lace curtains over the windows on either side of the door, though somewhat yellowed with age, were clean. A tall grandfather's clock at the top of the stairs suddenly rattled and struck six times. We all stared at it, hardly breathing, until it finished.

"When does Vincent Price arrive?" Poe muttered.

"What?" Ann said, turning her head suddenly toward him.

"Nothing." He grinned.

Dad looked at Carl. "Are you sure this has been empty for fifty years?"

He shrugged stoically. "Always thought it was. Musta been wrong."

We wandered into the living room (though I imagine it was called a parlor in its day) which opened to the left off the entry hall. "If this belongs to you, Professor," Ann said softly, "you should know if anyone's been living here."

He was genuinely confused. "Mr. Willingham's right. No one **has** lived here for fifty years. When I was last here, thirty-five years ago, I hired a man to look after the place. Apparently he's doing his job very well."

The living room/parlor was completely and neatly furnished in that blocky, ungainly style of the early twenties. Even so, it didn't actually look as if someone lived there; more like a display; the Sunday parlor kept spotlessly unused for company that never came.

"There's wood for the fireplace," Dad said, brightening. "I was afraid we might have to burn the furniture."

Poe wrinkled his nose. "Wouldn't hurt."

The professor came out of his mood. "Why don't you get the others from the cars and whatever else you might need while Mr. Willingham and I get a fire going?"

So we re-entered the downpour and slogged back to the cars. Ann smiled at me as we went down the porch steps. I missed one with my foot and had to grab the railing. Damnation!

When we returned with the suitcases, blankets, and everything else we could carry, Weatherly and Carl had a crackling fire going. That and the half dozen kerosene lamps scattered around the room made it almost cheerful. We all trooped in, bustling around, shedding raincoats and umbrellas, and looking around tentatively. Everyone was happily excited and seemed to regard the whole thing as an adventure.

"This is terrific," Linda MacNeal said with delight. "I was expecting spiders and rats." Poe's wife was twenty-two, blonde, pink and pretty — and very pregnant. Poe helped with her raincoat. I liked Linda as much as I did Poe.

"Either that, or some farmer would be using it to store hay." That was Judson Bradley Ledbetter, known professionally as Jud Bradley — he thought Ledbetter sounded a bit too hayseed. It was easy enough to tell he was Linda's brother. He was also blond, pink, and pretty, but with a dark undercurrent missing in Linda. I thought he was a bit overdressed and had obviously swiped his shoes from Carmen Miranda.

"Where are the ghosts?" Tannie asked, ready to get down to business.

"They don't show up till midnight," I said with a straight face.

"Stop it, Ben," Mom said. "You know she believes everything you tell her."

"You okay, hon?" Poe said to his wife. "You oughtn't to catch cold."

"You're the one who looks like you've been swimming with your clothes on."

He grinned. "I was expecting Fred MacMurray to paddle by in a rowboat."

"*The Rains of Ranchipur!*" Linda cried gleefully.

"Right!"

Mom wasn't one to let things go untended. "I have some towels in the suitcases," she said and fished out several. She handed one to Linda.

"Thank you," Linda said, smiling. "Just my hair and feet are wet."

"Is this your first?" Mom asked.

"Yes. It's all sorta terrific, isn't it?"

"Yes, it is," Mom said and laughed. "I felt the same way when I had my two. Here, sit by the fire and take off your shoes." She and Poe pushed one of the chairs closer to the fire and fussed over Linda. Then she gave Tannie and me each a towel with instructions to dry everything that was wet.

Mom was in high gear now that she had something to do. I guess that's one of the reasons she made such a good faculty wife. There are a lot of women who can't hack it. I've seen perfectly level-headed women go glassy-eyed at the thought of one more faculty tea; and assistant professors' wives seriously consider sticking their heads in the oven after being cut down by a **full** professor's wife — delicately and with no visible wounds, of course.

Mom says a faculty wife has to be one-quarter hostess, one-quarter scullery maid, one-quarter diplomat, one-quarter secret agent, and one hundred percent saint.

"If everyone is getting settled," the professor said in his role as

Insects in Amber

reluctant leader of the castaways, "I'll get my suitcases. I also have some food."

"I'll go with you," Dad volunteered. "We have some coffee in the car."

"Thank you," Weatherly replied. "There's a stove in the kitchen but, I'm afraid, no hot water."

"Clare, will you put some water on?" Dad asked. "We'll be right back."

"Of course."

They left and everyone was snuggling in quite comfortably. I got dry socks for myself and Tannie from the suitcase. Mom and Poe still hovered over Linda. Carl Willingham and Judson Bradley Ledbetter rotated themselves in front of the fire drying off. Jud soon gave up and went into another room to put on dry clothes, after fussing around in several matched pieces of luggage.

"When is it due?" Mom asked, not quite having exhausted the topic of babies.

"Five weeks," Linda said.

"We were on our way to visit Linda's parents in Wichita before she got too big too travel." Poe smiled a proud and slightly mystified father-to-be smile. "We live in Flagstaff."

"Oh, Poe," Linda moaned. "They're gonna be so worried when we don't show up. We were supposed to be there by eight."

"I know, hon, but there's nothing we can do about it."

"Would you like a blanket?" Mom handed her one before she could answer.

"Thank you, Mrs. . . ." She laughed. "I don't know your name."

"Clare Henderson. I guess that's the first thing we ought to do. That was my husband, Charles, who just went for coffee. My son, Ben, and my daughter, Tannie."

Everyone had the slightly nervous fidgets you get when you introduce yourself to strangers. Except me. I was looking at Ann Callahan just coming into the room from an exploration foray.

"My name is Tania Henderson," Tannie announced proudly. "After my grandmother."

"That's a terrific name," Ann said as she joined us.

"Thank you very much." Tannie smiled at her.

"You're welcome." Ann beamed back at her. "I'm Ann Callahan. From Albuquerque."

"Poe McNeal. I won't mention what the Poe is short for. My wife, Linda."

"That's my brother in there," Linda said, inclining her head toward the closed door, "Jud Ledbetter. He lives in Hollywood."

Mom raised her eyebrows questioningly. "Is he an actor? He's handsome enough to be."

Linda's mouth quivered with a suppressed grin. "He'll probably tell you he is," she said, "but he's a model. You may recognize the back of his head." The grin broke through and Poe chuckled. "He's been in a lot of commercials, but the camera is always on the girls' shiny hair or her gleaming white cavity-free bicuspids. All you ever see of Jud is the back of his head. If you'd like to hear a choice account of the doubtful ancestry of TV commercial producers and directors, bring the subject up." She and Poe both smothered laughter.

"Why are you laughing?" Mom asked in confusion. "He seems fortunate to me."

"Oh, he is," Poe controlled himself. "He makes money hand over fist—a lot more than I'll ever make. You see, Mrs. Henderson, Jud and Linda and I grew up together in Wichita. Jud and I were in the same grade. It's just hard for us to take him seriously. We know too much about him."

Poe plucked at his sodden clothes, unsticking the the fabric from his skin. "If you'll excuse me, I'll follow my beautiful brother-in-law's example and put on some dry clothes." He rummaged around in a suitcase and followed Jud.

"I take it your husband and brother don't get on too well," Mom said.

"No, it isn't that," Linda said, hitching the blanket higher around her shoulders. "They've seen very little of each other since high school, and Jud's changed a lot since then. I think the term is: gone Hollywood. It's nothing serious. Jud's airs amuse Poe and Poe's amusement irritates Jud."

"Would you care to join me in the water-boiling detail?" Mom asked Ann, suddenly remembering.

"Sure," she said. They took a lamp and went in the direction opposite Jud and Poe.

"I wonder when they read the will," Poe said when they came back.

"Huh?" I asked, because my mind was still on Ann.

"In the movies," he explained, "when a bunch of people are gathered in a spooky old house like this, they generally read the will. But there's always the stipulation that they spend the night. And then the beneficiaries are murdered one by one."

"Poe!" Linda frowned. "Don't talk that way. You'll scare Tannie."

"Nothing scares her," I said.

"Does too!" Tannie asserted.

"Either that," Poe continued undaunted, "or they're lured there by a mysterious host, who then murders 'em one by one."

"**And Then There Were None** and **The Thirteenth Guest**," I supplied.

"Uh-oh!" Linda laughed. "Poe's found a kindred spirit."

"Huh?" I said with another example of my brilliant repartee.

"Poe and Linda ask each other questions about old movies," Jud explained with no small amount of condescension. "If one can stump the other, he gets a point."

"It's a game we play on trips to pass the time," Poe said with a slight

Insects in Amber

narrowing of his eyes.

"May I play?" I asked.

"Sure." Linda laughed. "I'm not much of a challenge."

"Be warned, young man," Poe said, grinning. "You are opposing a master."

"Okay, my turn," Linda said and looked studious. "Let's see. Ah . . . how many times was Scarlett O'Hara married?"

Poe turned to me with mock exasperation. "You can see the kind of competition I have. You know the answer to that one?"

"Sure," I said and grinned. "Three."

"No points for Linda," he crowed. She made a face at him. "All right," he continued, preparing a zinger, "what famous star of B westerns once played the romantic lead opposite Greta Garbo?" he settled back with a satisfied smirk.

Linda looked at him suspiciously. "You're making that up."

"No, I'm not," he laughed.

"Johnny Mack Brown," Jud muttered.

An expression of abject betrayal settled on Poe's face. "How did you know?" he groaned.

Jud raised his pale eyebrows. "You mean that's right? I just said the most unlikely name I could think of."

"I was gonna say Lash LaRue," Linda said with a straight face. We were all laughing when Dad and Professor Weatherly came back. The professor had a suitcase and a picnic hamper. Dad had a cardboard box with instant coffee, styrofoam cups, sugar, powdered cream, and a bunch of other stuff. We were helping them unpack it all when Mom and Ann returned looking smug.

"Water's on," Mom announced. "With a little native ingenuity, feminine intuition, and a lot of luck, we figured out how to work that antique kerosene stove."

"Professor," Ann said with a slight frown, "does your caretaker live here in the house? There's food in the kitchen. Not much, mostly canned stuff."

"I don't know," he said with a befuddled look. "The man I hired lived in Hawley with his wife."

"Maybe some hobo has taken squatters' rights," Jud said.

"Wouldn't be nobody from around here," Carl said with assurance. "Folks in Hawley stay away from this place."

"You're here, Mr. Willingham," Mom pointed out. "Have you changed your mind about the place being haunted?"

"Never said it was haunted," he said phlegmatically. "Just said folks talk."

What happened then is difficult to explain. Poe and I had gone back to Linda at the fireplace. I was sitting in a chair next to Linda while Poe sat on the floor with his arms around his knees. Everyone else was at the table about ten feet away unpacking the professor's picnic hamper. I was thinking that he surely had brought a lot of food for some reason.

I felt it coming before it hit me, but I was so startled I didn't do anything to protect myself.

There was an impact. Then pressure; pressure that knocked the breath out of me. If I'd been standing I think I would have fallen.

My head flopped back against the chair. It couldn't have lasted more than a second, but the residue of cold fear was overpowering. The sweet chill of fear, drenched, infused with icy sugar water.

My eyes closed and I shivered uncontrollably. My arms were so weak I couldn't lift them. I never knew so much fear.

But not my fear.

One eternal second and it was gone; the pressure and the presence gone as suddenly as it came.

I could hear what everyone was saying, their tiny voices far away; and I knew what everyone was doing, not seeing them with my eyes.

In that chill second Ann gasped and looked around quickly, seeking a source. Of what? Everyone stopped talking and looked at Ann; Professor Weatherly with more interest than I could explain.

Then Linda looked at me. "Mrs. Henderson!" she shouted. "Something's wrong with Ben!"

Everyone gathered around me except Jud and Carl. Ann was shaken. They helped her to a chair. Tannie stared at me with eyes like saucers. Mom and Dan knelt beside me. Mom put her hands on my clammy face.

"Darling, what's the matter?"

I tried to open my eyes, but my eyelids fluttered like moth wings, and I couldn't focus.

"Ben!" Dad said, strain and worry harsh in his voice. "Son, say something."

"Mom?" I whimpered. I wasn't ashamed of whimpering. I was thankful I didn't scream.

Mom put her arms around my shoulders and pulled me against her breast, holding me like I was two years old. Dad had his hand on the back of my head. I opened up all the way, let down all the barriers. I sopped up their love and concern and compassion. I bathed in it, swam in it, drowned in it. I let the warmth of it wash over me, let it drive out the chill of that fear.

"What is it, Ben? Are you ill?" Mom asked softly.

"Oh, Mom, it was so scared!" I moaned against her shoulder.

"What was scared?" Dad asked in confusion.

My eyes focused on Ann over Mom's shoulder. She was staring at me, staring with surprised recognition. But she was no more surprised than I. Professor Weatherly was looking from Ann to me and back again like a startled owl. Then I saw everyone else was staring at me too, and I got a little embarrassed. I disengaged Mom's arms and leaned back in the chair because I wasn't sure I could stand up. But I didn't take my

Insects in Amber 179

eyes off Ann.

"I don't know, Dad," I said, trying to answer his question. "Suddenly, I felt . . . I felt . . . it was like I had my breath knocked out . . . and . . . there was so much fear."

"That's what I felt . . . only not so strongly," Ann said calmly.

Tannie slowly and tentatively took my hand in hers and looked at me with big round scared eyes. I grinned at her and winked. Her little face sort of exploded and she grinned back. Mom turned to Ann.

"Are you feeling better, Ann?"

"Yes, I'm fine."

Tannie suddenly perked up and piped, "It must have been a ghost." A little wave of nervous laughter rippled around the room.

"I think she's right." Poe grinned. "I've seen enough movies to know a haunted house."

"I've heard folks talk," Carl said with a nod of his head.

"You keep saying that," Jud grumbled. "Exactly what do folks talk about?"

"This house and what happened here fifty years ago."

"I knew it!" Poe cried and clapped his hands together sharply. "A house doesn't get a reputation for being haunted unless there's a story to go with it. What happend fifty years ago, a juicy murder?"

"First time I been in this place," Carl said, a little abashed at being the focus of attention. "Nobody I know's ever been inside. Seen it lots of times from the road. Used to be the main road before they built the highway."

"Well, what happened?" Poe squirmed.

Professor Weatherly was distinctly uncomfortable and wished he were somewhere else.

"Happened before I was born, but I've heard folks talk," Carl continued, warming to his subject. "The Weatherlys lived here. Had a right nice farm, folks say. That was before the Depression. Man, wife, two girls, and a boy. Real well liked, I hear, though folks say there was something peculiar about the boy. One night folks livin' close by saw the house all lit up kinda funny. Lights dancin' all over it and flames in one of the upstairs rooms. Thought the place was burning and rushed over to help. When they got here, there was nothin'. No fire, nothin'. They called. Nobody answered. They went inside and looked all over. Didn't find nobody. Just found that upstairs room where the fire was. They say it was the boy's room. The inside was all burned, but the fire was cold out. Nobody ever saw the Weatherlys or heard tell of 'em since."

"Hey!" Poe exhaled slowly. "That's even better than a juicy murder."

"Didn't they ever find out what happened?" Dad asked.

"Nope." Carl shrugged. "Not that I ever heard."

"Professor?" Ann turned to him. "You told me when we were stopped on the highway you used to live around here. In this house?"

"Yes, for a time." He fidgeted, then changed the subject. "Do you suppose the water's boiling, Mrs. Henderson? I'm ready for a cup of coffee."

"Oops!" Mom laughed. "I forgot about the water." She looked questioningly at me and I nodded. She hurried from the room. Ann continued to look speculatively at the professor but decided to let it drop for the moment.

"You said there were people living close by," Poe said hopefully. "Maybe we could walk to one of them and phone for a tow truck."

"And my parents," Linda added.

Carl shook his head. "Ain't there no more. Not many small farms anymore. Reckon there's not another house for four, five miles."

"Forget I mentioned it," Poe grunted and settled back.

Mom returned with a steaming kettle and put it beside the coffee stuff. We made coffee and sandwiches from the copious picnic hamper and went back to the fireplace.

All of us except Carl; he was standing at the window looking through the rain toward the cars. He was more worried and nervous than the rest of us. Then he turned from the window and joined us. He was frowning and worrying his cigar to a frazzle.

"It's real funny," he said. "I've been kinda keepin' an eye on the road. Hasn't been another car along since we got here."

"Maybe the water went down," Jud said in a bored voice.

"Not likely," Dad said. "It's still raining."

"The answer's very simple," Poe pronounced in mock gloom. "The ghosts lured us here for some diabolical reasons of their own and are now keeping everyone else away."

Professor Weatherly gave him a startled owl look. Well, well, the professor seemed to concur with that opinion. Linda laughed and shivered.

"Poe, stop! You're scaring **me** now."

"Not at all, young man." Weatherly rushed in to repair the breach. "Obviously, they've discovered the detour is also flooded and are turning the cars around."

Poe grimaced and laughed. "Spoilsport!"

Ann picked up the kettle and looked at me. "I'll put on some more water," she said and left the room. I followed her, kicking myself for not getting her alone sooner.

The door to the kitchen was open. I leaned against the doorjamb and watched her fill the kettle from the hand pump. She had short dark hair—actually not much longer than mine. She was tall, with long, very good legs. With high heels she would be taller than I, but she was wearing sneakers, I was five-ten, but I hoped to make it to six feet in a couple of years. I know I didn't make a sound, and she had her back to me.

"Hello, Ben Henderson," she said without turning around.

The kitchen was dark and gloomy even though one of the kerosene

Insects in Amber

lamps was burning. I had her alone and I didn't know what to say. So I pretended interest in the lamp.

"It's a wonder people didn't go blind with no more light than these things make." I gritted my teeth.

"They probably did," she said and lit the burner under the kettle. Then she turned and looked at me. She had a faint, slightly impudent smile on her lips. I felt as if I were standing there stark naked. It came so suddenly and unexpectedly, I blushed like a virgin. Then I blushed because I was blushing. The sensation was so erotic, I had to do some fancy mental footwork to keep from really embarrassing myself.

She laughed, but there was only fondness in it. "I'm sorry. I didn't mean to embarass you. I only wanted to see if you could pick it up."

"Loud and clear," I said, fighting the tingle in the pit of my stomach.

"You're a very good-looking young man," she said matter-of-factly. "You should be used to it."

"It was a little different this time. You **knew** I was picking it up."

She leaned back against the kitchen cabinets. Her voice was wistful. "Don't you sometimes wish you were like everyone else? Do you get sick to death of always knowing?"

"Yeah. Sometimes."

"You're very lucky, you know. Your family loves you very much."

"You don't have a family, do you?"

"No. They were both killed when I was little. I was adopted by an aunt. Did you see that?"

"No, not really. I felt sadness and a sense of loss when you mentioned my family. It had to've been something like that."

"My aunt and uncle are very good to me, but, unlike you, there's no warm, comfortable glow into which I can retreat when things get a bit overwhelming."

So I did something I'd been wanting to do since I'd found out Ann was like me. She looked at me with pleased surprise. "Thank you, Ben," she said softly, like white velvet flowing over burnished gold.

"Think nothing of it. Warm, comfortable glows supplied on demand."

"You're an idiot." She chuckled.

"It was real, you know."

"Yes, of course, I know," she said simply. Then she laughed. "And watch it, I've picked up that one before."

"Sorry." I grinned. "Involuntary reflex. Besides, you started it."

"You're not a child to me, Ben." I had again that feel of white velvet.

"I know. It takes a little getting used to, I guess. I thought I was all alone."

"Seeing yourself as others see you is true with a vengeance in our case. I guess the worst part of it is so many things are boring."

"Like card games."

"And school. Did you skip a grade?"

"Yeah."

"Me, too. I'm in my last year of college."

"One more year of high school. What will you do when you finish?"

She shrugged. "I'll probably do postgrad work and get my doctorate in psychology." A smile. "That's one field we're very good in." I looked at her and she looked at me. It was good, so good. But we had a problem.

"What do you think Professor Weatherly is up to?"

She frowned. "I don't know. I have a feeling all this has been contrived somehow." I felt the same thing, but I didn't say so. She knew. "He's my psychology professor at the University of New Mexico. When I stopped at that roadblock and he pulled in behind me, I was surprised, to say the least. He said he was on his way to Hawley, that he had lived near there as a child, that he owned some property and had come to settle some affairs." She looked around the room. "This seems to be the property and we seem to be enmeshed in his affairs."

"How did you happen to be here?"

She shrugged. "No reason in particular. After classes yesterday, I just decided to take a drive over the weekend. I don't know why. It seemed a good idea at the time, though I'm not so sure now." She looked at me and smiled. I felt the hum of violin strings. "No. It was a good idea." She lowered her eyes. "The water's boiling. We'd better go back."

She turned toward the stove with her back to me. "Ben? What you were thinking a moment ago. I didn't mind."

"I know," I said and took the kettle. She turned off the burner and looked at me. It never even occurred to me to blush.

On the way back to the parlor we found Tannie sitting on the bottom step of the stairway with one of the kerosene lamps beside her. She had her elbows on her knees and her chin in her hands. She had that perplexed expression she would get when she ran up against something too complex for her to understand. She was obviously waiting for me to help her out.

"Tannie, what are you doing wandering around?" I asked.

"I wanted to see the burned room," she mumbled with her mind still on something else.

"Did you find it?" Ann asked.

"Yes, thank you," she said politely, then looked up at me with a little frown. "Ben, what do ghosts look like?"

"I don't know," I said and laughed because she was so serious. "I've never seen one."

She looked at her toes and absently scratched her leg. "I always thought they wore sheets, or that you could see right through them. Now, I think they look just like people."

"What did you see?" I asked seriously, because I knew she'd seen something.

"There was a lady in the burned room. She was about two hundred years old and wore funny clothes." She looked up at me again with a puzzled little squint. Tannie related all this to me very matter-of-factly,

Insects in Amber

because she knew I never disbelieved her when she was telling the truth.

I put the kettle on the floor and sat beside her on the step. "What did the lady do?"

"Nothin'. She wouldn't talk to me."

I took her hand and stood up. "Come on back to the fire. Ann and I will go see."

Mom, Dad, Poe, and Linda were playing bridge. Carl was looking out the window again, and Jud was reading Rex Reed's **Conversations in the Raw**. Weatherly sat on the couch looking depressed.

"Mom," I said. "Tannie was exploring."

"What? I thought she was with you. Tannie, you know better than to wander off without telling us."

"Heck, Mom," Tannie sighed, expressing the triviality of her offense, "I was just talking to the ghost."

The reaction from Weatherly was so strong that I turned and looked at him. He was a severely startled man.

Mom smiled. "Sure you were."

"I'll be back in a minute," I said, still watching the professor. "Ann and I are gonna look around."

"Okay. Be careful."

"Sure." I retrieved the lamp from where Tannie left it on the stairs. "Tannie was telling the truth," I said. "She saw somebody."

"Yes, I know." Ann smiled.

I smiled back at her because it was the easiest and most pleasant thing in the world to do. "I keep forgetting. Professor Weatherly is definitely keeping secrets from us."

"I know that too. He wasn't telling the exact truth when he said he lived here as a child."

"Didn't he?"

"That part's true. He did. But he was evading the issue somewhere. Didn't you pick it up?"

"I wasn't thinking about it. I seldom read people without a good reason. It's usually too discomfiting and embarrassing. I just sorta close them out like a background noise you get used to and don't hear unless you listen for it—or, unless it's very strong, like when Tannie mentioned the ghost. I picked up an extreme dose of surprise and confusion. I don't think the professor was expecting to find anyone here."

We checked out several upstairs rooms, all bedrooms, before we found the burned room. One door, which should have led to the tower if my memory of its position was correct, was locked. I raised my eyebrows questioningly at Ann. She shrugged. The burned room had been a bedroom as well. It looked as if no one had touched it since the fire fifty years ago. The furniture and walls were charred in places but only scorched in others, as if the fire had raged fiercely for a few minutes and then been instantly doused.

But there was no old lady with funny clothes.

When we got back downstairs, Tannie was facing the others defiantly, and near tears. She turned and ran to me. "Ben, would you please tell these people what I saw?" she said with a quiver in her voice.

I knelt and took her in my arms. She put her arms around my neck and valiantly kept from crying. "I'm sorry, honey," I said softly. "When we got there she was gone."

"Do you think I'm imagining things, too?" The quiver had grown more pronounced at the thought that I, too, might be against her.

"Of course not," I said firmly. "She really did see someone," I said to the others. I stood up, but Tannie kept a grip on my hand.

"How are you so sure?" Judson Bradley Ledbetter asked with a supercilious sneer.

"Has the ghost made an appearance?" Poe asked with genuine interest.

"You'll have to ask Professor Weatherly about that," I said.

The professor frowned at me as if one of his own troops had turned on him. He fidgeted a bit and then sighed. "I can assure you there are no ghosts in this house," he snapped irritably. "However, you are due an explanation, as I see some of you are letting your imaginations run away with you. Before I explain anything, and I still can't tell you everything, I want to show you something." He went to the table where the bridge game had been abandoned.

"Why can't you tell us everything?" Dad asked, becoming a little bit irritable himself.

"You wouldn't believe me, Mr. Henderson," he said, sighing impatiently. "And there's no point in alarming you unnecessarily."

Poe grunted. "It's statements like that that alarm me unnecessarily."

"Mr. McNeal," Weatherly snapped, "there are no ghosts; you are in no danger. Please stop this wild speculation." Poe hunkered his head protectively between his shoulders and grinned at me. Ann and I cocked an eyebrow at each other. Weatherly was difficult. He was telling the truth, but I had a feeling it was only **technically** the truth. "Now, everyone," he continued and sat at the table, "gather around. Ben, you and two others sit down."

I sat opposite him, anxious to cooperate and find out what was going on. Ann stood behind me. Mom and Dad sat in the other chairs. Everyone else gathered around except Carl, who watched from the other side of the room. I had the impression he was staying close to the door, on the verge of bolting. Weatherly gathered up the cards and handed them to Mom. "Now, Mrs. Henderson, please shuffle the cards carefully and deal out four hands."

Mom gave him a quizzical frown but did as he asked. Weatherly picked up his cards and fanned them. The rest of us did the same. I had thirteen clubs neatly arranged in order, with the deuce on the left and the ace on the right.

Insects in Amber

"Now, Ben," Weatherly said, "tell us who has the winning hand if we were playing bridge."

"Dad," I said.

He nodded with satisfaction. "Correct," he said crisply and laid his cards face-up on the table. He had thirteen hearts. Mom had thirteen diamonds and Dad had thirteen spades. "Explain how you knew."

"I can't explain," I said with a frown. "It's like . . . like explaining sight or sound or smell to someone lacking them. Dad knew he had the winning hand, and I . . . felt . . . sensed him knowing it."

"Did you know exactly which cards he had?" Weatherly asked intensely.

"No. But it wasn't hard to figure out when I saw mine."

"Read everyone in the room, Ben," he said like a wire stretched to the breaking point. He never took his eyes off mine. "Your parents."

"Concern. Love."

"Tannie."

"She's still mad."

"Poe."

"Interest. Wonder."

"Linda."

"Love. Incomprehension."

"Mr. Ledbetter."

"Disbelief. Annoyance."

"Mr. Willingham."

"Nervousness. Stoicism."

"Me."

"Determination." I narrowed my eyes a little, and he knew I read more than that, but I didn't say anything else.

"Ann."

I hesitated. How could I put Ann into words? I couldn't, and so I just grinned like a sap. Ann put her arm around my shoulder.

"Ben . . . " Mom said in a tight little voice.

I hadn't really wanted my parents to find out like this, though my father had known subconsciously for quite some time. He'd never said anything; he hadn't wanted to upset Mom and didn't really want to believe it himself. Now they were both confused and frightened. I started to say something, to try to ease their worries, but Ann beat me to it.

"Don't you see, Clare?" she said quietly. "You and Charles think of Ben as an adolescent. So he acts the part to please you. It's difficult for us to be ourselves and not just the reflection of others. I went through the same thing. No one likes an uppity kid." She ran her fingernails through the hair on the back of my neck.

All I could do was grin and turn red. She hit me lightly on the back of the head.

"Ben . . . " Mom said again.

"I know, Mom."

"So, there you are," Weatherly said, getting us back on the path of his purpose, whatever that was. "Ann could have told me the same things. They are both telepathic and empathic, though Ben is the more sensitive."

"Telepathic." Jud snorted and poured himself another cup of coffee.

"Don't worry, Jud," Ann assured him. "We can't read your thoughts, only your emotions, your state of mind, and the like."

"But I also knew who had the winning hand," Weatherly barreled ahead. "I knew where every card lay, because I controlled the deal. If I hadn't, I wouldn't have known any more than . . . the man in the moon."

"I figured that," I said.

"How did you control the deal?" Dad had accepted everything completely.

"That, too, is difficult to explain," Weatherly sighed. "Ben and Ann are telepathic and empathic. My own ability is telekinesis, though I believe these days they are calling it 'psychokinesis.' "

There was a momentary silence. "What's that?" Linda asked wide-eyed. Poe had his arm around her and she leaned against him. Poe was quiet, absorbing everything.

"The ability to mentally control physical objects," Weatherly explained tersely.

"You mean mind over matter?" Linda breathed.

"Yes," he sighed, "I believe that is the popularized term."

Jud was pacing a short path on the faded carpet. "Let's see you make that shoe move," he snorted and pointed to Poe's still damp sneaker on the hearth.

Weatherly leaned back in the chair and tiredly ran his hand over his face. He broadcast resignation to the constant interruptions. He nodded and the shoe rose into the air. Mom and Linda gasped. Tannie was watching bug-eyed. Carl Willingham eased a little closer to the door. The shoe made a circle of the room and plopped back on the hearth.

"There's more to it than moving shoes about, Mr. Ledbetter," Weatherly explained impatiently. "Matter can also be controlled on a molecular level. Mrs. Henderson, lift the top card, please, and look at it."

She gave him a curious look and turned the card. It was the three of hearts.

"Turn it face-down again." Mom did so. "Now look at it." Mom exposed it once more. The hearts had been replaced by little yellow daisies. "It is now the three of daisies," Weatherly said without looking at it. "I could continue to perform carnival tricks until morning, but there are more important matters. There is something absolutely vital which I must do. I could not do it alone; not without the aid of a telepath. I have been searching for thirty-five years. I had just about given up hope. And then I found Ann. My dear, I must apologize for the way I maneuvered you here."

"Maneuvered?"

"Yes. I'm afraid it's turned into something of an imbroglio, however. I instigated your weekend drive by thinking it at you for the past two weeks. Naturally, you thought it was your own idea. I created the rainstorm, the roadblock, and the flooded detour. Of course, I never intended the rest of you people to fall into my little charade. Yes," he said and sighed, "I seem to have botched it rather badly." He brightened. "But, actually, it has turned out rather well. If things had gone according to plan, I wouldn't have found Ben."

"I don't believe any of this!" Jud flopped onto the couch and stretched his long, fashionably sheathed legs in front of him. He looked away with a sour expression.

"Really, young man," Weatherly said in exasperation, "creating a rainstorm, a couple of wooden barricades, an animated yellow slicker, and a little water over the road, differs from controlling a deck of cards only in degree. It's exactly the same principle."

"If you can do all that," Dad said suspiciously, "you could have gotten my car out of the ditch."

"Most assuredly, Mr. Henderson. But, you see—and I must apologize—it was I who put your car in the ditch."

"Why?" Mom asked.

"Oh, dear, isn't it obvious?" Weatherly whined. "In order to keep Ann here, I was forced to keep all of you."

"Why did you go through all these elaborate machinations, Professor?" Ann asked seriously. "Why didn't you just ask me to help you?"

"I couldn't take the chance. If you had refused . . . It was imperative that you come. I'm an old man, Ann. This is my last chance. If I'm unsuccessful again," his shoulders slumped, "then God help us."

Stunned silence spread over the room like a blanket and lay there. Then Ann spoke softly, "What is it you want me to do?"

"Please be patient with me, my dear." He sighed and ran his hand over his face again. His eyes were bleary from nervous strain, and his skin had developed a putty-colored pallor. I still didn't know what he was up to, but he didn't appear to be in condition to subdue an irritated kitten. "There are preparations that must be made before I explain fully. Imagine," he brightened, "after thirty-five years I find **two** telepaths."

"Just a minute," Dad said with a hardness in his voice I'd seldom heard before. "If Ann wants to help you with whatever you're doing that's her affair, but Ben is not to be involved."

Weatherly's chin set firmly. He was about to argue, but Jud jumped up to pace again. He rubbed his hands on the fabric molding his hips and said with nervous volume, "I think you're all nuts! You're sitting around talking about telepathy, telekinesis, and created rainstorms and . . . and . . . as if you were talking about . . . about the weather. All I've seen is a man, whose sanity I am beginning to doubt, do card tricks." He stopped and fixed Weatherly with a pale-blue gaze.

"Jud, please," Linda whispered in embarrassment.

"Don't forget the shoe," Poe said brightly. Jud transferred the glare to his brother-in-law. Poe grinned and raised his eyebrows.

Jud turned back to the professor. "If you can do all this hocus-pocus, will you kindly turn off the rain, get Mr. Henderson's car out of the ditch, and let us get out of this freak show?" His voice rose a little in volume with each word.

Weatherly matched him decibel for decibel. "I am not a magician, Mr. Ledbetter. I can't snap my fingers and **turn off** the rain. It took two days of careful manipulation to create it in the first place. Besides," his voice lowered to conciliatory tones, "there is no point in your leaving. You have to spend the night somewhere. It might as well be here. There are very comfortable bedrooms upstairs. If any of you wish to retire, I'll show you the way."

Jud wasn't giving up so easily. "You mean we stay whether we like it or not? My parents are expecting us tonight and I want to leave!"

"I'm sorry, Mr. Ledbetter. Take my word. It is impossible."

Ann and I looked at each other. We had both caught the same thing. He was telling the truth as he saw it. It **was** impossible for us to leave—and not because of the weather. But neither of us could get the real reason.

"Take it easy, Jud," Poe said sensibly. "We're so late now a few more hours won't matter."

"Okay, okay." Jud shrugged elaborately and sat at the now empty table. He picked up the cards and shuffled them. "You go right ahead with your spook hunt. I shall sit right here and play solitaire all night. I don't care if twenty ghosts come traipsing through here rattling chains and moaning their heads off. I shall be totally oblivious to them." He dealt out a hand of solitaire and pointedly ignored us.

Everyone looked at him with some amusement for a moment. His shouting match with the professor had done quite a bit to break the tension in the air. Then Mom sort of shook her head and said, "I know one young lady who needs to go to bed."

"Do I have to?" Tannie groaned. "Things are much too interesting to go to bed."

"Yes, you do," Mom said, laughing.

She took one of the suitcases and led Tannie out. Tannie said goodnight to everyone, kissed Dad and me, then gave me a defeated look. I winked at her. They left and Tannie came back almost immediately. "Mom forgot the flashlight," she said. Dad was about to hand it to her when we heard Mom gasp and drop the suitcase. We all scrambled into the hall. Mom was standing at the foot of the stairs with her hand over her mouth, looking up. The suitcase lay on its side at her feet.

"I saw someone standing at the top of the stairs," she said with a controlled voice.

Dad pointed the flashlight at the top of the stairs and turned it on.

Insects in Amber

There was no one there. The grandfather's clock suddenly rattled and began to strike. A startled squeak escaped from Linda. Dad moved the beam lower and caught a man descending toward us.

He was young, about the same age as Poe and Jud, dressed in rough clothes, with no expression on his dark, Slavic face. That's the way he appeared to my eyes. When I looked at him without using my eyes, he was a featureless shimmer. Dad kept the flashlight on him.

"It's Lester Gant," Carl Willingham said from behind us as if he were identifying a rabid dog.

The man reached the bottom of the stairs and stood looking at us, still with no expression. The clock stopped striking. For some reason, we all took a half step backward.

"You know him?" Weatherly asked, slipping back into the befuddlement he had only recently escaped. I had the impression he couldn't take very many more interruptions or complications.

"Is this the caretaker?" Dad asked.

"What?" Weatherly turned to him with a slight jerk of his head. "Of course not. That was thirty-five years ago. Wait, yes, the man's name was Gant. What was it? Horace? Homer?"

"Lester's father was Harold Gant," Carl supplied. "Is that it?"

"Possibly," the professor nodded and turned back to the dark young man. "Mr. Gant, is your father the caretaker I hired?"

"Old man Gant's been dead over ten years," Carl said. "Leastways, him and his wife disappeared."

"Ah," Poe widened his eyes, "more mysteries."

"You don't keep very close track of your caretakers, Professor," Dad said gruffly.

"What?" His head did another revolution. "Oh, the bank in Hawley handles all that. I suppose they gave the job to the boy when the father disappeared. Can't he talk, Mr. Willingham?"

"He can talk. Heard him myself," Carl stated.

And he did. Four words. I never heard him say anything else. "Missus will be down," he said in flat, colorless tones.

"Who else is here?" Jud groaned.

Weatherly sighed. "I imagine he means my mother, Mr. Ledbetter."

"Your mother?" Mom squeaked. "Why didn't you tell us your mother was living here?"

"I wasn't sure that she was." Weatherly sounded on his last legs. "I didn't expect she would still be alive."

Gant turned without another word and vanished into the darkness at the top of the stairs. Weatherly looked as if he had been kicked in the stomach. He had had one complication too many. After a moment, Dad picked up Mom's suitcase and escorted her upstairs.

"You want to go to bed, hon?" Poe asked his wife. "You must be exhausted."

"If it's all the same to you," Linda laughed nervously, "I'll wait until you go. I couldn't sleep up there by myself."

Poe grinned and put his arm around her. They all drifted back to the parlor, but I gave Ann a signal and went out to the front porch. The rain had stopped. I could see stars in the west and a smudge of light where the moon hid behind clouds. Frogs were screaming in damp ecstasy, and a few bold crickets had emerged from their dry hidey-holes. The air had the fresh, clean smell it gets right after a rain, pointing up the slight mustiness of the house. I took a deep breath and leaned against the railing, looking at the cars on the road at the bottom of the hill.

"Did you see it?" I asked when I felt Ann behind me.

"Yes. I've run across it a few times before. Apparently some people have natural shields." She leaned on the railing beside me.

I turned when I heard the door open, but I knew who it was. Carl Willingham nodded to us and went down the porch steps.

"Where are you going, Mr. Willingham?" Ann asked politely.

He stopped and turned, looking up at us. "Leavin', ma'am. Rain's stopped and I'd rather walk four miles than stay in the same house with Lester Gant. I can take magicians and mind readers," he dipped his head, "no offense, and even flying shoes, but he's too much. I'd advise the rest of you to do the same."

"What's the matter with him?" I asked, because he was genuinely frightened.

"Folks say he killed his parents. Never found 'em, no proof he did it, but folks know just the same." He nodded again and started down the hill. We watched him for a moment.

"Folks around here sure say a lot," I observed wryly and we went back in the house. Weatherly was sitting on the couch deep in gloomy thought. I had the impression of swirling, muddy water. Poe, Linda, Jud, and Dad were starting another card game. "Mr. Willingham just left," I said, certainly not expecting the reaction I got.

Weatherly jumped up and stared at me. "Left? What do you mean?"

"He said he was gonna walk to town," I said, completely mystified.

Weatherly was severely agitated. He moved around as if he couldn't decide which direction was the right one. "He can't leave!" he wailed. "He'll be killed! Stop him! Bring him back by force if you have to! Hurry! Hurry!"

Weatherly's anxiety was so strong and sharp that I ran from the room and out the front door. They all followed me, confused and frightened. Carl was almost to the bottom of the hill. I yelled at him. Dad and Poe were right behind me, not knowing what was going on. The others stayed on the porch.

Carl turned and looked at us curiously. His eyebrows rose in bewilderment at the sight of us bounding down the hill, floundering in the slippery mud, yelling like madmen.

Carl, the only one looking toward the house, was the first to see it. His eyes got big. He took a step backward.

Insects in Amber

Then I felt it, like static electricity in my head. I skidded to a halt on the muddy ground and fell to my knees with a grunt. I looked back at the house. Weatherly was waving his arms and yelling. The crickets stopped singing.

The house was surrounded by a glow, an iridescent nimbus, like a soap bubble growing larger and larger. Dad and Poe had stopped, looking at the house. Weatherly was screaming, waving us back. My head was singing with the sweet chill of fear, but not my fear. The air crackled with energy. I could feel the hair on my arms standing up. Sparks danced across the hill, flowing down it like a faerie river. I turned to look at Carl.

He stared at the house, backing slowly away. The static electricity in the air made his clothes cling to his skin. Then he whirled and ran. The energy pressure was growing unbearable.

Then there was light, an eye-burning flash, a fierce discharge. All the energy floating free in the air gathered at one point. It circled around like a whirlwind of fireflies, swept by me, contracted, converged at one point.

On Carl.

He screamed. Then he was covered with fire. He screamed and ran and burned. He beat at his clothes with his hands, beat at flames with flames. His glowing feet kicked through the damp grass and left little curls of steam that sizzled and disappeared.

Carl stopped his useless flailing and just ran, his arms stretching before him, seeking. Then he stumbled, staggered a few steps, and fell, still screaming. He kept moving, trying to crawl.

The screaming stopped.

Then the movement.

Carl was nothing but a shapeless lump, burning, sending a shaft of black smoke into the night air. The energy and the pressure was gone. The crickets started up again.

I had thrown up my tattered barriers, trying to shut him out, trying to block his agonies from my mind. Then, I think I felt the muddy ground hit me in the face.

I was moving, floating in warmth. Dad was carrying me as he had when I was three and had fallen asleep. I tightened my grip around his neck. Then he was prying me loose, putting me on the couch.

They were all crowded around, looking at me, except Jud. He was staring out the window, pale and shaken. Tannie, in her pajamas, was round-eyed with wonder. Ann put her hand on my forehead and pushed the hair out of my eyes.

Dad was standing a few feet away watching me. I had never known him to be so angry. "Professor Weatherly," he said in a low voice, "you told me there was no danger. I want you to explain exactly what's going on. No evasions. No promises. We'd like to make a few decisions for ourselves."

"I'm sorry, Mr. Henderson," he said with honest regret. "It's too late for independent decisions. There is only one course open to us."

"Did you hear what I said? I. Want. An. Explanation."

"Of course, Mr. Henderson." He fluttered like a moth. "Give everyone a chance to calm down and I'll tell you all I know."

"Jud. Come away from the window," Linda said. Her voice was hoarse and trembled a little. Jud turned without comment and sat in a chair.

"So the spirits are malignant after all, Professor," Poe said quietly.

"Be patient a few minutes, please. Let's get Ben back on his feet." He looked down at me with real concern on his face. "Are you feeling better?"

"Yes. I think so." I took Ann's hand in mine and squeezed it. Tannie looked at me with her little face pinched and pale. I grinned and winked at her.

"I absolutely refuse to give you a hug, Benjamin Henderson," she stated uncategorically. "You had me scared to death. I thought I was gonna be a widow."

Everyone laughed—more than it deserved, to be sure, but it broke the tension. Even Jud managed an anemic grin. Tannie sniffed. I sat up and held my arms out to her. She threw herself at me and sobbed on my chest.

"I'm sorry, honey," I said.

"Oh, Tannie!" Mom groaned, thankfully finding something practical on which to focus her attention. "Ben is covered with mud. You're getting it all over you." She extracted Tannie bodily. "Ben, go change your clothes and wash your face."

So I went to the suitcase and got clean blue jeans and a clean shirt. I was a bit wobble-kneed, but I tried not to show it. You can take just so much fussing. I went in a corner behind a chair and changed while they talked.

"Are you ready, Professor?" Dad asked, nearing the end of his patience.

"Yes, Mr. Henderson. Everyone get comfortable. I want to explain as well as I can what happened. Ben. Are you feeling it?"

"Yes."

"Describe it to me."

"There's really nothing to describe. It's just there. It's aware of us. And . . . it's just . . . there."

"That's right," Ann agreed.

"There's no hostility? No anger?" Weatherly asked as if he expected there would be.

"Not now," I answered. "It's frightened. I think it's always frightened. There was anger . . . no, not anger . . . panic, when Mr. Willingham tried to leave." I finished changing clothes and joined the group.

I was so busy concentrating on Weatherly, I didn't sense her

Insects in Amber

presence. Neither did Ann. No one knew she was in the room until she spoke in her brassy bellow. "Philip!" she brayed. "What are these people doing in my house?"

Everyone turned quickly. I felt Weatherly's resolve become as fragile as cobwebs. She stood in the doorway, surveying us. She wore a long black dress that reached the floor. It had a high collar that pushed her flesh into wrinkles around her sharp chin. The long-sleeved dress was unadorned but for a large cameo at her throat. Her hands rested on a silver-headed stick and her pewter-colored hair was piled on top of her head. Her skin was almost white and had a peculiar sheen—like a waxworks figure come to life. Lester Gant lurked behind her ramrod-straight figure, as inscrutable as ever.

"I'm waiting for an answer, Philip."

"It's good to see you again, Mother." He sounded like a little boy who had been caught doing something naughty in the bathroom.

"You're a fool, Philip," she said in her clarion voice. "You've always been a fool."

"Yes, Mother, very good to see you again," he said, sighing.

She speared him with a look and sat regally in a chair near us. She moved as if her spine were of one piece. Gant remained in the doorway.

"You've come to try again, have you." It was a statement rather than a question. The rest of us sat there with our mouths open.

"Yes," he said. "I was about to explain to these people."

"It will kill you as it did the man just now. I knew you were fool enough to keep trying, but I didn't know you were so obsessed as to endanger others."

"They are not here by design, Mother."

"How long has it been since your last futility, Philip?"

"Thirty-five years."

"So long?" she said a little wistfully.

"Professor," Dad said through clenched teeth, "we're waiting."

"What?" He started as if he had forgotten the rest of us. "Yes. Excuse me, Mother." He turned away from her. "You heard how it began from Mr. Willingham. I was ten years old. It was in my room that fire was seen. I had for some time been aware of my powers, but I thought everyone had them. After almost disastrously finding out that wasn't the case, that I was unique, I kept them secret and practiced. However, as you heard Mr. Willingham say, I didn't do it in time to avoid getting a reputation in the area for being . . . ah . . . peculiar. My powers developed with practice, but I was so immature."

"You were a fool."

"Yes, Mother. It happened the night Mr. Willingham told you about. I unfortunately thought I knew all there was to know. You see, I had just read Wells' **The Time Machine**. I . . . ah . . . I'm afraid I attempted to travel in time." He looked at us with an ironic frown.

"Why?" Dad asked a bit dumbfounded.

Weatherly shrugged. "I was ten years old and it seemed like an excellent idea."

"What happened?" Poe asked in rapt fascination.

"My powers were quite strong," he continued, "but my control wasn't. I didn't know at the time exactly what I had done, but I believe, now, that in some way I warped space. And something came through. It was ferocious. All fire and energy. It attacked me the same way it did Mr. Willingham. I tried to fight it but was successful only in saving myself. I ran out of the house and didn't return for fifteen years."

"He ran away and left his family to be destroyed."

"There was nothing I could do, Mother."

"Why did nothing happen to you, Mrs. Weatherly?" Dad asked.

Her head swiveled toward him. "I do not know why I was not destroyed, but I was not. It kept me like a souvenir. Like an insect in amber. I often wish I had been . . . destroyed."

Dad inclined his head toward Lester Gant, still standing in the doorway regarding us impassively. "What about him?"

"Mr. Gant is in no danger," she said with a slightly upward twist of the corners of her thin mouth. "Mr. Gant come and goes as he pleases. It knows he will return. Mr. Gant is a worshipper." I had the impression this was only a casual volley in an old war. Gant looked at her without expression.

"We were awakened by the commotion in Philip's room," Mrs. Weatherly picked up the story. "My husband and daughters reached it first. I saw them destroyed. I hid in the attic. When the neighbors searched the house, they didn't find me, and the thing didn't bother them. By the time I had recovered from my fright, it was too late. I was unable to leave."

"I returned fifteen years later. I was much stronger and completely in control."

"You should have seen the foolish expression on his face when he found me," his mother said with a slight pucker of her thin lips.

"You were here fifteen years?" Mom said in confusion. "How did you live?"

"Insects in amber require nothing," she answered flatly. "I do not eat. I do not sleep. I am not sure that I am even alive."

"The thing I brought here has no physical existence as we know it," the professor explained. "I think it sustains my mother with its own life energy."

"Is it the same for him?" Poe asked and indicated Lester Gant. I looked at Gant, still standing immobile in the doorway. His eyes were slightly narrowed and focused on Ann. I didn't think much about it at the time.

"Mr. Gant is here for other purposes," Mrs. Weatherly said with that tightening of her mouth which seemed to denote amusement. "Mr. Gant is here voluntarily. Mr. Gant has secret appetites."

Insects in Amber

Gant gave her a malevolent look and turned on his heel. She watched him leave, her porcelain eyes twinkling. She turned back to us. "Mr. Gant is blasphemed."

"What did you do when you came back?" Dad asked Weatherly, getting back on the subject.

"I'll tell you what the fool did," his mother brayed as Weatherly opened his mouth. "He tried to destroy it. But it had grown stronger also. And he ran again. Then, rather than letting the house fall down as it deserves, he hired Mr. Gant's father to keep it in repair."

"I did it for you, Mother. I couldn't . . ." She stopped him with a snort.

"What happened to Mr. Gant's parents?" Ann asked.

"Mr. Gant and I talk of many things, but that is not one of them. They moved into the house when he was a baby. It didn't matter to me. I never left my room. When Mr. Gant was about that boy's age. . . " she pointed a bony finger at me, ". . . the parents weren't here any more."

"What are you planning to do now, Professor?" Ann asked.

"My mistake was in trying to destroy it." He frowned. "I know now it probably can't be destroyed. But it must be stopped before it moves out of this house. I don't know why it's still here. I must communicate with it, find out what it wants. That's why I brought you, Ann, to communicate with it. You can't imagine the elation I felt when I found you. Thirty-five years . . ." His voice faded.

"How did you spot me anyway?" she asked.

"Tests." He raised his forefinger. "That's why I became a professor of psychology, so I could test students. Tests of all kinds, to thousands of students. Most of them had been somewhat altered to my purposes rather than the original author's, of course."

"What will communication accomplish," I asked, "other than to satisfy your curiosity?"

"Isn't that enough?" His eyes widened. "But I expect to learn much more. Much more."

"If it can't be destroyed," I asked, "what do you plan to do?"

"I must warp space and send it back where it came from," he said.

His mother looked at him speculatively. "Perhaps you are no longer such a fool." Then she shook her head. "No. You could have done it without involving the girl. You are still a fool." She stood and walked imperially toward the door. She paused and turned, both her hands resting on the silver-headed stick. "Do not let Mr. Gant know what you are doing." Then she went out the door and up the stairs like a wraith to disappear in the darkness.

"Mom," Tannie said droopily, "could I go back to bed, please? I'm sleepy."

Mom put her hand on Tannie's head. "Maybe you'd better sleep down here, dear."

"Why?"

"Isn't she frightened of anything?" Jud groaned.

Tannie looked at him, surprised at his ignorance. "My brother is here."

Jud grimaced and sighed. "I wish I had your confidence, kid. I really do."

"I guess we're as safe in bed as we are here," Poe said sensibly. "I'm ready myself."

I started for the door and Ann met me halfway there. I took her hand. We went back to the porch while the others bustled around preparing for bed. The sky had almost completely cleared. The night was bright out over the Kansas pasture land. I couldn't see Carl's body, if there was anything left to see. We sat on the railing.

"Ben," she said softly, "do you think we ought to be doing this? You know what happened to you when it killed Mr. Willingham."

"I've been working on that," I said and turned to face her. "Read me."

She concentrated for a moment, then looked at me in surprise. "You're completely shielded. I wouldn't even know you were there if I couldn't see you."

"When Mr. Willingham was killed"—the memory made my skin crawl—"I got the full blast. I've always had a shield of sorts. I don't pick up anything unless it's especially strong or I want to. Background babble doesn't get through at all. That's why I didn't spot you."

She nodded. "I wonder how many others there are, how many we've passed on the street and didn't recognize?"

"I've been trying to strengthen my shield," I continued. "It was relatively easy. It just never occurred to me to try. Here, concentrate on me. I'll let it down slowly. See how it works."

I showed her how it worked and she tried it. We practiced it for a while until she was as good at it as I was. She was quiet then, looking at me.

She stood up and stepped in front of me, facing me. She put her hands on either side of my neck. Tannie has nothing on me when it comes to looking wide-eyed.

"Ben . . ." she said solemnly, "I know what you're feeling about what you can do. You've never explored it before, never really tried to extend the limits of your ability. I know you're strong, stronger than I. But . . . be careful. Don't get in over your head with this thing. Don't get overconfident. Just . . . be careful."

I nodded, understanding. We looked at each other, not reading, just being physical. Then I slid my hands up her arms and interlaced my fingers behind her neck. I pulled her head down to mine slowly. She didn't resist. I kissed her very lightly on the lips, still not reading, enjoying the purely physical sensation. She pulled her head back and smiled at me. I stood up and let my arms slip lower down her back. I felt hers do the same thing. I kissed her again, harder. She kissed back.

We were sitting on the steps, not doing anything, not talking, just being together, when I felt it. It was like a hobnail boot in the groin. Fear

Insects in Amber

and pain, but mostly rage and anger. Ann got it too. She jerked and grunted and looked at me with pain. We jumped up and ran inside. I knew who it was. I did a quick survey of the house. Only one was missing.

I stuck my head in the parlor where the professor sat meditatively before the dying fire. "Where's Jud?"

He jumped at the sound of my voice and looked at me blankly. I repeated the question more insistently. "He's sharing a room with you," he said bewildered. "The second one on the right at the top of the stairs. What's the matter?" He rose and moved toward us.

"He's dead," I said over my shoulder as Ann and I ran up the stairs. We found him in the bathroom, on the floor, face down. He was wearing only gold jockey shorts. Blood was still seeping along the crevices between the white floor tiles. His blond fairness was now a pallor. Judson Bradley Ledbetter wasn't beautiful anymore. His shaving kit was scattered about as if he'd had it in his hands when attacked. I knelt beside him and turned him over. I shouldn't have. His chest and abdomen had been thoroughly worked over with a large-bladed knife.

Ann gasped and Weatherly let the air hiss out between his teeth. "Who could have done it?" he whispered.

"Gant."

"Why?"

"We don't know. Perhaps your mother does. She's in the hall."

She was standing there watching us, looking exactly as she had earlier. Poe opened the door across from us and stepped sleepily into the hall wearing pajama bottoms. "What's the commotion?" he asked, rubbing his face. Ann went to him and talked quietly. He looked frightened and hurried into the room we had come out of.

"Mrs. Weatherly," I said. "Jud Ledbetter has been killed." She turned her porcelain eyes on me but said nothing. "We've read everyone in the house except Gant. He's the only one who could've done it. We need to know why."

She narrowed her eyes at me then turned to her son. "Your foolishness is catching up with you, Philip. Mr. Gant is also a fool. He killed the wrong one."

"What?" Weatherly gasped.

"Don't be an idiot," she snapped. "Mr. Gant is protecting the thing." She turned back to me. "Young man, Mr. Gant will undoubtedly discover his error." She wheeled and walked away into the darkness.

"Ben," Ann whispered. "He meant to kill you."

"I'm trying to remember what we said while he was in the room. He knows that you and someone else are here to help the professor get rid of it, but you were sitting next to Jud when he mentioned it. That means he'll be coming for you next."

"We've got to find him," Weatherly whined. "He could ruin everything."

I gave him a disgusted look, but he didn't really mean it the way it came out. "I'll wake Dad," I said. Poe came back into the hall looking a little sick. Ann and the professor went to him.

Mom and Dad were both asleep. Tannie was on a daybed screwed up like a worm the way she always slept. I put my hand on Dad's shoulder and his eyes popped open. He started to say something, but I put my finger to my lips and motioned him to come outside. He got out of bed, careful not to wake Mom, and put on his robe, looking at me questioningly.

In the hall we explained everything that had happened. "Do you think Linda and your mother will be safe?" Poe asked.

"Wake Linda and put her in with Mom. Ann, stay with them and bolt the door." She nodded.

Poe was worried. "Don't tell Linda what happened to Jud. Not yet." He went back in his room and closed the door.

"Professor," I said, "you know the house. Where could he be hiding?"

He shook his head. "I don't know. Lots of places. I suggest we start downstairs and work up to the attic. Ben, can you read him at all?"

"No."

We started in the cellar and searched every hidey-hole. He wasn't down there and he wasn't on the ground floor either. Dad had his flashlight, and I had one of the kerosene lamps, so we could split up when necessary to prevent Gant from doubling back on us. Poe had a poker he took from the parlor fireplace. He grinned at me nervously and smacked it a couple of times in his palm.

We went back upstairs. Dad shone the flashlight down the hall. Gant was at the door of Mom's room crouched over the doorknob. He had a large butcher knife in his hand. He looked up at us and ran off in the opposite direction, through a door. When we got to it, it was locked.

"That's the stairway to the attic," Weatherly said.

Dad rattled the door a few times, frowning at it. It had one of those old mortise-type locks that could be locked from either side, but only with a key.

"Wait a moment," Weatherly muttered. The lock rattled and went **snick**. The door swung open about two inches with a lazy creak.

Dad glanced at Weatherly, then opened the door the rest of the way. He pointed the flashlight up the steep, narrow steps, but there was nothing except gloom and cobwebs. Dad took a deep breath and started up very cautiously. Poe was behind him with the poker, then the professor. I brought up the rear with the kerosene lamp.

The stairs entered the attic through a hole in the middle of the floor, a perfect place to get your head knocked off when you poked it up. Dad shone the flashlight around, keeping down as far as he could, ready to duck if Gant was waiting. When he motioned the rest of us up, I realized I'd been holding my breath.

The attic was a jumble of discards and had a fifty-year accumulation

Insects in Amber

of dust. The floor was velvety smooth, disturbed only by Mr. Gant's footprints leading into the pile of rubble, and little stitchery-like marks made by crawling beetles. Dad followed Mr. Gant's footprints with the flashlight beam but we couldn't see him.

Twenty people could have been hiding in all the clutter. I held the lamp high, trying to see into the darkness. It was practically useless; it lit everything beautifully—for three feet in every direction. And when one of us moved, he cast a shadow the size of Godzilla.

The rafters were draped with dusty cobwebs and spotted with little brown mounds made by mud daubers. The flashlight passed over a wasp nest the size of a dinner plate back in the corner. The yellow jackets stirred sluggishly, lethargic in the cool night air.

Dad kept swinging the flashlight around, covering as much of the attic as he could, but Mr. Gant was as invisible to my eyes as he was to my mind. He could have been hiding in any one of many places.

I was about to suggest we lock the attic securely and leave Mr. Gant to the spiders, when something toppled behind me.

We whirled in that direction. The flashlight caught Mr. Gant charging straight at us with the butcher knife drawn back. The whole thing couldn't have taken more than a couple of seconds, but I suddenly had a sensation of slow-motion, of Gant running at me through a narrow aisle between stacks of cardboard boxes, of the knife glinting in the flashlight beam, of his shirt flaring out at each step.

I remember studying his face, remember feeling surprise that it was almost emotionless, surprise that he wasn't slavering like a madman. All of this must have been only in my mind because my muscles didn't correspond. I just stood there like a dummy, watching him.

Then he tripped. His toe caught in a picture frame leaning against the stack of boxes. A startled expression crossed his face as his body got ahead of his feet. Instead of getting me with the knife, he rammed into me bodily.

My arms went up and the lamp slipped smoothly from my fingers. I grunted as the wind was knocked out of me. Then Gant and I landed on the floor in a tangle, but the lamp stayed in my line of vision, arching up slowly, very slowly. The thin glass chimney hit a rafter and shattered, then the base, the wick still burning, smashed against the trunk engulfing one end of the attic in burning kerosene.

Mr. Gant lost no time in getting himself untangled; he had landed on top. I was flat on my back. The next thing I knew he was straddling my stomach with the knife drawn back. I twisted as he brought the knife down, and I heard it thunk into the floor beside my ear.

Then good old Poe swung the poker with both hands as if he were chopping wood. It caught Mr. Gant across the shoulders. He yelled and arched his back, his face twisting with pain. He lurched up, gasping for breath, and staggered into the darkness, the knife still in his hand. He upset several piles of uncertain junk, bringing them down with a clatter.

Poe and Dad helped me up and I grinned thanks at Poe.

Mr. Gant was out of sight again, hidden by the darkness and the smoke. We turned to the fire. The whole end of the attic was burning furiously. The heat was rapidly becoming uncomfortable. We edged toward the stairs, but the professor was staring at the flames, deep in concentration. We stopped and watched.

A mist began forming in the attic, like heavy fog rolling in. It even smelled like fog. It grew thicker and thicker, closing in on the fire until, finally, it was completely obscured by the bank of white. The crackle of the flames gradually changed to a damp hissing and then nothing. I could no longer feel the heat. Little beads of water stood on the hairs on my arms, like a heavy dew. The thick mist swirled away as if in a wind and the fire was out. The end of the attic was blackened and charred, shiny with moisture. Drops of water fell from the rafters, thumping against the boxes and trunks and other debris. Weatherly sighed deeply.

"You're sure handy to have around, Professor," Poe said with a certain amount of awe.

"Carnival tricks." He perished the thought.

Dad swung the flashlight away from the burned area and started to say something. He stopped with his mouth open, looking at something. We turned. Gant was creeping toward us with the knife in his hand. Mr. Gant may have had his faults, but lack of determination wasn't one of them. He stopped when the light hit him. His eyes glittered like marbles. Weatherly was concentrating again.

I heard a harsh buzzing, and the wasp nest almost directly over Gant's head erupted in a yellow and black storm. I don't know what Weatherly did, but the yellow jackets swarmed all over Gant. He screamed and stumbled back, crashing through a pile of discards, swatting at the stinging insects. He kept yelling and threshing, and I guess Weatherly couldn't go through with it any longer because the wasps left Gant and settled back on the nest.

Then, unbelievably, Gant rose from the junk and started toward us again. His face and hands were solid with welts that grew redder and larger by the second. One eye was almost closed, but he came at us, staggering and stumbling, entangling himself in the clutter. He warded off the collapsing debris with one hand and held the knife in the other.

Professor Weatherly groaned. Then the knife in Gant's hand flowed a cherry red. Gant sucked air through his teeth and dropped it, clutching his hand with the other. The knife clattered to the floor. A curl of smoke rose from it. But, before another fire could get started, Weatherly did something to it and it was cold once more.

Dad kept the flashlight on Gant. He backed away, still hunched over his burned hand. We moved toward him. His eye was now completely closed, and the other didn't look too good. He still hadn't given up. He grabbed the base of the piano stool with his good hand and drew back to throw it.

Insects in Amber

Then he froze. The piano stool slipped from limp fingers and bounced off a three-legged table. Gant sucked in air like a fish. He clutched at his chest. I looked at Weatherly, then back at Gant. He breathed in great, roaring gasps, tearing at his shirt. He dropped to one knee, then doubled up and fell sideways into a rusty birdcage. He didn't move. We went to him. He was unconscious but breathing evenly.

I looked at Weatherly. "You could have killed him."

"Yes."

"What do we do with him now?" Dad asked softly.

The professor didn't answer for a moment, then looked up. "The closet in the upstairs hall has a strong lock on it."

So, we wrestled Gant down the steep, narrow stairs and locked him in the empty closet. The lock didn't seem to me any stronger than any of the others, but it worked and wasn't loose. The door opened outward, but there wasn't enough room for Gant to get much of a run at battering it down. If he tried, we would hear him. We propped a chair under the knob just in case and stood there looking at each other.

"Now what?" Poe finally said, plucking stray cobwebs from the hair on his chest.

"Everyone should go back to bed. There's nothing more to be done," the professor said.

Dad brushed dust from his robe. "How long to do you plan to wait before you attempt to send your monster back where it came from?"

Weatherly glanced at me, then looked morosely at Dad. "I don't know," he sighed. "Tomorrow, in the daylight, after everyone's rested . . . I don't know." He glanced at me again. "We must make sure everything is right. I doubt if we'll have a second chance." He looked at the floor, then back at Dad. "I'm terribly sorry all of you were involved in this, Mr. Henderson. Mr. McNeal. Terribly sorry." He turned and walked slowly toward the stairs.

"Clare and Linda will be very curious about all this commotion," Dad observed.

"Don't tell Linda until the morning . . . about Jud," Poe said in a strained voice. "She needs sleep."

"Ann has already satisfied their curiosity," I explained.

We moved Jud's body downstairs to the dining room and covered it with a sheet. None of us could think of anything else to do. Then we went back to bed.

I don't know how long I'd been asleep. I'm not at my most lucid when suddenly awakened. I found myself sitting in the middle of the bed wondering what woke me. Then I knew.

I ran into the hall, barefooted and in my underwear. The closet door was wide open. I never found out how Gant got it open without waking someone. I should have known his determination wouldn't have been dampened by a simple locked door.

I burst into Ann's room without slowing and skidded to a halt. Gant had his arm around her throat so she couldn't cry out. They stood near the foot of the bed. Ann was fighting him but he was too strong for her. He had gone back to the attic for the knife and held it at her breast. His face and hands looked like raw hamburger. He didn't even look at me, though I imagine he could barely see. His good eye was almost swollen shut. But he was lost in some fantasy of his own, and I thought I could detect an expression of rapture on his swollen face. He wasn't holding Ann as a shield or a hostage, but as a sacrifice.

I stood petrified in the middle of the room as he drew back the knife. My face contorted in rage and hate and I screamed a silent mental scream. I don't know exactly what I did, and I've never tried to repeat it. I drew on something I hope never emerges again.

My mind raged at Gant, blasted him with primal hate. Synapses opened like floodgates. The knife froze in the air. My fingernails dug into my palms. My body trembled uncontrollably. Sweat popped out on my face. My eyes locked on his. The arm around Ann's neck fell away. The knife slipped from his upraised hand. He took a step backward, staring at me uncomprehendingly with his red slit of an eye, his mouth slack. Ann stumbled away from him and got behind me.

I didn't stop because Ann was free. The vision of the knife buried in her breast was too vivid. I could have rationalized it as the only way, but I wasn't thinking at the time, only hating.

Gant backed against the wall, but his legs kept moving, trying to get him farther away. His head jerked back and forth, as if he wanted to loosen something clinging to his face. He put his red, puffy hands over his ears and breathed through his mouth. A low moan began deep in his throat. The moan grew slowly in volume and pitch until it was a shrill keening, ending only when his lungs were empty.

I hammered at the bright mirror surrounding him, beat at it, battered against it until it shattered, and I plunged through into his mind.

I thought I screamed, but Ann said later it was a whimper.

I threw up my shields and fought my way out, ripping and tearing, clawing my way free, slashing through the bright chaos and blinding disorder of Gant's mind. As I broke free I felt his mind dim and go black.

I felt like jelly and slumped to my knees. I couldn't get my breath. My arms hung limp and immovable. Gant was in a crumpled heap against the wall. Ann was beside me, kneeling beside me, her arms around me, feeling me.

A heartbeat began.

Oh, Ben.

Yes. My God! Do you know what I did?

I felt it. Part of it reflected off his shield.

Are you all right? Did he hurt you?

No. I was only frightened. You came.

We can do it now.

No. Not now. Later.

Insects in Amber

Yes.
The heartbeat continued.
They're all still asleep.
Yes. I never thought it could be so . . .
I know. I know.
I keep forgetting. Ann . . .
I know. Don't be sad.
We've lost something. But we've gained more, so very much more.
The heartbeat ended.

I put my arm around her. She leaned her head against mine and we went to my room. I closed the door behind me and leaned against it, looking at her. She stepped toward me. I met her halfway. We kissed, melded in mind and body. We undressed and moved to the bed, touching and loving. It wasn't only physical love, but I wasn't reading her. It was no longer necessary.

I was me.
I was Ann.
We were us.

When the sun came up we got out of bed and dressed. I went to my parents' room. Ann went to Poe's and Linda's. "Dad. Mom," we said. "Poe. Linda," we said. "Wake up. Get dressed and ready to leave. Pack everything and go out on the porch."

"Ben?" Mom said.

"Ann?" Linda said.

"Everything's okay," we said. "We're ready to help the professor get rid of his monster. Hurry."

Ann and I met in the hall and went downstairs. Professor Weatherly was asleep on the couch, tired and gray, slipping into despair.

"Professor," we said with my voice.

"What?" He sat up suddenly, confused. "Oh. Ben. Is it morning?"

"Yes."

"We're ready," the Ann part of me said.

"What?" He stood up, rubbing his eyes.

"We're ready to help you exorcise your monster."

He looked at us. "Something has happened."

"Yes. Ann and I are telepathically linked. It's permanent."

"Describe it to me."

"I'm not sure I can. I know everything Ben's thinking; I remember; I feel everything he feels."

"But there's more than that," I said. "I'm both of us and we're one of us. We're . . . well, essentially we're one person in two bodies. Yet we still retain our separate egos. Perhaps a better explanation would be we're two people cohabiting two bodies. I don't know how it would be with two men, or two women, but with us, it's . . . it's love."

"Yes," he whispered. "Yes. It would have to be, wouldn't it? Total love or . . . total loathing. There could be no other way."

"There's no way to really know what it's like without experiencing it," Ann said. "People who know only physical love are missing so much." We grinned. "Though, I guess there is something faintly masturbatory about it."

"This is absolutely marvelous." He beamed like a child on Christmas morning. "Will you allow me to study this further?"

We smiled at him. "Of course, Professor," I said. "As soon as the others are ready to leave, we can contact your monster. Your mother will not leave. Mr. Gant is dead."

"Dead?" He blinked.

"I killed him," I said. I locked my muscles to stop the trembling I could feel about to begin. "I willed him dead and he died," I said numbly.

Ann put her hand on my shoulder. "We're ready," she said. Vocalizing was slow and clumsy, but it was an old habit.

"Wait here," I told him and went to the entry hall. They came down the stairs with their suitcases and uncertain expressions, Linda crying, but trying to stop. Poe had told her about Jud. I herded them unresisting onto the porch. Mom and Dad turned and looked at me, frightened. I smiled. "Don't worry," I said. Tannie peeked back at me, saucer-eyed and solemn. I winked at her. She grinned and went on out. I closed the door and went back to the parlor.

"Are you ready?"

"Yes." Weatherly nodded.

"I hope what you find out justifies everything, Professor." We concentrated. A brilliant flash. A sheet of energy swirled around us, held away by the professor, and died out. "Take it easy," I said softly, "take it easy. It's almost insane with fright."

We touched that alien mind. Not entered, only touched. We would have been lost if we had entered. Its alienness was indescribable. There was no point of reference to human thought. We stared in awe at its great, shining, immature mind. Its alienness made details, even large details, impossible to grasp; but basic emotions, which must be common to all intelligent life, were clear to read. It was aware of our minds, but did not fear them. It feared only what was alien to **it**: Weatherly's **physical** assault.

A smile came involuntarily to our lips. "I'll be damned," I said aloud. "Do you know what we've got, Professor? It's a . . . a baby, if that's the right word. Its memory goes back millions, billions of years; so far it can't remember its origin, but it knows it's immature. The reason it's never left this house is because it's basically a frightened child. It only wants to go home. Send it back, Professor, while I try to keep it calm."

Another flash and another swirl of energy. "It's too frightened," I said anxiously. "I'm having trouble. It wants to go home more than anything, but you'll have to force it. It's irrational with fear. It's only been here a moment by its time-scale."

Ann left to get the others to the cars, away from the house. I waited until they were at a safe distance.

"Now. Force it, Professor."

Energy whirled around us like a tornado. The walls, the ceilings, the floors, the furniture, all were burning fiercely, except for the bubble in which we stood.

Weatherly opened a path through the inferno, a path from us to the door. "Go with the others, Ben," he said. I started to protest, but he shut me up. "You can do just as much from outside as you can in here. And I can do more if I don't have you to worry about."

He was right. I had no protection from the thing's physical energy, energy which I suspected was manifesting itself physically because it was **here**, not where it came from. I ran through the tunnel he opened and turned at the door. The tunnel closed and I couldn't see him anymore.

I hurried down the hill to the others, still in contact with the professor's monster. The just-risen sun gleamed on the still damp house, turning the weathered gray to copper, but flames poured from the parlor windows. Smoke billowed from other openings, the gray clouds also gilded by the sun. Flames suddenly spurted from under the eaves. The fire had gotten upstairs. Energy popped like lightning bolts.

All this I saw with my eyes and heard with my ears. What I saw and heard with my mind was different.

I caught a thought from the professor's mother, but shut it out quickly, unable to bear it. The monster thrashed in the professor's grip, frightened out of its mind, screaming pitifully.

I watched Professor Weatherly in the parlor but not with my eyes. He stood in a clear island surrounded by raging flames and energy. It began. The inferno cycloned away on one side of him and a tunnel opened, an endless, gleaming tunnel. He stood still, hunched in concentration.

I knew, suddenly, what was about to happen, but the professor was caught completely by surprise. There was nothing I could do to help him. I slammed shields around Ann. She jerked out of her trance and looked wildly about. She screamed at me, "No! Ben! Don't block me out!"

More energy popped. Everyone's clothing clung to their skin. I could feel my hair standing up, charged with static electricity. Helplessly I watched the professor force his monster into the tunnel.

He hadn't moved. He stood before the tunnel, surrounded by an inferno, hunched in concentration. Then, gradually, slowly, his body smudged outward, toward the tunnel. He felt it. He looked up. He strained away from the tunnel, held out his arms, warding it away. The distortion, the stretching outward continued. His arms were caught in it, extending to half again their former length, blurring toward the tunnel.

Then a particle of his little finger broke away and streamed down the tunnel like a shooting star. More particles broke free. The tunnel was filled with shooting stars, streaking to infinity.

I threw up my shield. Weatherly's terror was too great. But, in that last split second, I saw a comet roar away down the tunnel, and he was gone. The tunnel was closing.

I was aware of physical sensations only. I stood swaying, trying to keep from toppling over. Ann threw her arms around me. Dad put his hand on the back of my neck, not saying anything. I dropped the shields. Ann and I were one again.

"He did it," I said on an exhaustion high. "It's gone home. He sent it back. But it dragged him back with it. I was with him for a moment."

The energy was gone but the fire wasn't. The old wood of the house burned ferociously. Dad propelled us away, to the bottom of the hill, where the others waited numbly. We stood for a long time, saying nothing, watching the house burn.

Tannie had come to me and stood watching the house with her arm clutching my thigh. I had my arm on her shoulder. "What about you, Ann?" Dad asked.

"With me," I said.

"Yes," she smiled.

Tannie peeked around me, staring at Ann. Ann smiled at her and winked the same way I would. Tannie grinned like a supernova. She launched herself at Ann and hugged her.

The sheriff's car pulled up as we were about to leave. He was a nice person named Robin Walker. We told him a simplified version of what happened, a version he would believe. Ann and I made sure he believed it.

Dad backed the station wagon out of the ditch. I got in the yellow VW with Ann, and we went on to Wichita.

Waiting for Billy Star

Out here the wind is almost always blowing off the caprock. It's hot in the summer and cold in the winter, whipping sheets of sand like torn veils across the black asphalt of the highway. People out here don't have much time for the gentle things; the sun is too hot and the land is too dry and stingy. But they all remember Susanne Delacourt, even after ten years.

The record is still on the jukebox. I don't know why I left it there, but I wouldn't take it off now. It's just a recording of a hokey old song that was popular back then called "The Tennesee Waltz." Occasionally someone will play it; then a quiet will settle over the place, weather-worn faces will soften, ranchers and oilfield workers will gaze into their beer lost in remembering. Even the travelers who never heard of Susanne Delacourt will sense something and fall silent.

When the record is over, they'll look at each other and smile, sharing a sweet memory. Then a waitress will rattle some dishes and the talk will start and the moment is gone.

I'm no different from the rest of them—the ones who knew Susanne Delacourt. The wind was blowing that evening too, a cold norther coming off the caprock, working itself into a full-scale sandstorm. The sun wasn't quite down; an orange blur in the dust haze to the west, but the cars going through town already had their headlights turned on. The cars barreling down the flatland highway slowed reluctantly when they came to Caprock, Texas. It wasn't large enough to be much more than a hindrance to those hurrying on to Snyder or Lamesa.

The jukebox finished a record and, in the momentary quiet before the next one began, I could hear the sand flicking softly against the window. Harley Boone put his ticket and a quarter beside the cash register and slapped the toothpick dispenser. I rang up the dime for the cup of coffee he'd been nursing for half an hour talking to the other loafers and gave him his change.

Harley stuck the toothpick in his mouth. "You wanta change jobs with me tonight, Wade?"

Harley was a pumper who had to make the rounds of a dozen wells every night and he wasn't looking forward to it in that weather. I put my hands behind my head, leaned back on my stool trying to look as contented as possible, and grinned. My performance was lost on him; he'd already turned to watch Susanne fill coffee cups.

She smiled at him. "Good night, Mr. Boone," she said and took the tray to a table full of young cowhands in tight jeans trying their best to look like Paul Newman in **Hud**.

Harley watched her with a pensive little smile on his leathery face. He seemed to undergo a transformation; his beer belly disappeared, the permanently grease-filled creases on his hands faded, his coarseness sloughed away and he was young again and trim and handsome with a lifetime of promise ahead of him instead of a lifetime of indifference behind him. But it was only an illusion, a self-induced and contagious state of mind generated by the presence of Susanne Delacourt.

She affected all of them. Those young cowboys she was waiting on, so arrogantly aware of their own sexuality, acted like Sunday school children around Susanne. It hadn't been quite like that when she started working for me six months earlier. Everyone knew about her and Billy Star.

Billy Star wasn't his real name, of course. He apparently had the notion the name made the object; if he changed his name to "Star" he would become one. But he was only a second-rate rodeo rider. No one could understand why she loved him, no one could see what was so special about him. He was no better looking, no smarter, and certainly no kinder than any of the young cowboys she served coffee, but she loved him.

They had come in that night six months earlier to eat. He'd been riding in a rodeo at Lamesa and hadn't done too well. They were driving through to Fort Worth and he was already a little bit drunk. He was feeling rotten because of the rodeo and he talked a lot. So everyone knew he wasn't married to Susanne but that she was living with him. Then, when she went to the lady's room, he paid the check, got in his five-year-old Imperial, and left her.

Everyone in the place just looked at each other in stunned silence. Then they watched the door of the lady's room until she came out. She looked at the empty table, then went to the window and looked at the empty parking space. She didn't cry or get hysterical or ask questions. She just stood there for a moment looking out the window. The people turned back to their plates in embarrassment. Then she sorta squared her shoulders, came to the cash register, and asked me for a job.

I hadn't really needed another waitress, but I hired her anyway. I even let her have one of the rooms over the cafe. The place had been a hotel back during the oil boom in the '20s, but when I bought it I had closed it up as more trouble than it was worth.

Susanne probably had twenty propositions the first night she worked. She'd been living with a rodeo cowboy who had ditched her, after all, so most of the young bucks and a few of the older ones didn't see any reason why they shouldn't take his place. But she just smiled the way she does, not offended, and said she was waiting for Billy Star to return for her.

It took barely a week before everyone loved Susanne Delacourt— and hated Billy Star for what he had done. And no one could understand why she still loved him or expected him to come back. I even asked Maurine Eubanks, the other night waitress, but she just gave me a pitying look and muttered something about "men."

Headlights flashed on the window and I looked out. It had grown completely dark and the sand was so thick I could barely see the neon lights of the Caprock Motel across the highway. The two state troopers got out of the patrol car, shivered in the cold wind, and rushed to the door.

Just then the jukebox started playing "The Tennessee Waltz" and I looked over at Susanne. She was slicing fresh-baked pies with a wistful expression on her face.

The door rattled open letting in a blast of icy air. Pete Rankin's belly hung over the belt of his uniform making his gun hang crooked. "Wade," he said and pulled off his black leather gloves. Davey Boyd grinned at me and looked at Susanne.

She held up the hot peach pie and grinned. Pete and Davey sat at the counter, their leather holsters creaking from the cold. They came in every night at the same time; that's why Susanne had the peach pie ready.

Everyone thought something might happen between her and Davey Boyd. They hoped it would; he was the only man around everyone could agree was good enough for her. Davey was local. He was born in Caprock, graduated from the high school where he'd been a pretty fair football player, then got on with the state police. Everyone had always liked Davey and were a little bit surprised that they still liked him even after he became a cop.

"She likes my harmonica better than me," he said one morning sitting by the cash register over a cup of coffee looking sad and very young. Davey could play the harmonica better than anybody I ever heard. He could make it sing sweet and pure or he could make it cry like a broken-hearted woman and could bring a lump to any grizzled old throat.

One night when the jukebox finished a record and didn't start another one, he took the harmonica from his pocket while sitting at the counter and fiddled around with it a while then very softly began playing "The Tennessee Waltz." Susanne watched him with big sad eyes then, when he finished, put her hand on his in thanks. He looked around and saw everyone quietly listening and blushed.

Davey Boyd loved Susanne all right, and she liked him probably more than anyone else, but she loved Billy Star.

It was later that night ten years ago, nearly at closing time, when the new International pickup stopped at the cafe. The sandstorm was howling and the temperature had dropped nearly to twenty. The window was fogged and I had to wipe it off to see who had pulled in. I didn't recognize the pickup and I couldn't see much of the man who ran in hunched against the wind.

The cafe was empty except for me and Susanne and the cook back in the kitchen. I'd let Maurine off early because hardly anyone had been in since the sandstorm got going good. I was tallying the receipts and Susanne was stacking coffee cups. The door opened and he came in rubbing his hands together. The cook stuck his head out of the kitchen to see who it was and I could tell by his frown he'd already cleaned up.

The man grinned. "Am I too late to get something to eat?" he asked. The cook's frown deepened.

Susanne turned to look. The man's face lit with pleasure when he saw her, then it sorta crumpled.

"Susanne," he stammered. "What . . . what are you doing here?"

"Hello, Cliff," she said softly.

"Where have you been? Billy . . . Billy wouldn't tell us."

I should've known he was a rodeo cowboy by the look of him, but I couldn't figure what he was doing around here at that time of year. He and Susanne just stood there looking at each other while the cook glowered at me.

"The kitchen's closed," I said. "All we can manage is a hamburger."

"Oh," he said turning toward me, rubbing his hands on his thighs. "That's fine. Give me a couple . . . and coffee."

Susanne drew the coffee. He took the cup and went to a back booth. She finished straightening up, glancing back at him occasionally. He didn't look up; just sat hunkered over the table.

When Susanne took the hamburgers to the booth she sat down opposite him and they talked quietly while he ate. He finished but still they talked. The cook looked out at me questioningly and I nodded for him to go on home.

Finally the man got up but Susanne kept sitting there staring at nothing, no expression on her face. He came to the register and paid, then looked back at her.

"I'm sorry," he said.

"What did you tell her?" I asked, hating him for upsetting our tranquil routine.

He looked at his hands, then back at me. He sighed. "Billy Star," he

Waiting for Billy Star

said. "He's dead."

"What happened? The rodeo?"

"No," he said, and shrugged. "He was drunk. Ran his car into a tree. Yesterday, near Lubbock. His folks live in Lubbock. The funeral's tomorrow. That's where I'm going."

"Is Susanne going?"

"No. I told her I'd take her and bring her back, but she doesn't want to go." He frowned. "She said she'd wait for him here." He sighed again. "I wish there was something I could do."

"I'll take care of her," I said.

He nodded. "Thank you. She's special."

"I know."

He started for the door and turned back. "I'll stop in on my way back."

I nodded. He looked at Susanne sitting in the booth but she didn't look up. He went on out the door. I locked up and turned off the neon sign and watched the pickup back out and head west into the wind.

I went to the booth and sat across from Susanne but she didn't seem to see me. I put my hands on hers. Her eyes focused on mine and she didn't pull her hands away.

"Billy's dead," she said, her voice almost too low to hear.

"I know."

"Billy's dead," she said again, but she didn't cry.

"Is there anything I can do?"

She shook her head.

"Will you be okay?"

"Yes. I'm okay."

"I don't want to leave you here alone. I'll call Maurine. You can stay with her."

She shook her head again. "I'll be okay."

"You know Maurine will want you to stay with her."

"Yes. I'd rather be alone though. I'll be all right. You go on home."

"You're sure?"

She smiled and squeezed my hands. "Yes. I'm sure. Go on home."

So I left her there, still sitting in the booth, and drove the half mile to my house. I called Maurine and told her what had happened and asked her to check on Susanne in the morning. I went to bed and lay there listening to the wind and couldn't sleep. The air was dusty even in the house and I felt as if I couldn't breathe. An hour later I got up and dressed and went back to the cafe.

That was the last time I ever saw Susanne. The next morning when Maurine went to her room she wasn't there. The bed hadn't been slept in and nothing was missing. Davey Boyd tried to find her for months. I knew he wouldn't, that no one would ever see her again.

When I went back to the cafe that night the lights were turned off, but over the sound of the wind I could hear the jukebox playing. I tried to look in the window but the glass was fogged and I couldn't see. I opened the door as quietly as I could. It was dark but I could see by the lights of the jukebox. They were moving slowly, huddled in each other's arms. They didn't notice me, they were so absorbed with themselves, so I closed the door and left them there; Susanne Delacourt and Billy Star dancing while the jukebox played "The Tennessee Waltz."

2076: Blue Eyes

2076—Screenplay Cast of Characters:

BLUE EYES—About twenty years old. A warrior/hunter of the Wolf Clan, a happy-go-lucky young buck, secure in his own life and beliefs.

ROBERT SULLIVAN—About eighteen years old. A scholar searching for the truth through forbidden knowledge that could cost him his life.

FALLOW—About twenty-five years old. A horseman of the Badger Clan. Negro. A bitter outcast from his Clan.

RED TOOTH—The Prez of the Wolf Clan. A tough, leathery man nearing middle-age.

THREE TOES—The Vice-Prez of the Wolf Clan. Early thirties.

NIGHT RUNNER—The Proff of the Wolf Clan. Middle thirties, the keeper of knowledge with the power of life and death over those who stray from Night Runner's prescribed path.

LONG EAR—The Emdee of the Wolf Clan. About fifty, a healer of sorts.

BLACK SPIDER—The Prez of the Weaver Clan.

TRUE FINGER—The Vice-Prez of the Weaver Clan.

DARK WATER—Proff of the Weaver Clan.

GRAYBEARD—The Emdee of the Weaver Clan.

SWIFT WING—The Prez of the Eagle Clan.

WILD BIRD—The Vice-Prez of the Eagle Clan.

SHARP TALON—The Proff of the Eagle Clan.

LONE FEATHER—The Emdee of the Eagle Clan.

MIDWIFE—An Old woman of the Eagle Clan.

LONG KNIFE—A member of the Eagle Clan.

LONG KNIFE'S WOMAN—A woman of the Eagle Clan who gives birth to a mutant baby.

EAGLE TRADER—A dealer in antiques.

A MASTER WEAVER—An artisan of the loom.

WEAVER GIRL—A pretty young thing who is the object of Blue Eyes' amorous intentions.

RED CLOUD—A young warrior of the Weaver Clan.

GRAY FOOT—A young warrior of the Wolf Clan.

HIGH FLYER—A young warrior of the Eagle Clan.

EAGLE SLAVE TRADER—A dealer in captured lives.

WOLF SLAVE TRADER—The same.

LONG POLE—Sub chief of the Badger Clan. Negro.

STORYTELLER—An old member of the Wolf Clan who entertains the children with fantasies that pass for truths.

OTTER—A crazed member of the Otter Clan destined for the stewpots of the Wizards.

EXTRAS
Fifty to sixty members of the Wolf Clan; men, women, and children.

2076: Blue Eyes

Fifty to sixty members of the Eagle Clan; men, women, and children.
Fifty to sixty members of the Weaver Clan; men, women, and children.
Twenty to thirty Wizards; men, women, and children.
Three young warriors of the Badger Clan. Negro.
Twenty to thirty members of Robert Sullivan's people; men, women, and children.

2076—Screenplay Synopsis:

In the year 2076 A.D., almost one hundred years have passed since the Earth was conquered by the Overlords, an alien race which attacked suddenly from space, killing 99% of the Earth's population. The tiny remnant of humanity now lives in small nomadic Clans based loosely on the Plains Indians of the Nineteenth Century with a good many holdovers of the late Twentieth Century. The Clans live in uneasy truce and gather twice yearly for barter. Each Clan has a specialty: the Wolf Clan are hunters—meat, fur, skins; the Badger Clan deals in horses; the Weaver Clan in cloth; others are farmers, millers, winemakers, etc.—in an economy largely based, ironically, on an alien plant inadvertantly brought to Earth by the Overlords. The graybeard plant provides food, cloth, soap, and building materials.

It is at one of these Gatherings that the story begins. Blue Eyes of the Wolf Clan is a happy-go-lucky young buck, secure in his way of life and his beliefs. When the Gathering is attacked by a sniffer, a large robot which gathers human specimens for the Overlords, the Clansmen disable it and rescue the people imprisoned inside. Among them is Robert Sullivan from a group of people living in the mountains, trying to find a way to overthrow the Overlords and bring back the lost Knowledge. Blue Eyes takes him as his slave and their beliefs immediately clash:

Blue Eyes: 'The Overlords were sent, high and mighty Robert Sullivan, to destroy the Old Ones because they had become impure. They had become wicked and evil and sunk in wizardry. Their wizardry destroyed the land and they were wiped out by the Overlords. Now the Overlords sit in their towers with their all-seeing eyes to make sure the People remain pure and never again return to the old ways.

Robert Sullivan: 'The Overlords came from somewhere in space, I don't know where. They came because they wanted this planet for themselves, not to punish anyone. They hit every city, town, and village with some kind of radioactive gas. They killed over ninety-nine per cent of the population. Then they spent the next fifty years mopping up the stragglers. They have sensors that spot any kind of electrical or atomic energy. The Old Ones didn't have a chance. For the last fifty years the Overlords have been sitting in their towers letting the sniffers keep the population thinned out. We never knew they operated by scent though. That's a bit of information I need to get back to the keep.

It is this clash of ideology, combined with the fear of a humiliating punishment for a minor offense and an insatiable curiosity, that leads Blue Eyes to help Robert escape and return him to his people. But the trip is fraught with many dangers and adventures.

They set out on horseback to find Robert's steam car and camp the first night near a radioactive city. They are captured by people still living in clear pockets within the city, but the nearness to the radiation has caused them to mutate strangely. They escape the cannibalistic mutants but are unable to find their way out of the radioactive maze of the city. They rescue some mutated, intelligent lizards from a pack of giant rats and are later rescued themselves by the lizards and shown the pathway out.

Finally reaching the steam car, they head for the mountains but are attacked by a sniffer and captured. The sniffer is malfunctioning and they are not gassed into unconsciousness as usually happens. In the sniffer is another captive: Fallow of the Badger Clan. The Badgers are Negroes who have nothng to do with the other Clans except at the Gatherings and even then do not join the common encampment.

The sniffer takes them to an Overlord's tower where they escape the death usually meted out to unconscious captives. In the tower they make many wondrous discoveries, including the fact that the Overlords are dying. The sniffers and other machines are operating on their own, carrying out their pre-programmed functions, until they finally fall into disrepair while the Overlords sit at the tops of their towers, kept alive by more machines.

Blue Eyes, Robert, and Fallow barely manage to escape as the panic-stricken Overlord destroys himself and the tower. Fallow, an outcast from his own Clan, joins the other two in their journey to the mountains.

Once more in the steam car, they are confronted by about fifty Clansmen investigating the explosion of the tower. Accused of wizardry because of the steam car, the boys are taken prisoner. In the fight that follows, the boys manage to escape with the use of an alien weapon taken from the tower, but Robert is mortally wounded.

Robert and Blue Eyes have learned a great deal from each other and have become as close as brothers. Now, Blue Eyes fights to get Robert back to his people before he dies. They travel through the ruins of a vanished civilization and finally reach the keep—perched on a cliff near the crumbling Mount Rushmore. Robert dies as his people come down to meet them.

Blue Eyes: "Robert Sullivan. Don't go away from me. What am I gonna do? You know what an ignorant barbarian I am. You have to teach me about the Old Ones and about Science. We have to educate the Clans and kill the Overlords. We have to learn about the people in the bluecities. We have to put it all back together again."

Blue Eyes (novel) Chapter 1: The Wizard Child

Blue Eyes of the Wolf Clan scratched his nose with a dirty fingernail and yawned. He lay in a shallow gulley, his chin on his folded arms, looking over the edge through tall grass. The air was heavy and warm, honey-sweet with the aroma of new growth. The prairie was green with plump grass. Spring wildflowers were strewn over it like a shattered rainbow. Blue Eyes wallowed in comfortable lassitude and lazily watched the encampment by the river.

The Weavers were the first in, as usual, and apparently had been there since the day before. Their wagons were drawn in a circle and positioned, because they were the first in, nearest the river and the graybeards growing in thick clumps at the water's edge. Blue Eyes counted sixteen wagons; they had acquired a new one since the last Gathering. The small herd of horses tethered and greedily grazing nearby had increased. The number of goats in the graybeard-stalk corral seemed larger also, but Blue Eyes, a hunter of the Wolf Clan, could hardly be expected to count **goats**.

The Weavers seemed to be prospering.

"Sniffer **shit**!" Blue Eyes hissed softly and brushed an ant from his bare thigh. He scratched at the small, reddening welt. He frowned, wrinkling his totem, a blue dot withing a blue circle, painted on his forehead. He licked the tip of his finger and rubbed the sting, making a lighter spot on his browned skin. He flicked two more ants from his wolf-skin boot and saw the trail near his foot. He crouched in the gulley and moved a short distance, still scratching his thigh.

He found another spot that looked comfortable and, checking around a bit more carefully, lay down on his stomach. He shifted his knife and carry-pouch from under his hip, repositioned his bow and quiver of arrows, and squirmed around fitting his body to the contours of the ground. He pressed the grass down in front of his face and resumed his survey of the encampment.

There was almost no activity in the warm, still afternoon. Only the Weaver women at the pots were visible. They fed graybeard stalks into the boiling water while others pounded boiled stalks on flat rocks, separating the fibers, hanging them on drying racks made of other graybeard stalks. The smoke from the fires under the pots rose straight up in the stillness. The silence lay heavy like an old blanket, disturbed only by the lazy, rhythmic pounding of the Weaver women on the graybeard stalks, but even that seemed far away and half-heard.

Blue Eyes yawned again, scratching at the sting on his thigh.

It would be a good Gathering—the Overlords willing, Blue Eyes added hastily. The rains had come early; the sky was clear and cloudless. It probably meant a dry summer, but now, at the Gathering, it couldn't be better.

Weaver tents were erected both inside the ring of wagons and out. Those outside sported trading banners, but they hung like beards in the motionless air. Those inside, Blue Eyes knew, shielded the Weaver looms from the weather and they eyes of the curious. He grimaced. The Weavers and their silly secrets. Why would anyone **care** how the Weavers fashioned the cloth used by all the clans? Blue Eyes' own short, sleeveless tunic was made of the simple bluish-gray cloth woven on the Weaver looms from the graybeard fibers, but he had not the slightest interest in weaving it himself.

He did, however, like most young bucks of any clan, want a tunic made by a Master Weaver instead of the unadorned ones made by the Weaver women. But he was much too young to have amassed the fortune it would need to get one.

The pavilion was set up a short distance from the encampment with the Weaver totem, a spread-legged spider, occupying the central position. The other clans, with the exception of the Badgers who always made camp up-river away from the others, would circle the pavilion, setting their totems as they arrived. But always there was some extra privilege to the clan that arrived first and did the set-up.

A fat horse-fly suddenly found Blue Eyes' cheek to be irresistably delicious. He brushed it away, but it would not be discouraged. He waited until it settled, then swatted it with the palm of his hand. His preoccupation almost made him miss the new sound.

He listened intently and immediately made out the sound of horses and the creak and rattle of wagons. He looked to a low rise a mile away to the southwest and, after a moment, saw a rider come into view. Behind him came other riders, then the first wagon; three small boys drove a herd of goats; other wagons followed; trading banners swung lazily from swaying poles made of polished graybeard stalks; short-haired slaves walked beside the wagons; children too excited to ride ran ahead; yapping dogs raced about, spooking goats and irritating riders.

The lead horsemen carried the clan's totem and Blue Eyes squinted to make it out. It was an eagle, wings spread and claws extended.

The Weaver encampment suddenly came to life. People emerged from the tents and wagons to watch the newcomers; children ran out to meet them; dogs scrambled from shady spots to bark and run with the children.

Blue eyes slipped from his vantage point and sprinted in a crouch down the gulley away from the encampment. His horse, a dappled gray mare with Blue Eyes' totem painted on her flank, was tethered in the shade of a concrete bridge where a roadway of the Old People crossed the gulley. The black roadway was buckled and broken, bleached and crumbled by weather; grass and brush grew through the cracks, and a

2076: Blue Eyes

fair-sized tree had pried away a corner of the bridge. The earth had settled at either end, but the bridge had not collapsed.

The mare raised her head from nibbling sweet grass and snorted softly. Blue Eyes untied her and mounted with an easy leap. He sat on a blanket and used a rope bridle, both made from the fibers of the graybeard. He nudged the horse with his heels and clicked his tongue. The mare moved down the gulley at a trot. Blue Eyes swung his arm and grinned broadly, his long, almost-white hair bounced on his back and his pale eyes sparkled. He wasn't yet old enough that the Gathering was no longer a place of excitement and adventure.

He rode the horse out of the gulley and nudged her in the flanks again. He felt her muscles bunch as she raced across the prairie at full gallop. Blue Eyes yelled for the pure joy of it and swung his head, making his hair flop across his shoulders. Then he slowed the gray to a walk and stroked her neck. She snorted softly and bobbed her head. Blue eyes laughed and lay forward, putting his arms around her neck.

He patted her again, then straightened up and rode to the waiting Wolf Clan caravan with the dignity of an adult hunter and scout.

The Wolf Clan caravan differed little from the Weavers or the Eagles. It included fifteen wagons, fify-three people (counting slaves), thirty-two horses, an uncounted—at least by Blue Eyes—number of goats, and an ever-changing supply of dogs. The people paused at their preparations for the Gathering and watched Blue Eyes as he approached. Two men mounted their horses and rode to meet him.

He reined the mare and waited respectfully for Red Tooth, the prez of the Wolf Clan, and Three Toes, his vice-prez. Red Tooth was a tough, leathery man nearing middle-age. He had been Prez for as long as Blue Eyes could remember. He was well-liked and no one seriously considered challenging his office. Three Toes was young, only ten years older than Blue Eyes, and there were those ready for a challenge should something happen to Red Tooth. Both were dressed much like Blue Eyes, in the short sleeveless tunic, though Three Toes wore riding leggings. Each had his personal totem painted on his forehead. Unlike Blue Eyes, they wore bracelets and necklaces of wolf claws and teeth. Red Tooth wore a skirt of wolf tails, the symbol of his office. They both wore knives and carry-pouches. Everyone except babies in back-packs, even the short-haired slaves who were allowed nothing else, wore carry-pouches at their waists.

"Blue Eyes!" Red Tooth shouted as he reined his horse. "How goes the Gathering?"

"The Weavers are the first in—since yesterday. The Eagles are just pulling in. No others are in sight."

"No sign of the Badgers?" asked Three Toes who had earned his name from a Badger and had even less affection for them than anyone else.

"No," said Blue Eyes. "The ground is clean and the grass untrampled. We're the third ones."

Red Tooth nodded. "All right. Let's go in. May the Gathering be peaceful and prosperous—the Overlords willing."

He signaled the caravan. A horseman raised a ramshorn and blew a call. Women and children scrambled aboard the wagons and set them in motion; trading banners swung limply from graybeard poles; men mounted horses; slaves scurried about picking up dropped objects and keeping the goats from scattering; a rider raced ahead with the clan totem, a snarling wolf's head with bared teeth and curled lips, and gave it to Red Tooth. Children laughed and squealed; dogs yapped and goats bleated. The caravan rattled into motion.

Blue Eyes dug into his carry-pouch and rummaged around. He pulled out a wolf-tooth necklace and slipped it over his head, pulling his long hair outside it. He found, after more rummaging, the wolf-claw bracelet under the sniffercloth and pulled it over his hand. He would have preferred a greater show of wealth, but he was young.

Red Tooth waited for the caravan to catch up, then took his place at the head, the totem held majestically in the air. The Wolf Clan rattled and clattered and creaked and yapped and bleated across the prairie to join the encampment at the river.

The Gathering became organized chaos with the arrival of two clans at almost the same time. Slaves scurried to and from the river carrying bundles of long graybeard stalks, building corrals for the goats, carrying old, fallen graybeard stalks for the cooking fires, carrying clusters of graybeard pods to the women at the cooking pots, putting horses out to graze, helping the traders put up tents and set up the wagons to display wares. Children and dogs ran laughing and barking underfoot and paid little attention to adult reprimands.

Weavers and Eagles, anxious for the wares of the Wolves, waited impatiently, trying to get advance looks, trying to spot the choicest furs or leather boots before someone else got to them first. The Wolves were hunters; they traded in pelts, leather, tooth and claw ornaments, meat— salted or dried, boots, quivers, leggings, and bow strings, though there was some competition from the Weavers on bow strings. Most hunters preferred those made of gut, but those made of graybeard fibers were less expensive.

Blue Eyes led the mare to the river. As a hunter and scout he was not involved with the menial tasks of setting up camp; that was left to the women, the traders, and the slaves. There was almost as much activity in the river as in the encampment. Slaves and women from all three clans chopped the graybeard stalks with long-knives and caught them as the heavy cluster of pods at the top pulled them over. They hacked off the pods and set them aside, then peeled away the two-foot-long silky gray tendrils that hung beneath the pod cluster and stuffed them into bags for later use as bed-stuffing. No part of the graybeard was wasted, even the roots left in the ground sprouted new graybeards.

2076: Blue Eyes

The mare drank from the shallow river and snorted at the naked children splashing and playing in the water. Naked adults bathed in deeper pools, laughing and splashing with almost as much hilarity as the children. Other hunters watered their horses, not wanting to trust them to slaves, and looked with anticipation at the bathers.

Blue Eyes plucked a graybeard pod from a cluster carried by a Wolf woman. She scolded him and then laughed when he grinned at her. Blue Eyes had known for quite a while that his grin was the key to many doors, especially with women. He peeled the thin gray skin away and bit into the chicken egg-sized pod. He liked the graybeard pods even better than the potatoes the Digger Clan would be bringing to the Gathering, though the taste was entirely different.

He heard a feminine giggle behind him and turned. A Weaver girl with a jug of water on her shoulder pretended not to notice him. Blue Eyes chewed elaborately, grinning at her with his mouth open, letting juice dribble down his chin. He tossed the half-eaten pod casually into the river and wiped his mouth with his arm. He turned the mare from the water and walked back toward the encampment, watching the girl. He swaggered slightly, still grinning at her, letting his hips roll. He had known the effects he could get with that since he was fourteen; it had opened doors even his grin could not breach.

He matched his pace to hers, but still she pretended not to notice him. She wore her dark, silky hair loose to indicate that she was unmarried, not in the bun of a widow looking for a new husband, or the elaborate braids of a married woman. Her knee-length tunic was made of a soft, thin fabric, not the coarse trading-cloth. Her arm, raised to support the water jug, stretched the cloth across her breasts, making the nipples stand out like hard little beads. She was slender and graceful, just about the prettiest thing he had ever seen. He wondered why he hadn't seen her at a previous Gathering. Then he caught her looking at him from the corner of her eye.

Blue Eyes lurched aside suddenly and grabbed the arm of a small boy of the Wolf Clan racing toward the river. The boy yelped and stared at Blue Eyes with fright until he saw the expression on his face. The boy looked at the Weaver girl, who had stopped at the sudden movement, then grinned up at Blue Eyes with pure hero worship. Blue Eyes smiled benignly and handed the boy the reins. The boy trotted away, tugging at the unresisting mare, taking her to the ramuda.

The Weaver girl had gone on, but glanced slyly over her shoulder to see if Blue Eyes was following. He hurried to catch up with her, walking beside her a few steps, then going ahead and walking backward ahead of her. He followed the line of her hips with his eyes, then up to her slightly bobbing breasts, then over the soft angle of her neck and cheek. Her eyelashes were lowered. She pretended to keep her eyes demurely on the ground, but he was reasonably sure she was watching the way the muscles moved in his legs.

Then he stepped in a shallow hole and grunted as his foot came down hard. He took a quick step backward and threw his arms out to keep from falling. The girl quickly put her hand over her mouth to hide her smile.

Blue Eyes scowled at her, feeling his face getting red, but her smile vanished instantly to be replaced by a look of concern. He watched her a moment through narrowed eyes, but her expression did not flicker. Then he laughed and shrugged his shoulders and was so pleased with the girl he was just opening his mouth to ask her name when the ramshorn blew.

The sound caused Blue Eyes to stop, and he suddenly felt a sinking in his stomach. He had almost asked her name, the first step to an offer of marriage. He was interested, but not that interested. He turned and trotted toward the Wolf camp. The Weaver girl watched him with a pleased smile. He turned once and smirked at her.

When he reached the encampment, the official protocol party was forming. Red Tooth was standing impatiently, fidgeting as women and slaves arranged his finery. He was petulant and cross; the attendants darted in quickly, made rapid adjustments, and departed just as quickly. He wore his state tunic, red with an intricately woven Wolf totem on the chest, and with elaborate patterns crowding each other for the remaining space. The huge head of a timber wolf rested askew on his head with the pelt hanging over his shoulders and down his back. Little Hand, a Digger slave the Wolf Clan had been unable to trade back to the Diggers because of his crippled leg, attempted to straighten it, but he couldn't seem to get the movement of his hands coordinated with the movement of Red Tooth's head. With a growl the Wolf Prez cuffed him aside and secured it himself.

Red Tooth's long graying hair was in two braids, each caught in an intricately tooled band of wild-cowhide. There was a small red nick on his chin where he had cut himself shaving. He wore the skirt of wolf tails over the red tunic and was laden with tooth and claw ornaments. Satisfied with the result, a slave handed him a staff decorated with more wolf tails.

Long Ear, the emdee of the Wolf Clan, was in a simple white tunic with the Wolf totem on the chest and a bit of broken mirror from the time of the Old People glued to his forehead. He was a man of about fifty, short and rotund, but in no way was he jolly. He spoke softly and rapidly to his apprentice, so rapidly his painstakingly curled beard quivered. The apprentice, a boy almost to the age of manhood, stood silently with eyes downcast. His lips were pale, but he was stoic from years of practice. Blue Eyes felt sorry for him; it didn't pay to get on the bad side of the emdee.

Even less would he want to be on the bad side of Night Runner, the proff of the Wolf Clan. He was ten or so years younger than Long Ear, tall, with the face of a hawk, his beard almost to his waist, black and shiny and laboriously braided. His apprentice was a boy of twelve who basked in the older man's smiles as he helped arrange the proff's flowing black robes. Blue Eyes had seen the boy in tears more often than he had seen him smiling. Blue Eyes thanked the Overlords that he was a hunter and not an apprentice to these men whose minds had been made strange by the secrets of the Old People.

Blue Eyes joined five other hunters to form the honor guard. Water Foot, his best friend, was among them and they rolled their eyes in resignation, grinning at each other.

Red Tooth looked them over to see that everything was as it should be and shooed away the women and slaves who frantically tried to make perfect details more perfect. He signaled and one of the honor guard blew a pattern on the ramshorn. Similar ramshorn calls drifted in from the other encampments. The procession began to move with Three Toes leading the way, carrying the Wolf Totem. Red Tooth followed, then the proff and emdee. Long Ear still berated his apprentice, then snatched the satchel of herbs and ointments form him. He composed himself into an official demeanor and the apprentice beat a hasty retreat. Blue Eyes, Water Foot, and the other hunters brought up the rear. The women, slaves and apprentices breathed sighs of relief and retired to the nearest shady spot.

The Wolf Clan arrived at the pavilion almost simultaneously with the Weavers and Eagles. Blue Eyes suppressed a grin when he saw Swift Wing, the Eagle Prez. His feathered robe and headdress of state made Blue Eyes think of an exploding turkey, and he wore so many metal ornaments he clanked when he walked. Blue Eyes looked at Water Foot and their chins quivered. All those in the Eagle procession were heavily laden with intricate metal decorations of state; much finer than anything offered by their traders to the other clans.

Black Spider, the Weaver prez, wore tight-fitting black pants and shirt, delicately woven with a minute red pattern and bouncing with red tassels and fringes. Each clan carried its special art to its most elaborate extreme in the protocol ceremonies.

Slaves, making last minute adjustments to the pavilion, darted away. Seven folding chairs made of leather and graybeard stalks had been arranged in a row at the open front of the pavilion—the seventh would remain unoccupied; the Badger chief would not appear, but protocol declared he be provided a chair nevertheless. Seven other chairs were behind those; seven more to the right, and seven to the left. The Wolf and Eagle totems had been positioned on either side of the Weaver totem.

The three processions stopped twenty feet from the pavilion and waited. People from the three clans, those who had nothing more important to do, followed at a respectable distance and gathered in the background to watch the ceremonies. After a moment the totem-bearer of the Weaver Clan stepped ahead and turned at the front row of chairs to face the processions. He held the Weaver totem before him.

"I am True Finger, Vice-Prez of the Weaver Clan," he said sonorously. "May the Overlords go blind and deaf and the sniffers clog their noses with mud during this Gathering of the Brotherhood of the People." He stepped back to the second row of chairs.

The totem-bearer of the Eagles marched forward, clanking slightly, and swept a glare over the assemblage. "I am Wild Bird, Vice-Prez of the Eagle Clan," he boomed. "May the Overlords have their eyes and ears torn out by eagles and the sniffers fall into piles of rust during the Gathering of the Brotherhood of the People," he finished, topping True Finger in ferocity. He moved back with the Weaver vice-prez who gave him a malevolent look from the corner of his eye.

Three Toes moved forward. "I am Three Toes, Vice-Prez of the Wolf Clan. May the Overlords have their entrails eaten by black wolves and the sniffers suck up a family of skunks during this Gathering of the Brotherhood of the People." He joined the other two. Blue Eyes wasn't sure he had bested Wild Bird in his disdain for the Overlords and sniffers or not, but Three Toes, by the expression on his face, seemed to think he had.

Black Spider moved to the first row of chairs, a shimmer of tassels and fringes. "I am Black Spider, Prez of the Weaver Clan. The Law of the Brotherhood of the People must not be broken at this Gathering." He spoke off-handedly; his position made pomposity unnecessary. He sat in the front row of chairs with dignity and indifference.

The Eagle chief clanked and rustled; his indifference verging on boredom. "I am Swift Wing, Prez of the Eagle Clan. The Law of the Brotherhood must not be broken at this Gathering." He sat, secure that he had scored points in indifference by omitting a part of the invocation. A quiet murmur, quickly hushed, rippled through the gathered Eagles. Blue Eyes raised an eyebrow at Water Foot who wrinkled his nose.

Red Tooth strode forward, his tooth and claw ornaments ticking faintly. "I am Red Tooth, Prez of the Wolf Clan. The Law of the Brotherhood of the People must not be broken at this Gathering." Blue Eyes suppressed a grin. Red Tooth had topped the other chiefs by being so indifferent he did not bother even to compete.

The proff and emdee of the Weaver Clan moved forward together. Both were dressed, with the exception of the totems on their chests, identically to Long Ear and Night Runner. Their only vanities were their beards, styled and looped and curled and braided in unbelievable intricacies. Blue Eyes saw Long Ear scowling; his beard was obviously the least elaborate of the bunch. Blue Eyes felt sorry for someone.

"I am Dark Water, Proff of the Weaver Clan, gatherer and teacher of Knowledge and Master Weaver and Guardian of the Secrets of the Loom. Tough I am, tainted with the Forbidden Secrets of the Old People, I keep my Clan pure from Wizardry and protect them from the all-seeing eyes of the Overlords and the all-smelling noses of the

2076: Blue Eyes

Sniffers." Dark Water, like all the proffs Blue Eyes had ever heard, had a habit of talking in capital letters.

"I am Graybeard, Emdee of the Weaver Clan, healer of aches and pains and mender of bones. I have many new secrets to exchange with my brother emdees." They separated and sat in the groups of chairs to either side of the chiefs.

"I am Sharp Talon, Proff of the Eagle Clan, Master Smith and Guardian of the Secrets of the Forge. Though I am half mad with the Forbidden Secrets of the Old People, I keep my Clan pure and destroy Wizardry wherever it may appear. The Overlords and sniffers are eyeless and noseless against my knowledge." Blue Eyes sighed under his breath. Sharp Talon always said exactly the same thing Gathering after Gathering.

"I am Lone Feather, Emdee of the Eagle Clan, Master Healer with many secret herbs and potions to exchange with my brother emdees."

Blue Eyes attention began to wander. The sun was warm, the air was heavy and fragrant with the smoke from the cooking fires and the nutty aroma of boiling graybeard pods. He boredly scanned the assembled crowd and spotted the Weaver girl he had seen at the river. She caught his eye and smiled shyly. Blue Eyes got a smug look on his face and turned back to the ceremony, all his attention to protocol and duty.

"I am Night Runner, Proff of the Wolf Clan, Master of the Hunt and Teacher of Good Knowledge. I have long ago gone completely mad with the Forbidden Secrets of the Old People. I keep my Clan pure and seek out Wizardry and destroy it wherever I go. The Overlords are but blind moles and the Sniffers nothing but mice against my enormous knowledge."

"I am Long Ear," Long Ear said and touched his beard self-consciously, "Emdee of the Wolf Clan. My secrets of healing and mending are so numerous that it is doubtful my brother emdees will ever be able to trade for all of them."

As Night Runner and Long Ear took their places, the ceremony was over. The people dispersed, getting back to the serious business of trading. Blue Eyes looked for the Weaver girl, but she was not in sight. Two honor guards from each clan remained on duty, but Blue Eyes and the others began wandering off. He was headed for the Weaver encampment when he heard his name. He turned as Water Foot took him by the arm.

"Blue Eyes," Water Foot grinned. "I'm for the river. I feel like I'm carrying half the prairie on my skin. Join me. We're next on duty."

"Not now. I have other matters to attend to," Blue Eyes said and grinned knowingly.

"The Weaver girl?" Water Foot laughed. "Did you ask her name?"

"Of course not," Blue Eyes said in a tone that showed he was no infatuated cub.

"I find the river is the best place to make arrangements. When the sweet things see me without my tunic, I have only to choose among them," Water Foot said, puffing out his chest and tightening his buttocks.

Blue Eyes laughed. "Keep your knife at hand to fight them off."

Water Foot waved and trotted off toward the river. The clan leaders were in heavy conversation in the pavilion as slaves scurried among them passing out rough, hand-made cigars and lighting them with burning twigs. Blue Eyes started again for the Weaver camp, but was stopped by a new interruption.

An old woman, her elaborate braids frizzled and damp from perspiration, entered the pavilion in a staggering run from the direction of the Eagle camp. Her feet scuffled in the dust and she wheezed from exertion. She fluttered her hands and gasped for breath as she curtsied quickly to the chiefs and stumbled on to the emdees. Conversation stopped as they stared at her.

"Emdee! Emdee!" she croaked to Lone Feather. "Come quickly! Long Knife's woman is giving birth! She is having much trouble. I cannot stop the bleeding!"

Lone Feather looked at the other emdees and sighed at the responsibility of office. They nodded in agreement. The midwife scurried back toward the Eagle camp. Lone Feather took his satchel and followed at a stately pace. The old woman paused, returned to him, then scuttled ahead again. Blue Eyes, touched with curiosity, followed along after the emdee, as did a number of other people. The other clan officials, however, showed no interest and resumed their conversations.

Long Knife stood nervously outside his tent. The woman would pick just this moment to give birth, just the moment when he had important trading to do. A small crowd had gathered, mostly women and slaves. Long Knife fidgeted, seemingly unable to stop the movement of his feet. He would start toward the tent opening and then fear to see what was inside.

The midwife lurched through the crowd, shooing them away with her hands. They ignored her, but immediately moved back to allow Lone Feather to pass. He entered the tent. Long Knife looked after him with relief. The people pressed forward to peek in.

Blue Eyes stood on the edge, his interest waning. The Weaver girl was more important than all this. He only gradually became aware of the low moans of a woman, muffled as if a hand were held over her mouth. Those around the tent pressed closer.

Long Knife gasped, breathed in ragged flutters. Suddenly the moans became high-pitched grunts, then short, breathless screams of pain. There was a commotion in the tent and other women screamed, not in pain, but in fright.

The tent flap was flung back and the midwife ran out, whimpering, holding her hands as if they were contaminated. Two other women hurried out, both pale and one sobbing. A small whine escaped from Long Knife's tight throat. Lone Feather stepped from the tent. Blue Eyes was surprised to see the emdee so obviously shaken. His knuckles were white from the pressure with which he clasped the satchel of herbs and potions.

"Bring . . ." His voice cracked and he swallowed. "Bring Sharp Talon. There is Wizardry here."

The people drew back, little horrified, but thrilled, murmurs running through them. A slave ran to get the Eagle proff. "Long Knife's woman has been infected by a Wizard," Lone Feather said quietly, his voice barely under control. "She has given birth to a Wizard's child."

The people drew back farther. Blue Eyes, his eyes bright with excitement, moved closer, craning to see. Long Knife, his face the color of old ashes, stooped to enter the tent. Lone Feather grabbed his arm and pulled him away unresisting.

"No!" Lone Feather said sharply. "Keep away. Only the Proff has the Good Knowledge to combat Wizardry."

Long Knife turned slowly, stricken with the knowledge of what was to come.

Blue Eyes licked his dry lips. The woman in the tent still moaned, a sound that made the skin on his arms prickle.

Then Sharp Talon arrived followed by another crowd of people. The news had spread quickly through the Gathering. He entered the tent without a word or sideways glance. It was seldom that a combatter of Wizardry had a chance to do so in such a spectacular way. The crowd waited with a solemn and fearful hush. Blue Eyes edged closer, then stepped back quickly as Sharp Talon emerged suddenly.

The crowd shrieked and staggered back. The men paled and the women covered their eyes. Blue Eyes stared in fascination.

Sharp Talon held the baby by one foot, over his head like a cluster of graybeard pods. His eyes burned with fierce little flames. The baby's arms dangled below its misshapen head and the umbilical cord flopped around, staining the proff's black robes with blood. The baby's skin was a bluish color and didn't seem to fit together the right way. It was smeared with drying blood. The baby was quite dead. The eyes were big and black and open and seemed to stare at Blue Eyes.

He swallowed and took half a step backward.

Sharp Talon motioned two Eagle warriors into the tent. They hesitated only briefly, then went inside. The moans changed in pitch. The two men backed out, dragging Long Knife's woman by the arms. She was naked. Blood covered her thighs and trailed across the flattened grass. She struggled with feeble strength and tried to scream, but was too weak even for that.

Long Knife still stood with his back to the tent. His shoulders hunched and quivered, but he did not turn around.

The woman twisted around weakly, searching the crowd for him with glazed eyes. She found only his back.

Blue Eyes watched the defeat settle on her features and felt his stomach knot.

Sharp Talon motioned to the Eagle warriors. They grasped the woman's shoulders and held her to the ground. One of them took hold of her disheveled braids and pulled her head back. Sharp Talon, still holding the blood-smeared baby, pulled his knife, bent down, and cut her throat.

Blue Eyes winced. He wanted to shut his eyes, wanted to shut his ears to the sound of her breath gurgling away through her bloody neck. His stomach felt funny, but he knew this was right, knew that all traces of Wizardry had to be removed without mercy. He knew all that, but his stomach still felt funny.

Two slaves pushed through the crowd pulling a flat-bottomed two-wheeled cart. Sharp Talon tossed the baby on it as if it were a piece of rotten meat. The warriors picked up the body of Long Knife's woman and tossed it also on the cart. The slaves pulled it on, creaking under the weight, away from the encampment toward the open prairie.

Sharp Talon held up his arms for attention. "There is no longer any reason to fear," he said, satisfied. "The Wizard child is dead. The woman who has had intercourse with Wizardry has been punished. Once more I have cleansed the Clan of impurity. Go back to your work. There is no longer any reason to fear."

Sharp Talon turned to follow the cart. Lone Feather joined him, matching his stride. Several in the crowd followed them, but most went back to their activities. Blue Eyes watched the cart bounce across the uneven ground for a moment, then turned back toward the Weaver camp.

He took one last look at Long Knife, still standing with hunched shoulders, all alone.

Tom, Tom!
A Reminiscence
by Howard Waldrop

Tom Reamy was a large man, big-boned and heavy-set, but he moved with the ease of someone half his size. He had long fine hands, the first two fingers of the right hand stained yellow from the innumerable cigarettes he smoked each day. His dark brown hair was thinning out a bit, with streaks of grey showing, worn slightly long and partially combed back on the sides of his head. He wore thick black-rimmed glasses and he smiled a great deal, even when most of the people around him were looking woebegone. His voice was soft, surprising coming out of such a large man. He was kind and gentle, shy in many ways, and never intrusive.

He usually wore the same kinds of clothes. A light nondescript work or sport shirt with short sleeves, and darker-colored nondescript pants, with casual shoes of one sort or the other, the kind that don't need much care or attention.

I first met him when he was putting out his magazine **Trumpet** and I was helping out with all the comic book fanzines edited in Dallas. He was in his late twenties, and I was a callow youth of 17.

I remember him in those days by the places he lived. The house on Debbie Drive in exciting Plano, Texas. A home in a subdivision on the north side of Dallas. The first place I ever visited him was the bottom half of a converted stable behind a bunch of cedars of Lebanon in a spiffy neighborhood in Dallas.

He later moved to a trailer park north of Richardson. One Sunday in 1969 we all woke up to the news that a tornado had destroyed the trailer park north of Richardson. We tried to call all day, but the lines were down. About 4 p.m., several of us piled in cars and drove up there, with some vague notion of either claiming the body or helping Tom sift through his scattered wreckage. We found the trailer park across the street was gone, leaving the one Tom lived in untouched. Tom, in fact, was still asleep when we knocked on his door. I think we had an impromptu celebration. I remember playing **Risk** all night and not going to school the next day.

Risk wasn't Tom's game though—bridge, or one of its mystical progeny, was. I know absolutely nothing about the game, but I've seen Tom's face beaming over a fanned handful of cards and saying something which made the opposing players look disgusted and start adding up points, many times. At some SF conventions I've passed through the lobby or the party room, making that last grogged-out, gritty-eyed 4:40 a.m. swing through the place, and there would be Tom, wide awake and concerned over whatever was happening on the card table in front of him. Meanwhile, all the other players lifted their heads only long enough to play their hands before sinking back into their stupors.

At one side of Tom would be five or six empty Tab cans, and at the other would be cigarettes and an overflowing ashtray.

Tom, being a full-grown human being, had done many things before I met him. He'd been a movie projectionist, dispatcher at a concrete plant, skip-tracer for a collection agency (for three weeks). Mostly, from 1957 until the aerospace industry imploded, he worked as a technical illustrator for Collins Radio in Dallas.

Tom was an excellent artist. In the 1950s his artwork appeared in SF fanzines like Harlan Ellison's **Dimensions** and in the Dallas Futurians' own **CriFanAc**, which he edited from time to time. The Dallas Futurians were way before my time. Among others, they included Jim Hitt, Richard Kugle, Al Jackson, Greg and Jim Benford, Tom and the group was semi-run by a guy named Orville Mosher, a behind the scenes manipulator whom no one got along with. One of their last acts, after losing a Worldcon bid in 1958, was to elect Mosher president of the Futurians unanimously, and then disband the organization.

What those people did for entertainment between then and 1965, I don't know. It was that year that Tom and Al Jackson began editing **Trumpet**. Tom put his art, articles, movie reviews and considerable layout skills in it. He showcased the newest art talent of the time—Bernie Wrightson, Vaughn Bode, Tim Kirk, Jeff Jones and many others. He even adapted and got George Barr to illustrate an elegant comic strip version of Poul Anderson's **The Broken Sword**. There were articles by andy offutt, Jerry Pournelle, Harlan Ellison, David Gerrold, Robert Bloch. He got Richard Hodgens to come out of semi-demi-retirement and write about **Dr. Strangelove**. He did his own Westercon report, "The Adventures of Grady Goodmonster," which was everybody's first hint of just how well Tom Reamy could write.

It was a most elegant magazine, the envy of everyone. It was ruled ineligible the first year for the Best Fanzine Hugo because four issues hadn't been published yet. But **Trumpet** did come close to winning twice in subsequent years, only being beaten by Dick Geis's **SF Review**. *

---

* Ten issues of **Trumpet** were published between 1965 and 1969; about that time the problems in the aerospace industry and bidding for the Dallas worldcon began. **Trumpet** number 11 was not published until 1974. When Tom moved to Kansas City he started **Nickelodeon** and two issues were published before his death. A third issue was nearly completed and will be published under the title **Trumpet** by Tom's co-editor, Ken Keller. **Trumpet** 1-11 are long out of print. **Nickelodeon** 1 and 2 are still available from Ken Keller at 1131 White, Kansas City, Mo., 64126 at $2.00 per issue.

Tom, Tom!

Then along about 1969, we all went temporarily crazy and got involved in the Big D in '73 World Science Fiction Convention bid. One of the things we did to pull everybody's strings was to publish the **Dallascon Bulletin** and mail it free to over 6000 people. We were accused of trying to buy the bid. People said we were secretly funded from Argentina. They said we must be spending $2000 an issue in printing costs alone. But mostly people were upset because for the first time in science fiction fandom a city tried to win a worldcon bid by communicating and attempting to gain the support of so many people.

One of the posters we wanted to print was of Tom and Joe Bob Williams, dressed in white planter's suits, drinking mint juleps, sitting on the verandah of a columned ante-bellum home and smiling, while in the background the rest of the DaSFS people, in chains and raggedy clothes, lifted and toted and cranked mimeos and collated on a table set in the middle of a cotton field. Underneath would be the Big D in '73 symbol and the legend, "Love Us, Love Our Money."

I'm sorry the poster never got printed.

Suddenly I found myself drafted.

Just as suddenly, the Big D in '73 bid started coming apart at the seams, behind the scenes. Instantaneously, the bottom dropped out of the aerospace industry. What with out-of-work technical illustrators three feet deep in the streets Tom had begun writing screenplays and became briefly involved with a Dallas film production company. Nothing permanent came of it so Tom took his income tax refund check and drove to Los Angeles to make his fortune.

I didn't even know about it for awhile. I found myself too caught up with interesting and rewarding career-oriented jobs like guarding motor pools and closed PXs in North Carolina.

Tom was to spend a little less than two years in Los Angeles, working on films in any capacity from gopher to assistant director, writing screenplays, and seeing movies by the daysful. Tom Reamy was the most visually- and cinematically-oriented person I've ever known, and that's saying a lot.

It was the writing of the screenplays that turned him later to writing the stories. Tom's Hugo and Nebula nominated novel, **Blind Voices**, was originally a screenplay (**Professor Mephisto's Travelling Wonder Show**), as was "Insects in Amber" (**House at the End of the World**). "The Detweiler Boy" was taken from a screenplay Tom and I did just before the draft got me, which we called **The Screaming Night** or some dumb such title.

He wrote eleven or twelve screenplays, and they're all good. It was the chance to do movie work that took him to Hollywood, and it was the chance that one of his screenplays was going to be filmed that brought him back to Texas.

December 1972: I'd been out of the Army six months and was waiting to get back into college. I was in Dallas at some sort of comic book/movie convention held in the basement of a roadside motel on I-35.

Things were arranged so that, sitting at the registration desk, you faced these wide stairs coming down from the real world into the closed one of the convention.

People appeared like out of a mirage, only wrong-end first. You saw three-quarters of them before they could ever see you.

I was meeting new people, SF writers like Joe Pumilia and Lisa Tuttle for the first time, and it had been a long day. Tom had been gone from Dallas for almost two years, doing nobody knew what. Charlie Brown of **Locus** had run into him out there and mentioned him in a column. That was all the word we had in two years.

Anyway, I was looking toward the steps when some blue deck shoes appeared, then a pair of straight-legged pants (this when all the rage was bell bottom/wide flare/elephant pants). I held my breath. When the pants widened out and the bottom of a nondescript tan workshirt hove into view, I was sure.

"Tom, Tom!" I yelled, and jumped over the table, scattering badges and attendees in my path.

As the rest of him appeared on the stairway, other voices took up the chant behind me.

"Tom, Tom!"

I've never seen a more surprised look on the face of a human being in my life.

Later that night, while he was getting a Tab from a Coke machine, he turned to me.

"I didn't know what was going on when I got here," he said. "I didn't know how people would take me coming back, with all the hassle with Big D in '73 and all. I sure was glad when everybody was happy to see me."

He moved out to Woodson, Texas after Christmas, and I started getting this marvelous series of letters from him. Things were looking up for a couple of his other screenplays (**Insect God** and **The Screaming Night** were optioned for production in Malaysia, until someone absconded with corporate funds somewhere up the line). More importantly, he told me he had begun to write stories.

A couple of weeks later he sent me "Under the Hollywood Sign." It knocked me dead. He asked for criticism. I could only stutter and stammer and make a few generalizations in my answer back to him.

He wrote back: "Analyze Lou Rankin for me. You can come up with something more constructive than 'Icky'." He also told me he was starting another story with John Lee Peacock in it ("San Diego Lightfoot Sue") and still another unrelated story ("Beyond the Cleft").

His letters arrived in envelopes with a tan saddle oxford printed on them. On the oxford was a ladybug. (He must have found them cheap in some office supply store in Breckenridge.)

The stories went out and came back, almost selling. Damon Knight wanted a rewrite on "Under the Hollywood Sign." He made some suggestions and asked questions about the creatures in the story. Tom wrote

Tom, Tom!

me that, "Damon wants to know how you can rape an angel. Now I guess I've got to convince him that angels have assholes . . ."

One day one of the saddle oxford envelopes arrived. Only this time a word balloon had been drawn on it, and the ladybug was saying "Whoopee!"

The letter began:

"Just sold "Under the Hollywood Sign" to Damon and "Beyond the Cleft" to Harry Harrison. I was very disappointed to discover that HH only pays 3¢ a word plus royalties. Yuk, yuk."

His first two stories on the same day, and mention of where "San Diego Lightfoot Sue" and "Twilla" were. ("Twilla would go on to be a Hugo and Nebula contender in 1975, and "San Diego Lightfoot Sue" was to win the Nebula and be a Hugo runnerup in 1976).

All those written in the first six months of 1973, and no one had seen them yet but the editors and few writer friends when Tom brought them to the Turkey City SF Writers' Conferences. Everybody's mouth hung open for days after reading them. Tom just smiled.

"Hell," said Al Jackson, who had known Tom in Dallas since before the beginning, "Tom could write like that in the '50s. We just never could get him to mail any stuff off to the magazines."

Those first few months of 1973 were crazy ones for a lot of us. We were all—Steve Utley, Joe Pumilia, Lisa Tuttle, Jake Saunders, George Proctor, Bruce Sterling, Bud Simons, me—determined to sell stories everywhere, storm the field, eat all the dinners, break all the plates. We were all from Texas, and we had all started writing about the same time, in the last two years. We were as competitive as hell, yet we collaborated shamelessly with each other, sharing triumphs and rejections, commiserated, helped each other through personal crises. We talked story and writing day and night.

We had one thing in common, when it came to Tom's work, we were in awe, and most of us felt we were fighting for second place. We knew it. Tom didn't know it, but we knew it. We were as proud of him as if he were our own big brother.

There was one day, early on in his career, that summed up everything that Tom was, and would be, to me.

Some time in April 1973, my then-wife Linda, my then-daughter Teri Ann (four months old), my then-dog Rat and I piled into the old yellow '65 Ford station wagon we owned and set out for Woodson, about a hundred and fifty miles away.

As we drove west, the sky took on the appearance of the Gulf during hurricane season—dark clouds piled up in a solid wall a mile or two high. Squall lines, over arid west Texas. Very disconcerting. About forty miles out from Woodson the clouds passed and the sky took on a tinge like the bottom of Revere Ware skillet. In Texas that means you're going to have to eat a lot of dust for the next 24 hours.

The dust storm hit just about the time we pulled into the Reamy's driveway. The house was separated from the Exxon service station the Reamys ran by fifteen feet of side yard. Tom came out to meet us.

We said hello to Tom's folks, Ollie and Gertrude Reamy, and went inside. Tom's full name was Thomas Earl, but as Al Jackson once pointed out, everybody in Woodson pronounced it "Tomsurl". We talked for a while in the gloom. It was only two in the afternoon but it looked like dusk. The sun was just a red lump in a dirty sky. Tom and I decided to go out and scout locations for the movie. His screenplay, **Sting!*** looked as if it were going to be filmed.

We drove toward Eliasville, fifteen miles away, where the movie is set. Tom had me detour over gravel roads, stopping to show me the exact spot where the school bus scene takes place—a setting he remembered and described perfectly while living in Los Angeles the year before.

The dust was thick now, and the wind was rising. (I'll always associate Tom in this period with the weather. When we came to a Turkey City Writers' Conference at Woodson the next February, we learned that a) Wednesday, there was a tornado which wrecked part of the barn and the henhouse, b) Thursday it snowed, c) Friday, on our arrival, the temperature was in the 60s. By Sunday, when we left, it was in the thirties again.)

Eliasville, pop. 200, was just as Tom described it in the script—a town which had peaked during the oil boom of the 1920s and declined since. The only three viable businesses were a grocery store, a gas station and a cafe. They were surrounded by the shells of other buildings with 1930s Dr. Pepper and 7-Up signs still nailed to their storefronts.

Tom and I walked through town. He described to me angles, shots, pointing out the house on the hill that was to be Doc's office, the store next to the service station where Ira and Lester Tidwell would be playing dominoes when the meteor hit them.

Then, walking across to the cafe, Tom stopped.

"I just noticed the service station **isn't** directly across from the cafe. Hmm. Well, we could matte it in, or build it there," he said.

Knowing the number of things Tom had done in LA, like reconstructing the interior of a Ford Tri-Motor airplane for the film **Flesh Gordon**, I had no doubts he could move a service station where he wanted it.

There was a sign on the cafe door: "Closed from 3 to 5 p.m. today on account of the Bar-B-Q at the school."

On some back road somewhere, Tom had me stop the car. We got out and I followed him as he climbed a cattle gate that looked like it hadn't been opened in twenty years. (It hadn't.)

He talked about plans for the movie and how, since he came back, he'd found more things he wanted to put in.

"This is one of them," he said, as we emerged from the overgrown driveway before the Ultimate Abandoned House.

---

* In **Six Science Fiction Plays**, edited by Roger Elwood, Washington Square/Pocket Books, 1976.

Tom, Tom!

"Jeez!" I said.

"I thought you'd say something like that," said Tom, and smiled.

The house was huge and weathered a dark grey. It was an underslung two-story type you still occasionally see—the upper story starts halfway back and the whole thing is laid out in a long thin rectangle. The roof was tin. Strips of corrugated metal hung sideways and flopped in the dusty wind with noises like musical saws.

"I'm thinking of having something take place here," he said as we entered through a missing door. It was dark inside, and in some places the sky showed through. Old watermarked magazines, catalogues and pieces of cloth were strewn around. The whole place creaked like a ship at anchor.

"Isn't this a great place to have someone reach out and grab someone on the shoulder from offscreen?" Tom asked.

I could only mumble agreement.

He took me to another setting he'd found. I can't remember the exact name, but the sign above the entranceway said MINERAL BATHS. It was like stepping back into 1933. The dust storm helped too, lending the right Walker Evans light to the place.

There were cabins like the motor courts Gable and Colbert stayed in in **It Happened One Night**. Tiny places with an attached garage between each room in which no car wider than a Model T could park. These were arranged around some central building made of a material halfway between stucco and adobe. It looked like it had been ripped away from other cliff dwellings halfway up some mesa in Arizona.

The screen door on the place had no spring, and it was banging against the wall with every gust of wind. We went inside. There were people sitting around very quietly, their feet hanging off into a huge, shallow central pool of what looked to be very hot water. After a curious glance at us, they went back to watching their feet soak.

Tom bought me a Coke from the machine beside the front door. We drank while he told me the history of the place. He seemed to have found out everything about the establishment simply because he wanted to use it in the movie.

We drove back, talking of God knows what. We pulled into the driveway at real-for-true dark. The wind was howling.

That night, Tom cooked the best lasagna I've ever eaten. He said he used to get the urge to cook about once every three months, and Italian food was his favorite.

After supper, he and I went out to the service station to run it for awhile. I don't remember anyone coming by, but they probably did. There were no moon and stars. Dust was obscuring everything but the house.

Tom had some **Trumpet** and **Big D in '73** posters hanging in the station above the oil cans. He had sold several to curious motorists in the past month.

We talked of the stories he and I were writing, or were going to write, of the screenplays, of the production of **Sting!**, of anything else that came up. Both Tom and I were talkers, and we could talk of anything with each other. Tom drank Tabs and smoked cigarettes and I dropped redskin peanuts in my Nehi Orange and drank them, and we generally had a good time.

About 11 o'clock, we called it a night. Everybody but my dog Rat was asleep. The Reamy's house was the only light for miles.

Sting! was never made, of course. Half the things we talked of that dusty night we never did, or we put them aside, or transmogrified them into unrecognizable things. Other stories, other things took their places. We did our work. Tom moved to Kansas City, founded Nickelodeon Graphics with Ken Keller, published **Nickelodeon** with its nude centerfolds, worked with the Kansas City Worldcon Committee, wrote his Nebula and Hugo nominated **Blind Voices** and other stories, edited the MidAmeriCon* Progress Reports and Program Book, ran the film program at that Worldcon, was up for awards.

He was looking forward to moving either back to Texas or California and doing nothing but writing full time.

Of course, that never happened. I don't think Tom told anyone, except maybe his good friend Pat Cadigan, that he had had a mild heart attack in the summer of 1975.

One early November morning in 1977 he was found dead at his typewriter, seven pages into a new story.

He was 42 years old.

It's been two years now, and I can't think of Tom as being gone. I miss him. I find his name coming up in conversations, and people shaking their heads. I keep looking around for him.

I'll leave you with the happiest memory.

It is 1976, at MidAmericon. Tom has won the Nebula earlier in the year for "San Diego Lightfoot Sue". He is now up for the Hugo for that story, and for the John W. Campbell Award for the best new author of the last two years.

I have seen Tom earlier in his hotel room. He is so nervous he can hardly talk, the first time I have ever seen him that way. He finally has to ask all us well-wishers to leave, because our enthusiasm is getting to him, and he has to take a shower and change. He has shown us his outfit for the evening.

It is an incredible powder blue tuxedo, with tails, the kind Kurt Vonnegut calls a clawhammer suit. It has a white boiled shirt with a blue ruffled braincoral front. Narrow black patent leather shoes that look like obsidian mortar trowels. The whole outfit looks like it used to belong to Cab Calloway in the **Betty Boop** days.

And now, an hour later, Tom comes into the auditorium to take his place with the other nominees. Spontaneous applause breaks out.

The ceremony begins, and they get to the Campbell Awards. It is Tom's

---

* MidAmeriCon, the 34th World Science Fiction Convention, held in Kansas City, Mo., over Labor Day weekend, 1976.

Tom, Tom!

last eligible year ("Twilla" was published the year before). The competition is stiff and there is palpable tension in the air, more than I've seen at awards like this before.

The nominees are read, and MC Bob Tucker opens the envelope.

And says the magic name.

Applause comes in waves, and Tom Reamy rises, magnificent in the blue tux, and makes his way toward the stage.

As he walks through the hall, he is accompanied by a chant, which comes from me, from his friends, from other writers around us.

It goes:

"Tom, Tom!"

Howard Waldrop
August, 1979

San Diego Lightfoot Sue
and Other Stories
by Tom Reamy

This first cloth edition of the original manuscript text, published November 1979, is limited to a memorial edition of 2300 copies, of which 100 slipcased copies were numbered and signed by Harlan Ellison, Howard Waldrop and Leo and Diane Dillon on a specially designed tip-in illustration by Hank Jankus. Fiction text was typeset in 10 point Stymie, non-fiction text in 8 point, 8½ point and 10 point Avant Garde Gothic. Display type styles used are Aquarius, Avant Garde Gothic and Wexford. Typesetting by Nickelodeon Graphics, Kansas City, Missouri. Text paper is 60# ICP Neutral Natural, an acid-free paper with an extended shelf life. Dustjacket stock is 100# ICP Press Varnish Enamel. Binding material is Vellum Finish, C-Grade Roxite. This book was printed and bound by Inter-Collegiate Press, Mission, Kansas. Book design by Jim Loehr and Ken Keller.